BLOOD MOON RISING

Also by Richard Conrath

THE COOPER MOON SERIES

— Cooper's Moon —

BLOOD MOON RISING

RICHARD CONRATH

AUTHOR OF The Cooper Mystery Series

Published by Gulf Shore Press, St. Petersburg, Florida

Library of Congress Control Number: 2019900992

ISBN: 978-1-946937-02-5

ISBN: (e-book): 978-1-946937-03-2

Book Design (cover and interior) by Arc Manor, LLC

Published by Gulf Shore Press, 2019, St. Petersburg, FL.

Gulf Shore Books are available on Amazon and most bookstores near you. If the bookstore does not have the book, you may order it through them.

"THE FLESH IS YOURS, THE BONES ARE MINE."

An old Turkish proverb

Cooper, our protagonist, is the smoothest customer you'll ever meet, complete with a sharp tongue and a sharper mind, not to mention his fair share of faults and demons. Relentless in pursuit of justice and closure, "Coop" is the best combination of DeMille's Daniel "Mac" MacCormick (*The Cuban Affair*) and Connelly's Harry Bosch. Pick it up, buckle up, and read it like you stole it!

—TRISTRAM COBURN, Editor/Publisher

Lovers of the genre will find much to keep them engrossed. Readers will root for Cooper in his search for victims and the identity of the ruthless and mysterious killers. The author successfully raises tension with gripping descriptions and emotional dialogue.

—BOOKLIFE PRIZE (about *Cooper's Moon*)

A brilliant and exciting story. I can't wait for the final one—I hear it ends the trilogy with a nail-biting twist. Watch for the film—I imagine some production company will pick it up and run with it!

—KIKI AKIDO, Managing Editor, Gulf Shore Press

To my wife, Karyn, without whom this
book would not be what it is today.
It's been a long road, girl!

I t has been raining for five straight days now and the river is swollen, threatening to spill over the banks and inundate this small southern Ohio city. It's late autumn and this is what happens every fall. On the river. Rain, rising tides, flooded homes and people stranded on rooftops watching cars and animals floating down the river. People ask why don't they just move? The answer is because this is their home.

It's late, 3:00 a.m., and the waters of the Ohio are racing toward the Mississippi, the Blood Moon riding low in the sky now, watching the whole scene like a curious silver eye, casting its light on the waters and illuminating the flotsam that is beginning to jam the river and force it onto the shore. The people who were standing on its banks earlier in the evening have gone to sleep, hoping for a better day tomorrow, which means, of course, that the rain will stop.

What they aren't seeing now is a body, or should I say, parts of a body, washed against a pile of tree branches, bouncing like a rubber doll, one arm flopping as the waves from the torrent strike it. The other arm missing. Skin peeled back on the trunk. Her face, or what's left of it, is swollen and grotesque, the soft light of the moon unable to alter the fact that her body is decaying, the night breeze unable to hide the stench of rotting flesh. Her clothes are torn from the punishing waters, and her eyes, only holes now, stare into the night sky, as if anxious to release the secret of what had happened.

BEFORE THE WAR

1

LAWLESS

EARLY TUESDAY MORNING, OCTOBER 5

It had been days since I had gotten any sleep—or nights I should say. I was watching the red digital numbers on the clock sitting on my dresser. I had gone to bed at 11:11 p.m., the double hour. It was now 3:15 a.m. and I had been drifting in and out of dreams. They're always the same. I'm in the mangroves of the Ten Thousand Islands trying to get out, every waterway looking exactly like the next, the night cloaking avenues of escape in an impenetrable blackness. I've boated through these islands many times, but in my dreams they are strangers to me and only the sounds of gators slipping into the water are familiar. Those creatures scare the hell out of me. Sometimes I'm in shallow water, knee high, wading and tripping over mangrove roots, sinking into muck so thick I can't pull free. And the gators only yards away.

I have these nightmares oftentimes, ever since the disappearance of my son over eight years ago. They turn my nights into a kind of dream-hell, interrupted only when I wake. But waking is almost worse than the nightmare, because when I do, I see that Maxie is still gone and I almost wish the nightmares back again. Because I blame myself for not finding him. Eight years. I mean, I'm a private investigator for God's sake. Eight years? I would fire me if I could. But then...

And my cell rang.

The red numbers on the clock bore through the darkness like the eyes of a feral, angry black cat: 3:33, another double hour, almost. My cell continued to play out its tune. I checked the caller. Unknown number. I answered it anyway, wondering *Who the...?*

"Yeah?"

"Cooper?"

"You got it," I said, not happy. I mean, three o'clock in the morning?

"It's Jack."

It took a moment to process the name. Which Jack? I mean, aren't there a million Jacks?

"It's Jack Lawless," he added quickly, sensing I was struggling.

"Sure...Jack. Of course," I jumped in.

Lawless is a friend of mine from Concord College. His real name was Laighleis, a family name from Galway County. But nobody knew how to pronounce it so he changed it to Lawless when he came to the U.S. from Ireland. After a year at Georgetown University, he lived up to his name. He sat many a Saturday night in jail for drunk and disorderly and only by sheer luck was not tossed out of the university before he got his doctorate. I could picture him. Thin. Six-two. Light brown hair—receding. That mole just under his eye. And a lined face that showed hard living.

Like I said, he is a friend of mine, from Concord College in Muskingum, Ohio, where I used to teach philosophy. Where I used to live. Where I used to be married
and where I had a son, Maxie, that is until he disappeared
one day, right under my nose. Gone. Taken to God knows
where, eight years ago, seven years since my wife, Jillie, and
I broke up over the disappearance of our son—because
we blamed each other, of course—it always happens that
way—and seven years since I left Muskingum and came
to Miami to find Maxie. So far I haven't. Is that my fault?
I blame myself anyway even if it's not. Yeah. I think it was
my fault.

"I know it's early, Coop," he said, apology all over his
words. "A friend of mine…is missing." Silence.

"A friend?" I replied, wondering why a missing friend is
worth a phone call in the middle of the night.

"Yeah, a friend. I mean…you know…a friend."

"Oh, you mean a *female* friend." I was trying to catch
myself from sounding judgmental. But how could I not
since my friend here is married to another friend of mine.

"Kind of."

"I'm assuming Sonya doesn't know about her, right?"

"That's right."

Jackson and Sonya got married in a chapel at Concord
College. Jillie and I stood up for them.

"Okay. Go on," I said. "Tell me about this missing friend."

"About a year ago, I started seeing a girl at the university."

I nodded, then remembered he couldn't see me. So, I
said *okay*, and he went on.

"She's a graduate student in our program, assigned to
me as a teaching fellow."

"Did you ask for her?" I was hoping he would say no.

"I saw how talented she was and said I would be willing to take her on." He paused.

"And…?" Sometimes a pause can hang in the air for hours when in fact it was only seconds.

"And…you know…"

"You had a physical relationship?"

"Right."

"Okay, then what?"

"Then April began to get serious and I was worried that people would begin to wonder."

"That's her name? April?"

"Yes, April." He paused again. "What can I say? Sonya and I were having a lot of trouble and it just happened—I mean between April and me."

I didn't really want to hear all this. He must have sensed my impatience because he began to talk more quickly.

"Last week April told me she would be gone for a couple of days. 'It's a personal thing,' she said. She never said where she was going. That was Monday. This past Friday she was supposed to lecture in my Intro to Soc class. But she never showed. So, I called her. No answer. I went over to the department to see if anyone there had heard from her. The secretary said she hadn't heard from her at all. She was as surprised as I was. Said April is very responsible. Not like her at all.

"So, then I went to her apartment. But nobody had seen her since last weekend. I thought about calling the police. But what was I supposed to say? *See, this student that I'm having an affair with is missing.*" He paused. "I mean why would I be reporting a missing student to the police?" Another pause, like he expected me to answer the question. Then, "Somebody else would do that, right? Parents? Administrators?"

I didn't answer.

He had run the gamut of moods while he talked. Reasoned and controlled at first, but then argumentative and emotional.

"Do her parents know?"

"I don't think so. She's from Cape Town." Some more silence.

"Cape Town?" I wsn't sure I had heard him right.

"Yeah, yeah, Cape Town. That's right."

Jeez, I thought. Not that Cape Town was a problem. But it was a complicator. I mean a foreign student missing is different than an American student. You know, embassies get involved.

"Look, Jackson," I said, "April has been missing now for a week. She's an adult..." then I thought about what I was saying and stopped. Being an adult doesn't make her less missing. "What I mean to say is, she may have just decided to take a holiday. But you won't know until you call the police."

"The police already know."

"Then why are you calling me?" At three in the morning, I could have added.

"Because maybe the cops think I had something to do with her disappearance," he said, his voice trailing off, like he was wondering if I also thought he was in trouble.

"Who called them?"

"I don't know. Maybe her boyfriend who doesn't like me."

"She has a boyfriend?" I said. More complications.

"Yeah, another grad student," he added quickly.

I pictured Sonya and hated this whole thing.

"So, you want me to do what?" I couldn't help sounding impatient.

"I need your help. I want you to find her."

"The police are already looking, right?"

"Yeah, but they're looking at me right now."

"They know about your affair?"

"I think so. I think Adile told them."

"Adile? Who's she?"

"He. A student from South Africa. He's in love with her. April says they're just friends," he said, sounding like high school.

"From South Africa?" I said, surprised.

"Yeah. But they met here." He paused. "One more thing. April has a grant from the Ministry of Education to work on her doctorate with the understanding that when she's finished she would return as a deputy minister."

"Interesting." And I began to think, Homeland Security maybe.

"What's April's last name?"

"Januarie."

"That sounds French."

"It is. But she was born in Cape Town. She was runner-up in Miss South Africa," as though this last fact might tell me why he was seeing her.

"Is she Afrikaner?"

"No, mixed race. But she speaks Afrikaans." Small talk now.

"So, she's black?"

"No. Not black. She's considered Cape Coloured."

"Okay. Do you think Sonya knows about the two of you?"

"I don't know. Maybe."

"Maybe?"

"He paused. "I hope not…but yeah, maybe," he said, throwing that in again at the end.

I figured Sonya must know. That's too bad. But Sonya's smart. One of the brightest people I've ever met. She graduated high school in Saint Petersburg when she was sixteen, went to the University of Moscow where she earned her bachelor's degree and then a PhD by the time she was twenty five. A wunderkind. By the time I met her she was working on a law degree at Georgetown. She met Jackson there. We all graduated together, Jackson, Sonya, Jillie and I. And we've been friends ever since. And now this. Go figure. Life has a way of inventing its own endings.

"People in the department know?"

"I hope not."

Fat chance, I thought. *Oh, what a tangled web we weave...*

"You know how racist the Valley is, Jackson."

"I know," his voice slipping into anxiety. "Actually, I've been getting some crazy calls," he added.

"Yeah? Like what?"

"Oh, you know, crazy. One guy said something about not putting up with this kind of shit. I assumed he was talking about Januarie. Someone else called me a n-lovin' communist pig."

"Communist?" I said, ignoring the n-word. "Why?"

"Who knows? I teach a few sessions in class on the CPA—the Communist Party of America," he explained. "People in town aren't really happy with me."

He paused for a few moments, pulling in a deep breath. "One more thing. China disappeared last week..."

"Man, I'm sorry," I said.

China is Jackson's Chow Chow. He and Sonya got him shortly after they got married. Every morning China would come over to our house, scratch at the screen, and wait for a treat. Maxie was the one who gave it to him, would go to the fridge, pull out some special biscuits we saved just for China, open the door and toss them, one by one, into the yard, then follow the treats and China into the grass, the screen door slamming after him, with Maxie laughing and tumbling after the dog. They would play for hours when school was out—in the summer—from when the sun was low in the east until it rose toward high noon.

"Maybe he just ran away—"

"I found him in the woods behind our house yesterday."

My stomach turned. I thought of Maxie and China together in those same woods.

"Someone killed him. Throat cut. I can't talk about it. Sonya's freaked out…" he caught his breath, coughed, then, "She asked me about the calls—she got some too, and in her condition—it's hard for her to even get out of bed in the morning…"

Her condition? I hadn't heard.

Jackson hesitated, "and now our China."

I could feel him gripping the phone, waiting for me to say something, But I didn't. I stared out over the swamp emerging more clearly now through the darkness. There were predators there, waiting for a victim, apex predators, the crocodile and the python, who feared nothing—except humans, of course, people like me and men like Huxster Crow, a friend who lives in Everglades City who hunts them in season.

"You still there, Coop?"

"Yeah. Sorry. You need to call the police and tell them the whole story—I mean about April also. They probably already know, guy. April's more important right now than your worries about your reputation. In the meantime, I'll catch a flight to Columbus."

I heard him suck in his breath and then he began thanking me, said he would get my ticket, pick me up, buy me dinner when I got there, and pay me exorbitant amounts of money. I told him to calm down and get himself a beer.

"I'll see you tonight," I said.

2

THE VALLEY

It was 3:50 a.m. when I hung up. A half hour later I was still wide-awake, thinking of Jackson's story and listening to the sounds of the swamp. So I got up, booked an 11:45 flight to Port Columbus and began packing. I tossed in my Glock. The Oceanside cops still had my .38, confiscated during a shootout in Miami about a year ago. Had it been that long?

After that I went back to bed, tossed around for a while trying to catch a few more hours of sleep, and wound up watching the red numbers tick off the clock. I must have dozed because the next thing I heard was the alarm and the red numbers on the clock read 8:00 a.m. I lay there for a few minutes, letting the sleep flow from my body. I rolled out of bed, raised the blind on the window overlooking the Everglades, and watched egrets sinking their long, tapered beaks into the grass that grows wild in my backyard. I saw Herman, the old gator who lives in the mangroves near the wooden walkway to my dock. He was watching the birds feeding.

I showered, shaved, made some coffee, grabbed a banana and an apple from the fridge, some cat food for Sammy—he keeps Herman company when I'm gone—tossed my bag into the car and headed for Miami International.

I landed in Port Columbus at 1:30 p.m. and rented a car. I picked up Interstate 270 that circles the city and took Route 23 south to Riverdale. I figured a two-hour drive. It was warm, the late summer sun lighting up the countryside. The only scenery: farm land and an occasional advertisement on the side of a barn, Chew Mail Pouch Chewing Tobacco, in big yellow letters, Treat Yourself to the Best in white script beneath it.

Telephone poles flew by quickly on the four-lane highway. It's limited access in places, but mostly a country road. In the 70s, if you drove this road, you would pass small twelve-by-twenty-four-inch signs that advertised Burma Shave. The signs would appear in sequence, about fifty feet apart on the driver's side of the road so you could read them like flip cards. Each sign held a line of a poem, if you could call it that.

HE LIT A MATCH

TO CHECK THE GAS TANK

THAT'S WHY

THEY CALL HIM

SKINLESS FRANK

BURMA SHAVE.

As a kid, I would ride these rural roads, looking for walnuts with my dad, and watch for the Burma Shave ads. They're all gone now, just like most of the signs on the sides of the barns, except for the one I just passed, the old Mail Pouch sign, faded and barely visible. I was betting that the tobacco company wasn't paying the farmer ad money anymore.

3

THE RIVER

I passed the welcome sign to Riverdale, Home of the Big Red, shortly after 3:30 p.m. That would be the football team. Football was all the Valley had at one time. Recently, coal had taken a resurgence, the shale deposits putting millions into the pockets of farmers up and down the Ohio River. Now Big Oil had come to the Valley also. Competition for King Coal.

The population of Riverdale is around 40,000. Down from its peak of 55,000 in the 50s. That's pretty much the story throughout the Valley, the loss of the steel mills contributing to much of that. The jobs went and so did the young people, first to Cleveland and Detroit and then away from those cities when hard times came their way.

I found a diner on US 52, known in the Valley as the River Highway. A neon sign hanging over the road read Hole-In-The-Wall Bar & Restaurant and underneath it, Good Eats.

The Ohio River isn't far from the college where I taught in Muskingum, Ohio, about an hour and a half, driving fast. Jillie, Maxie, and I would head for Riverdale, say on a weekend in the fall, get tickets for a cruise on the riverboat, and spend the day. Dinner onboard. Listen to the entertainers at night—local talent—and watch the water fall off the massive paddles that drove the boat forward.

The people in this area are mostly river people, meaning they live and die by the whims of the water. It floods, they abandon their homes, they move back once the waters have receded, clear out the mud, tear down the wet plasterboard, dry the flooring, and start all over again. People from outside the Valley always ask, Why do they stay? You know, the floods and all. The answer is simple. It's their home.

The Hole-In-The-Wall was exactly what its name indicated, a small space with a few tables scattered in front of a bar. Several families were seated at two of the half-dozen tables. Everyone was big. Thick. Even the kids. This is Appalachia. So, there isn't a lot of money here to spend on organic vegetables and free-range chickens. A man at the bar motioned me to take a table, my choice, and went back to talking to a trucker who was downing shots and a beer.

A waitress in a black top and jean shorts came from behind the bar and asked what I wanted. I ordered a turkey burger plate, with special Hole-In-The-Wall fries and coleslaw.

"Anything to drink?" she said.

I told her a Coke.

"People from the university come in here?" I asked.

"Sure," she said. "All the time. They hang out here."

On a chance, I asked her if she ever waited on a girl named April Januarie.

"No. Never heard of her. Strange name. Don't sound American."

"South African," I said and watched her expression turn.

"She black?" she said. In the Valley, everyone from Africa is black.

"No, she's mixed…light skin."

"This part of the country, that's black," she said, turning for the counter.

People mount shotguns in the back windows of their pickups in the Valley. Mostly because they're hunters. But the guns serve other purposes as well.

I called Jackson.

No answer. I left a message.

4

THE UNIVERSITY

R iverside University is just a short distance from the Hole-In-The-Wall. My stomach was beginning to revolt against the fried food. I tried to put it all out of my mind as I drove up the curved road that led to the main campus. The university sits on several hundred acres of hilltop that overlooks the Ohio River. Prime property. You can see the river wind southward, appearing and disappearing between hills that rise on either side as it makes its way to the Mississippi.

The administration building is the first building at the end of the road, a gray stone structure with flying buttresses propping up the sides. I parked, headed for an oversized door with hinges that were larger than my arm, pushed it open, and walked into an open space as big as a courtyard, but dimly lit.

"Can I help you?"

It was a young girl, nineteen or twenty, short brown hair, sitting behind a long, polished, redwood desk to the right of the entrance. A moon was tattooed on one arm, a sun on the other. Wait till' you're seventy, I thought. Those cute tats will be wrinkled. Some books and papers were scattered in front of her. She had a pen poised over a notebook as she looked up.

"I'm looking for Miller Hall."

"That's the Soc/Psych building. So, as you leave here it will be the first building on your right." Then, "I'm a Soc major," she added.

"Oh, then maybe you know Dr. Lawless," I said.

"I sure do. I'm in his class. We have an exam tonight," she said, pointing to her notes. "Fun times, huh?" she said, shaking her head.

Miller Hall was faced with gray stone, just like the administration building. It was 5:20 p.m. Shadows began to creep along the walks and through the trees that lined them. Elms and oaks mainly. And I watched the shadows play over the faces of students who made their way through the doors of the building. I wondered which ones were headed for Jackson's class.

Inside the door, a wide stairway curved up to the second floor. The doors along the hall on the first floor were numbered, matching the numbers on a glassed-in directory. Jackson's office was on the second floor, rm. 209. I headed up. Room 209 was down the hall on my right. The door was locked, but a schedule of office hours and class times, attached to the wall to the left of the door, told me that Tuesday's class was at 6:30 p.m. Office hours from 5:00 to 6:30. It was 5:30. A sign on the door read, Man, the Loneliest Species.

"Cooper" came a voice from behind me. "Thanks for coming so quickly," he said, taking the last few stairs in one stride. Jackson is the same height as I am, but rangier, like someone who just climbed off a horse in New Mexico after rounding up strays.

"Come on in," he said, unlocking his door. "I missed most of my office hours. The last thing I needed to do was to listen to some student complaining about a C she got on a paper instead of a B. They even complain if they get an A-," he said, tossing his briefcase on his desk and motioning for me to sit.

"I'm going to cut my class short tonight. There's a quiet bar upriver where we can catch some drinks and we'll have a little privacy." He fumbled around in his pocket for a cigarette.

"You allowed to smoke in here?"

"No," he said, as he tipped a pack of Camels toward me and lit his own. I shook my head.

He watched me over the tip of the cigarette as he lit it, the end suddenly growing red, smoke coming out of the side of his mouth.

"The local cops called me this afternoon. I never got a chance to call them back. They stopped by my house." He took a long pull on the cigarette, held the smoke in his mouth for a moment, gazed at the ceiling, then blew it out. "Like I said, I'm a suspect—they call me a *person of interest.*"

"What did Sonya say?"

"She was in bed. Don't know what's wrong with her. Doctors think it's just fatigue."

"So, you haven't told her anything?"

"No. She's got enough to deal with."

"What did the cops say?"

"They wanted to know what I knew about April's disappearance—you know, where she might be, that kind of thing."

"Yeah. So, what did you tell them?"

"What I told you. I really don't know where she is. They asked me if April and I had a relationship—actually, asked if I was sleeping with her."

"And…?"

"I said, hell no. I'm not going to tell those bastards anything."

"Did they believe you?"

"I hope so."

"Okay…" I hesitated.

"What?" he said.

"It's like this, Jackson. If you want me to help, I have to know whatever you know. Have you told me everything?"

He looked hurt. "That's a strange question. Don't you trust me?"

"I just want to make sure you've told me all the facts, that's all." I watched his eyes carefully. They were fixed on mine. No flinching at all.

Instincts operate like a disease. They eat away at the recesses of your body, leaving subtle clues and speaking only in murmurs below the surface of your consciousness. We have to listen carefully to catch them. I stared back at him through the silence. Shadows began to creep over the windowsill and into the office.

The clock read 6:23.

5

"Where's this bar?" I said, looking at the clock. His class started in five minutes.

"The Corner Club. It's about five miles upriver on your right. You can't miss it. I'll meet my class for a half hour and see you there about 7:15. Okay?"

I found a Holiday Inn about three miles upriver that still had vacancies. It was next to a Dairy Queen that had either closed early or was out of business. My guess was the latter. That didn't bother me as much as the view of the abandoned steel mill across the river. The Valley is a depressed area. Depression can be a way of life here, especially when you see your job wiped out because it was shipped to Central America.

The clerk gave me a room with a river view. I could see the lights of the cars traveling Route 8 on the Kentucky side flowing like the river itself up and down the highway and disappearing into the blackness of the hills.

I was at the Corner Club at 7:15. Jackson came through the door at 7:45.

"So, Coop, what do you need to get started?" and he was pulling out his checkbook. No nonsense. No intros. This is not the Jackson I remembered. I was looking for some sensitivity for April. I didn't see any. Just concern about possible consequences to him.

"We can settle up later," I said waving off his check. He wrote one anyway and handed it to me.

"Plus your expenses and travel costs here," he added.

I nodded.

"So how do we get started?"

"What are the names of the detectives who questioned you?"

"A cop by the name of Passarelli. The woman's name, I don't remember."

I jotted down Passarelli's name.

"They grilled me pretty hard. They wanted to know when I saw April last and did we have a fight before she left."

"*Did* you have a fight?" I said.

"No." That made him angry.

"All right," I said. "Like I told you, I need to know everything you know if I'm going to help. The last time you saw April—what do you remember?"

"Nothing much. We were at a motel up the road." He stopped short. "Why are you looking at me like that?"

"Sorry." I was going to have to check my reactions at the door. "Tell me what happened."

"We…you know…" and he hesitated. I knew.

"And afterwards she said she had a class project and was going to be out of town for a few days—but she said she would be back for my class on Friday."

"And this was what day?"

25

"Tuesday night. I dropped her off at her apartment around 11:00 p.m. and got home shortly after that."

"Sonya wonder where you were?"

"She was asleep."

"Okay. So, after that you never heard from her until...?"

"I didn't hear from her at all after that."

"And you said you called her cell."

"That's right. It went right into voice mail."

"Remind me. You said you began to get worried when she didn't show up for your class on Friday?"

"That's right."

"What're you boys having?" said a waitress with the name Stephanie sewn on her blouse.

I ordered a Pinot Grigio. Jackson ordered whatever they had on tap.

"That's not much to go on," I said. "You might have some problems if April is more than missing. I suppose you've asked around?"

"No. I didn't feel comfortable doing that. The students who asked...I've just said, she's on a trip. Which she obviously is."

We drank in silence for a few minutes while I pondered the dearth of information:

Student disappears

Goes on a class project.

Wow.

"By the way, did you find out which class had a project?"

"I did. None of her profs assigned a class project and nobody questioned her absence. After all, students miss class routinely."

"No class project? Why didn't you tell me this before?"

"It never came up. But you're right. I should have."

"You told the police about China, I assume."

"Yeah. They as much as said, *So what?*"

The waitress brought our drinks. Jackson took a healthy swallow of his. I stared into the wine feeling that something was missing in this story. It's maddening how slowly a case can develop. The best place to get started is with the client. You need to pry into the client's private life to do that. In this case, Jackson's. So, if you hire a PI, count on that happening. That's what detectives do. They pry, spy, sneak around, break in if they can, and generally act like sleazy people. I don't like to think of myself as a sleazy person. I do humanitarian things—like catch unfaithful spouses and bring them to justice—I do that on the side to make some money. But generally, I try to stick to finding missing persons. I feel better about doing that.

"I'll talk with Passarelli tomorrow. In the meantime, you get some sleep, Jackson. You look like you haven't had any for about a week."

We sat in silence for a while, Jackson, raising his glass to the waitress for more and me sipping wine and thinking about what I didn't know. Maybe Passarelli would have some information. If not, then there was always surveillance. The only problem is I didn't have anyone to follow. Except, perhaps, Jackson.

6

JILLIE

It was late evening when I got back to the Holiday Inn. A long day. It had begun at 3:30 a.m. and I was beat. I hadn't eaten, so I checked to see if the restaurant was still open. It wasn't, but the bar was. I was surprised at how busy it was for a weekday night.

"The university," said the bartender. Maybe he was a mindreader. "The students and profs hang out here after their classes."

I ordered a beer. The bartender had a nametag that read James on it, but I could have sworn he was Chinese. I asked him if James was his real name and he said, "Sure boss."

I asked for a menu and watched my cell phone buzz and shudder.

"Hi Cooper," said Jillie.

I knew who it was. I recognized the number. I never told you much about Jillie. We met in graduate school in D.C., working on our doctorates. My main interest was the Pre-Socratics, like Thales of Miletus, who, in attempting to figure out what everything was made of, conjectured that it was water. And as the rising seas threaten to take over our coastline, he might have been on the right track. Jillie was interested in the French writers: guys like Sartre and Camus, existentialists who said that life is meaningless. Considering the confusion in the world today, they may have been right as well. So we would argue about what is right or wrong and sometimes never get to bed until early in the morning—and then have to skip class to get some sleep.

We did that a lot—until we got married. Both of us got job offers. I got one from Concord College in Muskingum, Ohio. She was offered a position at Ohio State University but turned it down. "I want to have kids," she said, "and be a stay-at-home mom." Then a position opened up at Concord College in the English Department. And so, together again, Jillie teaching down the hall from me.

We had a son in our first year. He disappeared in our seventh. We got separated the year after. That's the way it goes when you lose a child. I've seen it happen. You can't bear the sight of one another anymore—because you blame each other for what happened. I blamed Jillie for not watching Maxie while she was home with him. She blamed me for not being strict enough with him. *I have to do all the disciplining,* she would say. *You do the fun things with him. I get to do the nasty work.*

So that's who was calling. She does that on occasion. And sometimes I answer and sometimes I don't. Tonight, I answered.

"Yeah, Jillie," I said. "How are you?" and my stomach sank as I thought of the distance that had grown between us over the years.

And it sank again when she said, *I miss you, Coop*. Because I missed her too.

No, I still loved her. But it was a love buried in the loss of a child, one that would not go away. James slid my beer to me. I tried it and added some salt.

"I miss you too," I said.

"I hear you're in Ohio," she said.

"How'd you find out?" I said.

"A friend of ours from Riverside University."

"Yeah? Who's that?" I said, not sure I wanted to know.

"Sonya texted me."

I was afraid she would say that. Communication at the speed of light. A new world.

"I wish you would have told me yourself." Like we we're still married.

"I just found out this morning," I answered, like I was guilty of something. I wondered what Sonya had told her. "You okay?"

"No," she said. Matter-of-fact. Depression all over her silence. Sometimes it's so deep all you have are just flat statements. No feeling attached to them. You hope for a crack where some light can penetrate. And it doesn't happen. Then, "How about you?"

"No," I said as the conversation drifted. A breeze picked up outside, an October wind. Some rain was sure to follow, though the river didn't need more rain. It was already higher than it should be.

"Let's have lunch," she said.

"That would be good," I said. "I planned to call you."

More silence.

"How about this weekend," I said.

"Okay," she said. I don't know if she believed me. I wasn't sure I believed myself. But I liked saying it to her.

We talked for a while longer while the breeze picked up and I heard the beginnings of rain against the building. So, I said goodbye, talk to you in a few days, and hung up. I sank into the silence of the room and the pecking of rain against the window.

7

PASSARELLI

WEDNESDAY, OCTOBER 6

I was up early. Amazing for me. I'm usually not awake until 9:00. I took a quick shower, plugged in the coffee maker, and logged on to my computer to get a number for the Riverdale Police Department.

I got the officer on duty who wanted to know what I wanted. I told her Detective Passarelli. She asked me what the nature of my call was and I told her it was about the case of a local missing woman, April Januarie. She asked me who I was and I told her I was a private detective who had an interest in the case. She told me to wait a moment. In less than a minute Detective Passarelli was on the phone.

"Yeah? How can I help you?" Brusque and irritated.

"I was wondering what you might have on April Januarie."

"There's not much to say," he said. "So far there is no reason to believe that Ms. Januarie has come to any mischief. What's your interest in the case?"

"Got a client who's interested in her disappearance. Hired me to find her."

"Yeah? Who's the client."

"Uh-uh," I said. "You know I can't go there."

"You used to be a cop?" he said.

"Yeah, homicide. Miami PD."

"So, you know my buddy, DeFelice," he said, his interest picking up.

"Yeah. My partner for five years."

"That right? He's good people. You tell Tony I said 'Hey' when you see him."

"I will do that. How do you know him?" Small talk.

"I worked a case with him when I was a rookie detective in Miami Shores. Some guy killed his ex-wife over a cat. The husband lived in Miami; she was in my district. Anyways I'll let you know if something develops. My guess, she's with a boyfriend somewheres. Used the class project story as a cover." He stopped for a moment, then, "She seeing that prof?"

See this is where the trouble begins for a private detective. There is no way I'm telling Passarelli about Jackson and April.

"Have you asked him?"

"I'm asking you, Cooper."

"I've only talked to Jackson for a couple of hours. If I find out anything, I'll let you know."

Passarelli didn't say anything right away. But if he was suspicious, he let it pass.

"Okay. Just keep me up-to-date," he said, stiffly. I didn't get the feeling Passarelli was working very hard on the case. Cops get busy just like anybody else working a full-time job. Some are just lazy, some are hard workers who don't have the time to investigate. The case goes cold and everybody forgets about it.

"I just want you to know I'm looking into April's disappearance," I said.

"Feel free. Just let me know if you get something," he said. In other words, *I don't have time. Be my guest.*

8

THE UNIVERSITY

LATER WEDNESDAY MORNING

The Sociology Department is on the first floor of Miller Hall. The secretary was probably one of the students. She asked what I needed. I asked her if April Januarie had called in. She said just a minute and went into the office behind her desk.

A tall man, slightly hunched, with a lot of curly gray hair came out.

"Dr. Simmons," he said, holding out his hand. We shook and I told him my name.

"You're looking for April, I hear," pausing. "We haven't heard from her since last week and, quite frankly, we're concerned about her. Are you a detective?"

I thought, what the hell. "Yes," I said, letting that sink in. "I heard she went on a trip last week as part of a class project. But now I hear she really didn't."

"That's right," he said, then paused for a moment. "I'm not aware of any class projects. But April is a very responsible young lady. It just isn't like her to miss class like this, especially one she's supposed to teach. And I can't imagine her making up stories," he added. "She's missed a few classes lately because she's been sick. Nothing serious I understand. Other than that, she's a model student. One of our best. And a great help to Dr. Lawless," looking at me for a reaction. A little too long I felt. Maybe wondering about Lawless and April.

"I've already told the other detective everything I know. I don't have anything more to add." Then, "Have you talked with the students in her apartment? One of them may know something."

He waited a moment to see if there was anything else. I said no, thanked him, and headed for her apartment. The secretary gave me directions. It was an old red brick building that looked like it belonged in a ghetto—the white window frames pealing, some bricks missing grout, some missing entirely, like in a mouth that needed dental work. There was a door on the bottom floor with the word Office on it. I knocked. The hallway stunk from either mold or unwashed clothes. It didn't matter which; I held my breath. I was still holding it when the door opened.

A young man stuck his head out. "Yeah?"

"I'm looking for April Januarie," I said, finally taking a breath. The place still reeked.

"And you are?" he said.

"I'm a detective," I said. He blinked and slid a little more behind the door. Protection. It's interesting how seldom anyone ever asks to see a badge. They're intimidated. Most people have something to hide and so the first thing they think is *What did I do*? So, they don't ask. It might stir the water.

"I already told the police I haven't seen her. She left here last week. Hasn't come back. You talk with her friend yet?" He rummaged through his pants, pulled out a pack of cigarettes, and moved out from behind the door. He leaned against the doorjamb as he lit up, holding out the pack to me. I shook my head.

"Who's her friend?"

"He lives in the apartment across the hall. He's from South Africa, just like April. Name's Adile," he said, blowing smoke into the hall.

"You allow smoking here?"

"No, but then I'm the RA," he said smiling. "You might catch him before he goes to class. Third floor, room 207."

I thanked him and took the stairs two at a time. Catch him before class. Nobody answered when I knocked on the door. A man with red hair poked his head out of the next apartment.

"If you're looking for Adile, he's in class."

I walked over. Bright red hair.

"What class would that be?" I said.

"Intro to Soc. You looking for April?"

"That's right. Do you know her?"

"Sure. You a cop?"

"No. What time is the class over?"

The kid told me two o'clock. It was 12:45 so I got directions for the cafeteria. Leaves were falling now that October was taking hold. Most of the trees had begun to turn, some were already bare and had left the ground covered with a quilt of bright oranges, yellows, and dull browns. The whole scene a reminder of death. I noticed some walnuts scattered under one of the trees, their green shells already turning black from the dark meat inside the outer shell. That covering would stain the hands of those breaking them open to get to the nuts inside.

The afternoon was catching the chill of what felt like an early winter, so I buttoned the top of my shirt, pulled up the collar on my sweater, and walked more quickly across the campus. I was glad I wore jeans.

I was in time for the dinner buffet. I ordered sweet tea and helped myself to the Fall Special: turkey off the bone, mashed potatoes, gravy, cranberry sauce, and stuffing. It was as good as it sounded. I watched the students file in after their classes. It had been a long time since I had been in a college cafeteria. Seven long years. There were few good memories of those days. So, I drank coffee while I waited for the class to end and then headed back to the Psych/Soc building to wait for April's friend.

The redhead had described Adile to me: "He's kinda short, dark hair, and...well...he looks...uh... Middle Eastern," he had said, searching for the right word. No one of that description came out. I looked into the classroom and saw a short, dark-haired man talking with Jackson. That's got to be him, I thought. Then he turned and headed my way. Jackson saw me and waved for me to come in. I waved back and held up a finger—later—and called Adile over as he came through the door.

I introduced myself explaining that I was a detective trying to locate April and that I understood he was a friend of hers.

"That's right," he said. There was a question in his tone. And an accent. Like Ernie Els.

"Do you know where she is?"

"No, man. I don't have any idea," looking back into the room to see if Jackson was watching. The 'no, man' made me suspicious.

"Why don't I believe you?"

"I don't know. It's the truth," he said, shrugging.

"Okay," I said, "truth or not, your friend is missing and I have a feeling you can help me." I paused. "How about I treat at the cafeteria." The turkey was still sitting on my stomach. But I could try the pumpkin pie.

"I'm telling you man, I don't know anything," but he must have been thinking of the Fall Special, because he finally said, okay, to the cafeteria; he had some time before his next class.

We kicked through leaves that the wind had gathered into small mounds along the way. Some of the students I had seen earlier were leaving.

"So, you're with the police?" he said, as we entered the dining hall. Many South Africans—minorities especially—are leery of the police. Even after Apartheid.

"No. A private investigator. But I have no doubt that the Riverdale police will be talking to you—sooner than later," I said, and pulled two chairs over to a table in the corner of the cafeteria out of the way of the dinner traffic. "So, let's practice for that, okay?" He stared at me. I studied his eyes.

A Turkish cop once told me he could recognize a terrorist by simply looking into his eyes. *Gozler yalan soylemez!* The eyes do not lie.

Adile was no terrorist, but he was frightened of something.

9

IT'S ABOUT THE MONEY

What Adile was about to tell me would add to my nightmares—not only about Maxie but about every missing person out there. We live—and I mean most of us—in a sterile world.

"What?" I said, as Adile looked away. It's always the eyes. They give you away. He shifted in his seat and put his head down.

I reached across the table and took hold of his forearm. He tried to pull away. "Talk to me, Adile," I said, softly, but keeping a tight grip.

He hesitated. Then, "She's on a drug trial." He paused and looked around. The students at the other tables were studying.

"A drug trial?" I said. "How do you know that?"

Adile reacted nervously, taking in the whole room quickly. A girl at a table next to us was staring. When I looked at her, she dropped her head—back to her book.

He took a deep breath. "She told me. We've been volunteering—every couple of weeks—for experimental studies. Usually on campus. But sometimes we travel—you know, to another clinic or university. They pay our expenses." He had caught the attention of the other table again.

Adile's hands were shaking.

"Let's go somewhere more private," I said. I spotted an empty room off the cafeteria. It looked like a faculty dining area. I gave the students who were staring at us a look as I got up. They stopped. Once I closed the door to the private room, and we settled at the table, he relaxed—at least the shaking stopped.

"All right. Talk to me."

"We have been volunteering for drug trials now for the last six months or so. It's good money," he said, looking up at me. "The trials usually don't pay a lot. But if we do several a week, we could make fifty to a hundred dollars a week."

"Uh-huh. Not much but I guess it pays the bills," I said, encouraging him.

"That's right. Last week a drug company from out of town contacted April and offered her three thousand plus expenses to take part in a trial."

"That's a lot of money."

He nodded. "But I warned her."

"Yeah? Why?"

"Volunteers aren't supposed to do more than one trial a week…at the most! We did three the week before. And now this one."

"Why so much money?"

"More risky. The normal trial is no big deal. The runs that pay big money are more dangerous. You know, side effects, man. Besides she wasn't feeling too good. I don't know if she had a reaction to one of the other drugs or just caught a bug. I told her not to do it but—you know—she did it anyway."

"Did she tell you where she was going?"

"No."

"So I'm the first person you told."

"I was scared."

"Of what?"

"Man, if I told, we could get thrown out of school. We signed agreements with the university that we wouldn't take part in concurrent trials. I don't know if it's because they're concerned about our health or because multiple drugs in our blood might screw up the trial."

I shook my head. Unbelievable. "You're jeopardizing April's life by waiting until now to tell someone."

"Am I in trouble?" he said.

"Maybe. The police are going to want to talk to you," I said, reaching across the table and grabbing his arm again, "and you better pray that nothing happened to her. You held information back from an investigation. That's a felony." I held his eyes for a few moments, then let go of his arm.

"My God, a felony?" he said.

"Believe it, "I said. I let the silence set in. He looked out at the cafeteria as though someone out there might help him. But no one did. No one even looked our way. No one out there cared. But what did he expect? He didn't really care about April or he would have told someone about her little jog into the world of experimental drugs. He was only worried about being kicked out of school.

It was 5:00 o'clock when I left Adile, sitting in the dining room, staring at the empty tabletop. And it was eight days since April's disappearance and it was eight years since my son's and seven years since my separation from Jillie, and four years since our divorce, and now...every missing person case eats away inside. I can find other people's kids. I am so good at that. Why the hell couldn't I find Maxie?

A sudden wind tried to blow me across the parking lot as I headed across campus. I had forgotten the chill that comes with autumns in Ohio and pulled my sweater around my neck, hoping to block the cold from getting under my clothes and into my body. I hurried to the car, started it up, turned up the heat—full blast—and headed for the bar at the hotel to get a drink and call Passarelli. It was time to clear my mind.

10

CLUES

C lues are elusive. You have to dig them out. I sat at the bar sifting through the details of the case—there were more of them now. They came even more clearly as I sipped at the glass of Pinot. Sometimes at night, when I can't sleep because a case is driving me nuts, I go to my bedroom window that overlooks the Everglades and search for the moon. Sometimes it sits low on the horizon, backlighting some pines that live in a hammock several miles away. Some are bare, pushing their bony trunks into the moon, jutting out like toothpicks that need to be disposed of. It's those times I think of Maxie.

I drained a good part of the Pinot and was staring at the glass that was connected to my hand and… *We were in a park near the College, off main street, behind the Antique Shop, and in the middle of the green there was a water fountain, in the form of a lion, a lion with his mouth open, and the water spigot was in the lion's mouth and it worried Maxie. "Dad, what does a lion sound like when it roars," he said looking into the mouth, trying to decide if he was going to put his head in it and get a drink. I roared—loud—there wasn't anyone around. He jumped. I felt bad as I thought back—I shouldn't have scared him. I should have given him the hug that he was waiting for. That he really needed.*

But it was a memory now. And I pulled out a pen from my shirt pocket and began scribbling—new energy to search again—substitute April for Maxie—why not? I'm not getting anywhere with my own son—why the hell not focus on April. A woman who had just come in sat down one stool away from me as I started to line up the clues on a napkin. I used my left hand to block her view.

Affair with female student.

JL is holding back—something.

Student on a drug trial is missing—eight days.

"You must be a writer," she said. She was slurring her words. "Whyn't you give it a break, come over here and buy me a drink, handsome," motioning to the chair between us.

I ignored her and called Passarelli.

"Riverdale Police." A woman. I thought back to Miami PD and tried to remember how many women were in my division when I was there. I counted about ten in my head. Louise Delgado was one of them. We worked a case together last year—both of us almost getting killed. We're pretty close now. How close? I'll save that for later.

"Sir?" the voice reminded me.

I told her I wanted to talk with Detective Passarelli.

"He's not in, sir. What's your name, please?"

I gave her my name and asked her to tell Passarelli to give me a call when he came in.

I was on my third glass and the wine was beginning to taste like the stuff I used to drink in college when Passarelli called. The blonde leaned over as I answered the phone. "Go ahead and get it," she said, slurring her words worse than before. I wouldn't need another drink. It was all in the air between us. I said thanks and walked away so I could have some privacy.

"Don't play so hard-to-get!" she said, loud, so that the whole room would hear about our break-up. I shook my head, more to myself than to her.

"Whaddya need, Cooper?" said Passarelli. No small talk.

I told him about Adile and he said, "Christ, why didn't you call right away." Then paused, "You believe this kid?"

I told him I believed him, no reason not to. And that this new information didn't sound good for April, meaning that she was trying to keep the drug trial secret for a reason. Then I remembered the trial would have violated university policy. So maybe that explained it.

"Yeah, but I don't get it. Drug trial? That complicates things. And doesn't explain where she is now, does it?"

I admitted that it didn't.

"The kid tell you the name of the drug company hired her?"

I said, no, but I would see what I could find it out. Not to worry, he said. That was his job.

I ended the call and went back to the bar where my friend was still sitting.

"Changed your mind, huh?" she said, her breath not smelling so badly now. Maybe that was because mine was just plain sour. I nodded, ordered another glass, and went to my room.

I called Jackson. It went into his voice mail. "Why the hell didn't you tell me she was on a drug trial?" I said. "And don't tell me you didn't know," some anger leaking out. I couldn't hold it back. Didn't want to. And then I passed out. Must have been the wine. It always does that to me. Especially three glasses.

11

THE RIVER

It was about 4:00 a.m. when my cell rang out Pachelbel's Canon.

"Cooper?"

"Yeah," I said.

"Passarelli."

"Uh-oh."

"Afraid so." He paused. "Sheriff's Department turned up a body in the Ohio. About fifty miles south of here. I think it might be our missing girl."

I hesitated. The picture that Jackson had shown me—of April—it was in my head now.

"You still there?" Passarelli said.

I told him, yeah, I'm still here. But my mind was on the river, and April, and Jackson, and Adile, and the drug company that paid her for the drug trial—maybe that killed her. Or…maybe it wasn't her, I was hoping—for Jackson's sake.

"Why don't you tell me where you're at, Cooper. I'll pick you up," Passarelli said, then added, "Maybe it's not April. Let's wait and see." Mind reader.

47

But deep down I knew it was her.

Passarelli picked me up a little after 4:30 a.m. Not much sleep this night.

Route 56 runs along the river north and south. We headed south toward Riverdale and past the houses that lined the bank, rain making it difficult to see, the wipers working hard to clear the view ahead. The river was swollen. I had seen the river after spring rains, angry swells washing against the banks, trying to overtake the road. Earlier in the evening, a TV weatherman in red suspenders predicted the highway would be flooded by the weekend. But the highway was still open though the water was up to the berm in places. We sped past dark houses and overhanging trees while I stared at the outline of my face in the window.

Red lights bounced off the hillside as we approached a bend in the highway that overlooked an inlet below. There was a break in the guardrail that ran along the highway. A crime tape was strung along the road and the hillside overlooking the river. Sheriff's cars had cut off the highway at both ends, several parked at the crime scene at right angles to each other just outside the tape. Cops stood at the tape blocking a few news cameras trying to get closer. Some bystanders had already pulled to the side of the highway and left their cars to get a better look. Passarelli eyed them as he parked near the Sheriff's cars. He badged the cops at the tape and headed for the river where there was a small gathering of deputies and crime scene people.

"Passarelli," said Joe, introducing himself to the officer who was standing on the riverbank. He had been looking down into the water and glanced up when Passarelli came up behind him.

"Smith," he said. "I'm the one called you." Passarelli nodded.

"She's over there, Detective," Smith said, pointing down the riverbank at a body caught in the branches of a tree that had fallen over the bank and stretched into the river ten feet or so. "Mess, ain't it," he said, pointing to the chewed-up arms and legs hanging through the tree branches. "Looks like it had been stuffed in a heavy plastic bag. Parts of it are still attached to the body," and he motioned to the torn brown plastic hanging from the torso rising and falling with the wind and rain.

"At least it's in one place," I said, trying to hold back the food pushing itself up through my throat.

"Yeah, there's that," said Smith still staring.

"What makes you think it's our missing girl?" said Passarelli.

"Tattoo. Picture we had of her. She's got a flower on her left shoulder blade."

Then Smith waved to a man in a suit standing next to one of the county cars. "Sheriff, we're ready to bring up the body," he yelled. The big man nodded. There was commotion as another car pulled up behind the Sheriff's.

"That there's the ME, gentlemen. Y'all better step back. He's gonna want us to pull her up," said Smith. "That is, after he gets a good look-see," he added quickly.

The ME was short with grey hair and a gut that looked like he watched lots of football, beer in one hand and chips nearby.

He slid down the slope, hanging onto a fireman.

"Watch it, doc," said the tech bracing him as they both descended about six feet to the body. His one shoe was almost in the river as he searched over the body, finally finding a wrist.

"She's dead, gentlemen," he said.

"Wow," whispered Passarelli. "I can't believe it."

"Official words, officer," said the ME, looking back at Passarelli—like don't think I didn't hear you.

"You can bring the body up, boys," said the doc, turning to the firemen. "I'm done down here." He started up, almost sliding back down the bank as he reached the top. But he teetered then caught himself.

"Wish this damn rain would stop," he said, looking out at the water swelling and threatening to swamp the highway downstream where the road dipped to river level.

Two firemen with long boots and rubber coats eased down the bank carrying a large body bag. They began to untangle the girl from the limbs.

"Careful, boys! Get everything, including the plastic, and try to keep the body intact! And bring the branches if you have to," he yelled after them. "And don't fuck up my scene," he added as he turned back to us. "So easy to screw up a crime scene," he said, shaking his head. "At least we got pictures in case they do," growling the words out.

"Who called it in?" I asked the deputy standing next to me.

"That couple over there," pointing to a man and woman standing by a county car, its lights flashing crimson and white against the hillside. The man was talking to a deputy. The woman held a hand over her mouth, like she was watching a horror show.

The firemen laid the body on the ground in front of the ME. He shook his head as he stooped over and peeled back the bag—the eyes vacant holes. What had they seen? And what had they done to her? And I wondered about her suffering. I knew why I did. It's the kids that bother me the most—they are so unsuspecting, so naïve, so trusting.

One image stays with me: of a child in southwest Florida, at a car wash, the child standing outside waiting for the car to go through the wash cycle. The parents not watching. And there was a video that showed the whole thing. And it was brutally clear—black and white clear: a man taking the child's hand and leading her to his car, the girl looking up at him—walking out of sight. I wanted to jump into the video and grab her, millions of people watching just like I was—the video going viral. And all of us helpless to stop him—the man—watching the girl disappear from the screen.

The police found her body later.

One of the deputies held an umbrella over the ME as he worked.

"Long slit here—see?" said the doc, pointing to a long open wound running up her side and another across her lower back. The cop standing behind me coughed and choked. I moved away.

The rain was picking up again, creating a sea of mud by the riverbank; it caught at my shoes as I tried to lift them.

"Looks like someone's been doing some surgery on this girl," said the doc.

"April," I said. "Her name's April."

"Uh-huh," he said and continued to check the body.

"Definitely pretty crude surgery. More like you would expect from a butcher. Make you feel any better, I'm thinking she was already dead," he said, looking up. "But I'll know more after the autopsy."

"What do you think killed her, doc?" said Smith.

"I don't know," he said. "Let's see what we find tomorrow." And he packed up his kit and motioned to Smith.

"Might as well get her to autopsy." Then, "See you boys in the morning…first thing, if you want a front row seat." And he made his way through the mud, stepping carefully, his shoulders hunched over like a plumber carrying a load of tools—or maybe the weight of his job.

We sat for a while in the car, staring out at what there was of the night sky. It was mostly just rain and fog, October weather on the river.

"What the hell that girl get herself into?" said Passarelli, staring through the window into darkness. The police cars had quit lighting up the scene.

I shook my head and listened to the rain against the roof. He pulled out on the highway, past the ME's car, past the county cars that still blocked the road at both ends; past the dark houses that lined the hills on the way back upriver; past the trees hanging over the banks of the road, some of whose roots were bare, threatening to give way and release the tree into the water; past the rising river, six feet or more below us on the hills, but beginning to flow over the road as we dropped down into valleys; past the lights on the Kentucky side that were still visible through the rain; and finally into Riverdale, still above the flood, but maybe not for long.

"You wanna see the autopsy?" he said, as he pulled into the hotel's entry. There was an overhang there.

"No," I said. I've had enough of death.

He nodded. "Call me in the morning." And he pulled away.

12

KILL THE MESSENGER

I thought about Jackson as I stood there, studying the new thirty-foot sign, burning green and white against the black and the rain. That was a change, thinking back to the days when the hotel sign rested on top of a large, round, black steel pole.

It was 6:21 a.m. and the television stations would be breaking the big news soon in their early morning editions. I called Jackson. It went into voice mail. So I texted him to meet me at the hotel and gave him my room number. At 6:31 he texted me back.

"Be there at 7:30. What's up?"

"Tell you when you get there," I texted.

I got a frown back.

I showered, shaved, and made some coffee. While I drank, I stared in the mirror. I looked like hell. I couldn't believe the guy in the mirror. Did I always have those black bags hanging under my eyes?

I was pulling on my pants when I heard a loud rap. That's Jackson. No patience.

"You look like hell," Jackson said, coming in the door.

I nodded.

"I made some coffee. Black."

"That's good. What's up?"

I shook my head and told him to have a seat, pointing to a recliner in the corner of the room. I figured he would need the comfort. I handed him a coffee, pulled out a hard chair from the desk, and squared off so I was facing him directly.

"This is gonna be bad news," Jackson said, his voice flat. He sensed my tension.

"The police found the body of a young girl they believe is April about fifty miles downriver." There it was. No lead up. I didn't know any other way. I watched him react.

He stared at me at first, then, "That can't be," he replied, rising abruptly, some of his coffee splashing on his pants. He stared at the spill for a moment, almost as though he had discovered radium there, then dropped back down again, catching himself as he struggled to find the seat.

"That's just not possible!" he argued, shaking his head and throwing his hands into the air. "Not possible," he mumbled, and he was staring at the floor now, as if there were something down there that would clarify it all. "It's a mistake," he continued but with doubt in his voice, "that can't be April. I mean there are thousands of girls out there, hundreds of thousands." He was looking up at me for a reaction, his hands were shaking, his eyes red with questions all over the place. "How could the police know it's April for God's sake?" he argued, hands spread out, like he was pleading for me to agree with him.

All I could do was shrug, as if to say…?

Then, after a brief silence, he continued, "For sure?" begging, as if the possibility of it being April was right there now, right in front of him. And he leaned back in his chair, shielding his eyes with his right hand, while he gripped the arm of the chair with his left. Then, finally, he looked up at me, face wet, his eyes red and angry, and said, "No," shaking his head. Then he said it again, "No!" louder this time and then, "No! No! No!" over and over again, until all the energy it took to get the words out died, and only the quiet remained. And then Jackson Laighleis, the tough guy I had always known, pushed back into his chair, as though trying to disappear in it. And silence took over like it usually does when there's nothing left to say.

I went to my suitcase and pulled out a bottle of Jack Daniels Black. Grabbed a can of Planters Peanuts that I had picked up earlier at CVS, filled two glasses with ice, poured for each of us and sat back down.

Jackson picked up a Kleenex, wiped the snot off his nose, and drained his glass.

"It's her. I'm pretty sure," I said. The Jack Daniels burned on the way down.

He continued to stare at the floor as if he were still looking for meaning there.

The rain had stopped. The window looking out over the parking light was turning slowly from a night shade of black to a dull gray, the first sign of another day. No matter what happens to any of us, it's always a normal day to everyone else. The stock market will still open at 9:30, the paper will get delivered, TV anchors will report the news— today it will be April's death—men and women will be getting ready for work, all the time that April's parents will be wracked with pain when they hear, and mothers will still get their children ready for school, never dreaming that their kids may never get there.

And every year about 690,000 people are reported missing. Figure it out. That's about 1,890 a day. Of those, according to the FBI's National Crime Information Center, about 530,000 are children. Victims under eighteen. And that's about 1,452 a day, the majority, runaways or the victims of family abductions. They're usually solved. But others are the result of crimes like kidnapping or murder.

At the end of the day there are usually between 60,000 to 80,000 unresolved cases. And only a few of those will ever make the evening news. April would come off the list of the missing today and become another one of those solved cases. Good for the police reports. Too bad for her.

And I dwelt on past cases of the missing, of those who turned up dead or worse—mentally crippled by the ordeal for the rest of their lives. And the underground trade in body parts with its bloodthirsty, brutal, crude, dissection of a body—of almost anybody that's available—for money. Hey, it's a good business. Why? There's a price tag on each part: up to a hundred thousand for just the skin. And I couldn't help but wonder how April died. Toxic drugs? Her body just worn out from the trials? I thought of the movie, *Never Let Me Go*. Kids being raised for their parts—like in a junk car lot—and then thrown away—like April into the river.

We must have sat for over an hour, just drinking and thinking. Then, finally, Jackson pulled himself out of his chair and collapsed on the bed behind me.

I called the university and told the secretary that Doctor Lawless was sick and wouldn't be in. Then I dropped onto the couch in the outer suite.

Jackson shook me at 11:30 a.m. I tried to remember where I was. Neither of us said anything. The ice bucket was filled with water, so I dumped it, went down the hall, and filled it with more ice. There were some crackers and snacks in a basket on the table so we broke into those. I looked at the bottle. Half full. Jackson held out his glass. No ice. So I filled it, poured us both a drink and sat down again, saying nothing, Jackson still trying to find meaning in the floor. I stared at the rain that had started up again and was beating against the sliding glass doors. I wondered about the rising river. But this was a six-story Holiday Inn. All inside hallways.

By one o'clock in the afternoon we had finished the other half of the bottle and the rain had stopped. My brain was on a merry-go-round and Jackson had passed out again. I called Sonya. She seemed surprised to hear my voice. I told her Jackson and I had just had lunch and were hanging out and he would call her later. Why wasn't Jackson calling her? she asked. He's drunk, I told her, and so was I, and, when we sobered up, I would bring him home. She didn't say anything for a long time. Then she asked me when I would tell her what was really going on, a hard edge to her voice, and I said, maybe sometime soon. She said, good, and hung up. I could hear her anger in the slam of the phone. I tipped my glass to her. Don't kill the messenger.

Today was bad. But tomorrow would be worse. I hadn't said anything to Jackson about the condition of April's body. And it seemed that Sonya hadn't been listening to the news this morning—or maybe she had and April's name hadn't been released as yet. But it would be. And Sonya would wonder. And there goes another bottle of Jack Daniels—or two maybe. So, I turned on the TV to see what the pretty blondes who read the news were saying about the whole bloody case.

13

THE REPORTER

I hadn't drunk as much as Jackson. I think he had consumed about two thirds of the bottle. So, we left his car at the hotel and I dropped him off in front of his house. I sat in the car for a minute while he fumbled with the key and was interrupted by Sonya who opened the door into him. She looked out at me without waving, turned away quickly, and helped him into the house. The rain had started again. I looked down at the rising tide of the river.

I got back to the Holiday Inn around 9:00 p.m. The room was too quiet, so I headed down to the hotel bar. Before I got out the door my cell rang.

"Detective Cooper?"

"Yeah," I said. "Who's this?"

"Jason Eisenberg, *The Plain Dealer*," he said.

"The Cleveland *Plain Dealer*?" I said.

"That's right."

"How did you get my number?"

"Easy. I'm a reporter."

"What do you want?"

"I'd like to talk with you about the body of the girl that was found in the river this morning. I understand you were at the scene." Just like that. How do these guys get their information?

I didn't know what to say so I said this wasn't a good time. Before I could shut him up he pushed on about a series of articles he was doing. I ended the call.

My cell buzzed again. I didn't answer. Best way to handle a reporter.

It rang again. I let it ring.

I locked the door and headed for the hotel bar. It was quiet also. Strange for a weekend. I guessed there was nothing to celebrate. So I sat at the bar and ordered a glass of California merlot. A Holiday Inn lounge in the Valley is not a fancy place. A restaurant mostly with a bar for a few single people who didn't want a table. A man at the end of the bar was ordering a shot and a glass of beer. He downed the shot like it was medicine and followed it quickly with the beer. All in less than a minute. He rapped on the bar and ordered another. I watched him through this ritual several times until someone tapped me on the shoulder and said, "Detective Cooper?"

The guy standing next to me must have been no older that his mid-twenties, short, maybe 5'5", black curly hair and a round but handsome face. Maybe a college kid.

"Yeah?" I said.

"Eisenberg. *The Plain Dealer*. Remember?" and he held out his hand.

"You're kidding! You were already here," I said, irritated.

"I called from the lobby and, lucky me, here you are," he said, holding up his hands like, Here I am and here are you.

"Uh-huh, lucky," I said. "All right so you're here." I nodded to the seat next to me.

He hiked himself up onto the stool.

"I saw the report of the girl's murder on TV. Gruesome, huh? It's a national story now, you know. When I heard your name on the news, I remembered an *AP* wire story about a former Miami PD homicide detective named Cooper who chased kidnappers through the Everglades. That's you, right? Rescued a ten-year-old boy?"

He didn't wait for me to respond. "So here I am," and he looked at me like I should be excited to see him.

"He was twelve-years-old and his name was Eddie." I tried the wine. A little sweet but it had a nice bite to it.

I thought back on that case. Yeah, kidnappers, trading in young kids. Let your imagination run wild with that thought: cheap labor, sex partners, body parts. You buy them, you use them for whatever purpose you want. I couldn't dwell on it too long because my thoughts drifted ultimately to Maxie in the hands of some stranger.

"Mr. Cooper?" he said, watching me curiously.

"What is it that you want?" I said. "Look. You wasted a trip. I don't have any more information right now than you do."

He shook his head and shrugged. "I'm just trying to follow up. You know—a look at Cooper. Who is he?" Trying everything.

He had ordered a beer. But it was just sitting in front of him. He was playing with the salt shaker.

"Put some in your beer. It'll give it some flavor."

He poured and watched the salt disappear into the beer and turn into a white foam. I looked at his fingernails. They needed trimming.

"How long have you been a reporter, Jason?"

"About a year. This is my first job out of college."

"*The Plain Dealer*. A big paper for a first job."

"Yeah, and my dad didn't want me to take it. He wanted a doctor in the family." He was staring into my empty glass. "But he was happy that I went to Columbia. 'A good journalism school,' he told me. At least there's that."

"You ought to rethink that doctor thing," I said, paid for my drink, and turned to leave.

"Hey, I came a long way. Come on, gimme a break!" He looked hurt—like I owed him something.

"We'll talk, Jason," I said. "We'll talk. When I have something to talk about. Right now, I'm just detecting. And that's your story," and I headed for my room for some rest and privacy.

14

TONY DEFELICE

FRIDAY MORNING, OCTOBER 8

I had drunk too much. I get tired when I drink. So, I fell into bed just to rest my eyes and before I knew it Pachelbel's Canon was playing in my ear. I love that tune, but not at 7:01 in the a.m.

"Where the hell are you, Coop? I turn on the TV and see this story about a girl turning up dead in the Ohio River. I didn't think much about it 'til I heard the name, Cooper. That got my attention. And I think, No, not my *best* friend, Coop. He woulda tole me he was on a case in Ohio," said Tony DeFelice. "Isn't that right, Coop?"

Tony DeFelice was my partner for five years when we worked homicide with Miami PD. We grew up together in Cleveland along with a street-wise kid named Richie Marino and a couple of other guys from the east side. We formed our own gang—for protection. In Cleveland you were either from the east side or the west side. People from the east side felt like the people from the west side were just plain stupid. West siders felt the same way about east siders. It's all about where you live, isn't it?

We grew up tough because every day we had to fight our way home from school. Sometimes the fights turned violent. Richie was known for using a Cleveland Indians baseball bat to clear the sidewalk. DeFelice was just as tough as Richie. Today Tony uses a gun; Richie still uses his bat.

"So, when you comin' back to the big city, Coop?" he said.

"I'm up here a while. I've got a friend looks like he got in over his head."

"Yeah. No kiddin'. But it's not your case. You got cops up there can do that. You don't need the bullshit of workin' a homicide in Ohio. Besides you ain't licensed there. You hear what I'm sayin'?"

"Thanks, Tony," I said. "How's…?"

"She's right here. Wants to talk," he said.

"She" is Louise Delgado, a detective with Miami PD. Her job is to monitor gang activity in the city—as well as to keep track of what I'm doing.

"Coop. You stayin' safe up there in redneck country?" She sounded nervous.

"I'm doing fine, Louise," I said. I could feel the energy on the line. Louise and I were developing a kind of relationship. It was complicated though by my feelings for Jillie. Louise was aware of them.

"I got some weeks comin'…in case you need some help," she offered.

"Maybe," I said.

"You making any progress?"

"Not a whole lot yet. I'm still trying to figure out the cutting of her body. It was gruesome."

"You run into your ex?" I was waiting for that.

"Yeah. We had a talk…when was it?" I was stumbling. "Yeah, Tuesday night…I think. On the phone. About Maxie mostly." I didn't tell her Jillie suggested we have lunch.

Our relationship is—how can I put it?—still developing. It started with a kiss. She was recovering from gunshot wounds in a hospital after we both got caught in a shootout with gangbangers in Miami, in a place called the Hole. The streets are the neighborhood garbage cans. And rats come out and feed on the food that's strewn along them; or on a homeless person who died; or on someone who hadn't died yet but was too weak to fight them off. And then they scramble back into the giant red-brick apartment buildings and hide in the garbage there—the remnants of a Big Mac or a Wendy's burger, shit that one of the gangbangers left behind, the urine that penetrates the air.

I took a shoulder hit that still hurts when I raise my arm over my head. Louise took one in the side among other places. It was touch-and-go with her for a while. I was released first, so I stopped by her room to see how she was doing. Neither of us had ever brought up our feelings. But that day, with death just behind us, we kissed. I leaned down and she pulled my face to hers and we kissed. It seemed like it lasted for hours.

"Hmmmm," Louise said, still thinking about my talk with my former. Jillie is always there—always—in the back of my mind, no matter how hard I try to put her to rest.

I told Louise about Jackson and his wife, about April and about her work for a drug company. I said I didn't have much but could use some help in finding the people who paid April for the drug trial.

"Any ideas?"

"Maybe," she said. "I gotta friend who works for NIH. I think they keep a record of clinical trials."

"Friends in high places," I said.

"Former boyfriend," she said. Ouch, I thought. Touché.

So, I thanked her and told her I owed her another one. I figured she hadn't kept track of the other IOUs.

"Dinner," she said.

"You're a cheap date," I said.

"Not where we're going," she said. Then, "I gotta run. Another homicide—in gangland. One hundred and eighty-one so far this year."

"Be safe," I said. "You think you might be heading this way?"

"Plan on it," she said.

15

SONYA

I had just hung up from Louise when Pachelbel's Canon rang out again. Sometimes I just let it play itself out and then call back—I need the peace it brings to me. But I saw the number and it was Jackson.

"Hey, what's up, Jackson?" I said.

"It's Sonya."

I was jolted out of my Canon reverie. Hearing Sonya's voice when you expect your client is like realizing you're going the wrong way on a one-way street.

"Sonya!" I said, thinking fast about what to say.

"Yeah, it's me. I just saw the news. I need to know what's going on." No explanations. I told you. Sonya's sharp. Sonya Anikin. Top of her class at Georgetown Law. She's a sweet girl, beautiful, with those sharp clear features that are so characteristic of Russian women. Like Lara in Doctor Zhivago. I wondered why Jackson would cheat on her. But who knows what happens to people in their own bedrooms. I paused too long.

"Why are you here?" she said, deciding to help me out. Like she's the lawyer and I'm on the stand.

I still paused. Then, "Jackson asked if I would help him find April."

"That bitch," is all she said. I just told you, Sonya is a sweet girl. Silence on her side. Heavy breathing on mine.

"Looks like you found her," she said, her voice as flat as an Arizona mesa. There was so much silence now that I didn't have enough in me to begin to fill it, so I let it be.

"Is that all you're going to tell me, Coop?" she said. The lawyer in her talking. I mean, I would ordinarily say that Jackson's my client. But to Sonya? His wife? And she's a lawyer. She knows all about client privilege. So I asked her what she wanted to know. First one to speak loses.

"I know my husband's been seeing her," she said. "So, you can skip that part. What exactly do you plan to do now?"

It isn't as though we haven't been friends for these past eight years. The trips to the Valley that the four of us, Jillie, Jackson, Sonya, and me, took with Maxie—the paddleboat in Marietta, camping in Oglebay Park, fishing on the river, dancing in Wheeling Park...under the summer stars...so many of them in the blackness of the Valley's sky. There were no secrets then. There are a lot of them now. How time changes things. So much has passed in these eight years. I felt her anger, even though she didn't talk—a woman scorned—it left me with nothing to say. Which is what happens when you have secrets you can't share, even with someone you love. So much has passed these eight years.

I hung up. I didn't know what else to do. I didn't like myself for doing that. But really, what else could I do?

16

THE SUSPECT

I no sooner hung up than my cell buzzed. No Canon this time. I had turned off the ringer.

"They're taking me in for questioning," yelled Jackson. "They think I killed her!"

"They're just doing what's normal," I said, trying to calm him down. "Spouses and boyfriends are always suspects. If you've done nothing wrong, you've got nothing to worry about."

I felt guilty about saying that. Fact is you do have to worry. Justice has nothing to do with prosecution. It has everything to do with the kind of lawyer you hire. Innocent people go to jail all the time. In this case the police are looking at the data—of the 165,000 plus murders that were committed in the U.S. between 2000 and 2010 (excluding Florida—there were about 11,000 in Florida), about half of them were committed by someone who was related to or knew the victim. That's the sorry fact, but I wasn't about to tell Jackson that.

"What am I supposed to do?" he broke in.

"We need to find that drug company," I said, making it a joint effort. Always involve the client if you can. "You have any ideas?"

"I'll see what I can do," he replied, sounding more settled. Keep him busy, I thought to myself. Out of trouble and out of my hair.

"Get back to me if you get anything. In the meantime, get a lawyer!" I said. "A good one. And keep your mouth shut."

I figured it was time to call Huxter Crow.

17

THE INDIAN

"Yeah, who's this?" said the voice on the other side.

"One guess," I said.

"Coop, my old buddy," cried Huxter. "Where the hell you been? I figured you forgot your old friend, or else you was deceased." Uh-huh.

Huxter Crow is an old school Florida cracker. His ancestors were among the original settlers of Florida who came from Spain in the late 1700s. They were a rugged and lawless bunch of cowboys, much like those of the Old West, who moved about like gypsies and worked when they could to get by. They were known as Crackers. That name most likely came from the way they rounded up cattle, not with a lasso like the cowboys out west, but with a bullwhip they cracked over the herd. They were proud and boastful, and scoffed at modern conveniences like air conditioning and refrigerators. That was Huxter. In his past was Miccosukee Indian blood. His wife was a Seminole. That marriage lasted only for a few years. His last attempt at matrimony.

I met him when I was fishing in the Ten Thousand Islands. Near Rabbit Key. I heard shots. It sounded like they were coming from a camp on the island. A python was wrapped around a gator and a man dressed like a frontiersman was shooting at it—missing by a wide margin. He was also drunk. The python let loose and both disappeared into the water. Turns out the man's wife had just left him and he had set up camp on Rabbit Key to be depressed and alone. We spent the night drinking and talking—him telling me all about the misfortunes of his short-lived marriage. We became good friends after that—Huck calling me his shaman confessor. "Never forget what you done for me that night, my friend," he always told me.

When he learned I had left the MPD and opened my own private detective agency, he wanted to join me and help catch all them sonofabitch varmints. "Think of me as a pardner," he said. So I did. And I paid him. He just never got his license.

"So, what's up?" Like we had just talked yesterday.

I filled him in on Jackson's phone call. "The police found her body in the Ohio yesterday morning."

"Oh yeah? That musta been the one I seen on the news last night."

I nodded, forgetting I was on the phone.

"We get the news down here in Everglades City, you know." Defensive.

Huxter never went beyond ninth grade. But he's what you would call swamp-smart. He's lived there all his life and knows all about predators.

"You still there, Kemo Sabe?" he said, always reminding me he's part Indian.

"How soon can you get up here?" I said, thinking I could use him to keep track of Jackson while I tried to run down the drug company.

71

"I can get over there pronto. Give me a chance to pack my truck. Day and a half, I figure. Give or take." I told him where to meet me.

"And bring your alligator gun," I said.

I called Louise as soon as I got off with Huck. She answered on the first ring.

"So soon!" she said. "Does that mean you miss me?"

I nodded but didn't say anything. "Any news from NIH?"

"Not until you answer my question," she said.

"I did answer it."

"Oh really?"

"I nodded."

"And I'm supposed to see you nod?" Silence. I think she was mad.

"I'm trying to conserve language."

"How's this for conservation. Do your own research." I waited for the call to end. It didn't. I apologized.

She said, "Oh my God. First time." I nodded again.

The phone line was beginning to ice up, so I asked again about the drug company information.

"My friend,"—and she said 'my friend' like it should worry me—"didn't find any current drug trials run by any university in southwest Ohio. That doesn't mean there weren't any or that your volunteer didn't travel further out of your area. Because your client was murdered, he came up with a theory that it's possible that the trial wasn't a real one, but perhaps a way for some bad guys to lure an unsuspecting victim into their operation. It does happen. And..." she paused.

"And...?" I said.

"...my *friend*'—I was hoping she would stop with the friend thing—"said he was aware of a scam operation in the tri-state area that sought out clinical workers for the purpose of using them in illegal drug trials. He's heard they pay them well."

I was quiet for a while, letting that all sink in. I hate being a cop. All you see is crime. Drugs and prostitution— the everyday crimes. Husbands beating wives, and sometimes wives beating on the husband. And the children see it. Then there are the turf wars between gangs. And the killings. A lot of those in big cities—like Miami. And the white-collar crimes. What a pretty term for stealing money. If I didn't know better, I would think, from what I see every day, that there are no good citizens in this world. I rarely get to see a man like George Bailey in *It's a Wonderful Life*. Let me tell you something. That world doesn't exist. Not for me.

"Did your friend think they might be operating in the Valley?"

"No. But he guessed they're probably linked to the Russian crime syndicates. The Moscow gangs have begun to ship their business overseas. It's because the economy there is in the crapper."

After Maxie was kidnapped, I read a lot about human trafficking. Over 700,000 victims annually. The vast majority being women and children—I prayed that Maxie was not one of them. And Russia is one of the largest dealers in the sale of sex. So what Louise was telling me was not shocking.

A multibillion-dollar business worldwide, third only to the sale of drugs and weapons. But what surprised me most when I first read the FBI reports was that the United States was a major destination for trafficked victims.

"You still there, Coop?"

"Sorry. Yeah. What you said triggered some thoughts." I paused. "So, tell *your friend* I said thanks."

"Jealous?" she said. Then, "I will see you on Sunday. So get yourself ready."

"But Sunday's a day of rest," I said.

"Not for you," she said. "I'll be on the early morning flight to Columbus International. And no worries, I'll rent a car and see you in the afternoon."

I was about to tell her I would pick her up when she was gone. A woman of her own mind. I have to say I was looking forward to seeing her.

18

ANOTHER MISSING PERSON

LATER FRIDAY AFTERNOON

I didn't eat lunch. I had gone out to Kroger's in the shopping center near the hotel and picked up two bottles of Louis Jadot Beaujolais-Villages; Swiss cheese on special, $4.95 a pound, reduced from $12.99; a package of Ritz crackers, the large size; yellow mustard; a can of sardines; a bag of pistachios; and Bibb lettuce. I threw in a large Ohio grown tomato. All that back in my room was lunch. If you're wondering what I did with the lettuce—the sardines go well with lettuce and tomatoes. I finished lunch around 2:00 p.m., sampled the wine and cheese, and then, as always after three glasses of wine, I passed out.

My cell rang me out of my sleep for the third time today. I looked at the clock at the side of the bed. Eight fourteen. I looked out the window trying to figure out if it was morning or night. It was dark. So, I checked the time on my cell. It was p.m. At least I hadn't slept through the night.

"Hey, Coop," said Anthony DeFelice.

"Twice in one day" I said. "Did you leave something in my room?"

"That's really funny, Cooper. But seriously, we got a call down here in South District from a Russian who claims his granddaughter is missing. Reason I'm telling you is it sounds a lot like the missing girl case you're working on. The granddaughter's name is Taisia Federovich. She disappeared from the University of Miami campus about a week ago."

Another missing-person case. I didn't know if I could take another one. I thought I saw a shadow pass over the sliding glass doors that looked out over the courtyard below. It disappeared just as quickly. My thoughts drifted back to the day when I learned my seven-year-old son had disappeared. I remembered the feeling. Like a hammer slamming into my chest—a dull punishing blow that lasted for days. And after that? It was like an eternal night settled over me. And that was followed by eight years of emptiness.

"You okay, Coop?" My silence must have stretched too long.

"I'm okay. And you're calling me because…?"

"It's on our case load. But this is Miami. One of the highest murder rates in the country, right? So, searching for a missing person ain't going to rise to the top of the Captain's agenda."

"Who's working the case?"

"Frankly? Nobody right now. We got too much shit on our desks. Missing persons isn't on the board," he added.

"Why didn't Coral Gables catch the case?"

"They did. But the girl was living in an apartment in South District so they kicked it over to us. Hey, you know, it happens. Nobody wants to do the work.

"I think her grandfather knows that and wants a private dick to look for the girl. So, before you say no, hear me out. I thought of you for two reasons. First, you're already on a case that smells a lot like this one—and besides you got the time," he added, his voice rising like he was baiting me.

I didn't answer. A case in Miami…a case in the Valley. Far apart. What was I getting into? And a Russian girl. The last thought struck a chord. Both were college students, both were women, both were international. A puzzling coincidence.

"I'll think about it."

"The grandfather's name is Leo Federovich. He lives in Moscow. But he's on his way here to…well, hell, I don't know what he plans to do here. Probably cause a shitload of trouble. But that's the story, Coop. Can I give him your number?"

I was nodding to myself before I answered.

"Coop?"

"Yeah, yeah," I said, and gave him my cell phone number.

"I already know your fuckin' number, Coop. I called you! But thanks. I think this case will be good for you. Besides Lou knows the case. She'll wanna help. Give her a call."

I knew what he meant. A way to work out my issues… with Maxie. And besides, maybe one of the cases leads to him. Ever hopeful.

I called Louise and told her, "Don't come up. I'm coming down. Meet me at Miami International."

19

SATURDAY MORNING, OCTOBER 9

L ouise met me at arrivals. I loaded my bag into her
Jeep and we headed for Coral Gables.

"So, what're we doing here?" she said.

"Investigating," I said.

"Very clever," she said.

"I used to teach philosophy."

"Yeah, but that doesn't make you smart."

"But it does mean I'm clever," I said.

"Okay, clever one, tell me what we're doing."

"We're going to talk to a few university people about
a missing student. See if we can trick them into giving us
information."

"You should be able to do that. You were once one of
them, smart boy."

"Still am," I corrected.

I filled Louise in on Taisia as we made our way from
the airport to the university.

"Interesting coincidence isn't it?" she said. "Two college
girls go missing from their campuses, both international."

"Enough similarity to make you wonder, doesn't it?" Then, "On second thought, nah."

But it still got me thinking.

The University of Miami is in Coral Gables, an old, upscale section of Miami.

Big estate homes, palm-lined streets. Not too far from Coconut Grove, a popular night club spot for the students. I didn't make an appointment to see anyone. I figured we would surprise them.

"We don't have an appointment, I take it," Louise said.

"We don't."

I pulled into an open parking spot under palms that looked like they could be blown away by the next hurricane. Their fronds stretched into the sky above the tallest buildings on campus, their trunks diet thin. Like toothpicks with a hat on.

A grey-haired woman standing at her desk sorting through papers looked up as I went through a door that said, Dean, Academic Affairs.

"May I help you?" she said.

"Yes. Is Dean Sanchez in?" I said.

"She has someone with her at the moment. Who shall I say is calling?"

"Detective Delgado, Miami PD," I said. "I'm her assistant." Louise kicked me.

She stared at us for a moment.

"Oh my," she said. "Is something wrong?"

"Yes," I said.

"Oh," she said, obviously hoping I was going to share my secret.

"How long will it be?" I said.

"I will call her right now," she said and picked up the phone.

79

A short stocky woman with legs that looked like they could lift weights and a short frilly skirt, hardly what I had expected, came out of her office.

Then she held out her hand. "Dean Sanchez," she said.

I told her who we were and motioned toward her office. I could feel the secretary's ear invading my space. The dean noticed.

"Let's go into my office," she said.

"Good idea," I said.

Louise smiled and shook her head as we followed the dean's dress into the office. The room was well-appointed with walls paneled in a dark, rich-looking wood—walnut maybe; a thick, brown carpet; and a wide stretch of windows behind the desk that gave her a view of the campus. She was in control. I noticed Will Durant's *History of Civilization*—one of my favorites—sitting on the middle shelf of a floor-to-ceiling bookcase off to my right.

"How can I help you, Detectives?"

I told her we were looking into the disappearance of Taisia Federovich.

"Oh yes, Taisia. Poor girl. I hope nothing bad has happened to her," she said, shaking her head as she settled behind her desk. We took it as a sign to sit. So we did.

"Sorry," she said. "I should have…" and she waved at the chairs that we had already taken.

"No problem," I said. Louise crossed her legs and sat back. I don't think she liked her.

"I've talked to the police already. Several times actually, including the Coral Gables Police, the FBI, and someone from the Miami Police Department—I can't remember his name," she said, looking over at Louise.

"Detective Anthony DeFelice," Louise offered.

She nodded. "That's right. Thank you. So, I'm not sure what more I can say," looking over at both of us as she finished.

"Just a few questions," I said, "if you don't mind."

"Not at all. We are as anxious as you are to find Taisia."

"I know you've probably been asked this before, but I would like you to think once again about any problems that Taisia might have been having. Academic? Boyfriend, maybe?"

"No," she said quickly and definitively, "but I think Student Services might have more information about that sort of thing. She was in pre-med and, from what I've heard, doing quite well," she added, smiling as she said it. "I talked with the grandfather, Mr. Federovich, just the other day. I'm sorry to say, I didn't have any more information to share with him than I have to give you. He mentioned that he was hiring a private investigator to look into his granddaughter's disappearance. I assume that's you," looking at me rather than at Louise. I nodded.

"But it's all good," she said quickly. "We want to do everything we can to help find this young woman.

"It's hard to figure, isn't it?" she continued. "Successful student, socially involved, determined to make a difference in the health field, so much so that she regularly volunteered for research studies. She had such high aspirations for her…"

"Volunteered for research studies?" I said, surprised.

"Sure, many of our students volunteer for research studies. We are a major research institution. So, we receive a lot of money to carry out research—the Federal Government, private foundations, corporations. A lot of the research is scientific in nature—and many of those studies require or affect human subjects. So, our professors are in constant

81

need of volunteers," she said, matter-of-factly. "Their work is what drives our university."

"Was she involved in a study when she disappeared?" I asked.

"Well, I don't know." She paused, rose, and turned toward the bank of windows behind her desk that looked out over the campus. "Her advisor is in that building over here," she said. "The Cox Science Center," she added, pointing to a two-story across the green. "She would be the best one to talk to. In reality though, I must tell you, several of our students might well be volunteering for studies that we know nothing about."

"With another university?" Louise asked.

"Another university. A private laboratory. A corporation. I daresay there are thousands of research projects in the works every day, maybe more, all around the country. Even abroad," she added, turning away from the window, bemused, as if searching for a thought that had gotten lost somewhere in the universe.

"So, your students might be volunteering for projects not sanctioned by the university?" Louise continued.

"Oh yes; we have no way of monitoring their private lives. After all they are adults. They have left their parents' protection and are here, on their own."

I thought about what Dean Sanchez had said as we headed for the science building and wondered how many students nationwide were volunteering for experimental trials. I wondered if their parents knew. I even wondered if Taisia's advisor knew about her own student's involvement in a study.

"So, do you think that's where she's from?" asked Louise, smiling. She was referring to Doctor Joan England, Taisia's advisor. The secretary had given us her name.

I shook my head. That Louise.

We were standing in the hallway of the center looking for her office when someone from behind me asked if we needed help.

I turned to the voice. It came from a man who looked like a fence post, tall and thin. Slightly rounded at the edges. He looked like a student.

"Yes," I said. "Doctor England's office?"

"She's probably at the arboretum. Are you students of hers?"

"No," I said.

"Oh, I see. You might want to check her office hours; they're posted on her door. It's just down the hall," he added, pointing to his left.

I asked him where the arboretum was.

He pointed to an exit at the rear of the building.

"The Gifford Arboretum," he said, adding, "that's what it's called. It's through that door and straight ahead. You will enjoy it." And then as I began to turn away, he quickly elaborated, like a tour guide, "The Gifford specializes in exotic plants and butterflies, dragonflies, and damselflies."

"Hmm," I replied. "Thanks."

I had never heard of damselflies but my imagination ran away with me. According to my new friend, Doctor England spends her afternoons in the arboretum, observing several varieties of dragonflies.

"People actually spend their time studying these things?" said Louise, as we headed for the exit. "No wonder you're so weird."

"Research," I said. "All in the name of the advancement of science."

"Uh-huh. And I suppose that advancement comes out of our pockets?"

"Right. But aren't you glad someone is studying the damselfly? I mean how else would one know they even existed?"

"Yeah. I'm thrilled."

I was betting that the woman in a white frock coat, bending over a flowering red bush was Dr. England. She held up her hand to stop me as I approached and pointed at something in front of her. I didn't see anything at first. Then I saw a dragonfly hovering above a rush of crimson flowers. It flew away after a short time, its wings lost in the flurry of its own movement.

To say Doctor England looked like an academic would be too simplistic. There are all kinds of academics. A philosopher, for instance: jeans, shirt out, probably stained with mustard, and wrinkled. His jacket would be corduroy with patches on the elbows—maybe covering up real holes.

And then there was Doctor England, the scientist, dressed meticulously, a white lab coat over creased pants, a blouse buttoned almost to her neck. She was studying the insects through large, tinted glasses, much too big for her face, but they suited her well.

"The Sympetrum flaveolum," she said, staring at the dragonfly. "Otherwise known as the Yellow-Winged Darter," she added, without taking her eyes off her subject. The back of the dragonfly was bright red, near crimson, its sides and head tinged with yellow, its wings translucent. "You would never think of it as a predator, would you?" the doctor observed, almost to herself and still focusing on the dragonfly.

"May I help you?" she said, taking a deep breath and finally turning toward us. Her eyes were accentuated by the rose-tinted glasses.

"Doctor England?" I said.

"That's right," she said. "And you are...?"

"Cooper," I said, holding out my hand. "And this is Detective Delgado from Miami PD. We would like to talk with you for a few minutes about an advisee of yours, Taisia Fedorovich."

"I've already talked to a detective from Miami, I think," she said, looking at us through her glasses just as she had with the dragonfly.

"You probably talked with Detective DeFelice. We're following up," said Louise.

"I understand that Taisia volunteered for clinical trials here at the university. Are you aware of that?" I said.

"Yes, I am. She has been in several experimental studies here. She told me about them. Why do you ask?"

"I'm wondering if she was involved in any outside the university."

"I'm not aware of any. But I wouldn't have any idea of what she did on her own time. Are you seeing connection between the trials and her disappearance?"

"The university experiments. What kind were they?" I said. Louise was taking notes. Dr. England glanced her way, her brow raised in curiosity.

"Just to jog my memory, Doctor," said Louise, trying to assure her.

Doctor England nodded and continued. "They were conducted by the faculty in the medical school. One was a clinical trial...a sleep study, having to do with the effectiveness of a new drug in treating sleep disorders."

"Was she actually taking the drug?" I said.

"I'm not sure. You would have to ask the researcher that question. She could have been taking a placebo. As you might know, in a clinical trial an experimenter needs several kinds of subjects to carry out the study: a control group and an experimental group—the control group, the one not getting the intervention, and the experimental group, the one receiving the intervention, in this case the drug."

"I assume some studies might pose risks to the subjects?" I said. I was very familiar with the Belmont Report, the paper that generated the flurry of activity set in place by the feds to prevent abuse of volunteers in research studies.

"Absolutely," she said. "All studies pose a modicum of risk. Even the study that Taisia may have been involved in. Some trials, however, pose a much more serious risk than others. You've heard of the Stanley Milgram study?"

"I have. The subjects were ordered to administer lethal doses of electricity to other subjects, right?"

"Not lethal," she said, "but powerful doses nonetheless. Doctor Milgram was trying to determine the relationship between obedience and authority. His motivation was that he was Jewish and, being Jewish, was deeply troubled by what happened in the Nazi concentration camps—the guards arguing that they were simply following orders.

"The risks to the subjects in the Milgram study were considerable. One set of subjects was commanded to give shocks to other subjects held in isolation. The shocked subjects were paid actors who were only pretending to be shocked. However, those administering the voltage didn't know that. They thought they were actually administering the shock. The purpose of the experiment was to see how much voltage a subject would administer to the subject in isolation. Surprisingly, Milgram discovered that thirty seven of the forty subjects administered the maximum shock,

450 volts, when commanded to do so. Five hundred volts can cause internal burns."

She noticed I was drifting off. I felt like a graduate student in one of her research classes.

But she she plunged on again. "Needless to say, Doctor Milgram was roundly criticized by many of his peers."

"Uh-huh," I said, "I'll bet."

She took that as encouragement. "As a matter of fact, his experiments are part of the reason that the federal government legislated that researchers now have to submit their studies to an Institutional Review Board before they can begin their study. It's an ethics committee and is guided by principles outlined in the Belmont Report. We have such a committee at our university, of course."

She stopped and looked at me for a few moments. I was wondering what Taisia might have gotten involved in. She read my mind.

"Taisia was…," she stopped momentarily, "*is* intensely dedicated to the study of science. She is determined to become a research physician. I am almost positive that she has volunteered for more than one study. As a matter of fact, she asked me to help her get permission from several of her professors in order to travel to a lab site. I warned her to exercise care in doing that. She assured me she would," she added, quickly.

The look on my face must have unsettled Doctor England. I was struck by the increasing similarity of the two cases, Taisia's and April's.

"I tried to warn her," she said, looking at me sidewise as if trying to assure me she had.

I nodded. But she still looked worried.

"How can I find out about other trials she may have been involved in?" I said.

"I don't know, "she said, almost apologetically. "Do you really think that this might have something to do with her disappearance?"

"I don't know; we'll see."

I thanked her as we headed out of the arboretum.

"She had a boyfriend, you know," Dr. England called out after us. We both turned. I started back.

"A boyfriend?" I said. Another similarity.

"Do you have a name?" said Louise.

"Or at least I think he was a boyfriend," she added almost under her breath as though unaware of Louise's question. "He used to sit in on my bio class. But I haven't seen him around lately. He might be able to help."

"His name?" Louise asked again.

"Geza Petrescu," she said. "From Romania, I think."

I complimented her on knowing her students so well. She said he was a special kid and so was Taisia. It was easy to remember them.

"One more thing," she said, a pained look on her face that told me the news was going to be bad. She looked troubled. "There is a group of people, many of them students, who are known as *clinical workers*."

"Clinical workers?" I said, not liking the sound of that phrase.

"Yes. Clinical workers are people who regularly volunteer for clinical trials—more than they should—for pay. Most studies forbid their subjects from being part of more than one study at a time. These subjects, in order to skirt the regulations of a particular study, will travel, in order to take on more trials. Sometimes becoming subjects in as many as three to four different trials in a week." She was watching for our reaction, almost as though Lou would arrest her for withholding information.

"For the money," Louise said.

"They can make good money," she said. "The riskier trials can pay thousands of dollars to their volunteers. Of course, the pay is in proportion to the risk. But the risk to the subject's health can be considerable. Some students support themselves by offering themselves to research organizations as clinical workers."

"And…?" I said.

"I've been worried lately that Taisia and her friend, Geza, might be doing exactly what I've just described," she explained, her eyes telling me that she felt negligent in not reporting this earlier, "because of their frequent absences from classes this past month." I noticed just a trace of nervousness in her voice. A slight tremor on her lips.

My stomach dropped when I thought of Taisia's mother and grandfather. Clinical workers were easy targets for human traffickers. Trafficking in human bodies and body parts has become the second most common crime worldwide, just behind the drug business. And, in the United States, Florida is the hub.

The arboretum was beginning to close in on me, trees blocking out the sun, dense foliage pushing up against the trees. I knew what was happening. I could see Maxie's face as I left the garden.

"You okay?" said Louise as we escaped this paradise of rare animals and flowers.

"Yeah. This place. It's too dark."

"Let's see if we can get that phone number for Geza," Lou said.

20

PHONE CALLS

W e were back in the car with Geza's number when my cell went off again. I was about ready to kill the damn thing.

"Yeah?" I said. There was no name with the number.

"Coop! Where are you?" Jackson. "Are you in Ohio? I'm telling you, man, I need your help. I'm now officially a person of interest. Can you believe that?"

He was losing control.

"Slow down, Jack," I said. Louise was looking at me like *what the hell was going on?* I mouthed Jackson's name.

She nodded.

"Is Huxter Crow there?" I said.

"No."

"No?" I couldn't see Huck not doing what he said he would do.

"Now Sonya's asking a lot of questions," Jackson continued. "I need to know what to tell her. And I've been getting threatening phone calls ever since the big story about April in *The Plain Dealer*. The article implied that April and I were…you know. Somebody must have been talking to the paper. I told the police about the calls. They said they would look into them. Big deal. It'll never happen."

"What does the caller say?"

"Things like, communist, n-lover. I tell you I'm going to get a gun. And Sonya. I think she knows now—because of the *PD* story."

I told him I understood, that I was in Florida and would catch the next flight out. He said, thanks man, and he would pick me up if I needed. I said, no problem, I would catch a rental.

I booked a flight for Columbus International that left Fort Lauderdale at 6:05 p.m., arriving at 8:30 p.m. Louise said she would meet me there in a few days. I gave Huck a call. Straight to voice mail.

21

THE BLOOD MOON

Route 23 that runs from Columbus to the river could be the darkest highway in America. It's a rural road, with the wild stalks of harvested corn rising at times to the lower branches of the tree trunks, walnut, oak and elm that line Ohio's country roads. And the light…the light was limited to what little there was dropping from the moon, now hanging low in the sky, this ninth day of October. The Harvest Moon was now gone. The fields had been cleared of crops under its light. Tonight, I was driving under the eye of the Blood Moon. It's the first full moon after the Harvest Moon, called blood because of the reflection of the sun that turns it a shade of dull red. Native Americans say the moon gets its name from the blood of the prey that runs in the fields during the pre-winter hunt, turning the landscape scarlet.

Otherwise it was dark, darkness interrupted only by the outlines of the trees, by the skeletons of the cut corn stalks, and by an occasional barn silhouetted against the moon, and by the lights from the Volvo that cut a narrow path through the highway ahead.

I called Richie and left a message. A few minutes later my cell rang.

"Hey, Coop, what's up?" Richie.

I told him about the case, about Jackson, and the threats he was getting.

"You need me? I'm there. Gimme coupla hours to get to the Valley. Where you at?"

I told him where the hotel was and my room number.

"Be there before you," he said.

"Uh-huh." That's Richie. Always the kidder.

Richie is an old friend of mine. We both grew up in Cleveland, in a Catholic neighborhood, learned how to fight, Richie specializing in a Louisville slugger that his old man gave him. "Better than a gun, you use it right," his dad used to say. He got a gun when he was fourteen. But he still kept the bat.

A slow drizzle slowed me down, so it was almost midnight when I got to Riverdale. The river was riding high along the bank and angry, its swells visible even in the darkness. The water must be over parts of the highway south, I figured.

The bar was closed so I went straight to my room and texted Jackson. He didn't respond so I guessed he was finally calm enough to sleep—that is, if Sonya hadn't killed him yet. I called down to see if there was any coffee in the lobby.

"It's in the room," the front desk told me. Funny, the coffee in the lobby would have tasted better.

It was about 2:00 a.m. when I finally settled down. I pulled the Glock out of my bag and loaded it, ten rounds plus one in the chamber. I preferred the Smith & Wesson. But I liked the quick response capability of the Glock. Most law enforcement people do. I got out of my clothes, placed the Glock on the nightstand next to my bed, and fell asleep. And I dreamed.

22

EARLY SUNDAY MORNING, OCTOBER 10

S *he was sleeping on her side. Blond hair across her face. She was alone. In her dorm room. A man was standing in the hall outside her door. He knocked. But she didn't answer. I warned her not to answer. He tried to open the door...then...*

"You in there, Coop?" So quiet.

"What?" I looked at the clock. Four a.m. What the hell!

I looked through the peep-hole, saw who it was, and opened the door.

There he was, all 6'2" of him. Wide and tall. But all muscle and sinew. He was grinning and holding his arms out like I'm supposed to love his 6:00 a.m. wake-up call. He grabbed me before I could stop him, squeezed like a wrestler, pushed me away and said, "It's Richie, Coop! Richie's gonna take care of everything!" and he heaved his big bag through the door.

"When did you leave Cleveland?" I said, not believing he was standing there. At my door. At six-o'clock in the morning for God's sake.

95

"You called. I left. I'm your buddy, remember?" He looked hurt. "What?" He paused, his palms turned up. "It took me like, six hours. Walk in the park," and he dropped his bag on my bed. I wondered where I would be sleeping.

"Come here," he said and patted the bed for me to sit. "Tell Uncle Richie everything," and he waited with a smile, like things are good now. They usually are too. I looked for the bat.

"Bat's inna car, Coop," he said. Mind reader.

So we sat there, on the bed, Richie in his pressed black slacks with a white linen shirt and cufflinks and me in boxers and a tee-shirt, talking about April, and Taisia, and Jackson, and China, and the phone calls, and the old neighborhood, and how we ruled it, Richie and DeFelice and me, and how I went away to school and became a big shot college professor and look at me now, and what the fuck am I doing on a case in Ohio? and where the hell is DeFelice? We did this until 8:05 a.m.—I noticed the time as I fell asleep, Richie sacking out on the couch against the wall.

I had trouble seeing when I woke. The window facing the river was wide open, the sun blinding me. I rolled away from the light and tried to wipe the light out of my eyes. Richie was gone from the couch. He was standing in the doorway, grinning.

"Hey it's 12:30. Half the day's over, bud. Hope you're not gettin' overtime."

I didn't say anything. It was too early to talk.

"Figured maybe you'd like to join me. That is if you're not otherwise engaged."

That's Richie. He can be literate when he wants to.

"Yeah, yeah," I said. "I'll be right down. Close the door behind you."

We talked through breakfast about Jackson. About April Januarie. About China—Richie cringed—he loves dogs more than people. About the phone calls—Richie listened while he ate, carefully keeping his cuffs out of the soft-boiled eggs. He likes to dress well for meals.

"You gotta respect good food, Coop," he said, buttering his English muffin.

"Can't believe they don't have no fuckin' bagels in this place," he groused, looking around at the clientele. "Guess not," he said, and continued to butter his muffin.

"So, your friend, Lawless—what kinda fuckin' crazy name is that?" He looked up at me.

"Just keep an eye out," I said. "The man's freaking out. Maybe with good reason."

He responded without looking up. "Leave it to me. You got no worries." Richie loves food. When he's dining, he dines. He doesn't eat, he focuses. No interruptions.

I called South District while we were eating to see what Louise had learned about Geza. DeFelice answered.

"Where you at, Coop?"

I told him that Richie and I were having breakfast and talking about him.

He said I should tell that little dago bastard he could still whip his ass. I said I would do that—Richie looking at me but the speaker wasn't on. Thank God.

"And how is your father-in-law?" I said.

DeFelice's ex-wife had left her dad and the poor man was grieving so badly that Tony took him in. Tough guy, right?

"He's okay," he said. "Thanks for asking." He paused. Then, "So, Cooper—on this other case—you keeping the locals informed?" Always looking out for me. "Cause if you ain't, you're leaving the police, whose main job is to serve and protect" (still mad his old partner, namely me, left) "in the dark, you unnerstand what I'm sayin'?"

I said, no I hadn't done that yet—tell the locals, that is—but I would eventually, because in reality I didn't have much at this time anyway.

He said, "Uh-huh. And, by the way, here's your buddy. And stay safe!"

Silence. Then, "How was your drive, Coop?" Louise. I had the phone on speaker.

"Good," I said.

"You alone up there?" I think I detected a note of worry. Jealousy?

"No, Richie is sleeping with me."

Richie hit me in the arm so hard I dropped the phone. It hit the table and bounced for the floor. I caught it before it landed.

"Don't listen to this guy, Louise. He's a freakin' prevert," said Richie, leaning into the phone.

"Hmmm," she said. "That right?"

"He's exaggerating," I said.

"So, okay, Coop, you wanta know about Geza. So far nothing. He's not answering his phone. I couldn't leave a message because his voice mail isn't set up. A person gets a phone and they don't set up the voice mail. First thing I do." Obviously irritated.

"Isn't it fun?"

"Tell me about it," she said.

"I checked into credit cards. He doesn't seem to have any," sighing. "So that's the latest. How about you? Anything?"

I thought about saying *Yeah, I miss you.* But, Richie was right there—even though he was reading the paper—and I couldn't do it.

We talked for a few more minutes about nothing and then got off. Richie was looking at me, smiling.

"What?" I said.

"Nothin'," said Richie. "Nothin' at all. Just that you and Lou...I'm just saying" and he made a gesture, like, *Whatever*.

"Louise will be up here in a couple of days," I said. "You be nice to her."

Richie lifted his hands in surrender. "You know me, Coop. I'm a gennaman."

In truth—despite his tough exterior—he really was.

23

THE REPORTER

SUNDAY AFTERNOON, OCTOBER 10

"Cooper!"

"Yeah?" I said. It was 3:30 p.m. and Richie and I were back in the room after our late breakfast. He was sacked out on the couch in the front room of the suite—snoring. I was in the bedroom watching a football game. Browns/Pittsburgh. The Steelers were winning, 27-7. Yikes.

"Jason here," he said.

"Jason?" I said, knowing exactly who it was.

Richie opened his eyes, curious.

"Jason Eisenberg, the reporter!" he said, like, my God, didn't I remember?

"Oh, I said. The reporter. I thought you went back to Cleveland."

"I am in Cleveland."

"I still don't have anything, Jason."

"But I do."

"Yeah?" I said.

"Yeah," he said. "Something you should find interesting."

"Okay. Tell me about it."

"Face-to-face."

"What kind of information are we talking about, Jason?"

"Uh-uh, Coop. First, we meet. Then I tell."

I thought about it. Probably too long. Jason broke in.

"You still there, Coop?"

"Yeah, I'm here. Okay, let's meet. Tomorrow."

"Tell me time and place. I'll be there."

"The Holiday Inn near the University, 9:30 a.m. In the restaurant."

24

JASON'S CLUE AND MORE

MONDAY MORNING, OCTOBER 11

I had a hard time sleeping, tossing about and turning every so often to check the time on the digital clock on the dresser. The numbers stared at me, blood red in the darkness—all night. Two a.m., then 3:45, then 5:15. I was never sure if I had slept or not.

It's a strange feeling, not sure if you're dreaming or not, not sure if you're sleeping or not, not able to separate what's dream from what's reality. Take Maxie for instance. I think about him all the time, sleeping and waking. It doesn't make any difference. It's all a nightmare.

The day I was called out of class by the dean and told my son was missing was the start of it all—that bad dream. When I got home there was a police car in the drive. And Jillie, standing there on the steps of our two-story colonial with a wrap-around porch and finished attic where Maxie played. She waiting for me—anxiety cutting into her perfect face. I could see it even from the driveway.

I remember most of the details of that day. She shuddered against me when I held her. And I said soothing things like, *It'll be all right, don't worry*, when all the time I had no idea if things would be all right and I was anxious as hell. We would both be worried sick later. Both get ill quickly. Not able to fight infections because we didn't sleep.

Campus security searched the premises, even though Maxie had only been gone for several hours. They did it because they were our friends. They exhausted the woods behind the house. I did too. Jillie was frozen to a chair in the dining room, staring out at the hills that surrounded the house. Later that day, a number of my students joined in the search. So did the dean and our campus friends. By the next morning, the local police joined the search and sent out a notice to the Sheriff's Department about Maxie's disappearance. They sent some deputies.

I didn't go in to teach that day. The whole college joined the search as it continued through the second day. Townspeople also. News travels fast in a small town. Anthony Coppoletta, the local antique dealer who was a close friend, offered a reward to anyone who had information. Several more days went by the same way, Jillie and I drifting in and out of reality like two zombies in an old horror movie.

The FBI showed up a week later. I think it was a week, it might have been longer. They said they were here because our son was kidnapped. Several leads from local detectives indicated that. A neighbor had reported that he thought he saw our son get into a car. He couldn't be sure it was Maxie—thought it might have been. Couldn't remember much about the car—maybe it was a Ford—maybe. The person who reported it—I quizzed him beyond the point that I should have, angry at him for not noticing more: the license plate, was it Ohio? Did you see who was in the car?

"How could you not see?" I said angrily, the man looking distraught. "Didn't you see anything?"—sarcastic and nasty— "How could you not see who was in the car?" asking a third, maybe fourth time, until Jillie pulled me away and I never approached him again, until a year later when I was more rational, as rational as I could be. And he didn't know anything more then than he did before. But he was a weird guy. A little touched, according to the locals.

And I began to devote all of my time to the search and no one complained, least of all my students who continued to help. But later the dean became concerned that I couldn't do my job. And my friends in the department took over until I was able to pull it all together and get my mind back on my class. But I knew that wasn't going to happen.

"He's not dead," I kept telling myself, and told Jillie the same thing, every day. Even when I taught class, I searched for him in my mind. And then we began blaming each other, first in small questioning kinds of ways.

"So when did you see him last?" I would say. And she would say, "On the porch," and then I would follow it up with something as innocent as, "Did you check on him?" and I could feel the blaming in my voice, and she would look at me, confused at first, and then with rising irritation, "Of course I did." And then, "What are you saying? It was my fault?"

And I would say, "No, of course not, I'm just saying." But I wasn't "just saying."

And she would say, "You know you were never around during the day. Maybe if you were, you could have helped," and her face showed the anger that was inside.

"You're blaming me because I wasn't around?" I was angry and resentful that she would say that. And I could feel red blooming in my cheeks. And my blood pressure rise. Like two hundred over ninety. Damn.

And that's the way the year went. Until we couldn't take it anymore, couldn't stand each other, and we pulled apart. And nothing new on Maxie. He was just one big hole in our lives, a dark and painful one. And our marriage went out the window. It happens, you know. Just like that. You lose a kid, you lose your own life as well.

Jason was waiting in the restaurant, The Captain's Table, talking with the hostess when I got off the elevator. He must have made a fast trip down since he was early. I was hoping to catch a cup of decaf and wake up before I talked to him.

"You look like hell, Cooper. Didn't you sleep?" he said.

"No," I said. I could have added, "I never sleep."

We found a table by a window and away from other diners.

We drank coffee while I waited for breakfast. I ordered the Farmer's Special: biscuits and gravy, eggs over hard, rye toast and a glass of orange juice. Jason ordered a corned beef sandwich—"extra lean," he added. The waitress, whose hair was either frizzed or just not combed, looked at him like he spoke a foreign language.

"You are in Riverdale, mister," she said. "We got one kind of corned beef and that's what comes in a Reuben. You want a Reuben?"

"Yeah, that's fine," he groused. I could have told him there weren't really any Jewish delis in southern Ohio.

People don't understand Jewish in the Valley. It's kind of like a pagan religion to them.

"So, do you know anything about the Communist Party in the United States, Cooper?" he said.

"It still exists?"

"Yeah. The CPUSA. President is Sam Webb, a graduate of a Catholic university, by the way. It's still very active, but it's different today. After the disintegration of the USSR, the CPUSA lost a lot of financial support from the party in Russia. The former president of CPUSA, Gus Hall, had a falling out with Gorbachov's policy of Glasnost. As a result the party in Russia cut off funding the party here. They used to get several million a year to support their work in the U.S."

I nodded through it all.

"So?" I said, waiting for him to get to the point.

"Doctor Jackson Lawless is a card-carrying member of the CPUSA."

"I see," I said. "You're thinking that his politics is somehow connected to April's death and to the threats?"

He nodded.

"And just who would be so outraged with Jackson being a communist that he would kill him for it?"

"The Valley is run by a man in Steubenville. He controls everything that happens there. Among other things, he owns The Wheeling Horse Track, the biggest in the Valley. He controls dog fighting, cock-fighting, the bars, prostitution, and the government." Jason paused and watched me.

"And who is this man?"

"His name is Carmen Santangelo. He's connected to the crime bosses in Cleveland and Youngstown."

"So, what makes you think he would have anything to do with the killing of a girl from South Africa?"

"Not him necessarily, but a man who works for him, Kenneth Boyd, a redneck who is the head of a militia group in the Valley. That man hates blacks and communists—and Jews," he added. "And I wouldn't put it past him to kill a man—or his black girl friend—for just those reasons."

I leaned back in my chair and almost tipped it over, catching myself before it fell. Private detective falls over in his chair while considering clues. Even Inspector Clouseau wasn't as clumsy.

I didn't know what to say, so I said nothing. And I wondered what Taisia had to do with all of this. If anything.

Jason continued. "Dr. Lawless was part of an official trip to China to visit with the bigwigs of the CPUA. Interesting, huh?" He waited for me to react. I just listened. "I would think that would not be great news in the Valley, home of one of the most active militias in the country, Cooper. I'm figuring there is no way that someone like Kenneth Boyd doesn't know about that trip."

I thought about what he was saying: Marxism in the Valley. A deadly combination for sure. The Ohio Valley is all about unions, hardnosed living, guns, good clean work, isolationism, God and religion, and the hell with outsiders, including Jews, communists, gays, Northerners with those strange accents, and the Hare Krishna. Being a communist in the Valley is tantamount to putting a target on your back. Maybe that's what Jackson had done to himself, and to April.

"Where does Boyd live?" I said, trying not to sound too interested.

"So, you like what I'm saying?" he said, smiling.

"I'm listening, that's all," I said, figuring it was a lead of sorts. A hate-killing, maybe.

"I'm going with you when you talk to him," he said, looking at me steadily.

I stared out the window that overlooked the valley.

"I know where you can find him," he persisted.

It started to rain. It fell hard for a few minutes then turned into a drizzle, hitting the road that wound down the hill to the river, forming small rivulets that ran into gutters on either side of the road. It was fall now, so the days were getting cool, turning the leaves into a variety of colors. Take out your crayons and paint those trees as you will and they will still surpass any colors you can come up with—leaves of soft gold and brilliant yellows, deep crimson and browns that range from tan to the ochre tones of earth, and variegated shades of green as they begin their autumn change, like chameleons in camouflage, trying to hide from the bitter cold that will eventually kill them and drive them from the branches.

"Cooper," Jason said, bringing me back. "What do you say?"

"I say, let me think about it. And don't push." He backed off. I figured Boyd was a start. I had nothing else for the moment.

"By the way," he said, taking a bite of his Reuben and talking while he chewed, "I'm writing a series in *The Plain Dealer* about April's killing and her ties to Professor Lawless. The series will be running all week, including a front-page picture in the *Sunday Magazine*. 'Death in the Valley.' Good title, eh!" he said, pleased with himself. "Nothing like a little peek into the seamy side of life on the River in southern Ohio."

I was close to shoving the sandwich down his throat.

25

KENNETH BOYD'S CAMP

MONDAY AFTERNOON, OCTOBER 11

I decided to take Jason with me. He knew where Boyd lived all right. But he was not at his farm. He was in Wayne National Forest. Wayne is a massive tract of timberland that covers a large segment of Southeastern, Ohio and is shaped like a kind of inverted triangle. The southeast leg is formed by the Ohio River and ends in Marietta Ohio. Small towns like Lebanon and Stafford form the southwest boundary. And Woodsfield, the Monroe County seat, anchors the base of the triangle on the north. Boyd was in the easternmost section of the forest.

The sun was still high in the sky when we headed east up Ohio Route 7 towards the National Forest where Boyd trains with his militia. The only information that Eisenberg had was that he was somewhere in the eastern section of the forest. That meant we only had to search a little over 125 million acres to find him. Thank you, Jason. We were headed for Marietta, Ohio, about 180 miles away. It's the largest city southeast of the forest with 14,000 people and a riverboat, Jewel of the Ohio, a big sternwheeler that carries tourists up the Muskingum River through a system of four, hand-operated locks and two side-cut canals. It was the first system of its kind in the United States. Jillie, Maxie, and I took that trip—forty-four miles of river past small farm towns, and forests, and deserted mills—now a sad part of Appalachian life. I was hoping we could do that again.

We got to Marietta around 5:00 p.m. and took I-77 north toward Caldwell, another small town north of the forest. We cut off I-77 at Ohio 530, about twenty miles south of Caldwell and headed toward Lower Salem and Germantown. I figured we could stop there and get information about Boyd and his camp before night fell. I saw a sign for Lower Salem ahead and slowed down. There would be no hotel there, population 109, last count. There was only a post office, so I decided to head for Caldwell. A better chance of getting a place to sleep. I took the scenic route, Ohio 821, a two-lane road that skirts the forest and plays tag with the freeway. A more interesting drive than the freeway.

Jason was fast asleep, snoring. He had been for the last hour or so. So I was enjoying the loneliness of the ride, fences flowing like in a kaleidoscope, cows, standing in the field, and walnut trees hanging over the wire fences, their ripe fruit sealed in black shells and scattered over the road, waiting for kids with baskets. I was a gatherer when I was a kid, riding in the backseat of my grandfather's old Nash Rambler, dad talking in the front with grandpa, me riding quietly in the back—bushel baskets in the trunk waiting to be filled with walnuts, black gold to us, a deep black that stained our hands when we broke the shells away to harvest the nuts.

Driving these country roads again, and passing by fields and small streams, and stone bridges, and back roads that run off into the distance to God knows where, and old-fashioned signs, long worn by the weather, and long lines of telephone poles carrying phone service to the houses that appear now and then along the road, I'm reminded of the area just north of where we were and the creek that runs through the hills and valleys that rise and fall there. Leatherwood Creek. Memorable because of a man who suddenly appeared there—along the creek—about 170 years ago—nobody knew from where—and began to preach. His name was John Dylkes.

He appeared in the town of Salesville, a small village near the creek, and began to talk about the New Jerusalem, claiming he was the Messiah. No. More than that. God. And he preached under the trees near the town, and on the roads that ran from it, and in the fields that surrounded it, and near the waters of the creek itself, anyplace where there was an audience to hear. And he converted a lot of people, including several of the town fathers of Salesville.

I'm telling this story because John Dylkes was a fraud. Either that or he was God. I have a hard time believing the latter. Since Maxie's disappearance, I have had a hard time with belief of any kind. John Dylkes didn't help any. But somehow, deep inside, I can tell you I still hope and trust that someone out there will hear my prayers and someday will answer them. I pray it won't be John Dylkes.

I wondered if Boyd had ever heard that story.

We were in Caldwell by 6:30 p.m. A good time to find a motel and ask questions. Besides, I knew the town. My dad had taught English in the high school for several years before we moved to Cleveland. There's a bed and breakfast not too far from the Baker Glass Museum. Friendly people. Maybe someone would remember our family.

We pulled into the inn at 6:45 p.m. just in time to keep the darkness from burying us in the forest. Night does fall fast when the denseness of the woods blocks the sun.

"Just one night?" said the man behind the desk. Young or old. I couldn't tell. It's always hard with a beard.

"One night," I said.

He nodded and looked in his computer.

He finished registering us and said there was wine and cheese in the dining room. He pointed to his right where a few men were lined up at a buffet pouring wine for themselves. Hunters. There was a fireplace against the far wall that wasn't lit.

"We'll turn it on in another month," he said.

"This your place?" I said.

"Uh-huh. Been mine ever since I remember," he replied, smiling out of the side of his mouth. Country humor.

"How's the hunting?" Jason said. He was eyeing the men standing by the hearth who looked more like beer drinkers than wine tasters.

"What you hunting for?"

"Small game: rabbits, squirrels."

I felt like punching Jason. Dumb answer. Small game in the forest?

"Not many people come this way to hunt just rabbits and squirrels," the proprietor said, reading my mind. He was eyeing Jason curiously.

"We're looking for a friend who's camped out somewhere up here," I said, jumping in.

"He alone?"

"No, he's with a group of men. Maybe twenty or thirty all together."

"That's a lot of hunters. Only a few camps where there's that many people."

He studied me for a moment, as though he knew I had another question.

"Kenneth Boyd," I said. He pulled back. "That's who I'm looking for."

The man busied himself with something behind the desk.

Then, "If you're looking for Boyd, you'd best head into the forest just outside of Woodsfield. But you be careful. This is deer season. Sometimes the hunters can't tell the deer from the people. They get jumpy. Shoot at anything."

I thanked him and started to turn away.

"They call that area the Switzerland of Ohio," he continued. "Lots of hills and forest, denser'n hell. Easy to get lost in there. So you mind where you're goin'. Don't wanna see nothin' happen to you boys."

Jason looked at me as if to say, *what's he talking about?*

The man gave us the keys to the room and said we could pull up to the front door and unload there.

"Room's easy to find," he said, pointing at a stairway that led to an open hallway above. "If you step away from the desk, you can see it. Center of the hall."

Jason took the keys and headed for the car. As I started to turn for the stairs, the man leaned over the desk and whispered, "Is your friend an Arab?" stressing the 'A' as he watched Jason head toward the car.

I stared at him for a moment.

"Tretter, Robert Tretter," he said, holding out his hand. Sign of friendship, I guess. "I was just asking, 'cause folks down this way don't take to Arabs. We've got Lebanese folks settled along the river. But they're all good Christians." He paused. "You tell your friend to be careful. Nine/ Eleven ain't that long ago," and he nodded to emphasize his point.

"He's not an Arab. He's an American. Just like you and me," and I almost poked him in the chest to emphasize it. But I didn't.

"No offense, mister. Just friendly advice," he said, not backing down.

It was pretty clear that I had made a mistake bringing Jason along. Jewish was a little better than Arab. But not by much. I should have thought of that five hours ago. Too late now.

"What?" said Jason, as he dragged his bags into the lobby. He must have seen the look on my face—or on the Innkeeper's, now staring steadily at him from behind the counter.

"Nothing," I said, and headed for the stairs with one of the bags. "Let's get unpacked. We've got to be up and out of here early in the morning," and I turned back to Tretter and shook my head. He was back to work behind the desk. Fiddling with something. There was no winning this war. That's the Valley for you.

It was a large blue room, clearly decorated by a woman, hardly one where a couple of guys would hang out. I don't have any problems with my identity, though the ceramic washbasin and powder blue hand towels were a challenge. But we had twin beds, so no problems there, despite the flowery duvets and the blue sheets. I guess that's why they call it the Blue Room.

I decided to talk to Jason about what Tretter had said.

"So that's why you looked so strange. He thinks I'm Middle Eastern! I wonder what he would think if he knew I was Jewish."

"I'm not sure. That's why I'm not taking you with me to meet Boyd. I have no idea what he might do...or his friends. It's too dangerous."

"I'm not worried. I'm going. I mean, how can I write a story if I'm not there?" He paused, his eyes locking onto mine. "I'm going."

I shook my head and thought for a few moments. Then, "Okay. Have you ever used a gun?"

"No. Never."

I had two guns, the Glock and the .38. I wasn't going to give him either one. I didn't want him to shoot me, accidentally.

TUESDAY MORNING, OCTOBER 12

We got an early start in the morning and checked out after breakfast, breakfast being a cup of coffee and homemade breads—*Been baking since five o'clock*, the innkeeper said—lots of home-grown strawberry preserves and apple butter. It was about a forty-minute drive to Woodsfield, a small town on the northern edge of the Forest, population 2501. I had checked it out on the internet. Ninety-nine percent white. That means there aren't many other kinds of people there, including Blacks, Middle Easterners, Hispanics, or Jews. I guess being the county seat doesn't mean diversity.

We stopped at a McDonald's in town for coffee—and for information. The lady behind the counter looked to be about eighty. She waited on us like it was the best job in the world. I figured she wouldn't have information on militia so I asked for the manager.

"Can I help you, sir?" said a tall black man who came from the back of the kitchen. Things were looking up. Diversity after all.

I asked him about campsites in the area. I didn't want to ask about militia. He said a bunch of men were camping out in the northeast part of the forest. I waited for more.

"The entrance to the forest is just up the road," he said.

It must have been clear I didn't know where "just up the road" was.

He pointed to the highway we had come into town on. "Hang a right and the entrance is about a mile on your right. Can't miss it." I just love "can't miss it."

"And the camp?"

"Just follow the sounds of gunfire," he said, an amused look crossing his face as he said it.

"Really?" I said.

"Really, he said. "You have to be careful hiking out there. Those folks might think *you're* fair game." The second time someone told me that.

"Looking for friends?" he asked, talking low like it was a secret we shared.

"Uh-huh," I said, stretching the word a little.

"Friend got a name? I know a lot of people around here."

"Kenneth Boyd," I said, figuring there was no way he knew him.

"Mr. Boyd. Sure, I know him. He's been coming out this way for a decade or so now. What kind of business you got with Boyd?" Talk about suspicious.

"Oh, just business," I said. We watched each other for a few moments.

"James is my name," he said, and held out his hand.

"Cooper," I replied and we shook on it.

We talked for a few more minutes; then I checked the time on my cell and said we had to head out. I thanked him and headed for the door.

"Like I said, you best give them a holler, Cooper. Let 'em know you're coming. Those fellas shoot first, ask questions later," he warned as the door was closing behind me. That was the third time today.

"What the hell!" said Jason. "What kind of place is this?"

"It's Appalachia, Jason. It's just Appalachia."

26

THE FOREST IS DARK AND DEEP

Heading into the forest in mid-October is like driving into a fury of color. The leaves form a carpet of reds, oranges, purples, and yellows, all interlaced with greens and browns, making it hard to distinguish road from forest floor. We depended on where the underbrush was thickest to tell us where the trail was. We passed red maples that were now scarlet and orange, and beeches, their branches loaded with pure yellow gold. The sugar maples, probably a bright scarlet a month ago, were now a weathered orange, the white oaks, a dull orange-brown. Nature was painting the forest, as it does every year as it gets ready for the winter—it blows in sometime around Thanksgiving and transforms Wayne National Forest into a wilderness of bare trunks, their crooked limbs stark against the autumn sky. It's all a preview of what the world will look like when the Winter Moon finally settles over the landscape and the sun loses its fire.

Indian legend has it that the trees in the fall are red from the blood of the Great Bear that was slain and that the yellow in the leaves comes from the fat that splashed out of the pan as they cooked the meat. I wondered how much blood the hunters were spreading over the forest today.

"It looks like a campsite up ahead," said Jason, pointing through the trees to a clearing in the trail. I could see the backs of a few RVs ahead. As we rounded the bend, the campsite grew. Tents stretched into the forest beyond the clearing that I now saw was twice the size of a football field. We pulled into a parking area beyond the tents where several large RVs were standing. Two men fed logs into a bonfire in the center of the camp. They looked our way as my car hit stones and brush. Both men had on tan/green ranger vests—no sleeves—and camouflage khakis. They started to walk in our direction. Yeah. We were in the right place. These guys looked like genuine rednecks—militia types.

"What can we do for you boys?" said a tall lean man. He showed bad teeth. "Y'all lost?" He was peering into the car. A tattoo of a mermaid on his left bicep stared at me as he laid his left arm on my window. Semper Fi formed an arc over the fish-girl. The other man was making his way over to Jason's side.

"No, were not lost," I said. "We're looking for Kenneth Boyd."

"Oh yeah? And who are 'we'?" said the man with the tattoo, checking out the back seat. While he was doing that his underarm was almost in my nose and the odor was fast becoming a lethal weapon. I figured he followed the 'We shower every Saturday night,' rule

"Cooper," I said and climbed out of the car, pushing him back as I opened the door.

He stumbled and caught himself. "Fuck you doin'?" he yelled, his face red like fresh blood. He was tall but I was

119

bigger. The other guy had come around the car and was lined up with his buddy. We all stared at each other for a few moments.

"Just getting out of the car, bud," I said, like *fuck you*, back. Jason wasn't going to help. He was frozen to his seat.

Then, "What's happening over there?" a man standing on the steps of an RV parked near the forest about a hundred feet away, called out, breaking the tension. He was looking up so he could see from under his big hat—one of those Australian outbacks.

"Couple boys want to talk with Mr. Boyd," tattoo man yelled back.

"Oh yeah? What about?" the man with the hat yelled back.

"Didn't say."

"Ask him what he wants," the man said.

"Whaddya want, pal," he said, up close to my face.

"We got business with Boyd," I said, holding his stare. The man who hadn't showered yelled back my answer.

"All right. Bring 'em over," the other man said, not happy.

The guy with the mermaid on his bicep turned back to me. "You a reporter?" The fish girl's tail moved like it was alive.

"Nope."

He raised an eyebrow, then glanced over at Jason as he climbed out of the car. "He's one though, right?"

"Yeah," I said. He stared at Jason for a moment, then motioned for us to follow. The mermaid swam up his arm as he walked. Probably a trick he practiced for kids.

He stepped aside when we reached the RV and followed us up three steps where his buddy with the big hat was holding the door for us. A Glock was holstered against his right hip. He winked as I passed, nudging my arm.

The first thing I noticed was a collection of guns scattered on a table: handguns, a short-barreled Mauser, an automatic rifle that resembled an Uzi, and an array of hunting knives. A long wooden wall cabinet with a glass front showed another arsenal: rifles, more handguns, shotguns, and, beneath them all, a cavalryman's sword, sheathed and draped in a Confederate flag.

A tall lean man got up from a desk at the end of the RV. His hair was mixed with salt and pepper but his face didn't look old—forty-five maybe. Serious, like he didn't have time for this.

"You're the Florida dude looking into the murder of that colored woman, ain't you," he said, matter-of-fact. Right down to business. "And I suppose you have a connected reason to be talking to me about that," he said, and sat down. He waved at a couple of folding chairs for us to drag over to the desk. It was a neat desk. As a matter of fact, the whole RV was neat—like he had a cleaning lady come in just for us.

"Speak your mind," he said. "Got things to tend to," and he spat into a can near his desk. I guess I was reckless in calling him neat.

"Lemme save you some time," he said. "You think I might have had something to do with that girl's death," and he smiled as if he read my mind. He looked over at the man leaning against the door with the Glock, and laughed, "You see, Darren. I was right. Did I kill that negra girl?"

Darren looked back at him and shook his head. "No sir, Mister Boyd." He leaned out the door and spat. Manners.

"Are you a real live private dick, Cooper?" Baiting me. I didn't answer.

"Somebody hired you. Don't tell me. It's that n-lovin', communist teacher at the university, wasn't it?" More smiling. But he didn't read my mind. It was blank.

"He was messin' with that negra girl that was killed, wasn't he?"

"Cape Coloured," I said, the tension building in the room.

"You ask me, you oughta look to Jackson Lawless, you want to find the killer. He had every reason to. That's why he hired you. Hide behind your investigation," looking at me like I was just dumb.

"Your friend a Jew?" He was looking over at Jason. Jason's face turned crimson. I raised my hand in front of Jason to warn him not to react. This man was truly a piece of work.

"You're giving me plenty of reason to suspect you, Boyd. A hate crime, maybe."

Boyd reacted quickly. "The bastard's a commie, anti-gun liberal. I wouldn't be surprised if he wasn't a homosexual," he said, rising and spitting into a sink in the small kitchen behind him. Talk about neat.

"You like to hunt, Cooper?" he said, turning back around and wiping his mouth on his sleeve.

"I do," I said.

"What kind of guns you got?"

I said I mostly hunt people, so I use handguns. He noticed my Glock. Boyd looked over at the man waiting at the door as if to say you blew it, brother. The man held out his arms, palms up.

"Next time don't let nobody in here, Darren, less you frisk 'em. You got that!" he said, spitting out the last word. Darren nodded. Apology showing in the slump of his shoulders.

"Looks like our business is done here, Cooper," Boyd said coming around the desk, invading my space. "Bring

your rifle. I'll teach you how to shoot a real gun, you hear."
And he turned to Jason. "Never got your name," and he
held out his hand.

I was surprised Jason took it and told him his name.

"What paper you work for, Jason?"

"The Plain Dealer."

Boyd nodded as if thinking about that. Then, "Y'all
come back. We gotta teach these big city boys how to hunt,
Cooper," he said, turning to me. "Never know when it'll
come in handy."

Then he nodded to Darren who shuffled over to get us
the hell out of there.

We headed back to our car with three body guards, two
in back and one in front. A small group of men who had
gathered around the campfire now that it was blazing hot
stared at us—like we were aliens. Darren and his two buddies pushed us into the car and slammed the doors shut.
Nice hosts. Jason looked over at me like, *what the hell was
that all about?* I thought, Yeah, what the hell? I guess we
stirred someone's pot.

"I warned you, Jason," I said. He nodded. I saw fear
creep into his face. A first for Jason.

The colors were gone now that darkness had taken over,
the bright lights from the car bouncing off trees on either
side of the trail. I had to dim them several times so I could
spot the potholes in the road. The dense pines that had
crowded the road on the way in were now just a wall of
darkness. I made my way slowly, Jason's breathing notice-
able in the silence.

"We have a problem?" he said.

"Yeah, maybe," I said, and heard a pop as I followed
the trail around a gradual bend and under overhanging

branches. Then I heard another pop, followed by another and the snap of glass breaking. I thought I had hit something in the road. I looked over and saw Jason holding his hand over his chest, staring at it.

"What the hell!?" he said. "I think I'm shot!"

27

TUESDAY EVENING, OCTOBER 12

I hit the brakes to look, then realized the shooter was still nearby. So I told Jason to hang on while I hit the gas and sped away, the car bouncing over ruts and holes in the road. I almost lost the trail for a moment, narrowly missing a tree, then lost the road again, my right wheel riding the side of a ditch. I held the wheel steady against the slope of the embankment until I was able to pull back onto even ground.

Once we cleared the forest, I pulled off the road and helped Jason into the back seat. I stripped off his shirt, checked the wound—a shoulder shot. I tore off the sleeve of his shirt and made a pad to hold against the wound to slow the bleeding. Then I placed his hand on the pad and told him to hold it in place while I secured it with more cloth torn from his shirt.

Jason moaned, "Is it bad?"

The entry wound was small. So, I figured a .22-caliber rifle. The problem is the damage could be greater than a shell from a Glock since the bullet from a .22 usually doesn't exit.

125

When I was back on the road, I called Louise to find the closest hospital.

"What the hell happened?" she said. I told her in twenty words or less and said I needed the information fast. I stayed on the line while she checked. The closest hospital was in Cambridge, about forty miles away. Forty-five minutes, I figured.

The bleeding had stopped. Jason was lying with his head back on the seat, eyes closed. Maybe asleep. We were at the emergency room in thirty-nine minutes. Paramedics had him on a gurney and were wheeling him into surgery with me following, until a nurse stopped me.

"You'll have to wait here," she said, pointing to an area where a few people were watching TV. "The patient advocate will need some information about your friend. She will be out to see you shortly." I looked at the clock. It was 8:05 p.m. and black outside.

At 8:30 a nurse came out, said Jason was in surgery, and the doctor would see me when it was over. I watched the clock move toward 9:00. I must have dozed because when I looked again it read 9:25. No word about Jason, no sign of the doc. At 9:36 the ER doors swung open. A man in blues, cap in his hand, came over. I was the only one in ER.

"Mr. Cooper?"

I nodded and stumbled trying to get up. He put his hand on my shoulder and said it was all right. Then he sat sat down next to me. I was worried about what that meant.

"Your friend is out of surgery and is in recovery," he said.

I nodded, waiting for the bad news.

"He's had a nasty little gunshot wound, a .22-caliber bullet. It entered his shoulder and stayed there, but, fortunately, I was able to remove it without much trouble. The problem with a .22-caliber bullet is that it can roll around inside the body"—just what I was afraid of—"and, depending on where it makes its entrance, do some significant damage. As good fortune would have it, in your friend's case, that didn't happen. And…you did a good job of first aid," he added, smiling. "But the bullet did do some damage to the shoulder. He will need some rest and rehabbing before he has full use of it again."

"Permanent damage?" I said.

"No, he should recover fully. But it will be some months before that happens. It all depends on how well his physical therapy goes. The bullet tore into some muscle. That will require some healing time." Then he hesitated. "I've got to report this, you know," looking up at me over his glasses. I said that's exactly what he should do. He was relieved to hear that. "Some of these incidents are hunting accidents," he said. "I'm guessing you don't think this was one of them."

"That's right," I said.

I asked him when I could see Jason. He said in an hour or so.

After the wait I spent some time with Jason. I let him fall asleep, then headed for the closest coffee shop before I hit the road again. Jason had called his girlfriend. She was coming down to take care of him while he recovered. His editor was already calling about what happened. They talked for about fifteen minutes while I was still there. I was picturing the front page.

Plain Dealer Reporter Shot Investigating Murder of South African Student The kind of article with follow-up potential for a Pulitzer. Maybe it was worth the shot—for Jason.

28

RICHIE

I found a diner still open in downtown Cambridge near Kennedy's Bakery. Kennedy's has been operating in Cambridge for over eighty-five years. It was there when I was a kid. It's there now. My friends and I used to stop after school in front of the large storefront window that overlooked Main Street and stare at the pastries that were showcased there—fresh apple pies, smelling like an apple orchard; cakes of all kinds; pumpkin pies with Gingersnap Crust; cherry pies, the fruit deep red and overflowing the crust; donuts fresh from the ovens; it was all there that a young kid would want after a hard day at school.

Mr. Kennedy would come out of the bakery, look in the window with us, and ask if we saw something we liked. "Sure," we would say and point to a pumpkin pie or some other piece of pastry that made our eyes pop out of our heads and our stomachs ache.

"How much money you got?" he would ask, smiling down at us. He looked seven feet tall. My guess is that he was about five feet ten inches, most.

Five cents or so was all we ever had. So that's what we told him.

"Well, I think I've got just the thing you want for five cents," he would say, and he would go back into the bakery, take the pie, or whatever piece of baked treasure that we pointed to in the display case, and hand it over to us for a nickel—or whatever we had. I always thought everything was so cheap!

"Mr. Kennedy still does the same thing today," one of his kids told me recently, smiling and shaking her head.

There's not much open in downtown Cambridge on a Wednesday night. But the diner was still open. I found a booth near the front window and ordered a decaf and a piece of cherry pie I had seen on the way in.

"Is this from Kennedy's Bakery?" I asked.

"Sure is," she said, surprised. "You must be from around here." I smiled and nodded. I called Richie.

"Nothin' happenin' here, Coop. Where are you?"

I told him quickly about the reporter from *The Plain Dealer*, filled him in on Kenneth Boyd and the trip into the National Forest to his camp.

"Jeez, shoulda tole me you was leavin'." Like he was hurt. "I shoulda gone with you. I get up and you're gone!"

"On hindsight, you're right," I said. "Jason got shot."

"Shot! What the fuck, Cooper. Who shot him?"

"I don't know. I think one of Boyd's people."

"Where are you?" he said.

"So, you're not mad anymore?" I said.

"Hell yeah, I'm mad. Where the fuck are you?"

I told him.

"Get a room. I'll meet you there."

"Already have one I said. Hampton Inn on Georgetown Road, just off I-70 near the junction of I-70 and I-77."

"Good. Be there in an hour."

Always the optimist. It was at least a two-hour drive. But then…we're talking Richie.

29

THE PLAN

I was checked into the hotel by 11:00. I was worried about Huck. I hadn't heard from him since Friday morning. That was unlike him. So I called.

"So, you finally call your sick friend, Kemo Sabe," complained a sad voice on the other end.

"What happened to you?"

"Gator took a small bite out of my leg."

"What?" Huck had never had a gator get to him.

"How big a bite?"

"Doc sewed up the torn skin like a deerskin coat. Still smarts when I walk though. I still plan to get up your way this weekend. Threw the crutch away this morning."

Huxter is a natural born gator hunter, relentless when he's tracking them in the swamp. I went with him several times. It was on one of those trips when I developed my fear of those evil creatures. A damn gator grabbed my foot as I stepped out of our motorboat—I never saw him sitting there in the grass just off shore in the Ten Thousand Islands. Huck shot him between the eyes with his alligator rifle. Blew part of the gator's head off. Lucky he didn't take part of my foot with it. I guess he must have left his gun at home this time.

"Don't even think about travelling until that leg of yours heals up," I said.

He said, no problem, but plan on him being in Riverdale on Monday. Would drive his old Ford pick\up. That way he could bring all his guns.

I told him about the Holiday Inn and that Louise would meet him there. I wanted both of them to take turns surveilling Jackson.

"When do I get my private dick badge?" he said.

"Soon," I said.

"And that would be when, exactly?"

"Soon," I said. Private dick language.

Richie showed up at the hotel at about 11:15 p.m.

"Let's get a drink and talk about plans," I said. The bar was still open.

"You got plans?" said Richie.

"No, I don't have plans," I said, suddenly feeling tired.

Richie had a beer, I ordered a dry white.

"What you tell me, Coop, they got an army in there. Besides you don't know *they* shot Jason anyway," said Richie.

I looked around the bar and tried to think of a plan. There was dark wood everywhere. It reminded me of a gentleman's club in the south. The bartender was black, dressed in black pants, white shirt and a black bow tie. Nice touch. He served generous drinks.

"It's almost midnight. Let's get some rest. We'll visit Jason tomorrow," I said. "Maybe I'll have a plan by then."

"Uh-huh. You do better with no plan, Coop. Get some sleep." He looked at me with that old Richie look—but this time with a hint of sympathy there.

30

CARMEN SANTANGELO

WEDNESDAY MORNING, OCTOBER 13

The sun was hitting me in the face so I rolled away from it. The alarm read 11:25. It took me a few moments to figure out where I was. Hampton Inn, Cambridge, Ohio. My message light was blinking. It was Jason.

"I got a phone call this morning, Coop," he said. "A 740 area code. That's Steubenville. Guy left a message. Said he had read my articles and had some information for me."

"Yeah?" I said.

"I got a message to call back."

"So, did you call him back?"

"Yeah, no answer. So I left a message to call me back."

"And…?"

"Nothing so far."

"So, you got a message from a guy from Steubenville and you think this is big news?" I said.

"Yeah. I think so. Follow every lead."

"So you think you're a detective now, huh, Jason?"

"An investigative reporter. Same thing, Cooper."

He had a point.

"I'll be right over," I said.

"The name he left was Palazzo," said Jason as I walked in on him. He was sitting up and picking at some food on a tray that was rolled over his bed. "I've talked enough. My shoulder's killing me. Why don't you call him?"

I punched in the number on my cell that Jason read off his phone. No answer, so I left a message with my number.

"I guess we wait," I said.

My cell rang.

"Cooper," I said.

"Who the fuck's Cooper?" said a voice on the other end.

I asked him if he was Palazzo. He said yeah and so what. I told him who I was and that Jason was with me. I reminded him that he called. He said, oh yeah, you're right, and ain't you the private dick from Florida? I said I was. He said Mr. Santangelo would like to talk with you too. I said who was Mr. Santangelo?

"You don't know Mr. Santangelo? Where the fuck you been livin'? With your head up your ass? Everybody knows Mr. Santangelo."

A voice behind Palazzo told him to shut the fuck up and tell me to get my butt up to Steubenville. I guessed that was Santangelo.

"Mr. Santangelo has information about the murder of the girl in the Valley—Mr. Santangelo don't like people getting offed he don't know nothin' about, see?"

I nodded.

"You listenin', Cooper?"

I nodded again, but added an "Uh-huh."

"Okay. Mr. Santangelo also said he might be able to help with that missing girl too—what was her name? Tania?" said Palazzo. I asked how he heard about her.

"Newspaper," he said. Your friend the reporter." Like he read my mind.

"Her name's Taisia," I said.

"Yeah, yeah, okay. The point is when can the two of yous get up here?"

I looked at Jason. "I'm afraid it will have to be just me. Jason's out of commission for a while."

"Geez. Nothin' serious I hope," said Palazzo, like he really cared.

"Nothing serious," I said.

"Good. The Boss would like to see you today, Cooper."

"I've got no problem with that," I said, thinking about the time I would need to drive to Steubenville from Cambridge. I figured an hour and a half.

"It's noon now," I said. "How about three thirty?" That would give me plenty of time to pull my stuff together.

"That's fine. We're gonna meet across the river at Elbie's Big Boy in Weirton." I knew the one. "Mr. Santangelo likes eating at Big Boy's," he said. "A lot of windows there. Got a clear view of everyt'ing.."

I told him I would be there.

"Drive safe, kid," he said.

I called Richie.

31

"You still asleep?" I said.

"Not anymore," Richie said, sounding irritated.

"I need you to go with me to a meeting. Can you be ready in a half hour?"

"A meet with who?" he said.

"Whom," I said. "Carmen Santangelo. Recognize that name?"

"Nope. Whom is he?" said Richie.

"Tell you about it later."

I went back to the hotel. Richie passed me in the hall.

"Heading down for some food," he said. He was wearing his pin striped linen suit and a white shirt with the cufflinks showing. Richie likes to dress up when he's going to kill someone. He must have made a call to Cleveland about Santangelo.

I pulled on black dress pants, a white, button-down oxford shirt and grabbed my leather jacket. I loaded my Glock and held out my right hand to see if my fingers shook. They didn't. Sometimes they do. I never know if its nerves or just advancing age. Since I'm only forty-three, it must be nerves. I had been shot twice in the last year. I had enough of that. I pushed the Glock into a shoulder holster and strapped it on.

Richie was finishing up bacon and eggs in the restaurant when I got there. I ordered coffee, an English muffin, and a fruit cup.

"What the fuck kind of breakfast is that, Cooper?" he said.

"Diet," I said patting my stomach.

"No. This is diet time," he said, pulling back his jacket. I saw more muscle than fat.

Richie finished up the last of his eggs as I checked my cell for the time. I don't wear a watch anymore. I have half a dozen in my dresser drawer. Probably collector's items now.

"You ready to go?" I said. "We're not staying overnight."

"This what you're asking?" he said, pulling back his jacket to show his Browning HP JMP. I used it once on a practice range in my back yard in the Everglades. It holds 13 rounds of 9 mm shells. Good in a gunfight. I was hoping we wouldn't need it today.

"I called Johnny when we got off the phone," said Richie.

Johnny is a union organizer in Cleveland—among other things. Richie does 'odd jobs' for him.

"He told me Carmen Santangelo's a big man down here. Controls the action along the river from Youngstown to Cincinnati. Used to work for Johnny in Cleveland. Got his own gig now. Nobody to fuck around with. Palazzo—he's his shooter."

The drive up the river takes you past power plants that spew out smoke generated from coal—coal is King in the Valley—past deserted factories, their redbrick walls falling apart, their chimneys coated in black soot; past small river towns like New Matamoras, Powhatan Point, and Shady-side. I used to think they were pretty towns, now they look sad and deserted, just like the factories that employed the people who still live there.

A Dairy Queen sits next to a steel plant that runs along the West Virginia side of the river, downstream from Sha-dyside and Martins Ferry, Ohio. Richie, DeFelice, and I used to come to the Valley for football games when we were in high school. Cities in the Valley always had good teams and every year or so our school would travel and play them in a non-conference game. I can remember stop-ping at the Dairy Queen and running through the orange smoke that choked the air, dense as an early morning fog, to keep the soot off the cone. I never thought to cover my mouth and nose. I just wanted to protect the white custard from the pollution. It was pure poison.

But the smoke from the factories that polluted the Val-ley, that poisoned the lungs, that blotted out the sun in the day and rested at night so the moon could show its face, that choked you with a vengeance when you had to run through it, say for ice cream or just to walk to school, something as innocent as that, this smoke, deadly and filled with acids and chemicals of all kinds, was a sign of prosperity for the Valley.

So, the people looked for the smoke, enjoyed it, and knew, when they saw it rise from the gigantic stacks of the steel mills, that the Valley was alive and well. And on Sunday, when the mills rested and the smoke was gone, the people from Shadyside and Bellaire and Wheeling and Martins Ferry would go to church and thank God for their prosperity, and, by the way, for the smoke that witnessed to it.

Times have changed. Today the smoke is gone, and so is the prosperity. The towns that struggled to find a way to make a living…well, they're still here. But there is still coal, the black gold of Appalachia. There is that. And there's still Friday night high school football. There is that as well.

"Geez, what a depressing place!" said Richie, looking out the window. I agreed with him.

We pulled into the southern limits of Steubenville and headed for the new bridge on U.S. 22 that crosses the Ohio into Weirton and to the Big Boy restaurant. One of the best places to eat in Weirton. That's the kind of place it is. You go to Big Boy's on Sunday, you get dressed up.

The new, high-level bridge that spans the river stands in sharp contrast to its surroundings: the deserted factories that line the shore on each side; the empty store fronts, not even a 'for rent' sign in the windows; houses still suffering from the blight that the mills brought, wooden frame houses needing a paint job and leaning into each other, showing the strain of aging. And rust everywhere. Anything that's metal is brown with it. I guess that's why they call it the rust belt.

As you exit the bridge, you take the ramp to Route 2, Main Street, hang a left on Main, turn onto Freedom Way and there it is, Big Boy's. I parked the car as Richie jumped out. He's usually out before I stop. He waited for me half-way across the lot, feeling for his gun behind his jacket.

A waitress met us at the door.

"Are you Mr. Cooper?" she said. I told her I was and watched her eyeing Richie.

"He's with me," I said.

She nodded and led us to Carmen Santangelo's table. Carmen smiled and waved us over. There was a man sitting next to him that I didn't recognize. Palazzo, I figured.

"Have a seat, gentlemen," Carmen said, pointing to several chairs opposite him. It was a round table, with a white tablecloth, and six chairs pulled around the table. Fancy for Big Boy's.

"They fix it up special for me, Cooper," Carmen said, smiling and nodding his head.

"So you bring greetings from Cleveland, huh, Richie?" he said. We were still standing.

"Johnny sends his best, Mr. Santangelo," said Richie, hiking his pants up.

"You wondering how I knew about you huh, Richie?" said Carmen, grinning like he was winning a bet.

Richie didn't respond.

"Johnny gimme a call. Said I should treat you like a brother. Don't I know you from somewheres, Richie?" Old home week.

"I don't think so," said Richie, shrugging.

"No? Maybe not. Well anyway, sit," said Carmen, pointing to three chairs in front of him. Palazzo was sitting next to Carmen. There were two men at a booth by the front window, overlooking Freedom Way, watching us. Santangelo saw me looking over at them.

"I gotta lotta enemies, Cooper. Can't be too careful," he said, winking. "That's why I like this place. Normal people," looking around with his arms extended as if there were crowds around him. There was hardly anyone there. "And the view is good. Over there," he said, pointing out the window "you can almost see the river." But all I saw were run-down stores and a street that needed a water truck to wash away the dirt.

"How you doin', Coop?" said someone behind me. As I turned around, I was face to face with Kenneth Boyd and

141

his buddy with the tattoo. Carmen was smiling, like he was enjoying a show. Time froze for a moment. Richie stared.

"What's a matter, Cooper, you don't know Boyd?" said Carmen.

"I know him," I said. I wondered if my face was red.

"Were your boys out hunting when we left your place, Boyd?" I said.

"We always hunt, Cooper. That's why we're out there."

I nodded. "Were we in your sights?"

"If you were in my sights, Cooper. You wouldn't be standing here," he said, his gaze steady on me.

"Come on, boys, sit," Carmen said, extending his arms like he was welcoming us into his home.

"So, where's your reporter friend?" said Boyd, taking a seat next to Palazzo.

I didn't answer him.

"Boys, boys, let's smoke the peace pipe," said Carmen. "I know all about the shooting. None of my boys is responsible for any shooting of any reporter. Ain't that so, Boyd?" he said, looking over at Boyd, like he meant it better not be so.

"No sir, Mr. Santangelo. I don't know nothin' about any shooting. How's your reporter friend, Cooper?" he said, trying to be friendly.

"Shot," I said.

"Oh, that's too bad," said Boyd. I saw tattoo man smiling. I stared at him. He quit smiling.

"Who's your friend here, Cooper?" said Boyd, looking over at Richie, now sitting to the right of Carmen. Boyd and his tattooed buddy were facing him.

Richie's head was cocked to one side, staring at Boyd.

"You don't wanna mess with Richie," Carmen broke in. "You get him mad, he'll shoot you where you sit."

Boyd flinched. Richie stared.

"No offense," Boyd said, running his fingers across his chin and watching Richie as though he might suddenly draw on him.

Richie nodded.

"Let's get something to eat, boys," Carmen said, easing the tension.

He turned to Palazzo and told him to get the waitress to take our orders.

After the waitress left, Carmen turned to me.

"How much you make as a private dick, Cooper?"

"Enough to pay my bills and keep me happy," I said.

"Listen, you find the person or persons who killed that girl you found in the river and I'll pay you well," he said, patting his stomach like he had something valuable in there.

"All due respect, Mr. Santangelo, I don't understand why you care about a girl who's not even from here," I said.

"Mr. Santangelo has his reasons," said Palazzo, leaning into the table. "All he's sayin' is he's willing to pay you to find who killed her." I could see the gun under his jacket. Richie stirred. Santangelo held up his hand.

"I already have a client," I said, watching Pallazo. He was right handed.

"Yeah, and how much is that client paying you, Cooper?" Santangelo said. Then, "Tell you what. You think about it. Keep track of your hours and let Palazzo know how much we owe you, supposing, of course, that you agree to do this thing."

I was listening.

"I have a reason I want you to do this for me. I think I can help you with your case. I'm gonna give you that

143

information, but only on condition that you agree to work for me. You're gonna wanna know what I'm gonna tell you, I can assure you of that, Cooper," said Carmen. The whole table was locked into what Carmen was saying, including me.

"I'm listening," I said.

"A coupla boys from outta town are trying to take over my territory, Cooper. I think they may be the same guys killed your little commie girl," he said, forming his fingers into a house, staring at me over them. After a few moments he continued. The silence was for effect.

"Before you ask me who are these guys, let me say that's what I'm gonna pay you for. They're Russians. Came down here from Cleveland." He let that sink in. "Think of it," he said, throwing his hands up like he's incredulous, "a bunch of pinko commies trying to take over Carmen Santangelo's business!" Then he paused, watching for me to react. I didn't.

"Find them guys, Cooper, and I bet you find the guys killed your girl. Main thing I want is get those Russians out of my backyard." He paused, like he was thinking about something. Then, "Fuckin' communists. Got no morals."

"So where can I find these Russians?" I never thought of Russians and the Valley in the same sentence. Richie was leaning forward.

"They're here, Cooper. Up and down the river. You keep your eyes open, you'll see 'em, right Tony?" he said, turning to Palazzo.

"Right, boss," said Palazzo, looking up from cleaning his nails.

Then, "When we gonna eat!" yelled Carmen over to the waitress.

144

The young waitress, probably a college girl, brought out a tray—double-decker cheeseburgers, fries, cokes, the works—followed by another waitress with more food. Big Boy's. First class service. The afternoon had turned to evening by the time we left. The run-down houses were looking better as darkness settled over the Valley.

32

THE DREAM

We got back to the hotel around midnight. I rang for a wake-up at 9:00 a.m., turned over, and fell asleep. And I dreamed I was tracking Maxie's kidnappers. But I kept losing them. That's the way it always goes. I follow the road I know they took, and that leads to another, and that to others and they all run through unfamiliar towns and along unfamiliar country-sides, until finally I'm back to where I started. The highway never goes anywhere. And that's my road nightmare.

And sometimes I dream of being back at Concord College. There's always an undertone when that happens—an anxiety—the free floating kind—like I sense that something is wrong with my being there, but I don't know what it is—and I'm teaching—almost as if I am being given a second chance—and my family is there—Jillie and Maxie—but deep down inside, where all nightmares live and grow, there is that gnawing, that things are not right—and then I wake. And for a brief few moments I truly don't

146

know what is real and what is nightmare. Though in truth, there is no distinction. And I know it. Not for as long as Maxie is missing.

When the wake-up call came, I was sweating so hard my T-shirt and underwear were soaked. It took me about five minutes to finally realize where I was—in Ohio—not that far from where Maxie had first disappeared—about fifteen miles. Not far from the nightmare after all. And Richie, sleeping like a dead man in the other bed.

33

THE RUSSIANS

THURSDAY MORNING, OCTOBER 14

The morning was clear as Richie and I headed back to Riverdale. No breakfast. Just coffee. We took the longest but fastest route and jumped on I-70 to Columbus and then south on Ohio 23 which would take us to Riverdale. On the way we talked about our meeting with Santangelo.

"You've gotta be kidden' me," Richie said, shaking his head and staring at the endless fields and at the farm houses and barns that sat in them. "Damn Ruskies trying to take over The Man's territory." Then, "Are those fences electrified?" His eyes were following a line of barbed wire that bordered a field on his right.

"Not barbed wire fences. They don't need to be electrified. The barbs are enough to keep the cows in the field. If you see the wire running through small, white, cylindrical pieces of glass—those are electrified."

He nodded and kept staring.

"What we still don't have are the names of the Russians," I said. He nodded again and still watched the fence lines race by.

My cell played out Pachelbel's Canon. I can't tell you how much that tune calms my nerves. Musical Xanax.

"Cooper?" said the voice on the other end. It was Tony Palazzo.

"Yeah?"

"Mr. Santangelo said you want some names?" I nodded. "You hear what I'm saying, Cooper?"

"Right," I said.

"Well then, pal, here's some names."

And he gave me three: Kolya Shibalov, a guy by the name of Maks—he didn't know the last name—and Maryana Zorin.

"A woman?" I said.

"Yeah, a woman. These three work together. And don't underestimate her. She's a bitch. One of those women who would cut a man's balls off." A pause. "Okay? That oughta help yous."

I said it did and thanks.

"Let me know your expenses. I'll wire the money to your bank," he added. "And keep me informed, Cooper. Carmen don't like no surprises." Then he was gone. I wondered if those guys ever took an English class.

"You hear that, Richie?" I said. "The guy must have gone to the same school you went to."

Richie shrugged. "Hey, brains ain't got nothing to do with it, Coop. Look at you. Brains but no street smarts. Lucky for you, you got me around to watch your back."

"What do you think?" I said.

"About what?"

"Carmen and the Russians. Something about it I don't like."

"I don't know, Coop. At least we got somethin'. We got names."

"Yeah, you're right. So let's find out where the bad guys live."

34

THE GRANDFATHER

It was late morning when we pulled into the parking lot of the Holiday Inn in Riverdale. We were both tired and hungry so we dumped our bags in the room and headed for the restaurant.

My cell went off again. Busy day.

"Cooper." It was DeFelice. "The grandfather's flying into Columbus this morning. Thought I'd better let you know…"

"Columbus! What the…"

"I know. I know. The guy's crazy, Coop. Said he had to meet the man who's gonna find his grandkid. I tried to tell him. Wouldn't listen."

Great. "Okay, okay," I said. "Hope he's got a ride because we're heading back to Riverdale."

"Back? From where?" I had forgotten. DeFelice didn't know about our trip upriver.

"Cambridge," I said.

"Cambridge? What the hell you doin' there?"

I filled him in on Carmen Santangelo and his interest in April Januarie's killing. I also told him about the names of the Russians he had given us.

"That's crazy. Why would a guy like Santangelo give you names?"

"Yeah, I wondered the same thing."

"Be careful. I wouldn't trust him." He paused. "Richie with you?"

"Right next to me." Richie looked over.

"Good." Another pause, like he was thinking.

"You know, I'm thinking Santangelo might have a place down here—if he's the same guy..." Then, as if the reverie was over, "Like I said, yous guys be careful."

In Cleveland if you put an 's' at the end of you, you have a plural. Basic grammar.

"By the way, Lou 's flyin' in tonight. Told me to tell you. You knew she was comin', right?"

I said I did, I just didn't know when. Another surprise.

"Maybe it's supposed to be a surprise, Coop." Mind reader. In other words, *Get rid of all the girl friends.*

"Uh-huh. Funny."

I was looking forward to seeing her again, still remembering the time in the hospital. She pulled my face down to hers—no warning, despite all the bandages from the gunshots and the tubes in her body—and we kissed. I could hardly walk straight when I left her room. She smiled when I turned around. You owe me dinner, Coop, she said. Only the best, I promised.

We've been seeing each other off and on since then. Dinner. Movies—mostly Woody Allen and M. Night Shyamalan—our favorite, *Unbreakable.* And foot massages. And... so use your imagination. We've come a long way since the hospital. But we're still working on our relationship.

Richie and I had just ordered sandwiches in the restaurant when my cell went off again. You can run but you can't hide.

"Detective Cooper, it is Leo Federovich, and I am in Columbus." He paused as if he were waiting for a reception committee. Then, "Detective DeFelice called and said you are now in a place called Riversdale, is this true, sir?"

"Yes, that's right," I said. Richie, irritated, was pointing to our sandwiches. "I would have been glad to meet you in Miami," I continued, ignoring Richie. "No need to make the trip here."

"I understand Mr. Cooper. But this is better. You will not have to take time from your work to meet me. I will be in Riverdale in two hours—two o'clock."

I said fine and told him where to meet us.

"So we're supposed to pick him up?" Richie muttered through his food.

"Yeah," I replied, my irritation obvious.

He nodded and dug into his sandwich. A BLT. Chips and coleslaw on the side. He was happy.

35

THE RUSSIAN

First impressions are usually wrong. In the case of Leo that couldn't have been more incorrect. He looked like a strongman. Thick neck, angular face—the marks of fights evident in his cheeks.

"Detective Cooper," he said, as I opened the door.

Federovich was dressed nattily, like an American mobster: black suit, white shirt, tie pulled up tight against his large neck, his Adam's apple looking uncomfortable and confined. His black hair ran with traces of gray—it gave him that worried, kind of harried, look.

"You are the one who is going to find my granddaughter," he almost yelled, taking me by the shoulders, and clapping my arms. "Good. We will find the *Brodyagi* (lowlifes) who took her." He pulled away, studying me intently. "And when we do…I am killing them," he said, pushing two fingers into his neck.

Richie mumbled behind me. "Jeez. What the fu…?" I turned and glared.

If Federovich heard, he didn't let on. "Sit, sit," he said, gesturing to the chairs in the room like he was the host. "Tell me about my granddaughter."

We sat. There was a silence for a moment. He broke it. "Whoever has done this has broken Ponitka (the unwritten code). And so...," spreading his hands, like he had no choice, "we will respond with *razboiniki*." He noticed the look on my face.

"Violence for violence. They dare to take my granddaughter? No. No. No!" he yelled, his right hand exploding into his left. I felt my eye twitch.

"Do you have any idea of who might have taken your granddaughter?"

"Just my instincts, Mr. Cooper. It is how I have survived all of these years." He paused. "Tell me what you know. You are the detective."

"Did you know that your granddaughter was involved in clinical studies."

He seemed surprised. "Clinical studies? No. What are these clinical studies?"

I explained what they were. "Do you know a young man by the name of Geza? Maybe a friend of Taisia?"

He looked puzzled. "No, I don't know this person. Why?"

"He disappeared at the same time your granddaughter did."

Leo bit down on his lower lip and leaned back in his chair. "Go ahead, I am listening."

I told him about my visit with Carmen Santangelo, about how he thought some Russians were trying to take over his territory, and more importantly, how they might be responsible for stealing his granddaughter.

"Hmmm. Who is this Santangelo...?"

"Crime boss." I said. "Controls everything that goes on up and down the Ohio River."

He stared at me, his hands working against themselves, like he was kneading bread. Nervous, but hunching like a bear.

"I understand. *Pakhan*. Big boss. We have much crime in Russia since 1991." He paused momentarily, weighing his words. "So now there is no one to keep the law, Mr. Cooper. Only the *Pakhan*. And he is the law. And I know how men like your crime boss friend can lie. But this business about Russians?...I think this might be true. Maybe they try to take his territory." And then, almost to himself, "Maybe they take my Taisia." And the veins in his hands that were still wringing something, maybe someone's neck, were purple and swollen, and the tendons moved like ropes under the skin, like they had a life of their own, perfectly comfortable with killing.

"You know, Mr. Cooper, these *razboiniki* love the violence. They kill you for practice. Not like you and me..." He hesitated. "Not like you I think."

Richie cleared his throat and smiled. Leo noticed. He was thoughtful for a moment.

"Did this Carmen give you names?"

"Yes," and I told him about Kolya Shibalov, and Maks, and Maryana Zorin.

Leo was quiet for a moment. Then he nodded. "I am knowing both men. This is not good news. Kolya Shibalov is boss of the most dangerous gang in Moscow. They call him Myasnik."

I waited. "Myasnik means 'Butcher,' Mr. Cooper."

Stomach acid burned my throat as I thought of Taisia.

"He has meat supply business in Moscow. Illegal meat. So he got the name because he…" and he spread his hands and shrugged, "takes body parts of rival *razboiniki*. You see? Violence. It is part of our new culture. Teach lesson." He paused. "So, he is here in this country." And he nodded, then slapped his knees as though he had discovered a big truth.

I shrugged. "According to Carmen."

"This is very bad news, Mr. Cooper. And the other man, Maks," he continued, "I think this is Maks Remizov. Remi. One of Russia's new *pakhan*." He paused, resting his head in his big hands, then, looking up, said, "If Taisia is in their hands, Mr. Cooper, we don't have much time." And the tension in his voice revealed, for the first time, a shade of fear.

"And Maryana?" I said.

"I know nothing of her. Sometimes they can be the worst—womens. Gangs use the womens for kidnapping children. She takes them under her…*plashch*…? I don't know in English," and he mimicked putting on a jacket.

"Cloak?" I said.

"Ah, yes. I believe that is right. She takes them under her cloak," and he pretended to hide a child under his jacket, "and she delivers them not to safety, my friends, but to a *cipotctbo* where they are sold."

He was watching me carefully as he spoke—to see if I got it? And I did. I sure as hell did. I knew exactly what he was talking about. And I was thinking of the children in Ichiguro's book, *Never Let Me Go*. Children who were raised in a special school, a boarding school, Hailsham, a safe sounding name like for a British boarding school, a school like Eton or Hyde, where students from rich families are prepped for university, for the best ones, but these

157

children, the children at Hailsham, innocents in the cruelest of worlds, were being raised for a far different purpose, hideous and inhuman, and led to believe that they were special, led to believe that they had a privileged future, only to slowly discover, like the children in Leo's horrifying orphanage, that they were being raised to donate their body parts: their kidneys, their blood, their eyes even, to the school's wealthy clients, that they were no more than a junk yard of parts for aging cars. And the children of Hailsham remained innocent even to the end of their short lives, trusted their caretakers, their guardians, trusted like the naïve Golden Retriever, who blindly follows his master. And I thought of Taisia, and I thought of Maxie. And I knew they would trust. And that's what Leo saw in my eyes.

"Are you okay, Mr. Cooper?" The first note of gentleness in Federovich, the pakhan.

I sighed deeply, and nodded.

"A *cipotctbo*—how do you say?" and he tried to use his hands to describe something. "A place where you keep the children who have no mother—a *cipotctbo* (pronounced sirotstvo)."

"An orphanage." And my stomach dropped through the floor.

"Yes, Detective Cooper, they have such places in Russia. An orphanage," and he looked at me to see if he pronounced it correctly.

I had heard of traffickers using orphanages in Eastern Europe as holding houses for children sold into slavery. Maybe Mark Twain was right: Man *is* at the bottom of the scale of evolution. Predators. Apex predators. No competitors. The cruelest of the animal kingdom.

"Why your granddaughter?" Images of *cipotctbo* my new nightmare.

"Kolya was very important gang leader in Russia, Mr. Cooper. When the Rossiyskaya Federatsiya *razvalilsya*—how can I say it?—fell," and he plunged his hands violently downward, "the gangs take over."

I nodded.

"Yes. As head of Ministry, I wage war against gangs and put Kolya in prison. Maybe you see my problem?" He paused and sat back, his hands working against each other like they were enemies. "Now everyone in Russia is in gang," throwing up his hands as though they themselves were angry. "It is necessary to survive. Yes, even the President," nodding to emphasize that point. "I am old Bolshevik, Mr. Cooper. I make enemies. Even with the President.

"Russia suffers from money. Peoples turn to crime to make the money. Because of my position, I am able to travel—come to America. Most Russian peoples have no money."

"You said Kolya was in prison. How could he be here?"

"Remi was KGB. He and Kolya are *druz'ya*." He must have seen the question on my forehead. "Druz'ya," and he clasped his hands.

"So, maybe Remi freed his friend and they kidnapped Taisia out of revenge?"

"Yes. I think, maybe. And I fear they may try to sell her." He thought for a moment. But his hands told me all about him. The energy that came from them, the power, the relentless movement, as though they had a life of their own. They rested for a moment. Then, "Yes, I am sure of it. And so, we must act quickly. These are very dangerous peoples," he warned, raising his fist, his face crimson.

I nodded. "Just one caution, Mr. Federovich—"

"Please. Leo," raising his palms and shrugging.

"Okay. Leo." I paused. "Finding someone who has been missing for a month will be a challenge," I cautioned, not adding the grim stats for victims missing for more than a few days.

"I understand," he said, half listening. He opened his suit jacket and pulled out a few pictures.

"Her sixteenth birthday." And he held up a picture of a young girl, who looked maybe thirteen or fourteen, blond hair pulled together in a ponytail. She was laughing and waving at the camera. "And this is where she is living," pointing to a third story window in a red brick building, the stones stained from the pollution in Moscow. She was standing on the steps of the apartment building with her arm around an older woman.

In another photo she was holding a snowball, her arm back as if to toss it at the camera.

"Yes, we had a snow fight that day," he said, smiling and laughing gently.

He thumbed to another picture. She and a young man were about to take a T-bar up the side of a mountain. That smile again, her face full and flushed.

"She is very beautiful, is she not?" he said. "This was in central Turkey near Ankara," he explained, pointing at the slopes behind them. "It was our gift—her mother's and mine—before she goes to America."

I nodded. "Who's the young man?"

"A friend. Not Geza," he said. "I do not know this Geza."

I nodded. "May I keep one of the pictures?"

"They are yours, Mr. Cooper. For you to find my grand-daughter. You have found others. I am trusting you will find my Taisia." And he put the pictures—all of them—carefully back into the envelope and handed it to me. "Find her. Find my little Taisia," and he laid his hands on my shoulders and squeezed. Hard.

I wanted to tell him I would. But I didn't. Promises like that aren't worth the words they travel on. So, I didn't say anything. I let the silence run its course. And he focused on me for the briefest time.

Then, "But we must drink to our success, Mr. Cooper," and he pulled a bottle of Russian Standard Gold Vodka out of his suitcase. I knew that brand. Tingly to the tongue and it will knock me on my ass.

We didn't have vodka glasses, but we did have Holiday Inn glasses. And we drank—to success. And Leo toasted. To Taisia. To Detective Cooper. To Mr. Richie. To everything you could think of. And it was after three in the morning by the time we finished the vodka, Leo downing most of it.

You might wonder why Leo Federovich would waste time drinking while his granddaughter was missing. But Russians don't work until they have drunk, Cooper, Leo told me. It is a custom. To violate it is bad manners. And he held up his glass one last time, drained it, and slammed it down on the counter—so hard it shattered.

36

LEO'S PLAN

"Wha's our plan?" muttered Richie, the vodka taking its toll.

"Plan?" said Leo. "We don't need plan. We need men, men with *sisu*. You know *sisu*?" Richie shook his head.

"The Finnish have *sisu*. It is what keeps them free. It means, iron will. With it a man cannot be beaten."

"They were your enemies," I said. It came out enemas. You know, the vodka at work.

"I admire my enemies. I learn from my enemies." Leo had a neck that cut at an angle toward his shoulders. Like a strongman. It twitched as he stared at me. There was fire in his eyes. The vodka seemed to have had no effect on him.

"We will find them, Mr. Cooper," he said. "We will find them."

"And Mr. Richie, you will join us. Yes?"

Richie nodded.

Some kind of posse this was going to be: Richie, a hit-man; a dangerous Russian strongman; and me. I would save a spot for Louise. I was wondering why she didn't call.

162

37

L eo left to check into his room and Richie said he was heading to the bar. I had a chance for quiet time to try to get clarity about how to start the search.

My cell rang again. Maybe someone was calling with the answer.

"Hi Coop," said Jillie. "I want to meet." A few moments passed before I responded.

"Meet? Okay. What's up?"

"We need to put some things behind us." A pause. "At least I do. I think it would do us both some good."

I thought about it. My stomach was telling me not to do this.

"Our son is missing," she said. Anger rising there. "What have you...we... really done about it in the last few years? Me, I haven't slept through the night in eight years. I don't know about you—but this has been my life for the whole time."

I thought about it. She was right. What had we done together to find Maxie? So I said, "How about tonight? Six? That work?"

163

"Sure." Surprised. "Where?"

"Do you know the Village Bakery and Café on East State Street in Athens? The vegetarian restaurant," thinking it would be about half-way for both of us.

"Yes, I remember it. That's fine. But I need about an hour to get ready. It's 3:15 right now. How about 6:30?" I said that would work.

I hung up wondering what I was going to say to her. About Maxie I mean. We haven't talked about him much at all since our divorce. It's why we split in the first place.

I knew the drive to find missing persons was fueled by the need to find Maxie. But I also knew that I wasn't exhausting myself to find him anymore, perhaps, deep down, thinking it was useless—or just afraid that I would find him—dead. But the guilt for not looking? It hangs there just below my consciousness. And deep down I knew I had to commit myself to that search again. No matter what the outcome.

And if he was dead, well…I gave up on hell a long time ago. Let me tell you, it's here. You don't have to wait for it.

It was after 4:00 when I jumped on Route 23 north. By 4:30, I was heading east on Ohio 32 to Athens and the café on State Street. It would be a noisy place, filled with university students, all trying to lead a moral life by going vegetarian. That is until football season, then they all drink themselves into a stupor, turn cars over, and strip naked on balconies overlooking State Street.

It had been a while since I had been to the university. I had delivered a paper on one side of a debate—about the morality of the Iraq War. It was heated, I remembered that. My position—I was opposed to the war.

The cell buzzed in my pocket. It was Richie. I didn't want to discuss this trip with anyone. So I had turned off the ringer. This time I shut the phone down completely. I figured I would only be gone about five hours anyway.

State Street was crowded with students, many of them trying to get into bars with fake IDs. And, oh yes, it's a party school—third in the nation according to Monster College. I found a parking spot on the street about a block from the café and walked to the restaurant. It was cool, of course, because it was October, and the moon was still high in the sky. It was the Blood Moon now, the first moon after the Harvest Moon. A faint shade of red there, maybe from the sinking sun, maybe from the blood of the dead, who knows? But I could see it, and I could feel its pull even as I looked away.

Then I saw her. Seated at a booth at the front window, right under a neon sign the read, Open, and watching me, smiling, pulling back strands of blond hair, waving, uncertainly. Then I opened the door and faced her for the first time in seven years. I smiled back. How could I help it? Such a beautiful smile. I had forgotten.

She rose and put her arms around me, her face losing itself in my jacket. I had forgotten how smooth her hair was. We stayed that way for a few moments—until the waitress interrupted,

"Can I get you two lovebirds something to drink?"

A few students were staring at us as I sat down. They looked eighteen—max.

We both took a deep breath and stared at each other... until Jillie said,

"How have you been?" and she tilted her head as though she felt sorry for me. I wondered if I looked that bad.

165

"I've been well," I said, lying. "How have you been?"

"Should I lie or tell the truth?" She turned red, looked down, and then back into my eyes. I saw a cloud pass between us. Just for a moment. Then she looked away again, just as the waitress brought two cups of decaf and two waters.

"You two found time to read the menu yet?" she asked.

"A few minutes," I said, and she left with a smile that said *Take as much time as you like,* but she didn't say "lovebirds" again. Thank God.

38

THURSDAY EVENING, OCTOBER 14

The beginning of dinner was uncomfortable, all the feelings that had led up to our separation coming back. I let the silence sit there for a while. She broke it.

"So, Coop," she began. It sounded strange coming from her after these many years. "I've been thinking. Why don't we put all the bad feelings behind us, the blaming, the…" and she never looked up as she was speaking. And then as though that topic was over… "have you been seeing anyone?"

"No," I said, interpreting that to mean "now." Oh, what webs we weave…

And she smiled, that knowing smile that I had gotten so used to when we were together.

"You?" I said.

"Not recently."

I wondered where this was going.

"I was thinking that maybe neither of us was seriously looking for Maxie. Maybe we didn't really want to face up to what might be the reality."

"Being?" I said, irritation riding on that word.

"You know, Coop. It's been eight years. What are the chances?"

"Of what?" I said, pressing her on that point, knowing full well what she was going to say and not wanting her to say it.

"You know what I mean. What are the chances that Maxie is…?"

"Don't even say it, Jillie," I said. "I don't want to hear that word."

"Alive? Is that the word you don't want to hear? You know he's probably not."

"I don't know anything of the kind," I said.

"Then why aren't you looking for him? Or are you and you just haven't told me?" There was that old blame again.

"Every day of my life is spent thinking of him, wracking my brain for clues. Anything! Why do you think I'm doing what I'm doing? Looking for missing people. I quit two jobs to spend more time on Maxie." This is why we got divorced in the first place. The old anger rising again. Damn. I couldn't sleep because of it.

"But you're not really, Coop" she said, looking accusingly across the table.

"You said…"

"I know, I said no more blaming. Sorry. It's so hard," she said, looking down at the table as though something was there, then reaching across for my hands. She hesitated, then, "I still love you, Coop." A confession.

I wanted to say I still love you too. But I didn't say it. I just stared at her. After an uncomfortable silence she struggled for something to say and then, "Oh forget what I said." She was angry. Then, "What I really need is help to get through all this." She pulled back, seemed to study me for a moment, and added more softly, "Coop, if only to find out that he's really..."

"Don't say it," I said gently and squeezed her hands. "Don't say it. The thought of Maxie being anything but..." and I couldn't continue. We sat for what seemed hours. It was probably a minute—maybe even seconds.

People near us got up to leave. They turned away quickly when I looked up. I wondered if the whole place was watching. But they weren't. Life goes on.

"Then do something about it," she said softly, encouraging, her hands gently shaking mine. "Do something about it!"

Dinner came. I had a BLT Panini, with an apple instead of chips. I was watching my weight. Jillie, a Mediterranean salad. It was just small talk after that. We avoided talking about Maxie. But she would look up from her plate now and then, study me quietly and then continue to pick at her salad.

"Anthony Coppoletta says hello," she said without looking up. Anthony owns an antique store in Cambridge. We used to visit his shop on Saturday evenings and drink wine with him and his collector friends while he shared stories about his latest acquisition and the history behind the piece. I have an original 'Anthony' in my living room that I bought on one of those evenings. A black and white ink of a peasant woman on the seashore with her children, the mother holding her heavy skirts away from the waves, the oldest girl doing the same.

"Tell him I said, 'hi,' when you see him again," I said, missing those days.

I held Jillie tightly after we left the café, her head deep in my shoulder. She asked me to call her. I said I would.

169

"Thanks for tonight," she said.

"Thanks for kicking me in the butt about Maxie," I said. "I needed that." She smiled, nodded, and looked very tired. She walked down State Street toward a hill that banked toward several red brick dormitories. She turned once and waved. I wanted to tell her that I needed her—almost said *I love you too*. But I just waved back. Maybe she could read my thoughts.

39

THE SEARCH BEGINS

I had mixed feelings of anger and sorrow when Jillie left. I was angry at the kidnappers, angry at myself, angry at the slow progress of my current cases. I should have walked her to her car, talked with her about plans for finding our son. I was sorry that I hadn't told her how I still felt about her. Maybe when I find our son…

I pulled into the hotel at 10:35 p.m. I parked and headed for my room, listening to my phone messages. I had a few.

"Good evenings, Detective Cooper." Leo's voice. He was anxious to get started.

"Hey Coop, what's up? Leo's goin' nuts. Call me." That was Richie.

"Coop, I'm at the hotel. Where are you?" Louise. Oops.

"You out huntin' gators, Coop? Where in God's name are you?" Huxter. "Jackson's wonderin' why you didn't call him."

When I opened the door, Louise was resting on the bed. I had asked for a king-sized. Good planning. She was reading. In a sheer camisole. Looking at me innocently.

"Surprise!" she said and put the book aside. She studied me. "You look guilty."

I must have been thinking up excuses.

"Where have you been? No welcoming committee?" she said, looking hurt.

I hesitated. "Just some personal business to take care of."

"How was your dinner with Jillie?"

"How did you know?"

"I'm a detective, remember." That smile that was not really a smile.

I thought about lying. But didn't. It's a funny thing about lying. Sometimes it makes sense and is a good thing—for instance, when it's no one's business or you're saving someone's feelings. So, answering a direct question isn't always a good thing. But then if you do lie, will that person ever trust you again? So I didn't want to do that to Louise.

There was still a little bourbon left. Jackson and I hadn't finished it. I poured us each a drink. Neat.

"Trying to get me drunk?" she said. Still hurt.

"Just trying to say, I'm sorry." I touched her arm. She was still.

"I guess you've got a few things to work out with her," she said.

"I guess," I said.

She nodded, got up, and put on a terrycloth robe. I gave her a quick kiss—testing the waters.

"Let's see what we can do with those names you've got," she said.

I had jotted the three names on a tablet next to my computer. I used Firefox this time instead of Safari.

"I've already tried the national sex offender website. Nothing. I also searched my old standby for missing persons, *melissadata.com*. Nothing there either." Louise was bending over me. Her hair loose and falling on my neck. Jasmine, I guessed. The smell, that is.

"Let me see what I can do," she said and traded places with me at the computer.

She used Google first, typing in Remizov's name. Why not? Everything's on the net. A few Remizovs came up. None with the first name, Maks.

Using a few meta-search engines, she found a few Remizovs of various ages, one Marko but no Maks. There were a number of Marcs. Obviously, we would need a more sophisticated search engine, namely, Interpol. Most of the work of a private detective is searching for missing persons or things. That's been the focus of my work. It's crazy boring, done mostly on the computer. It's not the Hollywood PI kind of work. But this is reality. The fun stuff does happen once in a while—the confrontations when the person you're tracking doesn't like being tracked. And yes, sometimes you get shot at. It's happened to me—twice so far. But the fact is, it all starts on the computer. Most times it ends there.

She entered Maryana Zorin's name using *vivisimo. com*. There were a few matches for Zorin, but no Maryana. There was a Mariana Zorin from Romania. So we tried *altavista.com*. and found a few Zorins of varying ages. Again, no Maryana.

"Let me try Shibalov," I said and switched places. I Googled his name. A few Shibalovs came up. But only one with the first name, Kolya: Cleveland, Ohio.

"He might be our guy," I said.

"So, that's what we've got so far," I said, leaning back. "I'll call the license bureau tomorrow, see if I can shake anything loose there." I turned around—her face was

173

inches from mine. "You still have your Interpol connection, right? Maybe…"

"I'll call him, see what he has," she said. A little softness there. Finally.

I stood up and unwrapped her robe. She did not object.

Suddenly I felt Louise's hands turning me, pulling my face to her mouth. We kissed like we had dreamed of this moment forever, the room moving like an amusement park ride where the floor falls out and you hang suspended on the walls. We fell on the bed and rolled on each other like hungry lovers, Louise pulling my jacket off as we struggled with clothes.

I wasn't sure how long we lay there. Several hours I think. We had fallen asleep. When I woke, it was 1:30 a.m. Louise had her arm around my chest, her head resting on my neck. She woke when I tried to remove my arm.

"Did you have fun, detective boy?" she said, smiling through half open eyes.

"I did, officer," I said, and kissed her brow. "You might as well stay where you are, it's too far to drive home tonight," I said.

"Funny," she said, scooting out of bed and trying to look modest as she headed for the bathroom. She looked good without her robe on.

40

THE CHASE

I t was like rounding up a posse in the morning. I called everybody together: Leo, Richie, Huxter—I didn't have to call Louise. Just waken her. She had rolled over and fallen asleep again. As for Huck, he had been staying at the hotel while watching Jackson.

"The professor's fine on his own. He sure don't need me no more. Besides my rifle is gettin' itchy for some work, boss man." So, I invited him as well.

We met in the Captain's Table at 9:00 a.m. They were quiet as they drank coffee and waited for me to say something.

I filled them in on the events of the past two weeks, reminding everyone that Taisia's disappearance was rapidly approaching the point of a case gone cold. Told them about the trip into the National Forest and Jason's shooting; about the meeting with Carmen Santangelo; about the Russians: Shibalov, Remizov, and Zorin.

"Today we're going hunting," I said. "And we need to move quickly," watching Leo as I said it. He didn't react. "I would like to leave in about an hour," I continued, looking at each one of them. They all nodded. No talk. All serious. Like before a battle. It was so quiet I could hear my stomach talk.

"So where are we going, Coop?" said Huxter.

"Cleveland," I said.

"Got an address?" said Richie.

I looked over at Louise.

"The latest is, the guys we're looking for, Koyla, Remi, and Maryana are all in this country," she said, pausing for effect. "My friend checked credit cards and visas. Kolya *is* in Cleveland. That was his point of entry. Maryana and Remi entered through Miami. Interpol doesn't know where those two are now. But my contact said he would get back to me in a day or so. He did give me the most current address he had on Kolya."

"Yeah. Where's that" said Richie, his leg moving like it had a life of its own.

"South side. The Tremont area," I said. Louse nodded.

"Anything else?" said Richie, his leg now bouncing against the table leg.

"Koyla's nickname's the Butcher. He likes to cut people up," Louise said. "For body parts."

41

THE DEER HUNTER

It's about a five-hour drive from Riverdale to Cleveland. Huck and Louise rode in the back of Richie's Land Cruiser. Leo was spread out in the third row of seats. That worked well for him. Richie drove. "Nobody drives my baby but me," he said, "except you, Cooper." He loved his Toyota toy. I rode shotgun—literally—his 20-gauge Mossberg sitting between my legs. No one talked. We stopped for coffee in the Columbus suburbs at a Dunkin' Donuts. Richie had three.

"You going to call him?" said Richie, peering over his glazed filled donut.

"No," I said. "I want to surprise him. People love to be surprised."

Leo chuckled and nudged Huck. Huck stared at him like *What the hell is that about?* Leo nudged him again and laughed. They were becoming friends.

"Loosen up, Mr. Huck. Today we have some fun with this bad guy. Maybe I will kill him."

I drove from Dunkin' Donuts so Richie could catch some sleep. We hit the southern suburbs of Cleveland around 3:00 p.m. Interstate 71 that runs from Cincinnati through Columbus carried us all the way to downtown Cleveland. In order to get to Tremont, we had to jump off I-71 and take I-271, one of the outer belts of Cleveland that runs through northern Ohio's most lush countryside, by green hills and over a high-level bridge that spans a valley—a stream running through it hundreds of feet below—and by Hinkley Lake, one of a series of lakes and streams and parks and forests that comprise Cleveland's famous Emerald Necklace. A piece of nature's jewelry that hangs around the city's neck like a string of green pearls, hiding the crime and deterioration of the inner city. Just before entering Cuyahoga National Forest, I headed north on I-77, a north-south highway that runs from Cleveland to Columbia, South Carolina.

Interstate 77 skirts the inside edge of the Emerald Necklace and enters Cleveland through the southern suburbs: Parma, Brooklyn Heights, and Cuyahoga Heights, all ethnic neighborhoods that make Cleveland famous for its diversity. I jumped off the 77 at I-490, a smaller belt that took us into Tremont. The exit I was looking for was the W 17th Street exit. When we finally hit that exit, I was surprised to see a renovated Tremont area. Red brick buildings with white trim. Well maintained. Richie was rubbing his eyes. He had slept most of the way from the coffee stop.

"Nice," he said, looking around.

"So, this is Cleveland?" said Leo. "I am liking it."

I turned left at Starkweather. The street was white sidewalks, red brick walkways, and well-maintained commercial shops and apartment buildings, mostly redbricked and trimmed in white. Maintain the décor.

"I am in Saint Petersburg once again!" said Leo, pointing to the massive church ahead on the left. A light brownstone church, with dark brown trim and topped with the familiar domes of Orthodox churches. They were rounded like turbans with metal crosses rising from their peaks. There must have been a dozen domes shaping the skyline of the neighborhood. Several were green. Not a natural shade—the metal had changed color with the weather.

We came to a large church with a sign in front that read, Saint Theodosius Russian Orthodox Church.

"A famous church," I said, pulling the car to the curb on the other side of the street.

It was an old building, its stones holding the evidence of the pollution that poured out daily from the mills in Cleveland's Flats.

"What are we doin' here, Cooper?" said Richie.

"Yeah," said Huck from the rear.

"This is a great church, my friend," said Leo, pointing to the domes and the crosses rising from them. "This is cathedral. The Patriarch will be here."

"This is also where *The Deer Hunter* was shot," I said.

Silence.

"What the fuck is that?" said Richie.

"One of the great movies of our time," I said.

"Ah. The Russians and Americans in the war together and now here, in this place!" exclaimed Leo, his arms extended as if embracing the whole area: the golden-domed church, the cross sitting on top of it like a flag of Orthodoxy; and the whole neighborhood, now not only Russian, but populated by immigrants from Eastern Europe, toughened by decades of war and hard living.

He turned to Richie. "How could you not know this movie? Mr. Dinero. Mr. Walken. They went to mass in this church. This is their neighborhood."

Richie shrugged.

"There are many Russians here in Cleveland. Some of them are my friends. They get jobs in our steel mills. And some of them…,"pausing and shrugging, "they are like Koyla."

"Where are they now?" I said.

"I have lost track of them. The mills have gone. So are they I think." And he stopped for a moment. "Here we will find Kolya," and he looked down the street at the old houses that lined it, homes for the steelworkers at one time, now old houses leaning on each other for support.

I pulled away and headed down Starkweather. We were close now. Most of the houses and buildings that we passed were one and two-story, shingled, built in the 40s and 50s. Asphalt roofs, patched. Starkweather was narrow, its sidewalks cracked and lined with old wooden telephone poles. No urban renewal here.

We passed Lucky's Café on the left, a one-story red brick building with a large bay window, a red and white neon sign, blinking OPEN, hanging over it. The address we were looking for was about five blocks further down the street. I pulled up to a two-story, faded green house with two spindle-railed porches, one on top of the other, both stretching across the entire front. A good place to sit and watch a parade—or your neighbors as they strolled in the evening. Windows in the gables over the upper porch indicated an attic. Shingles were missing from the front and side, but the house sat there unembarrassed, like a man with missing teeth, smiling like he could care less about the gaps in his mouth. I sat behind a car that was parked in front.

A chain link fence guarded the house on its front and sides. There was an opening for a brown grass and dirt driveway. The same kind of fence guarded both sides of the street. There were large gaping spaces where a fence used to be and other places where it had been trampled or cut.

I pulled away from the curb, continued down the street, did a U-turn and parked under trees, with leaves turning burnt orange from the onset of fall, about a hundred feet from the two-story and behind a beat-up Chevrolet. We all stared at the house for a few minutes.

"So, what now?" said Louise.

"Go knock on the door," I said, and got out of the car, feeling under my leather jacket for the Glock. I turned my back to the house, checked the chamber and slammed it back in place. Richie slipped his shotgun under his coat. Huxter was carrying a hunting knife in his boot and a .45 in a holster strapped to his waist. Louise had a Glock that she carried off-duty. She was holding it with both hands at her side and following me up the front steps. I had told Leo to stay in the car. He refused and was right behind us. We must have looked like a SWAT team moving in. I hoped no one was looking.

I signaled Huck and Richie to go around to the back of the house. Huck put his hand on the chain link fence and leaped over it. Richie held his gun for him, looked at me and shook his head like *Is this guy crazy?* Richie slid through a hole in the fence further down the street, pulling his shotgun behind him.

I checked my phone. It was 6:59 p.m. now and streetlights were beginning to emerge. The moon was low in the sky. A waxing Crescent Moon. It was moving slowly to October's Full Moon, the Hunter's Moon. It wouldn't be long now. Blood on the fields. Blood in the streets. The cycles of nature have a way of repeating themselves.

42

THE HOUSE ON STARKWEATHER AVENUE

I never like to enter an empty house without knowing what's inside. To do so is to risk getting shot. I thought back on my experiences in the Hole, a gangland cesspool in lower Miami. Louise and I were ambushed by gangbangers there. I was a week in the hospital. Louise longer. That was the second time I had been shot. I wasn't looking for another.

Louise leaned her shoulder against the doorjamb—away from the door. She was about to knock when I whispered,

"On second thought, let's not knock." I pulled my cell and called Huck and Richie.

"Yo, Coop," said Richie. "We're ready when you are."

"See if you can find a way into the house from the back. We'll wait on the porch for you to enter. Once you're inside, yell and we'll come through the front door. We'll look for anyone you chase our way."

"You come on in if you hear gunfire, capisce?" said Richie.

Richie likes to wade into a fight head on. No hesitations. No questions. I trusted his instincts. I stepped to the other side of the door, opposite Louise. I motioned for Leo to get off the porch. He didn't.

My cell buzzed.

"Nothing so far. We're in the kitchen. Huck's going into the living room. I'm heading up stairs. He's gonna open the door for you."

The door opened and Huck waved us in, pointing to the stairs directly ahead. I could hear them creak as Richie made his way up. The sound of a shotgun shook the house and part of the wall lining the staircase above Richie disappeared. I ducked—instinctively—and moved to the railing side of the stairway. The second-floor hallway was open, a railing running along the open side overlooking the entryway. I could see Richie crouching just below the top of the stairs, his Mossberg pointed into the hall. Another blast tore into more of the wall over Richie's head, creating a dust storm of white plaster and dried paint. He slid back down the stairs, keeping his Mossberg trained on the stairs above him. Huck and Leo had moved into the living room and were peering up at the hallway trying to figure out where the shots were coming from.

Huck fired shots into the ceiling below the room at the end of the hall, spacing them so they had a better chance of hitting something. I heard movement overhead and then Richie made his move, rushing the stairs and unloading his shotgun into the hallway as he neared the top. Huck fired two more rounds into the ceiling. My ear-drums were numb from the blasts. Louise and I followed Richie, our guns leading the way. Then I heard someone running.

Huck took off for the front door, Leo with him. Richie, Louise, and I followed the noise. Then there was a crash, like an entire shelf full of plates breaking away from the wall and hitting the floor. It. came from the room at the end of the hall. I was the first to see a shattered window overlooking the side of the house away from the street. No porch overhang there to break a fall. Huck and Leo were standing over a man writhing on the ground on his right side and feeling for his back. He was yelling at Leo in Russian. Huck pushed hard against the man's chest so that he was now flat against the ground, and then buried the alligator gun into the Russian's neck. He quit moving. His back problem seemed to go away.

The three of us headed for the stairs to get outside and away before we caught the attention of the entire Cleveland police force.

"Shit, Cooper. All I need is to get tagged for acting without proper authority in another state," Louise said, breathing hard as she hurried down the stairs behind me.

No sirens, yet. Lights had come on in a few houses down the street.

"Let's get him the hell out of here," I told Huck. So we picked the man up by his shoulders and feet and carried him to the cargo space of the Land Cruiser where we dumped him. He screamed in Russian. I didn't need a translator.

"He says you are all mother fucking assholes," said Leo, smiling as he patted the Russian on the head, then smacked him in the face like he might do to someone he's going to punish. He leaned over and whispered in the man's ear. The man nodded quickly. Then Leo slammed the back gate shut, slapped the top of the Cruiser, and climbed into the back seat near the Russian.

Richie raced for the freeway. He sped through red lights, took corners too fast then accelerated like a driver pulling out of a turn at the Indianapolis 500.

I told him to slow down. We didn't need to spend the night in a Cleveland jail—especially with the Russian. Richie grunted and slowed. But he was pissed. I didn't care.

The moon was now high in the sky. There was no blood on its face, no blood on the streets.

43

FRIDAY EVENING, OCTOBER 15

Richie was back on the I-490 ramp quickly. No red lights flashing behind us. Once we hit the freeway, Richie floored the Cruiser and headed in whatever way the road led us. That happened to be east toward I-77 and downtown Cleveland. It used to be when you hit the city limits you could smell the smoke and ash from the steel mills and auto plants. Not anymore. The plants are gone—most of them—and the jobs and people with them. But Cleveland's downtown has been polished and it shines with its new sports stadiums: FirstEnergy Stadium for the Browns, Progressive Field for the Indians, and Quicken Loans Arena for the Cavaliers. And then there's the Tower City Center, a large complex of office buildings, a shopping mall and the Terminal Tower, once the tallest building in North America outside New York City. It rises in the center of Tower City like an aged but graceful structure from another century. The Tower is a classic piece of Renaissance architecture with Doric columns, much like those of the Roman Parthenon and topped by a dome and that by a spire that pierces Cleveland's sometimes sunny but more often grey sky: a symbol of hope for a city whose river was at one time on fire.

Then we hit Lakeshore, the east-west highway that connects to I-90 east of Cleveland which, in turn, links the city to other major cities on the way to Boston. We sped along the lake through light traffic, heading for the eastern suburbs, past Burke Lakefront Airport, past the Muni power plant that fronts Lake Erie, past Collinwood, one of many ethnic neighborhoods that make up the city, and finally into Euclid. I reminded Richie of Euclid Beach, an old amusement park, now dead and gone for several decades.

I asked Richie if he had any idea where he was going.

"Let's go to my place," he said. Richie has an apartment in an Italian neighborhood, Little Italy. People just call it Murray Hill.

"Good idea," I said. "Better than a motel. How's our Russian friend doing?" I said.

"Either dead or asleep," said Huck. "That gringo ain't movin', pardner."

Leo grunted: I saw him leaning over the back seat and staring at the Russian. "*Podonok*," he said , "you will tell me what I need to know," working his hand in and out of a fist. I didn't have to ask what *podonok* meant. Leo's face told the story.

Murray Hill is built on—you guessed it—a hill. Some of my favorite restaurants are there. Some are gone: The Golden Bowl, The Italian Gardens. The pizza shops are authentic. Of course. We're talking about real pizza. Each year in mid-August, the Hill celebrates the Feast, short for the Feast of the Assumption. Even though it's impossible to prove that the Blessed Virgin Mary was assumed into heaven—how would you do that?—the Italian community celebrates it with a colorful parade, gambling and auctions, carnival rides like the Ferris wheel and magic carpet, art displays and food booths with sausage and pepper sandwiches and Stromboli. It goes on for several days and ends with a procession where a life-size statue of the Blessed Virgin, wearing white and sky-blue robes, is carried through Murray Hill from Holy Rosary Church down Mayfield Road while a throng of worshippers hold up their rosaries and cheer as she passes.

If this were August, we would be following the procession down Murray Hill to the church. But this is October, and the only procession was into the various eateries that lined the streets. It was late. About 11:00 p.m. Lots of traffic and no parking places.

Richie lives in an apartment above one of the pizza places with an outside entrance to his room from a side alley. It was a metal stairway that looked more like a fire escape than a stairway. But it was wide and easy to climb. I backed up to the base of the stairs so Huck and Leo could drag the Russian out of the Cruiser while Richie hurried to unlock his door. Watching Richie run upstairs is like watching a truck trying to dance.

Believe me, getting a struggling Russian up a flight of metal stairs late at night without attracting attention is almost impossible. But there was enough noise from the streets that the racket we made fit right in. Besides Louise had bound his hands and tied a bandana across his mouth to shut him up. He still struggled against the bindings and tried to scream. Leo banged the Russian's head against the door as we entered the kitchen to quiet him down. I could smell the garlic and the odor of marinara sauce rising from the pizza shop below. My plan: get some food when we were done.

"Throw the bastard on the floor in the living room," Richie said, as Leo and I dragged him into the apartment. "And don't mess it up! I just cleaned it!"

And so there we were, in Richie's 'neat as a pin' living room, his couches covered in clear plastic, the carpet either new or just cleaned by Stanley Steemer, and the Russian, lying there, looking up at us, his eyes blood red. Angry or just from crying, I couldn't tell. I took off the gag and released his bindings. He massaged his wrists, then looked up and spat out something I figured was a curse. Ungrateful guest. I looked over at Leo.

"I think he said you are a capitalist ass," Leo said, nodding his head and smiling at me.

"As are you, Leo," I said, reminding him of the new Russia. "Ask him where Kolya is."

Leo asked him. The Russian spat at him. Leo smacked him across the face, bouncing his head against the carpet. The Russian tried to raise himself but fell back to the floor.

"Geez, my carpet!" yelled Richie, looking anxiously as blood dripped from the Russian's nose into the beige, thick carpet, turning the rug crimson under his head.

Leo bent down, grasped the Russian's throat in one hard and put his mouth to his ear. Fear can be deciphered in many ways. Through the stench that rises when the adrenalin glands let loose. Through the body as it tenses itself for danger. Through the eyes. The eyes can't lie. And they were all there in the Russian: the foul odor of fear, the tightening of the muscles, the deep blackness of the eyes that revealed terror in his very guts.

I started to say something to Leo, when I heard the Russian say,

"Kolya."

I knelt next to him. "What about Kolya?"

He spoke in broken English. "Kolya took money," he said. "All of it," and spit out blood onto the carpet. A tooth came with it.

"Geez! Gonna have to get a new carpet, asshole," Richie said to the Russian.

"What money?" I said.

"Money from sale. Kolya took it. I have nothing."

"Sale of what?" I said.

He shrugged. "You know," he said, holding up his hands as if embarrassed to say. I did know. Body parts.

"Who is the buyer?" I said.

"I don't know," he said, wiping his nose with his hand and staring at the blood he found there.

I showed him the picture of Taisia that Leo had brought with him. "Have you seen her?"

The Russian shook his head.

I showed him a picture of April. Same thing.

"You've never seen either one before?" I said.

"Nyet," he said, and he fell back into Russian. I looked over at Leo.

"He says he thinks his back is broke," he said.

"I'll break your back, you moron, if you don't talk to us!" yelled Richie. "Look at those pictures again," grabbing them from me and holding them up to the Russian's face.

The Russian jerked back as if he were getting ready to get hit. It didn't do him any good. Richie hit him across the face. Blood shot out of his nose again. Richie shrugged.

"Fuck him. Gotta replace the carpet anyway. His back's not broken. You want me to kill him?" Richie said pulling his gun and holding it to the Russian's head.

The fear I saw in his eyes said he believed Richie would kill him.

I waited for a moment as Richie pressed the gun against the man's cheek, his finger hard on the trigger, his shirt wet against his stomach.

The Russian was watching me as though I were the executioner. Richie and I looked at each other. I paused a little longer.

Then, "He deserves to die," I said. "But not yet. Gag the son of a bitch." I didn't want listen to any more of his crap. I walked away.

44

BLOOD ON THE FIELDS

It was late when we finished grilling the Russian. So we
decided to spend the night at Richie's apartment, tossing the Russian into a small pantry off the kitchen and
locking him in. Louise talked me into cleaning him up first,
the blood mostly from superficial wounds.

I asked Louise if she had called Interpol yet. She said
she had and was waiting for a call back. Richie gave Louise
and me his bedroom. "For the lovebirds," he said. He motioned Leo and Huck to the guest bedroom and said he'd
take the couch.

"I'll take the couch," said Huck. "I'm smaller'n you two
boys." Richie started to shake his head.

"Matters settled gents. Just gimme a blanket and a pil-
low and I'm good to go." Huck's a lot like Richie. When
he determines something, he locks onto it like an alligator
on a prey.

Suddenly the door banged open. "What the f... yous
guys doin', Richie?" A stocky man showing about fifty
years or so of age, carrying a small white dog with black
eyes stood in the open space, looking like he's pissed off.

"What? You kill somebody?" he berated us, "draggin' a body up the fire escape, making noise like to wake everybody up?" He was petting the dog all the while he was talking.

"Sully!" yelled Richie, forgetting the blood on the carpet, hiking up his pants, and walking toward the man with the dog like the guy was his brother. Big guys, Richie taller than Sully, bigger around the shoulders, but Sully with an arm long enough that he kept the nervous dog away from Richie's bear hug.

"You don't tell me yous was here? What? We don't know each other no more?"

"Last minute t'ing. What the hell is this?" said Richie, pulling away and looking at the dog who was staring back at him like he was a criminal, which he was.

"My new thing. Watching dogs. Whaddya think?" he demanded, looking around at us—like we were his crowd. "It's my retirement!"

Richie had talked about Sully Rossi known by the made guys as Sal "The Toe" Rossi. Not what I had pictured. An errand boy for the Cleveland crime boss, standing here with a Maltese in his left arm, stroking it like it was his baby.

"You must be Cooper," Sully said, nodding and still petting the dog who so far didn't have a name.

I nodded.

"So who are the rest of dese guys?" looking mostly at Leo who stared back with that frozen eye look I've seen from Russian gangsters in the movies. Like Viggo Mortensen, who isn't actually Russian but plays a good role.

"Leo Federovich," he said finally. "And who are you?" Leo demanded, like KGB.

Sully blinked and a twitch caught his left eye. Then, "Who's the dead guy yous was draggin' up the stairs"

I filled him in, the dog leaning in to hear.

"What's his name?" I said, reaching over to pet the nameless dog.

"Don't insult her. Her name is Fiffi," and he stroked her neck to ease the pain my question caused her.

I nodded. "Okay, then…" I began, trying to figure where we we're all going to stay.

Sully noticed. "Hey, yous guys are welcome to stay at my place. It's across the alley," he offered, pointing, like it's just outside the window, climb out and you're there. He paused, "but you keep the dead guy." Then he turned and yelled into the alley, through the closed window, into the night so that everyone in Murray Hill, awake or asleep, could hear him, "Nina, make up a coupla beds. We got company,"

"Okay, Sully!" a voice yelled back. I couldn't tell if she was happy or not.

"How's ma?" broke in Richie.

"She's good. Don't you never check on her? Whatsa matter wit' you, Richie? You gotta call your ma now and then!"

Richie shook his head. "Hey, I call her twice, three times a week. Sometimes every day. I asked you to look in on her. You doin' that?"

"Come on! You know I do. She's fine. Has trouble with the stairs. But she's good. She'll be upset you don't stop in."

"I'll see her tomorrow. Meantime, we're good here with the beds. Thanks for the offer. I'll check with you before we go. Okay?"

And Sully left with Fiffi and told me we were always welcome. "Got room when I'm not watchin' a bunch of dogs—my business you unnerstand. Just let me know. Nina can always make up a coupla beds."

Richie stared after him as Sully and Fiffi made their exit to the stairway that looked more like a fire escape. But who cares? That's what makes Murray Hill what it is. "You gotta love him," Richie said as the door closed behind the former hit man with the Maltese. "Him and Nina is good people."

After Sully left, Louise went into the kitchen to make coffee. I thought I would give my eyes a break, so I headed for the bedroom. The next think I knew it was 3:00 a.m. and Louise was sleeping next to me.

I got up to check on the Russian. I pushed open the door against what I figured was his body. He grunted as I shoved hard and pushed him away. Then, I shut the door and locked it, went to the fridge, and poured a glass of wine.

The door to Richie's room opened. There he was, in pajamas, his hair going east, west, north, and south.

"Whaddya doin'?" he said, rubbing his eyes and heading for the kitchen table.

"Can't sleep," I said.

This is the time when an investigation gets frustrating. You have a few clues, but no clear direction. I go to bed at night hoping my mind will assemble them into a meaningful whole. Morning comes, and no dice. Time was running out for Taisia. It might have run out a long time ago.

"You want I should talk to him?" said Richie. I knew what he meant.

"No," I said. "Let's see what Louise gets from Interpol. I poured a glass of red for Richie. We talked into the morning and watched the sun rise over Murray Hill. The Russian stirred in the pantry. *Don't tempt me*, I thought.

"The body parts business is pretty lucrative," I said, looking into my wine.

195

"Yeah?" said Richie.

"Yeah. A kidney is about a hundred grand, a heart a little less." I drained the glass and kept going. "Take a fertile woman. Each egg is worth about seven thousand." I let that drift for a moment, Richie nodding like he wanted me to go on. "So let's say she sells three dozen over a ten year period..."

"Yeah, yeah," he said. Interested. Maybe making a business plan.

"She could earn upwards of two hundred and fifty grand."

"Shit, Coop. We're in the wrong business!"

I smiled and told him he could do the same by selling his sperm, but it would take about three times as long and a lot more sperm donations than three dozen.

"No way," he said as he emptied his glass and poured another.

"Bone marrow could go for twenty-three million," I said.

"Jeez, that's enough!" He studied his wine, swilling it like a wine connoisseur. "So, what's my whole body worth?" looking up at me sidewise.

"The sum of its parts," I said. "People kidnap a kid and sell his parts just like they would if they were stealing a car and stripping it. The parts are worth a lot more than the car," my stomach pushing acid into my throat as I said it, images of Taisia and Maxie taking over my mind. Richie noticed.

"Forget it, Coop. Not the same thing. We'll get your kid," he said. He meant it and I loved him for it.

Light was beginning to creep through the living room window. I felt tired as I watched it slide across the floor. The morning had come and I had nothing but the Russian. We needed to get into his brain. Only one way I thought.

45

AND THEN THE SUN CAME UP

SATURDAY MORNING, OCTOBER 16

What I don't like about sunrises is they take away the mystery of the night. I think better in the night, find solutions to problems in the night. I love the shadows. More than that I love the moon. It's my guide, my muse. I miss it when the sun chases it out of the sky.

My cell almost knocked me out of my chair. I must have fallen asleep watching the sun come up.

"Coop?"

Louise was standing in the bedroom doorway in jeans and a white cotton tee holding her cell.

I looked at my cell. "You called me?"

She smiled. "I've got some info for you on Maryana and Remi."

"Great! That's fast. Your contact got back to you already?"

"Not Interpol. This came from DeFelice. I haven't heard from Interpol yet," she said. "He did a trace on Zorin, found a credit card in her name and is tracking it now. He thinks she's in Miami. He said he didn't know if it was your lady, but he'll get back later today."

"How about Interpol?"

"By the end of the day. Fingers crossed."

"What's up?" said Richie, pulling his head off the kitchen table and rubbing his eyes as he noticed Louise watching him, smiling.

"What?" he said.

"You guys sleep at all last night?" said Louise.

"Couple hours. I'm gonna talk to that bastard Russian soon as I get some coffee," he said, standing up and rummaging through the freezer. He pulled out a bag of coffee beans, ground them, the smell filling the kitchen, and started the pot perking.

It's a great aroma early in the morning, before life outside stirs, before the sun is on the horizon, before any food hits your stomach. The Russian must have liked it too because I heard him stir in the closet.

Then Richie searched in a bottom cupboard, pulled out a blackened, cast-iron pan, grabbed some eggs from the fridge, a package of bacon, and placed them carefully on the counter. Richie is a great cook. And he likes to cook. If you would visit Richie on the weekends, you would find him up early, 3:00 a.m., cooking sauce, and sautéing garlic until the odors penetrated every inch of the house.

But this was not the weekend. So, it was bacon, eggs and potatoes, Richie frying the bacon until it was crisp, laying each strip carefully on a paper towel, then cracking the eggs so the yokes didn't break. While they were cooking, he brushed the grease from the bacon over the eggs, salted them lightly until the yoke was covered with a white film, and finally, for the *piece de resistance*, used a spatula to transfer the treasure to individual plates. Through it all, Italian bread was baking in the oven and sliced potatoes and onions were sizzling in a separate fry pan. The smell was so intense that Leo and Huck seemed to rise simultaneously and appear in the kitchen, sniffing around like dogs for a bone or, better yet, like a cat chasing down the odor of salmon.

"A man's breakfast!" Leo exclaimed as Richie motioned him to the dining room table, set with orange juice, plates and utensils. In reality, we were camping, getting ready for the hunt. We ate like it was the last meal any of us was going to have for a long time, Leo telling Richie what a great chef he was, Huck nodding in agreement, but not lifting his head up from the plate.

"I could marry you, Richie," said Louise, "if you promised to cook like this every day."

"Promises, promises," said Richie, "I wish. No offense, Coop," he added quickly.

The Russian was pounding on the pantry door and yelling. I asked Leo what he was saying.

"He wants out and he wants food," said Leo, not interrupting his eating.

"He can get out and he can have food if he talks," I said. "Tell him that."

"Of course," said Leo. "But first…" He was admiring a piece of bacon. "Posmotri ne eto! (Look at this)" he said, mixing it with his eggs and eating quickly as though someone might try to take his treasure away. "I must take Richie back to Russia," he added, shaking his head in amazement.

It was still early when we finished eating.

"I think it's time," I said to Richie who took his plate to the sink, washed his hands, and headed for the pantry.

Richie dragged the Russian into the living room like a rag doll.

"Tell him what Cooper told you to tell him," said Richie, looking at Leo.

Leo leaned into the man's face and whispered in his ear. And all the while the Russian's eyes were locked onto something out there, like the monster in the closet that all kids worry about when mom kills the lights and shuts the door.

"What did you tell him?" I said.

"I said you would kill him if he didn't talk," said Leo, the Russian now watching me. Tense.

"Good," I said, nodding at the Russian. His eyes were empty, but his chin shook.

I went to pick up my jacket. My Glock was in a holster next to it. I pulled it out, walked over to him, and laid the barrel against his forehead. He screamed in Russian.

"What did he say?" I said to Leo, grabbing the back of the Russian's head and pressing the gun hard against his cheek, his mouth and eyes as wide as the Grand Canyon. He swallowed his breath.

"Kolya has taken Taisia to Miami," Leo said.

I pulled the gun from his head and pushed him hard to the floor.

46

BOYD

It was 11:30 when we got ready to head back to the Valley. Richie and Huck piled the Russian back into Land Cruiser after he ate and had a bathroom run, thanks to Louise who had been bugging me to allow it. It was a cool day, the weatherman predicting a high of sixty-five for Cleveland. Warmer in the Valley.

I gave Jackson a call.

"How're you doing?" I said.

"Where the hell've you been? I think the police might be close to arresting me, man. Have you got anything?" out of breath, like he had just run the Boston Marathon.

"Maybe," I said, trying to calm him down. "You and Sonya have room in your house for a few people?"

Silence. Then, "Probably. How many people we talking about? And what's going on?" he added quickly. Worried, confused, anxious, all at the same time.

"Six," I said. "I'll tell you all about it when I get there. Figure late afternoon. Call me if it's a problem for Sonya. Tell her we'll just be there overnight."

"Okay," he said. "But…"

"I'll talk about it when I get there," I said, and ended the call. His wife would be climbing a wall wondering what the hell was going on. I wasn't looking forward to facing her.

Any word from Interpol?" I asked Louise. She had just finished cleaning her gun in the living room. Richie had made sure she used plenty of paper to avoid getting cleaning oil on his carpet. *Worse than blood*, Richie had said.

"Nope, not yet. Probably tonight."

"Good. We're about ready to head out," I said.

My cell rang.

"Where are you guys?" said Jason.

"On the way back to the Valley. How are you doing?"

"Better. I'm out of here tomorrow."

"Good to hear. Glad you're healing."

"So, where were you?" he asked. Pissed.

"In Cleveland." Everybody wanted to know where we were.

"How did the meeting with Santangelo go?"

"Well…he gave us some names."

"He said he would do that. So what names did he give you?"

"Not yet, Jason. I'm still checking them out."

"Come on, Cooper. I'm the one got you the lead. I got a call from Boyd, by the way. Says not to print any stories about the Russians. Said it like he meant it. So I stopped the presses on that one. What else you got?"

"Off-the-record?"

"Of-the-record."

I didn't believe him for a minute. "We're heading to Miami."

"That's it? You're heading to Miami? Come on, why're you going to Miami?"

"Tell you later. Give me a call tomorrow. Maybe I'll know why." I was wondering why I even talked to this guy. A reporter. I should know better.

"I'm heading to Miami too, Cooper." Then, "I'll pick up a Merlot, and see you at your Everglades hide-a-way." He ended the call. I knew why I didn't like him. No manners.

We drove through the afternoon pretty much in silence. Richie, driving. Me, thinking about Taisia. Leo, quietly staring at the fields and telephone poles sliding by. Huck, humming. Louise, constantly checking back on the Russian.

Thoughts of missing kids worked their way into my mind. I tried to chase them away. Maxie was a future baseball player. He would toss a ball in the air and catch it for hours. Catch it. Throw it in the air again. Catch it. Until I would come out and we would throw it back and forth. He had a good arm for a seven-year-old. I wondered if that's what he was doing the day he went missing.

I still can't say kidnapped. That's too final for me. The ball was lying in the yard. No sign of Maxie—or of anyone else for that matter. Nobody found anything: the local cops, the sheriff, the FBI. The only lead was when DeFelice called about a child kidnapping ring in Miami. That was something—a stretch, but still… I went there anyway. That's how I wound up as a detective with Miami PD. And why not? That way I could investigate the gang DeFelice suspected. DeFelice and I busted a couple of bangers. Nothing. One of them laughed, like *Are you joking? We…? We stole some gringo kid from Ohio?* looking around at the others. Everybody laughed—until I shoved a gun up under his nose. He quit laughing.

I thought maybe I would look him up. For old times' sake. Stick a gun under his nose again. See if he still laughs.

It's funny how his face has stayed with me all these years. I've studied every aspect of it. Even the tatt on his neck. A crown. Blue with sharp points for a king's crown. A Latin King. Taunting me, even in my sleep. We'll have another talk. With Richie this time.

"We're here," said Richie. I must have fallen asleep because it was 6:05 p.m. when we pulled into Jackson's drive.

Richie was out first. Huck and Leo were right behind. I got the door for Louise who was checking the Russian's cuffs. She had used a tri-fold ASP disposable restraint made out of durable plastic. They're almost impossible to break and are easy to apply.

"Come on, buster," she said to the Russian, pulling him from the third seat. "Let's get you out of there."

Sonya was the first one out of the house when we pulled in. Jackson was right behind her.

"What the hell is this all about!" she said, waving at the gathering in her driveway. I looked at Jackson who was standing just behind her and shrugging at me.

Sonya looked anything but pleased as she watched Louise and me bring the Russian through the front door into the entryway.

"Who is this man?" she said, a look of disbelief on her face as she studied him from head to shoes. "What happened to his face?"

"This is one of the Russians we think was involved in the kidnapping of a young Russian girl—this man's granddaughter," I said, pointing to Leo. "He may also have been involved with the disappearance of April."

Without warning, Sonya slapped the Russian across the face, knocking him off balance. He tried to catch himself, Sonya screaming at him in Russian. He tried to say something but she hit him again. Richie grabbed Sonya and tried to pull her away.

"Jeez, what's wrong with this woman!" he yelled, Sonya still spitting out Russian at the man. The Russian looked lost, like a man searching for his car in a parking lot.

"What the hell did she say?" I asked Leo.

"She is very angry. She said he was coward—disgrace to country and accused him of murdering April."

Leo went to Sonya and talked with her calmly, leading her to an easy chair in the living room.

"You are Russian?" he said. Sonya nodded. "You are from Saint Petersburg?" he continued, smiling as he would at a child. "The Angleterre Hotel, what a beautiful hotels! The Place De Isaac. The Museum of Culture—oh, that is my treasure!" and he stroked her arm, trying to calm her.

We watched Leo, the enigmatic crime boss, bring Sonya back to sanity.

"Whew," said Richie. "Fuckin' crazy." We all nodded. *For sure*, I thought.

"Nice house," said Huck, filling the silence. "Wonder if they're any gators in that pond over there," pointing to the river and smiling to make sure we got his joke. In reality you can see the water from Jackson's backyard. His house rests on a hill that overlooks the Valley.

"Let's get this guy situated," I said, as Louise and I struggled to hold the Russian up. I turned to Jackson. He was staring at his wife like *Who the hell is this woman?*

Then he turned, shaking his head, "There's a bedroom in the basement we can lock." I had lived in Florida long enough to forget about basements. "He can't mess that up—and he can't get out of there," he added.

Louise and I walked the Russian down the steep stairway to the cellar. There was a meager bathroom there and a bed in the middle of a partly finished room, some cheap wall board covering cinder block, and the skeleton of floor-to-ceiling two-by-four frames that would eventually be covered with drywall to make a room. A stark prison.

"No word yet?" I said on our way out of the basement, referring to Interpol.

"Not yet," said Louise, shrugging. "I'll call that damn guy back again."

My cell rang on our way up the stairs.

"Yeah?"

"Cooper? Boyd here. How are you doing with the Russians?" I heard someone in the background talking to him. Palazzo.

"Why are you asking?"

"Mr. Santangelo wants to know."

I filled him in on our no-name hostage and on our plans. He said *good* and asked if we needed anything. I said *no*. Palazzo got on an extension and asked if I needed more money. I said I always needed more money, but right now I was good.

"Need a shooter, let me know," he said. I knew he meant it.

"How's that Jew-boy of yours doing?" said Boyd, back on the line. I could picture the grin on his face.

My eyes narrowed like an owl's who's ready to swoop down on a rabbit. "Someday, Boyd…" Then I let it slide, shaking my head—which he didn't see of course. *Hell with it*, I thought.

"Shut up, both a yous. Just find the sons of bitches killed that girl," said Palazzo, back on the line. Boyd was still there. I could hear him breathing. Then he hung up.

I didn't realize I had the phone on speaker. So, everyone was staring at me when I signed off.

"I hate that son of a bitch," said Richie.

The Russian was pounding on the floor in the cellar. *A full moon*, I thought.

47

THE BUTCHER

We went to bed early, Sonya assigning the sleeping arrangements. She and Louise stayed in her bedroom. Jackson was left to find a place to sleep. Sonya didn't help. Richie and I sacked out in one of the guest bedrooms. Leo and Huck in the other. I took one of the two twins, Richie the other. I fell asleep immediately and dreamed of roads that led nowhere—like my cases.

"Cooper!" I rolled over to see who was calling. Louise.

"I got the info on the Russians," she whispered, the beam from her flashlight in my face near blinding me.

"Damn, Louise! Turn that thing off, would you?" I complained, shielding my eyes with my hand.

"Sorry," she said, and stood there waiting for me to get up.

I struggled to get untangled from the blanket that had wrapped itself around my feet and sat up.

"What time is it?" I said, still not sure if I was awake. I looked to see if Richie was awake. He was stretched out like a log on the forest floor.

"Three o'clock," she said, smiling.

"My God," I said, remembering Jackson's call a week or so ago. This was getting ridiculous.

"My friend at Interpol, he's in Turkey now," she said, very excited—at three o'clock in the morning. "Kolya's got an apartment in paradise."

"Uh-huh. And where in sunny Florida would this be?" I said, rubbing my eyes but trying to be nice.

"Sunny Isles Beach, Florida."

"Really? That's a wealthy area." I was awake now.

"Yeah. Little Moscow. Perfect place for a Russian to hide. Eighteen percent Russian."

"You've been up all night getting those stats?" I said.

"Funny. Be grateful," she chided, screwing up her face at me.

"Absolutely," I said. "Anything else?" I whispered, finally getting used to the darkness.

She bent down, her hair falling into my face and kissed me. "Come on. Let's get a cup of coffee and I'll fill you in." And she guided me quietly to a bar that separates the kitchen from the living room. I could hear Huck snoring in the other bedroom.

There was still some coffee in the pot from earlier in the evening. It was strong.

"So, what else have you got, Lou?" First time I used that name. Tried it out.

"Lou?" she said.

"Is that a problem?"

"Maybe. Where did that come from?"

"Richie."

"No way. Only person calls me Lou is 'D'," She said.

"Oh, 'D'?" I said.

"Yeah, 'D'," she said. One of my best friends and I never heard this nickname. She continued: "Interpol has a history on Kolya. Nickname, Myasnik, you know, the Butcher."

I nodded.

"As you also know, he makes a living selling body parts."

"To whom?" I said.

"To who?" she said.

"Yeah, to whom?" I said.

She stared at me, the grammarian.

"Pharmaceutical companies and hospitals."

"I mean, how could that happen? Don't those places have a code of ethics?" I felt like a dummy asking the question. Where have I been living? I wondered.

"Hey, hospitals don't ask where the parts come from. They need them? They buy them. Pass on the costs to the patient and make some money as well. It's big business, and the need exceeds the supply, dude."

"So, he runs a parts business." I was thinking about April and her missing organs.

"Just like a body shop," said Louise. I remembered that analogy from an earlier conversation.

I didn't say anything for a while. I needed to find Taisia before the moon settled over her in a field somewhere. We weren't far from the fields of blood of the Indians. Our fields are more brutal than theirs. Our crimes more unforgivable. I thought about the kind of death such people deserved. I thought of Richie's kind of justice and that was not enough; I thought of hell, and that was not enough. Nothing could avenge this kind of crime. Especially if it was committed on my son. I needed to talk to that gangbanger again…about Maxie.

"Kolya had an enemy in Moscow..." She paused, "You listening?"

"What?"

"He had an enemy in Moscow—Kolya that is."

"Yeah. So?"

"He is *here* in *this* house tonight."

"Leo?" I said.

"The same. Leo was undercover KGB while he ran the Ministry of Culture. He hunted Kolya for years and was close to capturing him a year ago when he disappeared. So Kolya would have several motives for taking Taisia."

"No wonder he agreed with Santangelo about the Russians. He knew..."

"There's more. Maryana ran an orphanage in Moscow," she said. "It was her own. You get the picture."

"An orphanage. My God. A body farm for the Butcher." I remembered what Leo had said—about women as bait for children.

I tried to picture the scene. Kids in the lunchroom, talking and laughing, playing games during the day, trusting the counselors who played with them, then crawling under their blankets at night, safe from the evil of the world outside. Then one day, a stranger in the office talking about...what? An adoption? Then the ride in a car...or ambulance...or whatever...and the shock when the boy... girl...begins to sense danger...with that inner light that only kids have...when they sense they're no longer safe... and the confusion...that's the worst part...the confusion... in the mind of the child...

I was having trouble breathing. I got up and headed for the door and then I heard Louise calling me. I ignored her. "Cooper, I'm sorry, I should have..." and the screen door slammed behind me and I looked for the moon. Always the moon. There was just the blackness of the night sky merging with the darkness of my own thoughts. And I breathed that black air deeply and sat on the front steps and tried to block out the faces of children riding in cars with strangers. But I couldn't. Were they handcuffed? Were they terrified? And I knew they were, I just couldn't think about it, and I knew those thoughts would haunt my dreams tonight and I also knew I would waken and confront a worse nightmare—one that wouldn't go away with the sunrise.

I felt Louise's hand on my shoulder. "Come on, Coop." And she guided me into the house. Richie and Sonya were in the living room. I guess we woke everybody. "I'm on the couch," Sonya said. "You two take the bedroom." I didn't argue.

48

BACK TO THE EVERGLADES

SONYA'S HOUSE: SUNDAY MORNING, OCTOBER 17

The sun was in my face. It broke through the window like high-beam headlights, hitting my eyes straight on. It was still low in the sky. The house was quiet. As I started to rise, I saw a clump wrapped in a sheet on the other side of the bed. I lifted the edge of the sheet. Louise. She stirred.

"You okay?" she said, rolling toward me and pushing back the covers from her shoulders.

"I'm good. But what a night," and I wondered if I would ever have a normal one again.

I looked over at the alarm on the dresser. Seven-forty-five in big red letters. I looked at myself in a mirror over the dresser as I waited for Louise. She had gone into the bathroom. A face I hoped wasn't mine stared back at me. I pulled back the hair around my ears looking for gray. There was some coming. I used to be able to count the strands at one time. Now there were too many. The creases in my cheek seemed longer, the lines in my brow deeper. And the swelling under my eyes in the morning had gotten progressively worse over the years since Maxie disappeared. Lack of sleep. I took a deep breath and thought, *Who cares?* and turned to see Louise come out of the bathroom, a towel wrapped around her body.

"Don't worry about those lines, Coop," she said. "They make you look rugged."

"Like Clint Eastwood," I said.

"Like him."

"I like your towel," I said.

"I like your ass," she said.

"I like yours too," I said.

"Can't see it," she said. "The towel."

"You can now," I said, and undid it.

I started with a massage. No special oils. Just my hand on her neck. Then I worked my way down her back and moved to the feet.

"Wow," she said. "That's better than sex. Keep doing what you're doing." I did.

Then she did the same to me and kept doing what she was doing until we couldn't stand it any longer and fell into a deep embrace and then…then you can guess the rest.

We were lying on our backs, staring at the ceiling.

"What are you thinking of," she said.

"You."

"Prove it."

Come here," I said, leaning over and pulling her body into mine. And we started all over again.

LATER SUNDAY MORNING

It was almost noon by the time we were ready to hit the road again, Sonya not saying much, Jackson wondering when he would see me again. I told him I would call when we got to Florida.

Leo and Huck climbed into the second seat of the Land Cruiser after they loaded the Russian into the rear. Louise had cuffed him again and sat with him. Richie climbed behind the wheel. His car after all. I rode shotgun. I figured we would be in Florida sometime early Monday morning.

Richie and I took turns driving and dozing, the dozing turning into sleeping as night came and the hours rolled toward midnight and beyond. We cut off I-75 at the Florida Turnpike near the Villages, one of the world's largest retirement communities. Good place to play golf every day until you died. The turnpike took us all the way to Oceanside, a city just south of Miami, where I cut west on Midnight Drive that runs east-west through Oceanside and then swings north to a dirt road that leads into the Glades and to my home.

I pulled into my drive around 8:00 a.m. on Monday morning, every muscle in my body yelling at me. My cat was sitting on the front porch waiting for us. I have no idea how he knew we were coming. Sammy's an outside cat who lives under my back porch when I'm gone. When I'm home he spends most of his time in a screened-in porch in the back of the house. From there he can keep an eye on Herman, a ten-foot gator who hangs out in the mangroves at the end of my back lot. Not far from Herman is a dock where I keep my seventeen-foot Boston Whaler. I use it to fish the River of Grass—a name given the Great Swamp by Marjory Stoneman Douglas. It stretches east-west across the southern end of Florida and south-southwest toward the Ten Thousand Islands and the Florida Straits. I haven't explored it all because were talking over one and a half million acres of swampland, 60 miles wide and 100 miles long.

After we piled out of the jeep and locked the Russian in a small bedroom in the back of the house, I went to the fridge to get Sammy some food. He was following me the whole time. He looked so skinny I gave him the whole can.

"Done with your cat now, Coop?" said Richie, shaking his head.

"The cat is part of my family, Richie. Just like you are. If you were starving, I would feed you too."

"Cat food?"

"It's good for you, Richie. Let's check on the guns."

Leo, Huck, and Louise had thrown their bags in the living room and were in various states of repose. Louise looked at me like when are we going to sleep?

I said, good idea and showed Huck, Richie, and Leo the other guest bedroom. Huck saw the two twins and said he would take the couch. Louise and I went to my bedroom. She was gone in thirty seconds. Fully clothed. I was close behind. The numbers on the clock on my nightstand read a tired 10:00 a.m.

MONDAY AFTERNOON, OCTOBER 18

It was after three when I heard stirring in the kitchen. It would have to be Richie. I went out to check. It was Richie. He was wearing an apron. Did he bring one with him? He was stirring a pot on the oven, holding his face away from the steam, trying to sniff the aroma. He turned as I came into the kitchen.

"I couldn't find no spices," he said. "I found the clams, garlic, and olive oil. Couldn't find no Parmesan neither," looking around like it's got to be here somewhere. Richie the cook.

"So, what's the plan, bud?" said Richie as he stirred a can of clams into the sauce.

"We go to Sunny Isles and look for Kolya and the other two Russians."

"What makes you think they're there?"

"No other place," I said. "That's Kolya's address and, my guess, the other two are there too."

"Fair enough. So who's going to do what? Or are we all going to attack them at once, like on D-Day?"

"Let me go on the web and see what the street looks like. My guess, it's an apartment building. After that I'll have a better idea."

"Good," said Richie. "Food's ready."

Leo came out of the bedroom just as Richie was placing the pasta on the table in the eating area off the kitchen. It's a good place to eat. I can watch Herman from there. Then Huck showed up, yawning into his shirt sleeve, and staring at the pasta in the bowl.

"Am I gonna get some kind of systematic poisoning eating them canned clams." He had trouble getting out the canned clams. It came out clammed cans.

Richie looked at him—disgusted.

"You can starve, you want to, you dumb swamp rat. This is probably the best food you ever ate in your depraved life."

"Deprived," I said, trying to smooth things over.

"I mean depraved. That's what this crazy Indian is. He's depraved. He ain't deprived of nothin'."

Louise was watching the whole event from the open bedroom door. She came out and sat down next to me. "Is this going to be the whole trip?"

"I hope not," I said. "But, yeah, maybe."

Richie's dinner lasted into the evening, with three bottles of wine—or four, I lost count. After the effect of the wine wore off, Louise and I went to my second office, a corner of my bedroom overlooking the swamp, and logged onto my Mac. I used Google Earth to pinpoint the address.

Sunny Isles is between Aventura on the north and Bal Harbour on the south. Miami Beach is about ten miles south of Bal Harbour.

"We're talking about pretty high-priced real estate," I said to Louise. A far cry from Tremont and Starkweather Avenue that we had left just forty-eight hours ago.

"It's here," said Louise, looking over my shoulder and pointing to an apartment building on Atlantic Boulevard.

I recognized the area, not too far away from the Epicure Market on Collins Avenue—blocks away actually. The apartment building was a seven-story complex that looked like a Holiday Inn, only there wasn't any lobby or sign. I printed out the block where the little man from Google Earth had led me and we went back to the kitchen.

Richie was coming through the front door as we came out of the bedroom. He was carrying a large green duffle bag.

"Whatcha got there, Cleveland," said Huck as he watched Richie drop the bag in the living room. It's a small room, about ten by fifteen feet if you count the entry. There is a bamboo couch, two bamboo chairs and a coffee table. No TV. The only set I have is in the bedroom. I rarely watch it. All I have for reception are some rabbit ears.

We watched Richie as he bent over the duffle.

"Let's get this show on the road," he said, opening the bag. "Uncle Richie has brought some hardware. What are you carryin', Coop."

"My Glock. My .38 is still in Miami with the MPD."

He brought over a pistol, handing it to me grip first.

It was a Beretta 92 F/FS, used by US military and also by NATO troops. A semi-automatic 9 mm.

"Like?" he said.

"Where did you get this? This is military issue."

"I got my ways, Coop. Don't ask, don't tell," he said, smiling a wicked smile. "You can use the Beretta, Coop. I'm gonna use my old enforcer," and he pulled out his Browning HP JMP 50th. It holds 13 rounds. The Browning is a beautiful piece with ivory grips and a polished blue metal finish. If you look closely, you can see the Browning signature on the left side with a gold scroll background.

Huck let out a whistle as he stared at the gun. "Mind if I take a hold of that fire stick fer a minute?" said Huck.

Richie handed it to him with a warning to give it right back… "without any fingerprints," he warned.

I looked over at Leo.

"I don't need a gun, Cooper. If I get close, I break Kolya's back."

I nodded and looked over at Louise. She was carrying a Glock.

We talked and planned over some more wine until the night turned into early morning again.

"All right. Let's get some sleep," I said. It was three a.m. These late nights.

The silence of the swamp overtook the house as we settled in, Louise cradling against me. Huck was snoring in the living room. Richie and Leo were in the bedroom next to the Russian. I wasn't sure why we were dragging him around, but I had settled into dreams before I figured it out.

49

LITTLE MOSCOW

TUESDAY MORNING, OCTOBER 19

I recognized the house from the description. Don't ask me how. I had pictured it a hundred times: a three story, gray stone, grayer still from pollution, a wood porch stretched across the front, heavy door with a knocker, stain glass windows on each side, one of the panes cracked. I pictured the house, but I couldn't find it. And then there was the traffic. And streets running into each other. I yelled at the driver. Hurry! *And why wasn't I driving, I wondered?* It's down this street, *I urged the driver.* No, over there. *He was waiting for me. Maxie. I could picture him on the porch. But I was late and I knew I wouldn't make it. The traffic too heavy. The driver too slow!*

Then, a car pulled up in front of the house. I saw it all from a red light. And I knew we wouldn't make it. I screamed at the driver. He looked around at me. Frowning. I screamed at him again and leaped for the front seat.

I must have ripped the sheets off as I rolled out of bed, Louise calling out to me, "Cooper, what's wrong?" I was still tangled in sheets as I tried to kick them off. My

220

T-shirt and underwear were soaked, my chest pounding as I looked around the room, trying to place where I was. It was dark outside, darker than any night in a city could ever be. Nights in the Everglades are as black as pitch. No street lights. No car lights. No house lights. Only the stars and the moon. Not much of that tonight.

"Are you all right?" Louise said, holding the duvet against her breasts. The red digital numbers on the clock read 5:21.

"A nightmare," I said. "Maxie. I'm okay. Same damn dreams." I was still in shock, trying to separate the real from the nightmare. "Sorry about that."

We stayed like that for a few minutes. Louise rubbed my back for a few moments with *It's going to be all right, Coop. It'll be all right,* until I said I was going to get up. I loved her for saying it, but how in God's name she could believe it, I had no idea. She continued massaging my back and shoulders for a short time then rolled back into the duvet, covered her head, and fell back to sleep. I kissed her on the forehead. She murmured a *thanks*.

I went to the kitchen to put on some coffee and smelled it as soon as I opened the door.

"You up already?" Richie said, standing over the kitchen bar and pouring coffee.

"When did you get up?" I said.

"Never went to sleep. Just couldn't. So, I got up and made some java. Want a cup?"

"Decaf?"

"You gotta be kidden'. Decaf? Come on, Coop. We got work to do. Need to have some caffeine," and he poured me a cup. Black. No sugar. No cream.

I drank it.

"Don't say I didn't warn you. I get crazy when I drink this stuff. You know that," I said, running my hand through my hair and looking into the living room mirror to see if it turned gray overnight. Those nightmares were going to kill me.

"I ran off a picture of the building where the Russian's supposed to be," I said. Richie looked at me, puzzled.

"Google Earth."

"Ain't that somethin'. Man ain't got no privacy no more. Crazy country. What're we comin' to?" he moaned, sticking his finger into his coffee to test the temperature.

We sat at the kitchen table, part of my home office, and looked at the map of Miami. Sunny Isles was north of where we were. So we marked out our route as we talked about the plan. The building was built in a half-circle fashion, with sliding glass doors facing the ocean and Collins Avenue. Collins is the Ocean Highway, commonly known as A1A. You couldn't see much of the ocean from the top floors, since there were several blocks between the building and the water.

"My friends, you are up early," observed Leo, poking his head out of the bedroom, like he had kept watch through the early hours. "Are we ready for breakfast?" and he pushed a chair into the table next to me.

"Soon," said Richie. "Coffee?"

"I'll get Huxter up," he said, staring at the mountain of breathing blankets in the front room.

"He ain't gonna be happy," Richie warned.

But it was too late. The man from Moscow was already ripping off the blankets swaddling Huck, a smile sneaking across his face.

"What the hell you doin'?" yelled the sleeping mass, kicking at the disappearing covers to keep them in place. "I ain't done sleepin'."

"We are ready for breakfast," said Leo, dragging the reluctant Huck to the table like a kid truant for school."

"And the Russian better get a shower," added Louise, holding her nose. "And how about some eggs and bacon for the poor guy, Richie?"

Richie nodded as he stirred butter over eggs that sizzled and popped in the frying pan. But he wasn't smiling.

LATER TUESDAY MORNING, OCTOBER 19

We were on the road to Miami by mid-morning, the sun starting to heat up the day and the highway. Traffic and heat. Two dangerous components of Miami highways. Both at work today. Stirring up tempers. A/Cs in high gear. We worked our way over to Miami Beach by heading up I-95, jammed four to five lanes on each side all the way. I exited the freeway at the 854 that would carry us into Aventura, a northern suburb of Miami, known for its moneyed people and elite shops.

When we got to US 1, I headed south until I hit 856, where I turned east, past the Aventura Mall, across the Intracoastal Waterway and into Sunny Isles Beach. You know when you're in Sunny Isles Beach. It's the people. Women in tight pants, even on a hot day, with high heels and face lifts, walking their Maltese or Pomeranian dogs on leashes that sparkle with gems. We passed towers of glass and concrete that block the view of the ocean and house America's richest sunbathers. Only about thirteen percent of Sunny Isles Beach is American. It's a mix: English, Russian, Israeli, Italian, Polish, and German. More Russians than Americans. Thus the name, Little Moscow. Which is why Kolya would be here.

It was almost noon when we crossed the bridge into Little Moscow.

"You know anybody here, Leo?" I said.

"I do now. Let's find them," and the air carried the foul odor of revenge. I nodded.

We entered the beach on the north side, swung south on A1A, past the Trump Towers on the left and continued south looking for the building in the picture. We found it on a side street that was little wider than an alley. There were seven floors, each with balconies facing the street. They were arranged in a crescent shape around a black top parking lot. No Hyatt for sure. I parked on the street so that we could get away quickly if we had to.

The apartment we were looking for was 7001 A. That would be the top floor. The balconies on the seventh floor were double the size of the lower ones. Penthouse units. We sat in the lot facing the condos and studied the building for a few minutes. I climbed out and motioned for the others to follow me to the rear of the building. We left the Russian in the Cruiser. Louise had handcuffed him to a seat belt. Leo stayed in the lot to watch him. His idea. No one talked. All business now.

There was a fire escape on each side of the building in the rear. Trees blocked the view of the condos from the buildings lining the street behind the complex. We had some privacy.

"Huck, you and Richie go up the fire escape. Louise and I will go in through the front entrance. But wait here while we check on the front access and the location of the apartment."

Louise and I headed back around the building to the front entry. The double glass doors opened to a panel that listed each resident with his apartment number and a buzzer. No guard. The inside doors were locked. A young woman in shorts, T-shirt and running shoes came off the elevator and jogged through the front doors, nodding to us as she passed. I grabbed one of the doors and headed for the elevator. Louise was in front of me, already punching in the seventh floor.

"We're in," I whispered to Richie on my phone. "We're heading up."

The penthouse floor had no more security than the lower floors. There looked to be only four apartments. I turned left off the elevator and walked to the end of the corridor. Louise waited at the elevator. The second to the last door read: 7002 B. I checked the last door. Sure enough, 7001 A. I gave Louise a nod.

It was a heavy wooden door with scrolling on the sides, top, and bottom. A peephole in the top center. There was a lock in the door handle and a key fitting that indicated a bolt lock inside above that.

I returned to the elevator and we headed down talking about our strategy. Nothing much. Just break in and see who's there. Before I let the inside doors to the building close, I jammed a *Sunny Isles Living Magazine* into the space between the door and the wall, hoping no one would notice.

"So, what's the story?" said Richie.

Leo walked over from the SUV.

"The apartment is there, at the top on the fire escape," I said, pointing to the right side of the building, making sure in my mind that I was pointing to the correct end.

"Let's get the Russian," I said to Leo and Louise. I told Richie and Huck to go back to the rear of the building and give us ten minutes, then head up the fire escape.

Louise, Leo and I walked back to the Land Cruiser. The Russian was asleep, when we opened the back door. It was hot, the autumn sun still mean this time of the year. A sharp acid-like odor—the kind that comes from fear—poured out as I pulled the door open.

"Jeez!" said Louise, as she fell back from the smell, waving her hand across her nose. "When did this guy take a bath?"

Louise took off the tape, warned him to be quiet, and told him what he needed to do when we got into the building. He looked at the apartment building like he had never seen it before, then back at me. Questioning.

"Your friends," I said, Leo translating.

"This'll give you a chance to get some air," Louise said to the Russian. "So take advantage." He had no idea what she had told him.

Richie and Huck had followed us back to the Cruiser. "Forgot our guns," Richie said on the way over. The Russian's eyes went wide as he watched Richie pull his Mossberg out of the front of the SUV and check the load, pulling back the slide then slamming it back into place. The noise echoed through the empty parking lot. I cleared my throat and yelled "Jeez!" looking up at the windows above for any faces. None. The building was as quiet as a deserted tenement building in downtown New York City. Good thing, because what a watcher would see from his window would be a carnival beyond strange: Richie, trying to hide his Mossberg by holding it close to his leg, like trying to tuck in a kid with no blankets; and then there were Huck and Louise, pushing a no-name Russian in front of them with Leo bending into his ear and whispering harsh warnings; and me, checking the load in by Beretta and jamming it back in my holster. Then they would see us stopping in front of the entry doors, Richie and Huck disappearing around the right side of the building and Louise, me, and the two Russians getting ready to enter their building and shoot everyone. Lock your doors and keep your kids safe! They'd have to wonder where this parade was going, wouldn't they?

No one came out as Louise, Leo, and I entered the lobby with the Russian. Richie and Huck were already out of sight. The elevator was waiting this time. I hit the button for the seventh floor and hoped no one would be waiting when we got off. There wasn't. As we approached the door, I removed the tape and told Leo to remind the Russian about what he was supposed to say. The Russian nodded quickly that he understood.

I knocked on the door. Silence. There was a doorbell, so I rang that several times. Still no answer.

"Call them," I said. The Russian stared at me.

Leo translated. The Russian nodded, leaned forward, and spoke through the door.

Silence. I tried the doorknob. It turned. And we entered the apartment.

Then it hit me. The stench. Some people talk about the smell of death. A woman once told me she could smell sickness in a person. She said she could smell cancer—before it was diagnosed. I stayed away from her.

Louise pulled her Glock and led the way into the apartment, turning and holding her nose.

"Not good," she whispered, waiting for me to follow. I motioned for Leo to stay inside the door with the Russian and not move. I pulled my gun and followed Louise.

There wasn't any doubt about what I smelled. Autolysis. I had seen it at the Body Farm—it's on the campus of the University of Tennessee. One of seven in the country.

That's where researchers study the process of decomposition. A ghoulish job. You study how cells commit suicide. "It's kind of like the cells eating themselves," one of the docs explained. "But in reality they're already dead and simply releasing an enzyme into the air." Autolysis is followed by putrefaction. That's when you can smell the decay. I think we had at least one candidate for the Farm here.

As we passed through the living room, I heard a noise. We froze. I turned toward it and moved in that direction. The bedroom. I kicked open the door, swung the gun in an arc, and saw Richie and Huck—they had come into the room by way of the fire escape. I dropped my gun when I heard Richie slam a shell into his Mossberg. Huck had his rifle pointed at my head.

"Fuck, dammit Coop, say something next time! I mighta shot you," yelled Richie, his face scarlet. Huck dropped his gun and shook his head. "Helluva plan we had here. Headlines. Three men and a Miami cop shoot each other in some dude's apartment. Tried to interview them but they weren't talkin'," said Richie.

"Yeah, cause they was dead," added Huck.

I turned to find Louise. She came out of a bedroom

"What the hell stinks in here?" said Richie, surveying the room and stopping at the bathroom. I didn't want to go there.

Huck moved to the door and pushed it open. He jumped back or I should say he stumbled back.

"Damn!" he yelled, covering his mouth and trying to recover his balance all at the same time. The stench was horrific, like the odor of rotting meat under the hot sun. I holstered my gun, held my nose, and approached.

A man's body was splayed over the bathtub—in pieces. His eyes were gone, just holes now staring off into space.

Blood covered the tub, the floor, some spattered on the walls (don't let your children hear this part), his side cut open, a small amount of blood still oozing from the wound. His left arm was cut off at the bicep.

I had to turn away to breathe. The odor—now that the door was open, it took advantage of its freedom and swept through the room like a cloud of poisonous gas.

"Holy sweet Mary," I heard Richie mutter as I stumbled into him, "who's the prevert done this?" He caught hold of me and we both wrestled to stay upright.

"Shut that damn door," I said, "before we all die." Richie slammed it shut. That helped.

I went to the closest window and cranked it open. The air pushed in like a relief squad from the U.S. Cavalry. I stared at my hands as I filled my lungs, looking for blood—none.

I hadn't touched anything.

"You all right?" I felt Louise's hand on my shoulder. I nodded without turning around. I could feel the bile in my stomach, rising in revolt.

Someone was throwing up. I turned to see who it was and saw Huck's leather pioneer jacket slumped over the counter. Richie was standing at a window near mine, staring out over the city, leaning on his Mossberg. Not a sound from anyone as the seconds turned into minutes and I began to notice the smell again. The bitter odor of blood. I could taste it on my tongue—the bitterness, I mean.

"There's a note on the dresser," Richie said still facing the window. That silence again.

I looked around for the dresser, saw it, and rose to get it. Leo was already reading it. He had a firm grip on the Russian's arm. It tightened as he read, his face losing its color then quickly regaining it as he balled up the paper and threw it across the room, with the fury of a storm that had been threatening and then suddenly pours rain and hurls bolts of lightning against everyone in its way. Then thunder erupted as Leo looked at the ceiling and screamed. And it carried through the open windows and into the streets and burst through any silence that was out there.

I waited for a few minutes, for the moment when Leo calmed himself—and until my own chest quit pounding. Then Louise handed me the fallen note, still twisted and frail, the unfortunate messenger of very bad news. I opened it up, trying to restore it to something of its original shape. But…it was in what looked to be Russian.

I walked it over to Leo. "What does it say?"

He picked up the note, handling it like it contained some terrible disease and crushed it again.

"He will pay for this." His face was on fire. If I touched it, I would burn.

"Who?" I said, as calmly as I could.

"Kolya," he said, biting down hard on the name. Then, leaning back against the dresser, he continued like a defeated man: "He said, 'This will be your granddaughter if you follow me.'" His fists were clenched like a boxer's preparing for a championship bout, trying to beat the storm back. But the dam finally broke and he sobbed, quietly. He sobbed—like a proud man who was beaten down, embarrassed by his own failures. "And it will be my own fault if she dies."

Then he stared through the window that looked out over the shore of the Atlantic, and began to breathe more slowly, in time with the tide washing in. And a bird hit the window and fell. Probably to its death seven stories below. Life is so short.

230

"The Butcher," Leo muttered, still leaning against the dresser, still staring out the window, at the spot where the bird had collided with it. His eyes were veined and red. He couldn't hide it and wasn't even trying. "The Butcher," he whispered, and shook his head—as if he were already at his granddaughter's funeral, as if the bird were the messenger of bad news.

50

WHO IS TAISIA?

I went over to Leo and put my hand on his shoulder. He didn't look up—he just talked to the floor: "My wife has been dead for many years. So, I alone raised my daughter, Raisa. Many years ago my Raisa met a man, a foreigner visiting our country. They became friends. I thought that was all. He left after several months, but later returned. They spent nights together—without my knowledge." He looked up and shrugged: "So, I am a father alone, without my wife, and I make many mistakes. This was one of them." He paused, wiped his forehead with the sleeve of his shirt then shook it down so it fell over his wrist—wet from perspiration, and continued: "Then, this foreigner—I should have killed him—leaves Russia and my Raisa and later I discover my Raisa was pregnant, and now no husband..."

He stopped for a moment, as though struck by an idea, then, "yes, I should have killed him," and and he looked up at me again, his hands curled in fists, but, at the same time, bent over with grief. Sadness does that to us. It brings darkness into our world.

"She does not have other children," he continued, the darkness weighing like a demon on his shoulders. "I am her family.

"So, I help my Raisa raise little Taisia—oh, she is not so little now, I realize," he said, holding his hand out to show how tall she is. "But then...," and a smile filled his eyes, "she was so small I could hardly see her! Moya malyanpkayo byaondinka rebenka (*My little blonde baby*). She was so...," and he caught himself, "is..." and he didn't finish. "And now they have taken her. My enemies. My fault," he exclaimed, slamming his fist against the side of the dresser.

After some silence, he looked toward the bathroom.

"My God, the smell," staring at the open door. "Who is it?"

"It might be her friend, Geza," I said.

"I did not know her friend," he said. "I am sorry for him."

I called DeFelice.

"Yeah. What's up?"

I told him about the man in the bathtub and who I thought he was. He was quiet.

"Lunatics, he breathed into the phone. "You notify the locals?"

I said *of course*. Lying. He said, *uh-huh*. I said not to worry. He said he always worries when it's me. Then he hung up. I love talking to Tony.

I had forgotten the Russian. I didn't have to ask when I turned to Leo. "He is in the bedroom," he said, pointing to the room at the other side of the apartment. I wondered if he was still there. Leo read my thoughts.

"I have not killed him," he said.

When I checked the room, I didn't see the man. I looked at Leo again. "In the bathroom.," he corrected.

The Russian was lying in the tub, a large welt, growing on his head. I turned to look for Leo. He was standing behind me. He shrugged.

We dragged him out of the tub and laid him on the bed. He stirred, felt his head, and when he saw Leo, scrabbled away.

Leo grabbed his feet and pulled him back. Then, Taisia's grandfather picked the man up by the throat, the Russian's eyes inches from Leo's, his feet off the ground, flailing about like a fish struggling on a hook. I grabbed Leo's arm to stop him from killing the only person who might know where Taisia was, an arm as hard as unrefined ore. And I made a mistake because Leo dropped the Russian and whirled around at me, the new enemy, and I went sprawling, like a fly swatted away by a cow's tail.

I landed against a wall—hurt, but mostly my pride. And I watched as the fire slowly died in Leo. Then, the big man shook his head, apology in his eyes. A calmer man bent down and spoke quietly to the Russian who was struggling to catch air. Leo whispered, the Russian wheezed like a leaky bagpipe.

"Bol'shaya lodka," said Leo, finally turning to me.

I shrugged.

"A large boat," Leo translated, turning back to the Russian but still talking to me. "They go on large boat," he continued, and with his right hand grabbed the Russian by the throat again, trying to lift him. I tried to stop him when Richie burst into the room:

"What…?"

"Get him the hell out of here before the cops come—
or Leo kills him," I said, taking a lung full of air to try to
calm myself.

Leo ignored Richie, threw the man over his back, and
headed out of the apartment. I shook my head and nodded
for Huck and Louise to follow him. "Try to keep the guy
alive," I said and took another deep breath.

"Jeez," Richie muttered, watching the four of them
leave, "friggin' crazy man." Coming from Richie, that was
a compliment.

I finally had a silent moment. So I called DeFelice and
told him about the large boat. "It's probably in the water
right now," I said, "so we've got to catch them—pronto,"
figuring if that boat gets into the Caribbean, it's gone.

"Right. I'll call the Coast Guard." Then, "You called the
locals, right?"

"I'm on it, Tony."

"Uh-huh. Figured."

51

A few minutes later a man in a blue jacket and a white shirt appeared at the bedroom door. Richie and I were near the bathroom, checking out the bloody scene. The stench came at us like an invisible living monster.

"Cooper?" asked the man in blue. He was chewing on his mustache.

"Uh-huh," I had to skirt a bed to get over to him.

"James Olmos," he said, holding out a hand.

"Olmos? Miami Vice?"

"Yeah, yeah, I know," he said. "My parents loved that series. Why they called me James. Oh well. Live with a name, don't we?" Then, "Damn we need to air this place out," he said, looking for the source of the stench, the foulness of it growing by the minute.

I nodded behind me at the bathroom

"You know we have a low crime index here in Sunny Isles," he said, walking toward the offending odor. When we got to the tub, he shook his head. "Who the hell are you chasing, Cooper?"

236

"The Russian mob. They live right here in your sunny little town, Chief." He didn't smile.

"Sunny fucking Isles Beach," he replied.

"Makes you love your job doesn't it?"

He nodded. "Homicide. Miami PD, huh?" he said, looking sidewise at me.

"Uh-huh. Five years. You talked to DeFelice?"

He nodded. We had backed out of the bathroom—more like the terminal odor drove us away—and were heading for the apartment door and some air when the noise of an elevator opening and voices, followed by the scuffle of footfalls, echoed through the hallway. Moments later Leo, Huck, and Louise piled through the open door, Leo sweating and pulling up quickly when he spotted the uniform. He stared at Olmos, his mouth set to say something—you know, police in Russia—they usually mean trouble.

I was worried that Olmos would say, "Hey, you're the ones I saw hauling a guy across the parking lot." But he didn't. Thank God.

Olmos stared at me, waiting for an introduction, all the while, eyeing the Russian.

I started to fill him in about the kidnapping of Leo's granddaughter and...

"So how did you wind up here, looking for a missing granddaughter?" Olmos said, his brow creased.

Then, he looked over at Louise and nodded. "Delgado. You on duty?"

"Vacation time," she said. "Helping out." He nodded. Again. Just like on Miami Vice. Edward James fricking Olmos. I told you.

"What?" he said.

Caught. I was staring at the scars on his face. Probably acne when he was a kid.

"Nothing. Just thinking," I replied, embarrassed.

"Uh-huh," he said.

I smiled. "Olmos. Miami Vice." He scowled.

"My God. This place smells like a damn butcher shop," blew in a voice from the open doorway.

I turned. A man in blues, thin, smallish, smooth features. Women would say handsome.

"Thomas," he said, holding out his hand, and giving me that slow drawl you might hear from the Caribbean.

I looked at Olmos, then back at Thomas. "Don't tell me. Philip Michael Thomas?"

"That's right." Same smooth talk.

I couldn't believe it. "What are the names of the other cops in Sunny Isles Beach?" I said, turning to Olmos. "Don't tell me. Don Johnson."

He smiled. "Michael is marine patrol. I asked him to come along since you said the bad guys might be using a large boat. He's our Coast Guard here." He paused, looking at me sidewise. "One thing you didn't tell me—how'd you learn about this 'large boat' since there's nobody here but you and me and your buddies—and this guy can't talk?" he added, pointing toward the bathroom.

I thought for a moment. I wasn't gonna tell him about the Russian in the SUV. So...

"A hunch."

"A hunch?" He smiled. "You want me to go chasing around for a large boat on a *hunch*?"

I nodded. What else? Tell him? He takes the Russian into custody and we lose our only lead? So I stayed with hunch.

He shook his head. "Okay. I'm gonna hope you've got more than a hunch goin' here. So Thomas is supposed to run around the intracoastal looking for a large boat? Don't suppose you have a description in this hunch-vision of yours, do you?"

"I'm waiting on a contact at Interpol to give me more. When I get it I'll pass it on. Best I can do."

"All right. But just so you're clear. This homicide's in my town. No interference, and that includes…" and he poked his finger in my chest, "withholding information, okay?" I moved his hand away. We had a stare-contest for a moment. Then, I nodded.

"Keep me informed," he said, holding my eyes to make sure I got it. I bit on the side of my lip. I didn't nod this time. Cops. It's all about territory.

"Fucking asshole," Richie said, as Olmos walked away. If Olmos heard him, he ignored it.

"Okay, where's the body?" The voice came from a thin, Asian man, standing in the doorway to the apartment. Back to reality. Dr. Wann, the Dade County Medical Examiner. We had worked together on a number of homicides.

"What you doing here, Cooper?" he queried, pulling on a mask and gloves. "Stinks in here."

"Same thing you're doing, doc." We walked toward the bathroom, Olmos and Thomas right behind. I wondered where Leo had gone.

"Any ID?" asked Wann, kneeling down over the body. "God, someone did a number here, boys. And—in case you wondering—he's dead."

"How long?" said Olmos.

"Too early to tell exactly, Chief. But I would say eleven to twelve hours." He stood up. "See here? Rigor mortis.

Almost complete. Usually complete in twelve/thirteen hours. So, eleven/twelve hours is close." Then, "You guys hang out, okay? Got some work to do here."

I was happy to get out of there.

I almost knocked Thomas over when I turned around. He was right at my shoulder watching the ME. I apologized. He shook it off.

"So, you think these guys might be using a get-away-boat?" he said, studying my face.

"I think so." He was still staring. I needed to check a mirror.

"A hunch you said?"

"I have a source I can't divulge right now. But I promise you they have a boat, and a big one, not a get-a-away."

He thought about that for a while. "We got a fast boat—but it can't run down smugglers. And it can't go in the deep stuff out in the Straits where the big boys go." He paused, trying to figure something out. "But what I can do is take my little twenty-five footer and see if any big boats are floating in our water that shouldn't be there. Okay?"

I nodded. "Let you know if I find something," he added, trying to make me feel better.

"Yeah. Better sooner than later. A couple of hours might mean a girl's entire life," and I couldn't keep Maxie out of my mind as I said it.

I left the body of the kid I figured was Geza to the ME and the cops. It's their job. Hell, I'm just a second-rate private investigator who most cops hate anyway and who can't even find his own son.

52

The day was wearing on when we exited the apartment building, now deadly quiet. And I was wearing thin with it. We settled in Richie's SUV and I hit the A/C. The cool air helped our tempers which were rising in sync with the temperature, now pushing ninety. It was unusually warm for this time of the year—mid-October—and the hurricane season sinking with the sun now sitting low against the western Everglades.

Louise and Huck were in the second seat, leaving Richie to sit with the Russian in the back row. I headed out of the parking lot before the cops could ask more questions. They wanted a full report from me at the station in the morning. DeFelice had settled Olmos's concerns about us. He filled him in on the case. He explained that the FBI was still investigating but hadn't gotten anywhere. He told them I was one of the good guys. Olmos had asked me why I had left the MPD. I told him the short version. I didn't feel like rehashing the whole kidnapping of my son. We were becoming best friends. All in about a half hour. Male bonding.

I turned to Leo who was with me now in the front seat. "Tell me more about Taisia. There's more to this story, isn't there?" I was wondering what the hell else he had done to those guys?

"Yes. It is a long story, my friend," said Leo.

"So tell me the whole story. It might help us find your granddaughter."

He began in a drone, as though he were still depressed. "I was division head in the Ministerstvo Vnutrennikh Del. You know it as the MVD. The Ministry of Culture." As he spoke he stared out over the ocean as if transfixed by a memory of a happier time long gone. Louise and Huck were listening quietly in the back. I steered toward Ocean Highway, as he spoke, and headed south along the shore toward Miami Beach.

"During those days, Communism was very strong in Russia and I was valuable recruiter of foreigners. Then your Senator McCarthy began to make troubles for members of Party in America. It became difficult to recruit in the United States.

"We infiltrated organizations with our own people who had earned green cards, even Catholic seminaries," he said, looking my way. "You seem very surprised."

I sure as hell was.

"We planted over 1,000 men in your schools," he added, again glancing my way. "Shocking?"

"Absolutely. Did those young men become priests?"

"Yes, many of them."

I was trying to picture priests I had known in the past who might have been Communist party collaborators. It was a disturbing thought.

"I am sure that you are wondering what all of this has to do with my Taisia's kidnapping."

I nodded. "Go on," I said.

"Because of our great success, I become important person in MVD. Soon a young man comes to work for me. His name was Remi." Some light at the end of the tunnel.

He took a deep breath, stared up at the towering apartment buildings that lined the ocean side of A1A, and continued:

"Your developers have taken away the ocean from you, haven't they?" I didn't respond. He sighed as he watched the towers of condominiums slide by. A gathering of sea gulls rose suddenly between two of them, both all-glass structures, their tops soaring into the clean, blue Miami sky. The gulls floated like gliders out over the ocean. They disappeared behind another building.

"After collapse of USSR, crime was our way of life. Gangs controlled even the internal operations of the country. Everything.

"So my new job? Get rid of the gangs. And so I made enemies," and he shrugged like a he was trapped by his own deeds.

"Kolya and Remi," I said.

"Yes. Remi is one of the big boys in the gangs. A *lider bandy*. But see…" and he turned toward me, "I am old school. MVD controls everything. You would say KGB. Same things. So, with these new guys, anyone part of old Russia has to go. And so Remi and his gang, he helps criminal peoples like Kolya get power to throw me out.

"They are both—I mean Kolya and Maks Remizov— the most dangerous mens in Moscow. They are *Cert*.

Devils!" And he lost it for a while. Leo, the deliberate and cold Russian, was as red as his own flag. He continued, his calmness was belied by his fists that were working as though they had a life of their own, like creatures in a white heat.

"Kolya is butcher. He uses fishing knife." He demonstrated with a cutting motion. "And Remi is butcher's helper," his fists still feverishly kneading themselves.

"And you went after them?"

"Yes. I chased them."

"And they hated you for that."

"Hate is not strong enough. Hate is for humans. They are not humans. I locked Kolya up in Moscow prison. But Remi freed him—with KGB power."

"So I hunted for Kolya like a tiger. This *pak*. This curse. And I catch him on a *ferma*—I think you say farm—outside of Moscow, in a house, protected by his men. You see, Kolya was head of *Krasnaya Mafiya* for Moscow and area surrounding. I think you call city-burbs."

"Uh-huh. Suburbs."

"My policemen surround the camp with much shooting. Many men were killed—mine and his. When it was over, we took Kolya prisoner. He was put in prison for crimes against Russian peoples. Muscovites were very happy that we captured him, this man who killed many thousands of peoples, like a—how do you say?"

"A maniac," not knowing what else to say. What other word is there for men like him?

"I see. So, all the peoples of city were happy when this maniac was in jail. But he threatened my family when he went away to gulag. So when he got out, I was afraid for my daughter and my grandchild. So, I sent Taisia to America where she could be safe…we thought she would be…," his words drifted away like a lifeboat losing itself in the sea.

"So, you think they wanted to get back at you, and they…"

"Took my little Taisia!"

And his shoulders slumped as he finished, "I am afraid this is my fault."

53

KOLYA

"I think it will rain," Leo said, as he watched storm clouds building over the ocean. They rode one on top of the other, gray on black, the white clouds now gone. Streaks of lightening shot through them, followed by volleys of thunder rolling in the distance.

"You have taken her to make me come to America," Leo muttered—to his enemies, I assumed. His head was bowed and his fists were working once again.

"But you underestimate me," he continued, in an undertone, "I will find my granddaughter, and I will kill you— with my own hands," his voice rising and echoing through the Cruiser. And those hands, they seemed to have a life of their own—swear to God!

"Jesus," Richie muttered from the back of the car, "I'd hate to have that guy for an enemy."

We had been driving along Collins Avenue, which is Ocean Boulevard, as Leo talked, passing Bal Harbour and Surfside. When we hit Miami Beach, I took the 907 and slid along Biscayne Bay and the palatial homes that line the shore, and then on to I-195 which spans the Bay

246

and connects to I-95 and the mainland. I took 95 south through the heart of Miami until the freeway ended at Dixie Highway—US 1—sometimes billed as *America's Number One Highway.*

"Where the hell we goin'?" said Richie.

"Back to Oceanside," I said.

"Why?"

"Make plans."

"You ain't got a plan," said Richie. I could feel his smile on my neck.

"You got one?"

"Yeah. Same as yours. Get to your place, grab a beer, jump in your hammock, and look at the Everglades for a coupla hours. Somethin' will turn up."

"I second that, hombres," said Huck. "Time to reconnoiter." Huck loves big words. Actually, he's smart. He just pretends he's not.

"You know what the hell that word means?" said Richie, leaning over Huck's seat. Back at it again.

"I'm smarter'n you think, white man."

Richie turned away, shaking his head.

"We will lose time, will we not?" said Leo, his voice edgy and worried, "going to your house again."

"No. We're going to regroup. Plan our next steps. Takes some thinking…"

"And some drinking…" said Richie.

"…and some preparation," I corrected.

It's the calm before the war.

54

TUESDAY EVENING, OCTOBER 19

The sun was sinking over the swamp as I jumped on the north-south expressway that links I-75 to the southern end of the Florida Turnpike. The city of Oceanside begins where the Turnpike intersects Route 1 and extends all the way to the Everglades. The car was silent now as the setting sun turned day into dusk and the shadows of the evening played with the streetlights lining the highway. I headed west on College Avenue past the home office of the Oceanside Police Department, past Saint Augustine's Catholic Church and the Diocesan Seminary, and to Midnight Drive that runs north-south at the city limits. It is the last main street before the Everglades. I headed north on Midnight Drive until I came to the dirt road that takes me to my home.

If I didn't mention it before, I actually live in the Everglades. It's one of the original houses in the Great Swamp. An old Florida cowboy built it about ninety years ago when Miami was little more than a nest for mosquitoes and alligators. Today you can add pythons. Maybe as many as seventy thousand. Who knows how many? You can't find them.

It was completely dark by the time I pulled into the drive. No lights anywhere except from the headlamps of the Land Cruiser.

"We here, pardner?" said Huck, yawning.

"We're here," I said, fighting off a yawn of my own. I killed the motor and went around to the back of the SUV. Leo and Huck had already gotten out and Richie was right behind them. Leo and Louise reached into the back of the Cruiser for the Russian.

"I'll remove that gag, now," she told the Russian. "But keep your mouth shut when I do." Leo translated.

He nodded.

Richie was heading for the front porch.

"Hit the light would you," I told him. "The switch is on the lamp itself."

"How in the hell am I supposed to see the damn thing? Ain't no light!" he said.

"There will be when you turn it on," I said.

Louise removed the tape and the handcuffs. The Russian coughed violently for a few moments. Then he straightened up, felt his back—it wasn't broken by the way—twisted his torso as he would before a workout, moaned a little, and rubbed his wrists. I was beginning to feel guilty about how we were dragging him around. I gave him some water from a bottle I had pulled out of the SUV. He drank like he had been in the desert for a week.

I asked Leo to tell the Russian he should be thinking of where we might find that boat in the next few hours. Leo nodded and leaned into the Russian's ear, a threat in his voice as he spoke. Probably added a few words of his own. The man shook his head and shrugged, like he didn't know. He looked over at me. If he was looking for understanding he wasn't getting any.

"Bring him in the house," I said. Leo and Louise dragged him up the porch steps. Richie had turned on the light and was waiting for them. He looked over at me for the key.

"Door's open." I never lock it. It's too remote. Nobody around here. And Sammy protects it anyway. He had come from behind the house and was rubbing his body against my leg. Probably thinking, back so soon? Sammy followed the procession into the house, purring his way to the refrigerator. He waited. Letting me know he was hungry.

"I'm going to the back porch and grab some cold ones," said Richie. He picked up a package of crackers and some cheese along with a bag of chips from the pantry, dumped them on a plate, and headed out the back door. Only darkness would greet him there. The light had burned out. I hadn't replaced it.

"Where's the light?" said Huck as he followed Richie out the screen door.

"Burned out," and I thought of Simon and Garfunkel's old song, *Hello darkness my old friend.* I was humming the tune as they headed into the night to a hammock that stretched between two palms just off the porch and a deck chair that sat near it. They knew where it was. Even in the darkness. Past drinking experience.

I fixed a ham and bologna sandwich for the Russian and gave him a Sam Adams. Don't ask why. Guilt? Then I got him settled in the back bedroom overlooking the Everglades so he could get a good view of Herman in the morning. Louise helped secure him to the bed.

"Knock if you have to use the can," she said, Leo translating.

When the house was quiet again, I told Louise and Leo to join me in the backyard. They both begged off, opting to turn in for the night.

So I grabbed a chair off the back porch and joined Huck and Richie. They were sitting in silence, drinking and looking out over the Everglades.

"Grab a cold one," said Richie, pointing to a cooler.

"Made yourself right at home, huh?"

"Mi casa su casa," he said.

He had a point.

We sat in silence. I've had many a dream out here under the Everglades sky. My eyes were tired. Sometime during the night, I fell asleep.

55

THE COMING WAR

In the hours just before the beginning of the war in the Persian Gulf, CNN's cameras scanned the Baghdad sky, filming buildings sitting in silence, the lights of the city clearly visible against the black of the night. No sound, only the drone of the CNN newsmen as we waited for the first attacks. Then came a sudden explosion of shells and rockets over the city, and the noise: the air raid sirens, the whine of missiles homing in on targets, the chatter of commentators watching the sky light up with tracers tracking incoming aircraft, and through it all searchlights probing the night for jets—but they were nowhere to be found—while below, buildings erupted into fire and poured out smoke, huge clouds of it billowing over the city. The war had begun. But before that, it was calm. I should say a tense calmness that came from the TV screens that brought the city to our homes that evening—before all hell broke loose, that is. And no one slept while it went on—that night. But tonight…I slept. That is until Richie shook me.

"Wake up, Coop, let's get some coffee," he said, turning and heading for the house. It was dark. I checked my cell.

Three o'clock in the morning—I thought of the old B.B. King song:

> *Now, it's three o'clock in the morning*
> *Can't even close my eyes*
> *Lord, three o'clock in the morning, baby*
> *Can't even close my eyes*
> *Richie, you're killing me.* (The last verse is mine.)

It was quiet as Richie, Huck, Leo, and I sat around the kitchen table, staring into our coffee and thinking. Planning for a war. And you don't talk before a war. You think. You think about the possibility that you might get killed. You think about the chance you'll be killing someone else. Taking a life—that should be reserved for God. You think about the possibility one of your friends sitting around the table with you might get killed. You look at each one of them as you think about it. And you see them looking at you also, and you wonder if they are thinking the same thing you are.

So we thought. And we stared. And we drank coffee, and we listened to the house— which you could do because there was no noise—and we breathed deeply, and then, one by one, drifted off to bed, not a word among us, like ghosts. And I slept until early morning. No alarm.

My dreams woke me up. Louise was next to me, sound asleep. I could smell coffee brewing. Had to be Richie. So, I joined him in the kitchen. His HP Jump Browning was on the table along with his Mossberg. And the cleaning equipment and the smell of oil. And my guns were there too, broken down and smelling of gun oil. My Glock and the Beretta.

I sat down without a word. Death was in the air. It always seemed to be when Richie was around.

"How we gonna find that boat, bud?" said Richie breaking the silence, still cleaning.

"The Coast Guard is looking for suspicious vessels," I said, not expecting much to come from that. I mean, how do you find a suspicious boat? Big old pirate flag on its mast?

"What about the marine cop?"

"Haven't heard anything."

"So that leaves our buddy, the Russian."

"Leo will talk to him when he wakes up."

I called DeFelice.

"The FBI contact you?" he said.

"No. They back on the case?"

"Yeah. Sunny Isles police chief called them in. By the way, he asked me why Louise was with you guys. I told him she was working private." He paused. "Walk carefully, buddy. You tell Lou the same thing." Edgy.

"How's your father-in-law," I said, trying to get off the subject.

"Getting more senile all the time, Coop. Thanks for asking," his voice softer now. Tony's wife deserted the old man and DeFelice is taking care of him. Feels responsible, I guess. But anyway, I think he really loves the guy.

"Neighbors found him trying to get into their house. Old guy got mixed up. You know, houses look the same. He was looking for my Ex. Jeez, Coop, been a year since she left. They told him she don't live around here no more and he goes berserk. Claimed they was lying—said they was hiding her out. It's sad."

"Ouch," I said. I let the silence drift for a while.

Then, "What's new from the Coast Guard?"

"Nothin' yet. Your buddy, Captain Welder, said if you're looking for a big boat in harbor, you oughta check out the Fort Lauderdale Marina." I already knew that. And it made sense. It's the biggest one on the east coast of Florida.

Richie was staring at me when I got off the phone. "So where are we going?" said Richie.

"The Lauderdale Marina," I said. I went back to the bedroom to wake Louise.

56

KORABYAP

(THE BIG BOAT)

LATE WEDNESDAY MORNING, OCTOBER 20

The Lauderdale Marina was about an hour from where we were, give or take. So we took the scenic route, the old Tamiami Trail, to the coast, then up A1A to the marina, giving Louise time to check with Interpol.

The agency has the largest database on criminals in the world. The U.S. center is located in D.C. and is connected to the Department of Justice. The home of Louise's contact. You might wonder why Interpol is so important to me—the seeker of lost persons. A no-brainer. Besides being a database, Interpol also helps locate missing people or abducted children. If the kidnappers are foreign nationals, Interpol is especially interested. Kolya Shibalov was on their list of 270 of their most wanted people. And so they've been anxious to help locate him. Taisia was not yet on their list. I was hoping Louise could get her on.

My cell rang out my favorite tune. It was from Phillip Michael Thomas, the Sunny Isles cop with marine patrol duty.

"I think I've got something here, Cooper," he said. He sounded excited. I was surprised he was volunteering information to a P.I.

"I know you wonder why I'm sharing this information with you." I called that one right. "See I've got my own investigation firm on the side. I know what you guys go through." Moonlighting. "Besides you can do some things we can't, so the Chief is cool with it. Only thing, I wanna be part of the job."

I told him *super* what did he have.

"I've got a contact with Interpol in D.C." I wondered if he had the same contact Louise had.

"Okay," I said, pushing him on.

"Maks Remizov, one of your boys, is connected to the FSB, the Federal Security Service—the old KGB, as you probably know. The word from Interpol is that Remizov was able to get both Maryana and Kolya into the U.S. in the years after the collapse of the USSR when hundreds of Russian émigrés got into this country. Story is they took a trawler across the Bering Strait in the summer—that's when the weather conditions are most favorable—and entered the States at Nome, Alaska. Since Remizov is an international criminal, Interpol has been tracking his movements in the U.S."

"That is great news," I said. The best I'd had in a long time.

"Okay, here's more good news. Kolya must have brought a lot of money with him because there is some indication he paid for a yacht conversion down in the Canal Zone and went into business. Interesting, huh?"

"Business? Fascinating," I said, my excitement growing.

"What?" said Louise. She was riding up front with me and leaning into my cell.

"Oh yeah," he said, "especially because the boat is here in my backyard." I could feel his smile over the phone.

"Backyard?" I said, stunned. "Where?"

"The Lauderdale Marina," he said. Mind reader. That's where we were headed.

"Do you know the dock space?" This was getting too easy.

"Do I know my name?" he said.

"Okay. Where is it?" I said getting tired of his 'you guess what I'm going to say' game. He must know Huxter.

"Better yet, Cooper. I'll take you there."

"Good. We're driving. I figure we can be at the marina in an hour. That would be about 11:00 a.m."

"How about I meet you at the Fort Lauderdale Hilton on Southeast 17th Street," Thomas said. "It's next to the marina. I can be there at twelve noon."

I told him we would meet him in the dining room.

We got to the Hilton a little after eleven, parked, let the Russian out of the back of the SUV, and headed for the dining room.

The Hilton has a panoramic view of the intracoastal waterway and marina. I saw a boat that must have been over eighty feet docked along the waterway in front of the hotel. The advertisement for the marina said it could dock boats from 50 feet to 150. I figured I was looking at several million dollars in the yacht sitting in the water. At least.

We found some tables outside the restaurant overlooking the intracoastal. Stools were arranged around a square cupola sitting in the middle of a deck about the size of a tennis court where a bartender was serving drinks. We took one of the metal tables scattered around the bar. The Russian looked pleased. His hands were free. Louise had removed the handcuffs at the SUV. She hadn't taped his mouth. He pulled up a seat next to me, as far away from Leo as he could get.

I told everyone the good news from Thomas as we waited for someone to take our order. The Russian picked up a menu from a holder on the table. It was a drink menu. I ordered him a Sam Adams.

57

THE HOTEL HILTON

"Cooper!" cried a voice across the patio. He was walking quickly toward me, holding a paper in his hand and pointing at it. Jason Eisenberg. Another man was following not far behind.

"Have you seen the morning *Herald*?" he said.

"What are you doing here?" I said, not believing what I was seeing.

"We came to see how you were doing," said the man behind him. Kenneth Boyd.

Jason threw the *Miami Herald* down in front of me. A front-page story about the kidnapping: the Russians, the killing of Taisia's boyfriend, and me, a private dick, in the middle of it all. An AP wire story, credited to Jason Eisenberg. I couldn't believe it. I gave Jason a screw-you stare.

"There's more inside, Cooper. Pulitzer Prize stuff," he said, ignoring my irritation.

I just shook my head. Damn! What could I say? It was done.

"And Mr. Santangelo's gettin' restless, Cooper. We ain't heard from you lately," said Boyd, stepping around from behind Jason. I stared at him. The day was heating up and my mood with it.

He pulled up a chair next to me. Jason was still standing.

"Who's this fella?" he said, eyeing the Russian.

I folded my arms on the table and stared at Boyd, wondering why he was here. He didn't have to come to Florida to protect Santangelo's interests.

Richie moved behind Boyd, laid a hand on his shoulder, and squeezed the trapezoid until Boyd, all 6'4" of him, rose to face Richie, his face red, a sharp contrast with his white hair.

"I ain't got no quarrel with you," he said, pushing Richie's hand away as they squared off. I stood up and moved between them. I felt like a man trapped between two bears about to tear at each other.

"Asshole," I heard Richie mutter, as he shoved himself away from me, loud enough for Boyd to hear. Boyd tried to push around me.

"Trouble here?" I heard a voice behind me. A tall, thin man was making his way across the plaza wearing a Marlin's baseball cap. Easy to spot. A big M across the front of the hat. Rare in Florida. Nobody's a Marlin fan here. Except Phillip Michael Thomas who was walking toward me.

"No problems," I said, warning Richie and Boyd with a quick look. Boyd was evaluating the newcomer.

"I got a problem. You see the paper today?" Thomas said, clearly agitated.

"I just did," I said, nodding toward the paper spread out on the table.

"The AP story about the case you're on," he continued.

"Uh-huh. Meet the reporter," I said, nodding at Jason.

"You stirred up a lotta trouble with your story, fella. Homeland Security decided these guys are a threat to national security." Then he turned his anger back on me. "They called the chief this morning. Said this is their case now. So now it's outta our hands," Phillip Michael Thomas complained, his palms up like I had just screwed him.

"So...? What about the boat?" I said, ignoring his drama. I motioned for him to sit down, get a life, chill.

Thomas grabbed a seat next to me showing his reluctance to be appeased by yanking it out and sitting down hard. He noticed the Russian. He looked like he was about to say something, then went on:

"Long story short, the Russians you're looking for are a threat to national security. That and the kidnapping of a foreign student and the killing of another, it all adds up to federal involvement."

"Yeah, but the FBI is already involved."

"I'm just saying—Chief Olmas told me to relay the message to you, Cooper—and your friends," and he looked at the others around the table. "Y'all are done here."

Richie was glaring. "Douche bag," he muttered, under his breath. Thomas heard it and looked quickly over at Richie. But Richie was looking out over the water like an innocent bystander.

Leo stood up, walked to the railing overlooking the Intracoastal Waterway, stretched his body out as far as his 6'4" frame would allow him, and strained to look up the waterway.

Then, loud enough for us all to hear, he said, "Out there is my granddaughter, maybe in that boat down there," pointing at something beyond our sight. Then he turned to face the man who had brought the bad news. "I will not sit and drink vodka while my little girl is in the hands of those devils. I will not allow her to think that I sit by while this… this thing is happening to her. And you…" turning toward Thomas, "you tell me to do nothing! Let me tell you this. I will not stand by. I will find them and when I do I will kill them. And then I will take my granddaughter back to Russia with me and never come back to your country again!" And he turned back to the water, raised his fists, and brought them down on the wooden railing he had been leaning on with such force that it splintered and gave away, parts of it falling onto the tile of the plaza and parts falling into the water below. Then Leo caught himself, like a storm interrupted, and turned toward Thomas, his eyes on fire:

"I will do whatever I have to do to save my granddaughter, sir."

58

WHERE IS THE BOAT?

W e stared at Leo for a few moments, then Thomas leaned over to me.

"Holy Christmas, is that man for real?"

"You better believe it," I said. "Holy Christmas?"

"You're going to have to restrain him," he said, not moving in his chair.

"Uh-huh. So I take it, you're not going to help us now?"

"Like I said, it's not my case anymore," and he held up his hands to show me how helpless he was.

"Where's the boat?" I said.

Thomas shook his head. "If I tell you, then you and your boys are going to go after it. I can't allow you to do that," he added, softly, looking over at Leo to see if he heard him.

"You're going to sit here and do nothing when you damn well know there's probably a kidnapped girl onboard?"

"Not so loud!" he whispered. "All I know is I looked for the boat and it's no longer in the harbor."

I was struggling to keep from strangling him. But I couldn't. It would be like beating up on Christmas.

"Let me guess," I said, getting even more exasperated, "you actually saw the boat leave the harbor—and you never told me."

He got up.

"I didn't say I saw it leave," he argued, defensively. "I said it was not at its slip any longer. I don't know where it is."

"Why don't I believe you? You told me a couple of hours ago it was in the marina. Were you lying?"

He looked miffed. "I didn't see it, Cooper. I was going on what the marina staff told me. They must not have known it was already gone."

I shook my head. "All right. Forget it." Passive aggressive—I know. "But you led me to believe you would help and I'm holding you to it."

Thomas nodded. "I understand and I'm sorry." He paused. Then, "I just don't have any more information. I'm hoping the Coast Guard will be able to intercept them. But it's a big ocean out there."

"What kind of a boat do you have?"

"The Marine Pearl. It's a twenty-five-footer we use in the Intracoastal Waterway. It's not meant for an ocean chase," he added quickly. "The Russian boat's fast. It'd be easier to chase down that bad boy on one of our jet skis."

We all stood around looking at each other for a minute or so.

"Well, while we're waiting around here, the bastards are in the ocean heading for wherever. Maybe back to Russia for all we know," said Jason. We all looked at him, like what the heck was he still doing here?

"What?" he said. "I'm part of this thing. I got the first lead. I wrote the story. I'm staying with it," he insisted, all the while looking at me for reassurance.

I nodded—against my better judgment.

Richie said something under his breath.

Huck just cleared his voice and looked up at the sky, "Git yerself killed, sonny boy," looking sideways over at Jason.

"I'm in it, one way or another," stated Jason, giving Huck the angry kid's stare.

I rang DeFelice.

"What's up, bud," he said, answering on the second ring.

"When did you get caller ID on your cell?" I said.

"You're kiddin'," he said.

"Yeah," I said, and then told him about the Russians and the boat.

"I'll check with the Coast Guard, Cooper. Don't you do this yourself, you hear?"

"I hear you, Tony," I said.

"That means you're staying on dry land?"

"Maybe," I said, and ended the call. As I did, I noticed the Russian watching me and had an idea.

"I think we're done with this guy," I said to Leo, pointing to the Russian. "Tell him we're going to drop him off at the condo where we found him."

Leo pulled the Russian aside and told him something. I wasn't sure what it was. But I could tell by the man's reaction that it was probably close to what I had said to tell him.

"Who's this guy?" said Thomas, pointing at the Russian.

"Just a guy we picked up. A friend of Leo's."

He didn't look convinced but didn't say anything.

"I think I'm done here. Homeland Security knows about the boat. So it's out of my hands. The same applies to you," he warned.

I nodded. But he didn't believe me. I could tell. He adjusted his Marlins cap and walked back the way he had come in.

What we did was load the Russian back into the SUV, drove to Sunny Isles, and dropped him off in the parking lot of the high rise where Taisia's boyfriend had been killed. I gave him his wallet and cell phone and got back into the Land Cruiser. He stood there for a short time, staring at us, then began to back away toward the apartment building as I pulled out of the lot. When we were out of sight, Huck and I jumped out and headed back to the apartment complex. We got there just as the Russian turned away from the apartment and headed back toward Ocean Highway. If he would have been paying attention, he would have seen us. He walked south when he came to the main drag. We followed.

He stopped at a diner, looked up and down the street, no doubt checking to see if someone was following, and then entered the restaurant. It was 5:50 p.m. The edge of darkness was just beginning to creep over the streets when we settled on a spot across the highway under towering date palms that fronted the luxury high-rises overlooking the Atlantic. We found a bench that faced a walkway leading to one of the towers where we could sit and watch the diner and be relatively safe from being observed.

About a block south of the diner was an Italian restaurant. Its lights were just coming on to fight back the shadows of the oncoming night. A black limo had pulled up to the entrance, the driver jumping out to hold the door for his client. A tall thin, blonde in a short, tight, white dress and high heels was the first one out. A big man with thick gray hair, white shirt, and black pants climbed out behind her.

"Wonder if they have coffee to go?" said Huck, still staring at the couple.

"Why don't you check it out," I said, bringing my attention back to the diner. I could see the Russian at a booth fronting the street, talking on his cell. He signed off abruptly when the waitress came over. She stared at him for a few moments, maybe having trouble figuring out what he was saying, maybe noticing how strong his body odor was. Finally, she left and he broke out the cell again, looking out over the street as he talked. Waiting for someone.

Huck was already across the street heading for the Italian place. He was back in about ten minutes with two steaming mugs.

"No Styrofoam?" I said.

"No way, mi amigo," he said, "place's too fancy." He handed me a cup.

"Decaf, right?" I said.

"You betchum, Red Ryder. Sugar and milk's already in her." Then, "You know that blonde is a heck of a lot purtier up close than she is from far away. That fella she's with looks like her grampa! She don't look much more'n about twenty years old."

An hour had passed since the Russian had entered the diner. He got up and walked to the door, opened it, and looked out. There was a young girl and a man walking a dog. That was it. Traffic on the street was sparse, but then it was only Tuesday. Not a big day for restaurants.

A car pulled into the diner's lot. An elderly couple got out and helped each other to the door. The Russian went back to his table and pulled out his phone again. He was shaking his head, looking disturbed. The waitress had been watching him from behind the counter. There were only a few people seated at the tables, though the bar itself was mostly full. She brought coffee over to him again. He sat and drank.

He leaned into the window when he spotted a black Mercedes pull into the lot. It was a 300 series. One of my favorites. Boxy look. The black sheen of the car's finish strutted in the lights of the diner. It could have been pulling up to the Academy Awards.

"Looks like that got his attention," said Huck, pointing to the Benz and then to the window of the diner where the Russian was peering out. A woman climbed out. She was tall, maybe 5'10", in a dark leather jacket and skintight leather pants. The pants reflected the light from the diner as she walked. Just like the car. It was about 8:00 p.m. and there was a chill in the air. I was sorry I hadn't brought my jacket. It was in the Land Cruiser. All I had on was a light polo with a T-shirt under it. Huck was smart. He had his deer skin jacket and pants. Daniel Boone in the big city.

The woman sat down opposite the Russian, looked up at the waitress, and ordered something. Then she turned her attention to the Russian, leaning forward and waiving her hands around like someone giving a servant a lecture about not doing something right. Then she leaned back in her seat, looked around the diner, and then out the window, as though she was looking for someone. We were hidden from her now, the darkness having settled in.

I had never had a clear picture of Maryana. But this woman behaved exactly as I would have expected. Cool, deadly serious, and focused on what she was doing. The Russian got up and headed for the rear of the diner, looking back at her, nervously. A bathroom call. He stumbled against one of the bar stools on the way.

The woman was still surveying the darkness, peering up Ocean Boulevard where the glass of the towering buildings facing the ocean played with the lights from the highway fronting them. Waiting for someone? She looked our way, keeping her gaze in our direction. We both melted into the shadows as far as we could. Then she looked away again. Probably admiring Donald Trump's towers not far from us.

The Russian came back from the bathroom, returned to the table, and then they both headed for the cash register, the woman picking up the check. He was talking to her the whole time, like he was trying to appease. They headed for the Mercedes. I called Richie.

"They're leaving. Pick us up now."

I saw the lights of the Land Cruiser as it pulled out of a parking lot just north of where we were. He picked us up as the Russian and his friend melted into the sparse Tuesday night traffic heading south toward God knows where—but we would soon find out. We followed their tail lights—staying about fifty yards or so behind—and soon Ocean Highway became Collins Avenue where the high-rises mixed with restaurants and the traffic turned denser. They finally turned into a gated luxury townhouse complex about a mile down beach on the ocean side of Collins. Expensive real estate.

Richie whistled. "Some serious money here, son." I looked at my arm. Imagined $100,000. I wondered if I would really miss it that much. Pay off my mortgage, one arm at a time. Richie pulled over to the other side of the road as the guard let them through. After they had cleared the entrance, he pulled up to the gatehouse. I showed the guard my badge.

"Private investigator?" he said. "So…?"

"I'm investigating a case that involves the two people you just admitted. I need to get in."

"I don't know," he said, looking confused. I pressed on.

"Listen, I'm a private investigator, right? And this lady in the back," pointing to Louise, "is a Miami PD detective, okay?" He nodded, but still uncertain.

Louise pulled her shield and stuck it out the back window. He nodded again.

Before he could say anything, I continued: "I'm licensed by the State of Florida, to investigate crimes, find missing people, and provide that information to the lawful authorities who have hired me—just like you are to man this gate."

He looked back at Louise.

"Open the gate," she said. Cop's voice. She was still leaning out the window and holding up the shield, like *Move it, buster.*

He nodded. "Sorry. Just trying to do my job."

"So are we," said Louise, as the gate went up and Richie pulled in.

"Great security, huh?" said Richie, pulling his mouth sidewise into a smirk.

"Yeah," I said, showing my irritation. "Thanks for the help," I said, turning back to Louise. "Shield helps." She nodded.

Richie pulled into a circle that enclosed a large ornate fountain. Water was tumbling out of a boy's mouth, filling the pond beneath his feet. Richie parked in a visitor's space in front of a two-story, Mission Revival building with a stucco finish. I asked Huck, our tracker from the Everglades, to find out where our friends had gone. He hopped out and was back in less than three minutes.

"Got 'em," he said. "The Benz and the unit. Car's parked in the drive of a multi-bird townhouse." *A multi-bird townhouse?* Another Huxterism, I figured.

"Address is twenty-four hundred," he added in a whisper, acting like a P.I. doing reconnaissance.

Richie locked the Cruiser and we followed our tracker, on foot, the tassels on his deer skin jacket jumping as he walked.

A red cobblestone street formed a circle in front of the main building. Behind the building was a boulevard lined with townhouses on each side. Thirty-foot palms rose to the rooftops of the homes, towering over gas street lamps that flickered over the street. A ghostly scene at 8:30 p.m. I saw the Mercedes about three-quarters of the way down the street parked in the drive of a townhouse on our left. A light shivered in the second story window. The front lawn was in darkness, except for a dim light cast by a street lamp about thirty feet away.

"What now?" said Richie as we stared at the house. We were about three buildings from the townhouse and out of view of the lighted window. Since there were five of us standing there, we couldn't maintain that position long without attracting attention. So we needed a plan. Some of the buildings looked to be three-unit structures, others were two. The one we were looking at was a two-unit. The distance between the buildings was about twenty feet or more. So I pointed to a space between two buildings up the street from the 2400 building. Richie, Leo, and I headed there. Louise and Huck hung out in the front.

Behind the buildings was a playing field that stretched out to a development on the other side—about a hundred yards away. To our left and just behind the main building was what appeared to be a sports complex. Some tennis courts and a pool. Several players moved under the meager lights hanging above the courts, like figures in chiaroscuro in a mobile painting. The other end of the field, off to our right, was totally dark.

We headed in that direction—into the darkness—making our way carefully out onto the field so as not to get too close to the house and be spotted. We were now about a hundred feet from the rear of the townhouse and directly behind it. A light suddenly appeared on the third floor. We were still in darkness. The garage took up most of the first floor, though there was a window in the back side of the building, about mid-level to the garage, higher than a ground level window would ordinarily be. I figured it to be an extra room. An office perhaps. A good place to start.

I checked the frame above the window. No sign of security contacts. The window opened easily. My guess, the owners figured they had a gate and a guard to keep them safe. Big mistake. Richie struggled with the narrow space then reached down to help me up. I made it through easily with a boost from Leo. The big man stayed outside. He was clearly too big to fit through the space. Besides, who needs an entire invasion force to enter a house?

"Voices," whispered Richie, and pointed toward a stairway leading up into the main house. We were clearly in an office. A faint light filtered down from upstairs into the room. There was a desk to my left with several laptops on it.

File cabinets flanked it, a copy machine rested on top. On the right side of the room, there was a door. I wondered if it led into the garage. I opened it. It was too dark to see anything. I felt for a switch on the wall outside the door. Found one and hit it. Bingo. It was a closet. Boxes were stacked inside and to the right of the door in a corner.

On closer investigation, the boxes were of similar size and all marked UPS. I opened one. What I found inside jumped out at me like a nasty dream: boxed sets of surgical tools. I pulled the boxes out, one by one, and opened several, carefully and quietly. One box contained a metal ruler. Another, six operating scissors, each about six inches long. Another, all sizes and shapes of forceps, the light, dim though it was, bouncing angrily off their handles, as though it knew their purpose. Then I tore open more boxes, less careful now, more angry, trying to breathe away the horror of it all. Two serrated knives. Two Mayo dissecting scissors. A pair of forceps with a ratchet. I knew what that was for. A variety of clamps, including a bone-cartilage clamp. My skin burned when I held them. Some needle-nose pliers. A bone mallet.

Each instrument was clearly identified. Two Hibbs Osteotomes. Two Hibbs chisels. Do I need to explain? Towel clamps. Three or more retractors. And three Frazier Suction Tubes. Good Lord Almighty. A veritable supply store for surgery.

I turned around and Richie had opened the door, staring at the collection of tools I had laid out. I turned off the light immediately.

"Shit," he whispered. "That what I think it is?"

"Yeah," I said, shaking my head at the array of tools. "I think we'll find the same stuff in the rest of the boxes."

I packed up the boxes again, hastily, and turned back to the window where we had crawled in and motioned for Richie to follow. He paused, like, *you leaving this stuff?* but followed me back outside anyway.

Leo moved out of the shadows. Louise and Huck were with him.

"What?" said Huck.

I told them what we had found

"She's going to have to deliver that hardware to the boat. So we'll babysit this place until they come out."

We divided up our time for surveillance, Richie agreeing to take the first shift. The rest of us would stay at a nearby hotel until our time to keep watch came. I was convinced she would take the tools and the Russian to the boat tomorrow. Don't ask me why. That hunch again.

Richie dropped us at a Hampton Inn about a half-mile away. I had informed the security guard on the way out that we were doing surveillance. He said, *Sure man, cool.* He was a young black man, taking courses at the local community college in criminal justice. He asked if I had any openings in my firm. I said there was nothing now. But I would call him if I did. *That's cool*, he said, and scribbled down his cell number.

THURSDAY MORNING, OCTOBER 21

Huck and Louise spelled Richie through the night. Two-hour shifts. I took the early morning watch, parking near the entrance and picking a spot under a palm across the street and out of the line of sight of anyone leaving the building. The plan was, when the woman and the Russian left in the Mercedes, I would follow in the Land Cruiser and give Richie a call. The key to surveillance is not to blow your cover. Once that happens, it's all over, baby. I would make sure that didn't happen.

At 7:36 a.m. the woman, still dressed in black—jeans now—and in the same leather jacket, appeared at the entryway of the building. The Russian was right behind her carrying boxes I assumed were the same ones I had seen last night. He loaded them into the trunk, the lady holding the lid for him. The Russian went back into the building and a few minutes later he came out with another armload. They were planning a lot of surgeries.

The woman slammed the trunk lid and they got in. I crossed the street and headed behind the townhouses, hurrying across the field, past the swimming pool and tennis courts, and through a narrow passage between the main building and the row of homes behind it. I got into the SUV just as they were approaching the exit. The security guard gave me the high sign as I passed him. I gave him a nod and thumbs up. He smiled.

The Mercedes turned south on Ocean Highway. I waited for a few cars to pass before I followed and called Richie.

"I'm behind them," I said. "I'll come back and pick you guys up when I find out where the boat is."

"You got it, bud," said Richie. "Don't do this alone," he warned.

The Mercedes was staying just above the speed limit. Two cars ahead of me.

My cell again.

"Coop."

"Hi Louise," I said.

"I just got some information from Interpol on Maryana."

"Good. What have you got?"

"Word is she's Kolya's girlfriend and she sounds like a psychopathic cold-blooded bitch," she said, blaring into the phone. After she calmed herself, she continued: "She"—surprised she didn't say *the bitch* again—"ran an orphanage in Moscow that took in kids who were strays or just poor. Strays mostly so they wouldn't be missed. And she ran a boarding school there. So parents who didn't have money left their children with her—you know, free education. And then when the poor unsuspecting parents would come to pick them up a year or so later, the kids would be gone! *Adopted*, the bitch would say—can you believe it? Fact is, she sold them to her boyfriend." And she paused like this was more than her brain could handle. Then, "That's it. I can't talk about this anymore," and she let out a sigh, deep and hollow.

"I understand." How could anyone tell that story and not feel it?

"Did you get a description of this monster?" I said.

"Yeah. I got a picture on my iPhone. She's the wicked witch of the west—brown eyes, hard face. This looks like a prison picture. I wouldn't wanta meet her at an orphanage door. Some stats: she's thirty five years old, five feet ten, 135 pounds."

"Sounds like the woman in front of me," I said, trying to shake the images of the orphanage from my mind.

The Mercedes was still two cars ahead. We were on A1A in the town of Surfside and had just passed through Bal Harbour and about a thousand of the nation's wealthiest people while I was on the phone with Louise. Miami Beach was just ahead.

"You still there?"

"Uh-huh. I can't tell where this woman is headed," I replied. "We're in Miami Beach now. You guys need to rent a car—now. I don't want to get too far ahead of you."

"We're already on it," she said. "Richie took a cab to a rental agency and should be back any minute."

Miami Beach was crowded this morning, skateboarders weaving in and out of traffic on Collins Avenue, ignoring the cars and the horns. Welcome to South Beach. Guys holding hands, girls, with almost no clothes on, hawking seats in the restaurants facing the ocean. An entrée, only $9.99. Any entrée. The thing they don't tell you is the drinks are $25.00—each. They tell you that at the end—when the bill comes. I know. It happened to me. A guy next to our table, from the Caribbean, kept complaining about his bill, warning me and my companion: "Damn bill's over $300," throwing up his hands and yelling to me and everyone in the street, "It's a rip-off!" I nodded. He smiled, enjoying his tirade, and continued it, laughing and cursing the *damn thieves*. The woman with him looked embarrassed—so did the woman with me.

A girl was running into the water at the beach, no top. A guy with an 8mm camera followed her closely yelling out encouragement and directions. She seemed to enjoy it, smiling and dancing in the sand. But maybe that was all part of the act. I was staring and she noticed.

The Mercedes swung off the beach and took the 836 to the mainland. Wild goose chase? She caught I-95 south that cuts through downtown Miami, past office buildings with neon towers. At night they light up blue, green, and yellow soft, bathing the city in color—it's beautiful really—but they hide all larcenies, assaults, batteries, and murders that take place in the streets below them.

The freeway caught up with US 1 just north of Coconut Grove.

I called Richie.

"How's that rental coming?" I said.

"Just driving off the lot, buddy. Got a Durango."

"Good," I said. "It looks like we're headed for the Keys. I'll call you as soon as I'm sure. Right now, follow 95 to US 1."

"I'm on my way," he said.

I checked my gas. Half a tank.

59

KEY LARGO

I was right. A half hour later we were exiting the Florida Turnpike—we had picked it up at Cutler Bay where US 1 intersects the turnpike—and were now heading into Florida City. I remember a ticket I got there. Ran a red light—by mistake. Told the guy who stopped me I was a cop. He said, "So?" I told him he needed to have more respect for the uniform. He gave me a ticket anyway. He apologized later when he ran into me at South Station in Miami—*Just visiting,* he said. Surprised to see me. *Apology accepted*, I said, and punched him in the arm. Hard. Laughing like I was good with it. He was still rubbing his arm when he left. He didn't know whether to laugh or not.

From Florida City the Russians jumped back on US 1 and headed south on what's now called the Overseas Highway, overseas because it stretches for over a hundred miles over open waters between the Straits of Florida and the Gulf of Mexico. When you descend on US 1 past the eastern end of the Everglades and approach Barnes Sound that separates the mainland from the Keys, the boundless expanse of the Straits and the Atlantic Ocean open up and you enter the highway via a ten-mile bridge that empties into the first of the Keys, Key Largo, and serves as the starting point of the Overseas Highway. The black surface of the Mercedes reflected the light of the noon sun as it headed out over the Bay into the Florida Keys.

"Where are you, buckaroo?" said Huck as I picked up my cell.

I told him and asked where they were.

"We're coming out of South Miami and heading for the Florida Pike, hombre. Keep your eyes peeled. We'll be on you faster than bees on a honey bear."

I heard Richie say, *Gimme that damn phone.* Then, "We'll be in Largo in about an hour most," he said. "Let me know when you stop."

"Will do," I said and watched the Mercedes disappear into a line of traffic. I caught up with it and kept a Jeep Cherokee between us. The first of the Keys was visible in the distance, about two miles away.

My cell buzzed again. I had turned off the ringer because I had heard the Canon enough already.

"Yeah," I said.

"Mr. Cooper?"

"That's right."

"Hi. Mr. Cooper, this is Officer Cleveland Wong. Homeland Security. Where are you now?"

Just like that. Where am I now? Where were his manners?

"Where am I now?" I said.

"You're looking for a young girl, I understand."

I told him that's right.

"We need to talk," he said.

'I'm on a bridge," I said.

He was silent for a moment. "I'm with ICE. I've been assigned to investigate the homicide of the young man you found in Sunny Isles Beach, Florida. The young girl you're looking for is part of our investigation as well."

I thought about it for a moment. So Immigration and Customs Enforcement is involved. I loved the acronym, ICE. Sounds so…what? Cool? I remembered when Rodriquez first announced the agency's inception—a merger of U.S. Customs and Immigration and Naturalization.

He broke in again. "Where are you now? And don't tell me you're on a bridge, Mr. Cooper," he said with an edge to his voice. Wong must have been the one who called Olmos.

"I'm pulling into the Keys right now. Where are you?"

"In a heliport in Miami. There's a good bar in Key Largo, right side of the Overseas Highway, used to claim it was the bar where Casablanca was shot. The Caribbean Café. I'll meet you there in 45 minutes." How was that supposed to work? Where would he land?

"I'm following a car with a woman who was involved in kidnapping the young girl I'm looking for. I need to continue to follow her. If I don't, she's gone." I hung up. My cell rang again. I didn't answer it. So arrest me.

The Mercedes pulled into a gas station just off the bridge on the left side of the highway. I passed the station and pulled off at Lake Surprise Road, the first street on my left. I turned the SUV around so I was parked facing the highway, just far enough from the road to be out of sight, and waited until they reappeared. The Mercedes passed me about ten minutes later. I waited for a car to pass behind it and pulled back onto the highway.

The traffic got denser suddenly and several other cars pulled out in front of the car ahead of me as the driver slowed for intersections. I was ready to pass him when the Mercedes turned suddenly onto a side street on the right. It disappeared behind a restaurant on the corner. I got to the intersection just as the Mercedes turned into the first street on the left and disappeared from view. I looked at the street sign. Avenue A. Colorful name.

I made a left on Avenue A just in time to see the Mercedes making a right. I pulled up to the street. First Road. The Russians passed an open field on the right and pulled into the drive of a two-story. I backed away from the road so that I was about ten feet from the intersection, and parked behind a buccaneer palm. Its fronds, with a growth of yellow summer flowers, gave me some cover.

Richie keeps binoculars under his seat. I used them to peer through the branches and watched the woman and the Russian step out of the car. The woman checked her shoe—broken heel? —and then they both headed up a short stairway to the porch. Overhead was another porch that fronted the entire upper floor. I saw a curtain part in the side window on the upper floor. A face appeared momentarily when the car door slammed and then disappeared when the Russians reached the porch. I wondered if this was Taisia.

60

THE FACE IN THE WINDOW

THURSDAY AFTERNOON, OCTOBER 21

It was midafternoon now. The sun was heading for the west and the moon was trying to force its way through a thin layer of clouds on the horizon. A First Quarter Moon. Seagulls played over the rooftops of houses fronting the Straits, diving and soaring back into the sky like planes in a dogfight.

As I reached for my cell to check on Richie, it went off.

"Cooper?" It was Cleveland.

"We must have gotten cut off." Oops. But I was grateful for the excuse.

"Sorry about that," I said. "By the way. A personal question. The name Cleveland? I hope you don't mind. The reason I'm asking—I grew up there."

He laughed.

"I did too. I was born there and my father wanted to honor my birth in our new country. So…Cleveland. Talking about names, Cooper…?"

"I know," I said. "Same name—first and last—blame my father."

"Yeah, I guess we both should." Laughing again. "Okay, back to business. Where are you now?"

"Hiding and surveilling," I said.

"Where are you surveilling?"

"Key Largo. But a helicopter would scare the hell out of the people I'm following. It's a lot better if I do this myself. Quietly."

No response. Then, "Right. I can come by ground and be there in three to four hours."

"The Russians may be gone by then."

"Good point."

"Have you located the boat yet?"

"No. There's a lot of water out there, Cooper. Tell me. What makes you think you're following the right people?" Here we go again.

"A hunch."

"A hunch?"

"That's right." He was silent for a few moments.

"Okay. Any *hunch* about where this *so-called big boat* is?" He had definitely been talking to Olmos.

"None whatsoever," I said.

"Let me know if you get one." And he ended the call.

I could hear the noise of a helicopter in the distance, the whipping sound of its rotors receding as I turned back to the Russian house. I called Richie.

"Yeah, what's up, boss?" he said.

"Okay. Our friends have found a home and I'm sitting down the street from it. Where are you?"

"Just coming off the bridge." A pause. "Entering Key Largo. Where are you?"

I read off the intersection. He was pulling in behind me in less than five minutes. I walked back to the rental, a black Jeep Durango. Louise was in the front.

Richie rolled his window down. "Did I do something wrong, officer?"

"Your license," I said, smiling for the first time today and holding out my hand.

"Too bad you ain't in Cleveland," he said. "I mighta give you a hunnert."

"I'm one of the good guys, Richie. I would have taken fifty." He snorted and Louise smiled.

"How you doing, babe?" I said, looking across Richie to Louise.

"I'm doin' fine, babe. How you doin'?" giving me her tough guy voice.

"Okay. Touché," I replied, pulling back from the car.

Richie's Jeep was concealed from 1st Road by a house. No one on the street seemed to be paying attention to us. So we took turns watching and waiting. There was no activity at the Russian's house. A few cars passed, none turning onto 1st Road.

The moon slowly emerged more distinctly as the late afternoon turned into early evening, the sun diving with the birds for the horizon.

A Key Largo police cruiser pulled up next to me. I was in the Land Cruiser. The cop rolled down his window.

"I called you guys earlier this afternoon," I said. "I didn't want you screwing up our surveillance."

The cop nodded. "You guys want some donuts?" he said, smiling. Fucking with me. "How long you gonna be here?"

"I don't know," I said. "Your vehicle is pretty visible."

He rolled up his window, waved and moved on. I looked back at the house to see if anyone came out. No activity. I called the Key Largo Police again to remind them of what we were doing. The officer on duty said, "No problem."

"Damn," said Louise, shaking her head. "All we need."

I watched the darkness moving in off the ocean, slowly overtaking the waves pushing shoreward, and I watched it as it crept toward the houses along the streets leading to the beaches, and I watched it as it moved up the walls of the two-story and into the window where I had seen the face, and I thought I saw it one more time before darkness swallowed it up and I knew that we had to get in there before the night was over.

I walked over to Richie's Jeep and motioned for him to roll down his window.

"Ready?" I said, leaning in. Leo and Huck, dozing in the back, jumped and looked around as though getting their bearings. Richie reached behind his seat for his bat.

He noticed me watching him, concerned. "No worries," he said, pulling back his jacket to reveal the Browning HP JMP.

"Okay, then let's do it," I said.

There were no streetlights. But there was the fall sky, full of stars. I could almost picture our forms, backlit against the moon as we headed toward the house, Richie with his bat, Huck with his alligator gun, Leo with Richie's Mossberg, and Louise and I out in front of this grim procession.

"I'll take the back of the house," whispered Louise, as we neared the porch.

I nodded. "Take Leo and Huck with you. Richie and I will cover the front."

So Richie and I mounted the steps to the front porch—no sound at all. Amazing because they were wood. I waited for Louise, Huck, and Leo to clear the side of the house, then tried the door handle. It turned and we moved into the darkness. It was after midnight. I was hoping everyone was asleep.

The first thing I noticed was the smell of alcohol. *Not here*, I thought. *Surely not here!* Then flashes of light exploded like popcorn in the darkness, and I dropped to the floor just inside the doorway, protecting my head like a man caught in a hail storm. I couldn't tell where the shots had come from. But before I could move, someone shoved me out of the doorway, cursing and moving into the room, his form slowly becoming visible. I had dropped my gun when I hit the floor. I was scrambling to find it. Then I heard the sound of something hitting the floor in front of me.

"Richie?" I said in a loud whisper.

"Here," he whispered. And I strained to see where he was. Then a large form emerged in the diminishing darkness, a baseball bat in hand. He was bent over a body lying at the base of a stairway.

We both jumped as shots exploded in the back of the house.

"Damn. Stay down," Richie whispered. "This one's out cold. Maybe I hit her too hard. They musta seen us."

I eased out of the entry area and into what looked to be a dining room just to the right of the doorway. My eyes were getting used to the darkness so I could now discern the general layout of the first floor. There was a living room to the left of the entryway. The stairway that fronted the entryway led to an open hall that overlooked the front door. A railing ran up the right side of the stairway, across the front of the second floor hallway, and ended at what I assumed to be a bedroom.

A bar separated the kitchen from the dining room. I stayed below it. Richie had left the unconscious woman and had moved next to me.

I took a quick look over the bar and pulled back as a shotgun exploded from the kitchen.

I wondered where the hell Louise, Huck, and Leo were. All we needed was to shoot one of them. I held up a hand to warn Richie. He grunted.

We waited. I knew that whoever was in the kitchen was trapped between the five of us.

Then the kitchen door exploded and a shot gun blast lit up the kitchen sending debris flying into the dining room.

'Richie? Coop?" Louise's voice, low and hoarse. "Where are you?"

"Over here," I whispered loud enough to stir the undead. "By the bar," louder yet, but throaty. Then a light came on in the kitchen.

"It's the Russian," said Louise, standing over a body, a puddle of blood gathering around him. "I guess we won't be dragging him around any longer," she observed. She was right. And we never even knew his name.

"I was tired of carryin' that varmint around anyway," said Huck, staring at the remains of the Russian. His head, what there was left of it, was turned further right than it should be.

"Where's this woman? Maryana Zorin?" demanded Leo. Nobody paid any attention. We were all fixated on the widening pool of blood.

Then Leo joined in the staring. I bent toward his ear. "In the entryway. For all I know, Richie killed her with his bat."

Almost immediately Maryana begin to stir, as though she heard us talking about her, a low gurgling sound bubbling from her throat. I rushed over—don't ask me if I cared—and turned her on her side to stop her from choking on her own vomit.

"Damn woman. Shoulda killed her," Richie muttered behind me.

"Watch her," I told Richie. I had heard a sound from the upstairs hall. I looked over at Louise. She heard it too. We moved slowly up the stairway, Louise leading the way. We had only the light from the kitchen, dim along the stairway, the upper hallway dark. As I cleared the top step I saw a young girl, sitting just outside the door of the room at the end of the hallway. Louise gasped. A young boy was with her also. Was this Taisia? She drew back when she saw the guns in our hands, clutching the young boy against her body, his arms wrapped around her.

"We're friends," I said gently to the two children and looked for a hall light. Louise found it.

The children scooted into the corner where the rail met the outside wall of the bedroom. There were some red stains on the girl's dress. Blood?

"Is there anyone else here?" I whispered to the girl, moving closer to her, carefully so as not to alarm her, like approaching a deer to pet it. She shook her head—barely. Unsure about us. I wondered if she understood what I had asked her. I turned to Louise who was hovering over my back.

"Does she speak English?" Louise said softly.

I shrugged.

The girl looked into my eyes and nodded. There was such darkness there. Then she was rubbing the boy's back, murmuring softly to him, and staring through the rail. She was looking at Maryana. She turned back, her eyes meeting mine once again.

"Is she dead?" the girl whispered. An accent there I couldn't identify. She was watching me and chewing on her finger.

"No," I said.

"Oh," she said, disappointed. "She was going to kill us," she added, almost as an afterthought.

"Did she hurt you?" I asked as I drew even closer, bending over now so I was at eye level. The blood on her dress clear now.

"Yes," she said. "I wish you had killed her."

"What did she do?" I said, afraid to hear her answer.

"She had a doctor operate on me," she said. I heard Louise murmur, "Oh, Cooper." Tears started to run down the face of the young girl as I crouched down in front of her. The boy was shaking so hard I could feel it through the floor.

"What's your name?" I said to her.

"Tania."

"And your brother's?"

"He's not my brother. We just call him Sly."

"We?" I said.

"At the orphanage," she said.

"At the orphanage," I said, repeating it, the horror of what she was saying sinking in. I put my arms around them both as I settled next to them on the floor and said that everything was going to be all right. I was staring at the Russian woman now, and then at Leo. I could tell by the look on his face that he wanted to kill the woman and was only waiting for me to give him a sign. I gave no indication. Maybe I wanted him to kill her. *Go ahead, Leo*, I thought.

Then Richie said, "We need to keep the bitch alive. Find out where the rest of the bastards are…and Taisia." Cooler heads. Maryana looked relieved for the first time since I had seen her.

"Maybe you'd better clean up the mess in the kitchen," I said from the balcony, still holding onto the children. I should have put my hands over their ears. But they had probably seen more than I had in a lifetime.

Louise stayed with them, scooping them into her arms and murmuring into their ears. I went down to help out.

"I'm going to feed him to that big gator I seen in the backyard, Coop," said Huck, pointing toward the kitchen where the Russian was bathing in his own blood. Maryana was watching and listening, curled up like a child hiding from some monster in her room. Her eyes open as wide as a four-lane highway. I think she understood.

"Quiet!" I whispered, and pointed to the children who had clearly heard him. They looked terrified.

"Sorry," he said.

"Take the woman with you," I whispered. "Let her watch." I've been noticing a coldness settling over me for the last several years. I didn't like it. I was changing. I needed to find my son.

I nodded to Leo and Richie to give Huck a hand. Louise was looking down at us as if to say, *What are you doing*! I headed back up the stairs. She shook her head at me as she watched the three men drag Maryana out of the room.

I sat next to Louise. She looking at me like, *How could you*? I just shrugged. We stayed with the girl and boy, Louise now talking with them softly, asking about their home— *No, we don't have one.* Father and mother—They both shook their heads. Any family?—*No.* None?—*No.* Louise turned to me, her cheeks wet, looking utterly ruined. The children were watching my face intently. I told them not to worry. But I worried. Who would take care of them?

Then a scream shot out from the rear of the house, so shrill the children jumped. Louise and I both did too. I felt a chill. What had they done? Leo came back into the entryway, his bloody shirt now damp with sweat. "She wants to talk," he said.

"Okay. Bring her in," I said, leaning over the rail.

Maryana's legs buckled under her as Huck and Richie dragged her through the entry way and into the living room, her face white now, like a corpse. They dumped her onto the couch.

I've watched a lot of horror shows. The directors of those films could never get their actors to duplicate the pure terror in those children's eyes. I asked the girl what had been done to her.

"A doctor took one of my kidneys," she said with a coldness I have never seen in a child—the terror gone now. Interesting. I had heard about how moods change rapidly in those who have suffered traumatic shocks. Tania was fourteen years old, at most, but she had lived a lifetime in hell. Enough pain for a whole world.

I was talking with a priest friend of mine about hell one evening. He said it was still part of Church doctrine. He had no idea that it was really right here.

"That was Maryana's idea?" I said.

"She *told* the doctor to do it," the girl said.

"How long ago was this?" I said.

"About two weeks ago," she replied, matter of fact, looking down at Maryana, her eyes not wavering. Maryana must have sensed something because she looked up and saw the girl, who was now standing at the rail, looking down at her, and she took in a sudden breath that sounded like a rale. And her eyes drifted to the blood on the girl's dress and then to the boy who was now standing next to her. What did I see in Maryana's eyes? It was hard to tell. Fear, maybe, mixed with coldness. I had never met a monster before—not like her. In all my years working homicide—in one of the most dangerous cities in America.

"She was our foster mother," the girl said, still watching Maryana. "And she made that doctor operate on me." Angry. Bitter. I felt sad for her. I half expected to see the doctor standing next to Maryana.

"Did the doctor operate here?" I said. All eyes in the room on Tania.

"No, they did it on a boat," she said. "It's a very big boat. She was going to take us back there tomorrow," and she dropped her eyes, shuffling her feet nervously, then looked up at me. I had never seen such sadness. "But I guess she won't do that now," she said. Some hope, at last.

"No, she will never do that again," I said, and thought that I might have to kill this woman myself. There's that coldness again settling over me.

61

THE BIG BOAT

*O*h, she'll be going there tomorrow, but without the kids, I thought to myself, and looked up to see the others nodding in agreement. ESP. The boat would have to wait for the moment though. We needed to get the children to a doctor. We threw the woman into the rear of Richie's Durango. Leo jumped in the back to keep an eye on her. I was hoping he wouldn't kill her on the way. Huck, Louise, and I and loaded the two young kids into Richie's Cruiser and I headed for my house in the Everglades. We had to drop off Maryana. When we got there, the outside lights were lit, both front and back. I didn't remember leaving them on. Maybe Sammy.

Richie and Leo unloaded Maryana from the rear of the Durango.

"Take her to the porch in the back of the house," I said coming around to the rear of the Jeep. "We'll talk with her there." She was watching me warily. Leo and Richie each grabbed an arm and rough-handled her toward the rear of the house. I watched their forms disappear around the corner, the woman struggling as Huck yanked her along by the hair. Maybe he was looking to scalp her.

"Show her my friend if you see him," I said, referring to the ten-foot gator that lives in my backyard. He was old and never bothered me. But she would not know that.

Louise helped Tania and Sly out of the Cruiser. The children stood dumbly in the drive, rubbing their eyes as they took in the house and the land surrounding it. There is no other house on my street, if you could call it that. In reality it's a dirt road flanked on one side by undergrowth that shields my cottage from the lights of the main highway, and on the other by the now impenetrable darkness of the Great Swamp. With the moon behind us, you could see the edges of the mangroves that stretch across the back of the house, sealing in my land from the swamp.

Louise took Tania's hand. The girl was hanging onto Sly like a desperate mother protecting her only child. Louise helped them up the three wooden stairs onto the porch, murmuring softly as they turned to make sure she was still behind them. Louise looked back when they got to the screen door.

"It's open," I said. "I never lock the door." She looked at me momentarily—maybe wondering about the wisdom of unlocked doors—but shook her head instead and led the children into the house.

I jumped as something brushed against my leg. I looked down and saw Sammy rubbing himself against my foot and purring. He rolled over and I scratched his belly and under his chin. He was satisfied after a few strokes, rolled back to his feet, and meandered toward the house. He looked back several times and meowed to see if I was following. I knew what that meant. Food. So I went to the pantry, found a can of Friskies, opened it, and spooned a half-cup of tuna mix into his bowl.

"We need to clean these poor children up first before we take them to ER," Louise said as I came into the living room. I agreed.

"Look at them," she said, pointing to the children huddling in the middle of the room. Lost. Like kids from an orphanage.

"Let's get you two into the bathroom and into a tub," Louise said. "Sly, let your sister go first and then we'll get you cleaned up after, okay?"

Sly nodded bashfully. "She's not my sister, ma'am," he said.

"That's right. I forgot, Sly. But she's like a sister, isn't she?"

He nodded and dropped his eyes to the floor.

I called DeFelice while Louise was busy with the children.

"You're in trouble," was the first thing out of his mouth, "otherwise you wouldn't be calling me at midnight."

"Stop it, Tony. I'm the best partner you ever had." Then, I filled him in on our raid on the house in Key Largo. And I told him about the kids, leaving out the dead Russian. Only the gator knows about him.

"Damn. That's a fricking crazy story. But I gotta say, good work, partner!" he admitted. Still friends I guess. "Cleveland call you?" he said.

"He did. He doesn't know the latest..." A call was coming in. It was Cleveland.

"Speak of the devil, he's calling me now. Catch you later," and I flashed over to Cleveland.

"So what's happening?" said Cleveland.

"We picked up the Russian woman, Maryana, and two of her victims—a couple of young kids." I left out the information about the dead Russian. "We're taking the children to the local ER. Did you find the boat?"

"No to that, Cooper. We're done for the night. The locals can help you with the kids, by the way. Didn't find your girl, huh?"

"No. Sadly. Just two more sad victims of the bad guys. It's a wonderful world out there, Cleveland."

"Roger that, Cooper. What do you plan on doing with the woman?"

"I have an MPD detective with me. I'll let her handle it."

He was quiet for a moment. Then, "Don't go chasing after a boat without letting me know. We need the Coast Guard for that. Understand?"

"I do," I said, and ended the call.

Louise was already leading Sly out of the bathroom by the time I got off the phone. Tania was standing in the hallway, waiting for them. Both children were wrapped in towels and shivering. Louise was shaking her head and pointing to Tania. *Poor girl* written all over her face, the edges of her mouth turned down like a sad jack-o-lantern. She patted her eyes like she was wiping away tears. I nodded, *I know*. I was glad I didn't have to see the damage the doctor had wreaked.

"They'll be dressed and ready to go in a few minutes," she whispered.

I nodded and called the Oceanside cops.

1:30 A.M.

A police cruiser was parked in front of the ER, its lights flashing in sync with an emergency truck that had just pulled in. I parked in the circle that swung into the ER receiving area.

A doc met us on the way in. Two cops were with him, one tall and one short. I looked a little closer. I knew them. I had met them on an earlier case. Sandy Neumann—300 lb.—forty five years old, and Randall Flagg, a tall skinny guy with bad teeth and enough pockmarks to look like he had been hit with shrapnel. The EMTs rolled Tania through the ER doors and into a corridor that led to receiving rooms, the doc talking with her the whole way. Sly was hanging on to the rail of the gurney.

"Here he is. The private dick," said Flagg, nodding his skinny, balding head, and smiling like isn't he funny? "So, you're the one called it in."

"That's right." What else do you say to a wise guy? You're an idiot?

"So, fill us in, Cooper," said Neumann," pulling his pants up over his stomach. "What've we got here?" Then he noticed Louise. "Detective Delgado! I didn't recognize you at first. What are you doing here?"

"Workin'," said Louise. "Same as you, Neumann."

"Out of your territory, ain't you?" a knowing look floating across his fat face.

"No more'n you," she said, ignoring his game.

Louise is the special detective assigned to gangs in Miami. Since the neighboring departments don't have the personnel to dedicate to one area, like gangs, they use Louise through a special agreement with Miami PD. That included Oceanside. Neumann shut up.

I filled them in, talking to Neumann more than Flagg. That bothered Flagg—how could I tell? His mouth twitched, making the pockmarks dance. I left out the dead Russian and Maryana, walking the fine line between withholding information and serving my client. But I would confess later. I needed the woman to find Leo's grand-daughter. Simple as that.

"Okay. So what're we supposed to do with the kids? We ain't no orphanage," said Flagg, his mouth twitching again when he talked. There go those pockmarks again.

"No kidding?" The man's an idiot.

Flagg looked at me sideways, like was I serious or sarcastic? I glanced over at Neumann who sighed and shook his head.

"Look, Social Services is probably going to take charge of the kids, Flagg. But then you ought to know that, being a police officer here in Oceanside." Flagg was getting red. "In other words, it's not your problem," I said.

Neumann was nodding his head. "No problem, Cooper. We know that," he said, looking at Flagg like he truly was the idiot I thought he was.

"Louise, how you doing?" Neumann said, turning to her. Change the subject.

Louise said she was doing fine, blah, blah, blah, and not to worry, everything's cool. Neumann nodded. Flagg stared at her, then at me.

"Okay," he said. "Then we're out of here," and they both headed for the exit. "Keep us posted," Flagg added without turning around. Big man.

It was 5:05 a.m.

"Who's the responsible person here?" said the doc coming out to the visiting area through the double doors. I said, we were, nodding at Louise.

"You can follow me," he said, looking over his glasses and heading back through the double doors. It was a large space, more like an office with shoulder high modular walls, smelling of alcohol and teeming with nurses, techs, and docs moving from one small receiving room to another, the docs giving orders to the nurses and talking with the patients lying in cots inside. The receiving rooms were scattered in a circle around a central control station. We followed the doctor into a room on our right. There was no one in there. Just the three of us.

I saw the question rising in his eyes as he turned around. He was wearing jeans and tennis shoes.

"Easier on the feet," he said, noticing my eyes on his shoes.

"Tell me about those kids," he said, looking back and forth between Louise and me.

I told him I was a private investigator and that Louise was an MPD detective, that the children had been kidnapped, and that the police would be wanting to talk with them. I also said the only thing I knew for sure was that Tania had told me her kidnappers had taken a kidney and that a doctor had done it.

The doc shook his head. "Damn. He did a pretty bad job of it. I'm afraid we're going to have to go back in and see what the damage is."

I was staring at his nametag.

"Chavez," he said, and then quickly, "no relation."

I nodded. Thank goodness.

"Who's going to take responsibility for the kids?" he said.

"We will, for the time being," I said, and then looked at Louise who was mouthing, *really?* What had I just volunteered us for?

He nodded. "Good, the hospital staff will contact Social Services. Not to worry. I want to thank both of you for what you've done for these kids. You saved their lives."

We both nodded.

"Our job," said Louise, and looked away before I could see her tear up.

The doc assured us a hospital staffer would take care of the children until Social Services came. Louise looked at me like *can we really leave them?* I leaned over and told her we didn't have much choice, did we? She shrugged.

The children were already fast asleep in separate rooms. We peeked in on both.

"The boy just needs some rest and nutrition," Chavez said. "I have called in Dr. Murphrey for a consult on Tania. He's the best surgeon in the Valley," he added, trying to assure us—he must have seen the pain in our eyes. "He'll be here first thing in the morning."

He walked over to Tania's bed and checked her chart. Her eyes fluttered.

"How's the sleepy head?" said Chavez.

Tania nodded that she was okay. She had seen us come into the room. I saw the inkling of a smile catch her eyes.

We were standing next to the bed. Louise squeezed Tania's hand. "You're going to be fine," she said. The girl smiled, a faint, brave one.

Louise looked at me as though she wasn't sure she would be able to leave.

"We'll be back," I said to Tania—I meant it also for Louise. "Got some bad guys to catch."

The nights are never the same after an experience like this. In the darkness, in the silence that comes with it, thoughts and memories return, and they continue, oh yes, they continue, and they don't leave until the sun rises—and even then the taste of them stays with you through the day. But it's better then—when the sun rises. It's better, because

of the distractions of the day. But when the night comes…
It's the same story all over again.

I thought of that as I held Louise. "She'll never get over
it, Coop," she said, her voice muffled in my clothes. I didn't
say anything. What was there to say, *Yes, she will?* And we
stayed that way—my comforting her and she leaning into
me—until the emergency vehicle whose lights I had seen
in the distance pulled into the drive where we were standing. I walked Louise to the Cruiser with my arm around
her shoulders, trying to keep the early morning chill away.

"So what's next?" she said, as we pulled away from the
hospital and the children.

"Maryana," I said.

"Yeah? So what's your plan with her?" I was on Midnight Drive now.

"She's going to tell us where the boat is."

"Uh-huh. And how you gonna make that happen?" The
old Louise, back again.

"Oh ye of little faith," I said.

"Spare me, Cooper."

"Herman," I said.

"Herman? You mean…?"

"Yeah, that Herman. I think he's hungry."

62

HERMAN

It was after nine o'clock when we finally got back to the house. We had stopped for coffee at a Dunkin Donuts to wake up. Richie was the first one out the door when we pulled in. I looked past him and saw Herman lying in the new sun near the mangroves. He likes to hang out in the water beneath the walkway to the boat dock when darkness settles in. This time of day he drags his ten-foot body up on land, well away from the walkway, to a clearing where the sun can beat down on him. He appears to sleep, but I swear I can see one eye open all the time, watching. He has survived by being alert. *What about my cat?* you might ask. My cat has lived with Herman for about seven years now—give or take. He sleeps under the deck behind a wooden grid that fences in the open area below the back porch. They watch each other. I have seen them. But it's a friendly relationship—as long as Sammy far enough away.

"What did the doc say?" said Richie, anxiety riding his words like a concerned uncle.

304

"He says he has to operate again," I said.

Richie gritted his teeth and shook his head. "Fuckin' butchers."

Huck and Leo were eating in the kitchen when we walked in.

"Not good, huh?" said Huck. Leo looked up from his plate, worry in his eyes.

I just shook my head. Louise filled them in while I went to the kitchen for a glass, pumped some ice out of the refrigerator door, and filled it with water. I thought about the day ahead. Richie had followed behind me. He put an arm around my shoulder and asked what's next. I told him about Herman. He smiled.

"The gator," he said.

"The gator," I said.

"Let's take her to the back porch," I said.

Leo went with us to the back room where Maryana was lying on a bed, her hands and feet bound with duct tape. There was no need to gag her. Mine was the only house around. I told Leo to ask her about the large boat. He did. She shook her head. So, it looked like alternative 'B'. Herman, was the next step.

I cut off the tape and helped her from the bed. She struggled to get her balance.

Then we took her through the kitchen to the back porch, Huck helping, Leo and Richie following. Louise was sitting on the couch in the living room. Not approving.

"Don't do this, Coop," she said. I told her not to worry. She shook her head and waved me off like *You're going to do what you're going to do anyway*. She was right.

Herman was stretched out near the walkway, his ten-foot frame fully visible. I pushed Maryana into a rattan chair facing the mangroves.

Maryana was watching me intently, the color in her face now gone. I pointed to Herman. That coldness that I talked about before—it was back. I was growing to distrust myself. My own judgment. She must have seen it in my eyes, because she scooted her chair back, her feet forcing it toward the porch wall, away from me and away from the edge of the porch and Herman. Would I really feed her to a gator? My mind said, *no*, but my body, in a deep freeze, said, *absolutely*.

Leo pulled Maryana and her chair back to where it was, Maryana's gaze fixed in horror on Herman. A condemned prisoner eyeing the gallows. The movement must have caught the attention of Herman, because he moved slightly, one eye, half open, now turned toward the porch. Maryana lurched from her chair. Leo caught her arm and pushed her back down.

"Korabyap," he screamed into her ear. She froze …this woman, cold and treacherous, now in terror of a retired gator. She turned to Leo and pointed in the direction of the Florida Straits. Leo nodded and questioned her more quietly. He was clever—all that MVD interrogation experience. She responded in Russian.

"The boat is in Straits," he said, calmly, and with the satisfied demeanor of a man who had won a major war. His eyes never left her.

Maryana's blouse was wet now, soaked from the sweat that rolled down her face like water on a melting iceberg. The anger and aloofness that was there before was gone.

"Ask her how she planned to get to the boat." I was talking to Leo but focusing on Maryana. "And tell her we know about the surgical tools," I added, never taking my eyes off her. My tone delivered the message as much as my words.

I saw the coldness returning as she studied my face.

"Yaoaka," she said, her voice low, barely audible.

I looked at Leo and nodded. *She knows some English,* I thought.

"A small boat," Leo translated, nodding back and smiling at my discovery. "She uses a small boat."

"Ask her where it is."

She pointed toward the water and again spoke to Leo.

"The boat is docked at the marina. But she doesn't want to go with us. She's afraid they will kill her," and a smile crept across Leo's face, as though he had discovered a secret he could use—KGB stuff.

"Fine. Then tell her we'll leave her here. She can stay with Herman. Keep him company. Maybe I'll tie her to the damn palm over there," I said, pointing to a Canary Island Date by the dock. "Tell her that."

Leo didn't have to tell her. He smiled as he watched her staring at me. She had gotten my message. Fear makes mind-readers of us all.

63

YAOAKA

LATER FRIDAY, OCTOBER 22

It was late afternoon when we set out for the Keys once again. I drove Richie's Land Cruiser with Maryana in the cargo section and Louise—"Let's go get 'em cowboy,"—riding in front with me. Maryana seemed happy to see Herman disappear in the distance as she stared out the rear window. Richie, Huck, and Leo followed in the Durango. Richie seemed to like it more than his Cruiser.

It's a short hop from my house to the Keys. We jumped on the 997, otherwise known as Krome Road, that runs north-south and parallel to Midnight Drive. From there it was only a half hour to Florida City, home of my traffic ticket, and to US 1 and the Overseas Highway. We hit the bridge over Florida Bay at half past five and were back in Key Largo by six.

The sun had made a serious descent over the Keys by the time we arrived at the house on 1st Road. I wanted to make sure the Russians hadn't dropped in while we were gone. We also had one more piece of information to get: the position of the Russian ship. I suspected that Maryana had a radio in the house that she used to contact Kolya.

There was no activity. It was still as we left it, darkened now by shadows thrown by the sinking sun. The window where I had seen the young girl only a day ago stared at me as though it were alive. I stared back, expecting to see her face there again. But there was no life in that window this evening.

Louise was the first one out of the vehicles. She headed for the rear of the Jeep, opened the door, and dragged Maryana out by her blouse and let her fall on the ground. The sinking sun caught Louise's face, red with shades of black where shadows fell. She glared down at the woman, standing over her like a hawk over a chicken about to tear it apart. Louise's fists were wound tight, her eyes wild and wide. Then she buried her fingers into fat of the Russian's arm as she got in her face: "We need to do to you what you did to those children."

Maryana struggled to talk back through the duct tape. She couldn't. There was blood where Louise's nails were biting into her arm.

Richie came up behind Louise and pulled her away, shaking his head. "You gotta calm down, babe," he said. "Lots of time to get even with this bitch. The night is young."

Louise's face was still flushed as Richie led her into the house. Then Leo took hold of Maryana and rough-housed her toward the steps, cursing at her in Russian. Huck followed, his rifle bouncing against his back. "Don't never want to cross that woman," he muttered, as he followed Louise into the house. "She got a temper, don't she!" he said to nobody, chewing on something in his cheek.

Louise and Leo were waiting inside the door in the darkness. Louise was calm now, back to her old cop attitude: "Let's check the house. Make sure no one's here," she said, as I came through the door.

We searched the entire house carefully. No one there. No radio either.

Leo had deposited Maryana on the living room couch. We all gathered around her like in an Agatha Christie mystery, waiting for a confession.

I elbowed Leo. "Ask her where she was going to meet the boat and how she was going to contact them." Then, "And ask her if there is a radio in the house."

She was watching me carefully, her face twitching.

I would recognize the word, Korabyap. And of course, radio. It's the same word in English. Leo was standing over Maryana like a wrestler, his arms crossed. Then he spoke, harshly:

"The boat! Where is it? And where is the radio?" And he was now bent over her, his hands locked on her shoulder like a vice. Is there a radio?" All in English. She was trembling in his grasp. But no response.

He rose, turned to me, and whispered. "I think she might know English. Maybe playing mouse with cat."

I shrugged. "Maybe." That would be interesting. We had to be more careful about what we said in front of her. "By the way, it's cat and mouse," I said, smiling.

He grinned and nodded. "But I am close, no?"

I thought I would try out Leo's theory. "Tell her I will feed her to the sharks if she doesn't tell us and we'll find the yacht ourselves." Bad cop.

She didn't react.

Leo then told her in Russian. She shook her head violently and replied at a pace bordering on hysteria. I guess that answered our question.

Leo shrugged. "She is no cat and mouse, it seems. She says she will tell us the position of the ship if we guarantee that she will be safe."

Maryana said something else to Leo. I heard the word 'radio.'

"No radio here. It is on the yacht. That's how she contacts them," Leo said.

We loaded up the vehicles once again, Richie and Huck taking Maryana with them in the Jeep, Louise and Leo riding with me in the Land Cruiser. I swung onto 1st Road and headed back to the Overseas Highway.

Maryana had told Leo that the yacht was docked at the Pilot House Marina which is located about ten miles west of the bridge leading to the Keys. She said she would be able to give us the general position of the super yacht once we were at sea and close enough to make radio contact.

The Pilot House has a popular restaurant with a glass bottom deck where you can chew on conch fritters and watch creatures of the sea swimming under your feet. The marina wasn't far away. We were on the road no more than fifteen minutes when we came to the turn-off for the Pilot House.

The marina consisted of a scattering of beige, metal buildings spread on a large piece of land at the corner of North Channel Drive and Seagate Boulevard, two roads that protect the northern edge of Lake Largo where the marina sits. Boulevard doesn't really tell the story because *this* boulevard is crowded with buildings on both sides, and is not wide like you would picture a boulevard to be. This one housed boats of all forms, sizes, and makes, some sitting on trailers, others piled on top of one another in storage just off the lake. It was barely a two-lane road so I had to maneuver the Land Cruiser carefully around the boats and trailers crowding both sides of the street.

The marina itself faced Lake Largo, a body of water that's only about 400 feet wide and 500 feet long. The single entrance to the marina is through a channel that flows from the Florida Straits. I had driven my boat into this lake several years ago from Key Largo when I was searching for good fishing water. On the way out to the Straits, we would be passing a series of smaller channels on our starboard side. Houses cover every inch of available land in those channels, each with its own boat dock, each with its own chairs so the owners can sit and watch the traffic heading for the ocean. We would be passing that way in the next few hours. Weather permitting. A breeze was blowing in from the ocean.

I turned to Huck. "There a storm out there?"

It's still hurricane season in Florida until the end of November. Some devastating storms have hit the Florida coast in October. Take Katrina, for instance. It started as a relatively innocuous tropical storm, hit Miami, drove across South Florida and into the Gulf. It picked up energy there and swept into New Orleans and the northern coast of the gulf like Goethe's mad dogs of war.

"Just a tropical storm in the Caribbean. Still east of Cuba. No problemo, amigo," Huck said, picking up his rifle and staring out at the water that was beginning to stir.

"Are we going to be able to go out in this stuff?" I said.

He looked at me for a few seconds, shook his head, and said, "You're truly a dude ain't you, Coop. You're talkin' to one of the original (pronounced oreeeeginal) cowboys. This here's a *baby* storm that's comin'. Nothin' to fear."

In point of fact, Huck was never one of the original Florida cowboys, though he is one of the last. His grand-daddy and his daddy were. But the original Florida cow-boys—they were a lot older than Huck—herded cattle in the upper Everglades. Songwriter, Dillon Thomas wrote and sang about the last of those cowboys. They were in Florida 100 years before there were cowboys on the west-ern prairies. But the Florida cowboys were different. They used whips instead of lassos to herd cattle, cracking the whips over the heads of the cattle as they herded them. That's why we call them 'crackers'. Huck was a cracker. It's questionable that he ever herded cattle.

But enough about Huck. I told you about his history because he is, in a sense, like the originals, a straight-talking, no-nonsense, man-of-few-words, honest man. A cracker would say he was a true gentleman. "Not many of those around these days. Most of them guys out there don't have good morals to 'em," a cracker once told me. And Huck is my friend, a tough man, not afraid to shoot the bad guys. But always the gentleman if he has to do it.

64

I t was a large yacht for a so-called 'small boat,' forty-five feet, more or less. It was docked behind the Nautical Consignment Gift Store almost out of sight from the road, just the prow sticking out beyond the building. We parked in front of the store on a sandy lot and made our way to the dock, avoiding the propellers hanging off the backs of several boats, and past an idled lift truck used to raise and lower boats from their storage racks. The wind, blowing harder now, kicked up some sand in my face. There was a storm out there for sure.

Huck climbed on board first and turned around to help the others.

"Grab my hand," he yelled to Louise above the noise of the wind. It was beginning to kick up waves and scatter water over the deck.

A gust caught her hair as Huck pulled her up. He grabbed her as she slipped on the wet deck. Leo followed with Richie right behind him, the two of them turning to help Maryana aboard. She hesitated at first, then took their hands. Huck went directly to the Captain's chair to start up the engines. "Let's get her out in the water before this ka'ino blows in." Two 350 Mercuries roared, tossing water against the dock. I cast off the mooring ropes and jumped on board.

"Ka'ino?" I said.

"Storm, dude. Hawaiian."

We headed into the dark of Lake Largo, our running lights reflecting off the water, idling past the buoys, green on our right. We stayed at 'no wake' speed as we entered the channel and headed for the Florida Straits. It was too dark to see any chair-sitters watching us on the shore or down the fingers of the waterways that shot off the main channel.

I computed it would take about three hours to reach the big boat. We would first have to pass over the Pourtales Terrace that stretches for 213 kilometers from Key Largo to the Tortugas. There's plenty of water over the Terrace, about 180 meters at its shallowest near Key Largo. And then it gradually builds to a depth of 450 meters in the deepest part of the Straits. The Terrace is thirty-two kilometers at its widest and creates a kind of triangle as it stretches along the southern shore of the Keys all the way to the Tortugas. We would be driving over the upper end of the Terrace as we headed for the open waters of the Straits.

"The wind is rising," said Leo, as he looked out over the channel. The Hunter's Moon was out. It sat on the horizon like a lantern, spreading a silver path in front of it and creating a road of light that ran down the channel and out into the Straits. We followed it.

An hour passed between the time we left the channel and headed into the Straits. Moving at about twenty knots, I figured we should reach the big boat in several hours. We were headed for a point between the Pourtales Escarpment and the Mitchell Escarpment, two deep slopes in the Straits caused by millennia of erosion and land movement. They lie between the Keys and mainland Cuba. We would cross the Pourtales before we reached our destination. At that point, I figured, we would be about fifty miles from Havana when we made contact with the boat—that is if Maryana was telling the truth.

"Where are we, Huck?" I said, climbing into the pilothouse. I held my watch to the cabin light. It was almost 11:00 p.m.

"I figure we're about here, pardner," he said, referring to a point on a chart he had spread out in front of the wheel. "We're south of the Terrace and headed here," he added, pointing to Elbow Cay and a few small islands almost in the middle of the Straits, about sixty kilometers from Veradero, a city southeast of Havana. If Cuba is an extended index finger, Guantanamo is at the knuckle and Havana and Varadero are on the top of the finger.

"But we'll change course before we get to Elbow and head here," he continued, dragging his finger across the chart between the two Escarpments. "That is, if that commie lady is tellin' us the truth," he said, looking at me with his eyebrows raised.

"How's the storm?" I said, listening to the wind blow against the bridge. The waves were striking the hull with more force than when we first pulled away from the marina. He shrugged, like no big deal. I told him to get an update on the weather and went below again, thinking if Maryana was lying we would have some serious problems. I called Cleveland Wong.

"Where the hell are you, Cooper?" he said.

"In the Florida Straits heading for what I hope is the Russian boat."

Silence. "You're heading for the Russian's boat—and you never called me."

"I did call you. That's why we're talking," I said.

He replied quickly, "I meant call me if you got information on the boat, not go after it yourself, Cooper," sounding pissed. "You are interfering with my investigation. You need to let me know where you are." I didn't hear the sound of the helicopter anymore.

"You back in Miami now?" I asked.

"That's right. Most sane people would be where I am given that there's a tropical storm out there in the Caribbean." A silence again. "Let me ask you," he continued, "were you planning to board the ship and take them all prisoners?" using sarcasm to win his point. An unfair argument. I didn't answer. Might piss him off more. And, honestly, I didn't have a plan when we found the boat. Probably board it and take everyone prisoner.

"This is a little late, Cooper. Sounds like you guys are on your way." I heard a frustrated sigh. "Give me the general location of where you think the Russian boat is and tell me where you are," he said, his voice rising and falling like an angry parent. I didn't care. We needed help.

I gave him the information and thanked him for his help. *Yeah, yeah*, he said.

"I'll call the Coast Guard and dispatch a cutter there—you're in international waters now. The location you gave me for the Russian boat is in Cuban waters. I'm not going to be able to protect you there. And you realize this could cause an international incident if you get captured?"

I nodded.

"You listening to me, Cooper?" his irritation coming through loud and clear even over the noise of the storm.

"I'm listening. Precisely why *we* should proceed. It's going to be a lot harder to explain why the U.S. Coast Guard is in Cuban waters," I argued. Then, I lost him. The storm. Good thing. I had rented an Iridium Sat Phone, The Forbidden Territory plan, for $199 a week. That gave me 360 units or about 180 minutes. I'm not a rich PI. So the storm did me a solid.

We were heading for an area about twenty miles offshore from Varadero, Cuba, which is about forty miles east of Havana. Dangerously close to the Cuban mainland.

65

THE POURTALES ESCARPMENT

Once we escaped the Pourtales Terrace and were in the open waters of the Straits, the seas seemed to get rougher, the moon dodging in and out of the clouds. It was either beginning to rain lightly or the spray from the waves hitting the boat broadside was creating a constant wash over the deck. It was hard to tell.

"We're approximately a half hour from the coordinates, mate," said Huck, dwelling on the word, *approximately,* for a moment. "Maybe less, maybe more, depending on this damn weather." He had to yell over the noise of the motors and the wind. I nodded.

The spray, or rain, stopped for a few minutes as I strained to see lights in the darkness. We couldn't be any more than about ten miles or so from the boat. I looked at Maryana who was standing at the rail on the port side looking toward what should be mainland Cuba. But nothing was visible through the denseness of the storm.

"Dammit!" screamed Huck as the boat lurched starboard. "What in thunder is that?"

He trained a spotlight on a small wooden boat with a sail rigged clumsily in the center on a collision course with our yacht. As it came closer, I saw a man rise up with a rifle, but not pointed at us. I heard a shotgun blast from our boat and an explosion of water in front of the dingy.

I strained to make out the scene unfolding in the sea. "What the hell? Pirates?" I said, asking no one in particular.

"Damned if I know," said Richie, pumping another shell into his Mossberg and firing again.

Screams came from the little boat as the shell trimmed off part of the bow. The man in the boat dropped his rifle and yelled out in Spanish.

"What did he say?" I asked Louise.

"I don't know. I couldn't hear over the wind."

"Them boys is illegals. I think you mighta just sunk their ship, you damn fool!" Huck said to Richie. I wondered who was steering our boat. I looked over at the helm. Leo.

"Fuck do I care," Richie said. "Serve's 'em right for being out here. Where they goin'?"

"Probably Chokoloskee Island," Huck said. "Place is loaded with pirates and thieves. But they got a long ride, pardner. Probably won't make it in that piece of crap now that you put a hole in it," and he looked at me, like what are we going to do.

The boat with its passengers, five in all, was being tossed around in the water like a toy, the five passengers sitting with their hands over their heads and trying to keep their balance. They were surrendering. Great! Where would we put them? I could see that the boat was now lower in the water than it had been just a few minutes ago. I looked at Richie. He shrugged as if to say, *What the hell are we supposed to do?*

"All right. Wave them in," I said to Louise. "And, Richie, keep your shotgun on them…just in case."

The man laid his rifle on the floor of the boat. "And make sure you take that man's rifle," I yelled to whomever was listening.

Leo grabbed the boat as it eased against the yacht's swim platform off the starboard quarter. There were molded steps there to climb to the aft deck. But to get there each person had to scramble around a tender tied down to the platform. The constant wash of waves over the deck made the footing treacherous.

Leo held the boat steady as Richie, who had climbed onto the tender, helped a young woman up onto the platform and to the stairs, her dress clinging to her body like a wet suit. A young boy was next. I climbed down to the tender and grabbed his arm as he struggled for balance on the platform. He grabbed a cleat, steadied himself, and climbed the stairs to the cockpit.

The prow of the boat was now banging against the yacht, so Richie stretched over the tender and helped Leo swing the boat around so that its side was flush against the swim deck. I yelled for Huck to steady the yacht. But I don't think he heard.

There were still three passengers on the little boat. The man with the rifle was trying to boost an older man and a woman onto the deck—without success. So I climbed into the boat to help. I boosted each one of them onto the platform. Louise, who had climbed onto the tender to take my place, helped them up the ladder.

"Hurry the fuck up!" yelled Richie. "I don't think we can hold on much longer." Leo looked over and nodded. They were both stretched out over the tender, their arms fully extended, their feet locked against the top step of the ladder and struggling against the wind and the spray from the wash of waves to hold on to the wooden boat.

I climbed out of the boat, got a handhold on a tie-down cleat, and pulled the rifleman onto the deck. His face was worn—lined maybe from summers under the sun in the growing fields. But he hauled himself over the deck and up the ladder with ease then reached back and helped me. Richie and Leo had let loose of the boat and were watching it toss and turn through the waves until it finally disappeared like a lost soul. Then they scrambled over the dinghy and climbed up the ladder.

"I need a drink," were the first words out of Richie's mouth as he collapsed onto the deck. Leo grunted in agreement.

The Cubans were sitting against the bulkhead, shivering, their arms wrapped around their bodies like babes in swaddling clothes.

"Let's get out of the storm," I said, sliding the glass doors that led to the galley and salon.

The man who had held the rifle was staring at the furnishings: a full galley with beige cushioned seats around a highly polished dark wood table, stainless steel sink and appliances, and cabinets proud of their rich mahogany finish. Beyond the galley was a luxurious salon, with matching beige couches and chairs gathered around a center table. The entire space was enclosed in glass that, in the day, would provide a panoramic view of the Straits.

The Cubans were settled near the rifleman, huddling against each other to keep warm. The older man and woman stared at the water that dripped from their clothes to the plush carpet. I felt like saying not to worry. I looked over at Louise.

She nodded and began to herd them below deck by way of a carpeted stairway. What they would find there was nothing they would ever have seen in their lives: a long, carpeted companionway with three five-star cabins. But, hey, this is a million-dollar boat, even though it's a just chaser for the seventy-five-million-dollar super yacht the Russians drove. Probably like the kind of boat Paul Allen would have chasing his one hundred and fifty-million-dollar mega yacht. Money. It made me think of what the writer, Henry Fielding, had said: "Make money your God and it will plague you like the devil." That made me feel better at least until I followed the Cubans down the stairs to change out of my own soaked clothes and saw the VIP bedroom once more with its massive heart-shaped bed and large screen TV. Fielding. What does he know?

We found some dry clothes in the closets in the three bedrooms. Mostly bathrobes and wrap-around towels. But there was some swimwear and leisure clothes—these people were always prepared. We scraped enough together to get everyone into something dry.

I was getting ready to talk to the man with the rifle when Maryana appeared with Leo.

"What?" I said.

"She wants to know where she can sleep."

"Later," I said. "Stay with her." He nodded and took her topside. Everybody else seemed to be staring at me. We were gathered in the VIP cabin. Big enough for a honeymoon suite. Richie, Louise, and Huck were sitting on the bed. The Cubans were sitting on built-in, cushioned seating and staring at the furnishings.

"Let's all go up to the salon, get something to eat, and find out who these people are," I said.

323

The refrigerator was well stocked. Obviously Maryana was prepared for more than a trip to the big boat. After all it was a luxury yacht that probably had a crew ordinarily. I was sure she wouldn't drive this yacht alone.

Louise had taken Maryana to the fly bridge where she handcuffed her to one of the seats. Leo was keeping her company.

There were some meats and bread in the freezer, enough to make sandwiches for everyone. While we were eating, Louise asked the Cubans where they were headed. The leader with the rifle spoke rapidly, pointing south.

I heard a grunt and looked up to see Huck standing near the ladder. "Leo's got the wheel," he said, assuring me the boat was in good hands. "Them boys are lyin'."

Louise ignored him. "The man said they were heading for Elbow Cay but they got lost," she said.

"Sure," I said, shaking my head. "That's the best he can do? Elbow Cay? That's south. Besides, there's nothing there. No way. They weren't heading south, they were coming from the south."

"I think he mighta meant Key Largo, you ask me," said Huck.

"Anybody speak English?" I said to the five refugees.

"Hablas Englis?" I tried again, this time stopping at the rifleman.

"Poco," he said, holding his thumb and forefinger close together.

"Como te llamas tu?"

"Santiago Cavallero."

I smiled. "Cavallero. A horseman."

He nodded vigorously and replied, "Si. I am horseman," in broken English.

"Yes. And you are also illegals trying to get into the United States," I replied, and then realized that he probably had no idea of what I was saying. He responded in Spanish. Too quickly for me to understand. So I turned to Louise.

"He said they are lost," she replied.

"What am I supposed to do with you?" I said, more to myself. None of the five answered.

"Que estas diciendo?" he said, puzzled.

I turned to Louise again. "Ask him if he has seen a big ship."

She did. "Has visto un gran barco en el aqua?"

He shrugged his shoulders. "Tal vez," he said.

"Donde?" I said.

"Por ahi," he said pointing directly south toward the central part of the Cuban mainland. That was not where Maryana told us the boat would be. I heard Huck grunt. I looked over. He was shaking his head.

"They're claiming they saw a big boat out there. But it's nowheres near where that Russian woman said it would be." I had forgotten about Huck's Spanish. "What that means, amigo, is that boat of yours..." I don't know how it became mine, "is about ten miles short of where we're headed," he said, pulling at his leather jacket. "Damn lucky we run into you, pardner," he said to Santiago, the rifleman, who was now nodding at Huck and smiling broadly. I was sure he had no idea what Huck was telling him. "Saved us over an hour, Coop," Huck continued, looking out at the seas. "That is if he ain't lyin'. One of 'em is, that's fer dang sure." He hesitated. "Too bad you didn't bring one of them lie detester machines with you, Lou. Sure would help." Louise looked at him like he was insane.

"Lou?" she said.

Huck shrugged. "What DeFelice calls you." I couldn't believe it.

The waves were tossing us about now that we were drifting. No question but that the storm was powering up. I told Huck to check the weather again and take the wheel back from Leo.

"Cuan grande era este barco?" I said, turning to Santiago. He stared at me.

"Talk to him, would you?" I said to Louise. "My Spanish sucks.

"Yo te mostrare donde el barco es si…" began Santiago Cavallero. Then he hesitated, looking at Louise.

"He said he would show us where the boat is if…"

"Yeah?" I said. "If what?"

She looked back at the immigré wannabee. A man we had just rescued.

"Si nos lievara a Chokoloskee Island," he said.

"Chokoloskee Island?" I said.

"What did I tell you, Kemo Sabe!" said Huck, shouting from the galley—he hadn't gone up to the bridge yet. "Good place. Smugglers. Drug runners. Illegals. You name it. They're there."

"Who's steering this boat!" I yelled back. He disappeared through the glass doors.

Louise shook her head. "No can do, Coop. Totally illegal."

"Tell him we'll do it, " I said.

She looked at me surprised and a little angry. "Federal crime, Coop. No way."

I knew she was right. I told her to tell him that I would talk with Immigration if he helped us. Refugees from Cuba shouldn't be a problem—I was hoping. She told him. He smiled.

"Te llevare a la embarcacion. Puedo mostrarie desde la cubierta," he said to Louise. I turned to her.

"He said he would take us there. He can show us from the bridge," she said. I waited for the storm to subside before heading to the fly bridge since the stairs are on the aft deck. I saw a break and motioned for Santiago to follow me. I almost fell back on him as a wave hit the boat broadside. But we made it and entered the bridge lounge soaked again, shaking off water like a couple of wet dogs.

I asked Huck to show the rifleman the map and ask if he could identify the general area where he saw the boat. He pointed to an area off the coast of Bahia de Santa Clara, a peninsula east of Havana that sticks out like an eel into the Straits. If he was right, then Huck was right: the location was a good ten miles east of where Maryana told us the Russian boat would be.

"You trust this dude?" said Huck. "If he's right, we got our liar."

I shrugged. "This is like the old TV show, 'Who Do You Trust?' My guess, Cavallero. Let's go with him." Santiago smiled. He not only knows English, he can read a chart.

Huck swung the wheel south toward the peninsula and opened up the engines. The boat jumped in the water, cutting into waves now running five to six feet high. They slammed into the bow, delivering blows like a heavyweight boxer. I felt like I was driving a jackhammer into a slab of concrete.

"Hang on cowboys. It's gonna be a rough ride," Huck said. "We're headin' straight into it."

We hit the waves hard as we crossed their crests and came crashing down with a thud as we hit bottom. This went on for about a half-hour as the boat shuddered its way through the storm, my brain bouncing from one wall in my skull to the other. Headache time. A jackhammer headache.

We were headed south-southwest, past the Rompidas Ledge toward Santa Clara. We would be driving east of the Mitchell Escarpment, directly toward the Cuban mainland.

"Aqui!" yelled Santiago, pointing through the rain that was blowing over the deck, making visibility difficult. A light. Very faint. A wink of an eye in the night. Maybe ten miles away. Lights from the mainland? I couldn't tell. It was time to call Cleveland Wong.

I had tried to reach mainland U.S.A. on the boat's radio earlier. I wasn't able to get through. Maryana had said she was able to call the Russian super yacht by phone once she got close enough since they had a satellite system on the boat. The access to phone service at sea is provided by MTN Satellite Communications, the first company to offer a stabilized Very Small Aperture Terminal (VSAT) satellite solution for ships at sea, including service to super yachts. Our yacht didn't have that capability but it could pick up the satellite signal once we were close enough to the big yacht.

I had given our radio frequency to Cleveland before we left land. I had hoped he would call. The storm was interfering with my sat phone. So far, nothing. So I told Huck to try to reach the Coast Guard station in Miami on the radio. I took over the wheel. We were now south of the Pourtales Escarpment and no more than ten miles from the Cuban coastline. I strained to keep track of the light, but the wind and the rain played havoc with the wheelhouse window. Even the Clear View Screen couldn't spin fast enough to clear away the spray.

Huck played with the radio.

66

DARK WATER

The distant light danced in and out of the weather playing hopscotch with the waves. If this was our ship, I had no idea how we would board it.

"You have any plan on how we're gonna board that damn ship?" said Richie, climbing the ladder and joining me in the cabin. Mind reader.

"None," I said. "When I see the boat, maybe I'll figure it out."

"Uh-huh. The one time I don't like your plan," he said, checking the load in his shotgun.

"Why are you carrying that thing?"

"Sharks," he said.

"There are no sharks onboard, Richie."

"See," he said, smiling.

I shook my head. "Very funny. That's an old one, by the way."

"As old as you, Coop?" he said, still smiling.

Then, "I got 'em!" shouted Huck, raising a fist.

"That's great," I said. A voice crackled over the radio.

"Give them our coordinates. Tell them we may have spotted the Russian boat."

"Aye, aye, cap'n," said Huck and chattered into the radio.

"And tell them to call Cleveland Wong." I pointed to the agent's cell phone number that I had jotted on a pad. He shouted into the radio again.

"You don't have to shout," I said. "Doesn't bring them any closer." He ignored me. I was hoping I would hear helicopter rotors overhead before too long. Homeland Security was looking better all the time.

"Damn, I lost them," Huck said.

"No problem. At least you made contact."

"That light's getting closer," said Richie, who had staked out his territory in the sky bridge lounge. "How far away you think it is?"

"Hard to say. Eight miles, maybe."

"Think it's from the mainland?"

"No. The mainland's too far away. I'm thinking a boat," I said, hoping it was our Russian friends.

Louise joined us, shaking water out of her hair, and dropping down next to Richie in one of the loungers. Santiago was right behind her.

"Where's Maryana?" I said, suddenly aware of her absence. Louise had taken off the cuffs to give her a break, figuring she wouldn't be going anywhere out here in the deep dark Caribbean.

"With Leo," she said.

"Think that's wise?" I said, remembering the scene at the house.

"Why? What's he gonna do? Kill her?" Louise said.

"Yeah," I said. "I think that's exactly what he might do. Her first, and then the others when we get to the boat."

A wave about ten feet high crashed over the deck blinding us momentarily until the windows cleared. The rain was slashing into the boat with a new fury.

"What the hell! What's the story with this storm, Huck?" I said as he fooled with the radio.

"Got us a tropical, amigo," he said, shrugging his shoulders, like no big deal. "Courage is bein' scared and saddling up anyway, bucko." He kept playing with the radio.

"Who said that?" I said. Huck the cracker philosopher.

"The Duke," he said. I turned around. Richie had snorted and was shaking his head. Those two.

I heard the radio crackle again. Then, "Cooper. Sounds like you got yourself into a jam again." A voice from the past.

"Captain Welder?" I said. Thank God. I gave the wheel to Huck.

"The same," he said. "What are your coordinates?" I gave them to him.

"You're in Cuban waters," he said. "That's a problem. Copy?"

"Copy that," I said. "And we need some help."

The wind was blowing up the ladder, making it difficult to hear. There was only static for a few moments. Then,

"Hang on. Do not approach the Russian boat. Copy?" I said I did and then lost contact.

Huck looked away from the wheel, then turned back quickly as a large wave hit the boat straight on, swamping the deck.

"Damn," I said. "Sure this is just a tropical storm?"

"That's right, Kemo Sabe. A live one. About a 65 mile an hour breeze out there, he exclaimed into the wind. Then, "Whoa, horsey!" he yelled, as we got hit by another wave. Then a breather once again.

"So we going after the boat, boss man?" said Huck, relaxed at the wheel for once.

"We're going," I said. "We'll get Taisia off there if we have to ram it."

"Just like the Everglades, huh?" said Richie from the cheap seats.

I nodded. About a year ago we had been chasing smugglers through the Great Swamp. They had turned on us and started firing. I throttled up and aimed for the smugglers' boat. We hit them broadside, splitting their boat in half. Sounds crazy? It worked. I damaged our boat but totally wrecked their smaller boat. That wouldn't happen here. The Russian super yacht was more than three times our size, 155 feet to our 54.

"I'm going to get Maryana to contact her friends through SailMail. We should be close enough," I said, handing the wheel to Huck. I went below to look for her.

The rain had stopped, so when I descended the ladder, I looked out at a sea that was black except for the moon that seemed to ride just below the cloud cover—our own personal lantern. It was steady against the rise and fall of the boat as if it were also riding the waves. I thought of George Carlin: "There are nights when the wolves are silent and only the moon howls."

Leo and Maryana were on the aft deck, Leo sitting at the bar drinking—vodka I assumed—watching her, and Maryana leaning against the bulwark at the stern of the boat and looking out over the water at the Blood Moon.

Earlier she had shown me an Apple computer on board that was set up for SailMail, an email system supported by yacht owners who want to communicate with each other on the open seas. It operates at frequencies that allow operators to communicate within hundreds of miles of each other and uses satellite or its own private network of SSB-Pactor radio stations. Not something I had ever used on my 17-foot Boston Whaler.

I joined Leo at the bar and sat down on the other stool. "Any problems?"

"Of course not," he said. "She is ready to cooperate," and he raised his drink as he said it.

"Good. Bring her below. Let's send a message to her friends on the big boat." I paused. "You watch carefully. Make sure she communicates what we ask her to."

His hands clenched and unclenched as he sat, almost as though they had a life of their own. "Not to worry. She is careful to do everything now," and he was watching her as he spoke. She turned and looked at us. She understood.

67

THE LARGE BOAT

We were standing over the computer watching Maryana log into the mail system. She looked up at me.

"Tell her to say that she will not be leaving shore until the storm subsides," I said. She typed in a message. Leo nodded.

"Have her ask for their exact coordinates." She understood what I was asking because she hesitated. "Have her ask now," I said sharply, leaning into her ear. Leo leaned over and translated, his face in hers. She typed again. A short message. Leo nodded.

"Good," I said. "Let's see what they say."

A half hour passed and there was still no reply. Maybe they're like me and don't read their emails. I headed back through the galley to the aft deck. The sky was still starless—make no mistake, the storm was still out there—but the moon was visible, hanging like a lantern over a harvest field. I turned toward the coast of Cuba and there in the distance, winking at me just above the waves, was the light. A little nearer now it seemed.

I hurried up the ladder to the fly deck and told Huck to cut the motors to a fast idle. We were running without lights but I didn't expect to meet any traffic in the Straits at this time of night.

Santiago and Louise had just climbed the ladder and were standing next to me.

"Are we still on the right course?" I said to the rifleman.

"No," he replied.

I turned to Louise. "Does he know what I'm talking about?"

She smiled, shook her head, and then translated what I had said.

"Si," he said. "Maybe."

"Maybe," I repeated. "Great."

"Ask him if he had seen anyone onboard."

"Has visto a alguna persona a bordo?" said Louise.

"Si," he said and held up two fingers on each hand. Interesting way to count.

"Did they see you or say anything to you?" I said, looking at Louise.

"No dijeron nada," he replied, not waiting for Louise.

I smiled. "You know some English, eh, horseman?"

"Un poco," he said, holding out his hands, palms up, as if to say, *why not?* "I have some English," he said, half smiling.

I went below again to check the computer screen. Everyone followed except Huck. Leo was standing over Maryana's shoulder, looking at a message on the screen. He pointed to it as we all came through the galley.

A SailMail message had lit up the screen. I could see the numbers and degrees—a universal language. Leo read silently first. Then, "These are their coordinates," he said. For the first time he showed some excitement.

335

I went back to the fly bridge to check the coordinates against the map. Huck was leaning over me as I did.

"Bingo, boss! That must be the Russians," he said, as he looked out at the light that was bouncing in the distance like a star floating on the waves. We were the two Magi.

68

VNYZAPNOY NAPADYNOYE
SURPRISE ATTACK

The coordinates indicated that the Russian boat was about five miles away. Huck eased the boat along faster, just above fast idle, the running lights still off. The light had become more indistinct now, with the waves building to five and six feet. The storm seemed to be raising its nasty head again.

"What's with this storm, Huck?" I said, taking the wheel.

He shrugged. "Mother Nature. Changes like the moods of a woman, eh?" Huck, the philosopher.

I looked around the bridge at the empty seats. "Where's Leo? And Maryana?" Again thinking about the big man's threats.

"Not here, boss."

I rushed down the stairs to the aft deck and there was Leo. He had lifted Maryana over the rail.

"Leo," I yelled through the rain.

He didn't move. "She was trying to send messages to her friends," he yelled back, his voice dead. No affect.

"I stopped her. They would kill my granddaughter," he screamed, above the storm. He turned toward me, anger, strangely mixed with worry in his eyes. As though he wasn't sure about what he was doing but the anger was ruling. I was only about ten feet away—afraid to move.

"Don't do it, Leo!" I said, calmly. Both Richie and Louise had come above.

Maryana tried to hit the big man, screaming as she swung. But it was like she was hammering against a hurricane. He raised her higher and tossed her over the starboard quarter. I watched in horror as she disappeared into the sea—just like that—into a whirling, swelling, cauldron of water. A black hole. That fast. Not a sound. Gone. As if a massive wasteland of quicksand had reached up and swallowed her. And I...well, I was standing there watching, caught midway between trying to stop him and trying to take in what I was seeing—like a mannequin frozen in a store window, locked in the pose he was built to hold. Yeah, like that.

"My God!" gasped Louise. She was right behind me. And all I could hear was Leo muttering, "They would have killed her. They would have killed my Taisia." And he too was frozen, looking over the rail at the waves, larger now, tossing water over the deck. Soaking him.

"Let's get him inside, Coop," Louise said. "He's going to die of exposure." And she shrugged. I mean, what else was there to do? except to say what Macbeth said to Lady Macbeth about the murder of Duncan, "I have done the deed."

"You can arrest him later," I said, knowing full well that she wouldn't. Couldn't.

"Deserves what she got," said Richie. "Bitch is a goddamned killer."

The three of us hustled Leo below and out of his wet clothes. He was like a man who had lost his mind, repeating over and over again that Maryana was trying to kill his granddaughter. Maybe she was. Maybe that's what she was trying to relay to Kolya: *They're coming to get her. Kill the girl.* I wondered if Leo, like Macbeth, would ever sleep again.

···❖···

Fifteen minutes at fast idle had narrowed the distance from the super yacht to less than a mile. I told Huck to cut the engines to slow idle and let the yacht drift with the storm. The wind was pushing us in their direction.

At a half mile, I was able to discern the shape of the Russian ship, though the rain made a clear view impossible, even with binoculars. It was long and sleek, its stern low to the water. That would be the best place to board, I thought—the stern. I thought I saw a helicopter on the top deck and put the binoculars on it once more. I had to leave the cabin to get a clearer view since waves were washing up over the foredeck and obscuring the view from the window. I had seen right. There was a helicopter positioned aft, its tail hanging over the lower deck and its rotors turning slowly in the wind.

Huck swung the wheel so that we were heading toward the Russian boat on the starboard side. No one onboard the boat seemed to notice our presence as yet. The only sign of life, the running lights showing through the darkness and a cabin light below deck. The crew must have turned in for the night. I checked my watch. It was 2:15 a.m. We were now about 500 yards off the stern of the super yacht and holding steady.

I told Richie and Louise—Leo was still unreachable mentally—to break out the tender that was lashed to the swim platform. We would use it as a boarding craft.

We all stood on the aft deck eyeing the rear of the Russian yacht. Despite the rain washing against the binoculars, I could make out a name scrolled in large black letters across the stern as it rose and fell with the waves. The Bering Cross, aptly named for the Bering Sea that it crossed to get here. According to Louise's contact in Homeland Security, this boat used to be a trawler that Kolya had reconditioned by a company specializing in such work based in the Panama Canal Zone. If Expedition Yachts did the conversion then the Russian yacht would be fast, easily getting up to forty knots an hour. For a boat over 150 feet long that's incredibly fast. Our yacht, A Meridian 541, could only reach thirty-four knots an hour, max—even though our boat was only fifty-three feet long.

Huck had reluctantly agreed to stay with the yacht. Louise and Richie would go with me in the tender. A small invasion party. Leo would stay with Huck.

We pulled on our life jackets.

"I will go with you," said Santiago in halting English, serious.

I looked at Louise.

"Tell him he should stay here with his people. They will need him more than we will."

She turned and told him.

"I will go with you," he insisted, and made a gesture that he needed a gun.

"Let the little fucker come with us. We may need him," said Richie.

"Si, the little fucker will go!" said the man whose name meant 'horseman', a smile covering his entire face. I stared at him, the wind blowing the rain into his face now, and nodded. I motioned for Louise to get him a gun. She went below and came up with his rifle.

Richie had his Browning HP JMP 50th that holds 13 rounds of 9mm shells.

I was carrying a Glock 19 9mm with fixed night sights. It holds 15 rounds. A good choice because its black finish makes it almost invisible at night.

The seas were churning up more every minute so I knew we had to get into the water quickly or not at all. We shoved the tender off the platform, Richie and Louise holding the little boat fast to the yacht as we prepared to board.

I wondered about my sanity. Was what we were doing crazy? Trying to float a small boat close enough to a yacht that was large enough to be called a ship, and in a storm no less, a tropical storm, that seemed to be gathering strength every moment.

"I'm goin' too, pardner," said Huck, appearing suddenly. And I'm bringing Leo with me. He's good. "Y'all gonna need extra guns." No debate. Just like that. "Someone else can run this tin can." He was already putting on a life preserver and handing one to Leo, who seemed more with it. I knew Huck was right. We would need both of them. But who was running the boat?

Huck must have read my mind and said: "While y'all were trying to rope this thing," pointing to the tender, "into submission, I commissioned that Cuban man and his missus to keep this tub in place."

Santiago was standing close enough to hear.

"No problemo," he said to me. "El hombre es un capitan de barco."

I stared at him.

"Me entiendes?" he said.

I said I did understand, but shook my head in frustration. Talk about last minute.

"Okay, then, let's go," I said to the crew of wet bodies that circled around me.

"Leave your guns with me. I'll hand them to you when you're onboard. You first," I said to Santiago, pointing at the little craft being tossed about in the waves. He looked unsure.

"You can do it. Like this," I said, easing one leg into the craft.

He nodded. I held his arm as he eased off the platform and into the boat. Once he was in I handed him his rifle. Louise climbed in after him. Then Richie eased in, almost toppling the boat with his weight.

"Holy shit," he said as he righted himself. I had to agree with him.

Leo lowered his big body next, after handing me the Winchester that Richie had given him. I handed him his rifle after he settled and then Louise's Glock. I followed, my left leg hitting the water rather than the floor of the lifeboat. Richie and Leo grabbed me before I went into the sea. There were six of us in the boat now. Crowded. Huck handed me the Glock and his rifle. He then tossed the line to the young Cuban boy whom had called up from below and climbed in near Richie, the force of his weight carrying the boat away from the yacht, some water splashing into the tender.

"What the hell!" whispered Richie in a muffled scream. "Whoever learned you to board a damn boat! Sit your ass down before you drown us!"

I don't know if I told you, but Richie can't swim.

Immediately the wind and waves grabbed the dinghy and carried us into the sea, Richie hanging onto the gunnels like he was doomed. Luckily, we moved closer to the superyacht. I got the 14 hp motor started, its noise drowned out by the storm. We were now no more than three hundred fifty yards from the Russian yacht. Leo and I used oars to help stabilize the little dinghy and plow through the waves. Some were more than five feet high. At one time I lost sight of the ship and panicked, fearing we had been blown off course. I caught sight of it again when the moon broke through the spray. And there it was. Big.

"We ain't gonna make it, bud!" whispered Richie, totally panicked. As I said, Richie can't swim, so he's always been terrified of the water. But now this was a mother of a storm, driving us toward a giant of a ship, no more than fifty yards away now, still dark against the almost impenetrable blackness of the sea, and looking menacingly impossible to board. Despite all that, Richie had screwed up his courage like a man facing death and glared into this tropical storm like he was back on the streets of Cleveland's lower east side, ready to fight with his baseball bat. And then a wave hit us, almost swamping our tiny craft, as if to show us, including the intrepid Richie, that we weren't going to make it. Luckily, the force of the wave drove us within yards of the Russian ship, a superyacht, and I looked up through the spray that the storm was driving into our face, at this massive yacht, its tail soaring over us, as black as a Pteranodon, a flying reptile, from the Jurassic age, 80 million years ago. Angry. Daring us to board.

I cut the motor as we drew closer to the stern of the massive yacht, the wind now doing all the work to bring us in. Huck threw a line out and snagged a tie down on the stern. On the first try—a Florida cowboy. He looked at me and grinned.

Huck was up first as he reeled in the line and pulled us against the swim platform on the boat's stern. He jumped out and secured the tender to the super yacht, tying down the line with a triple figure eight. I threw him another line and he tied that one down as well. Santiago scrambled onto the deck next and reached down to help me.

I flopped onto the deck, grabbed onto the rifleman's hand, and, once I got a secure position on the platform, took the guns from Richie and Leo and passed them to Huck. He pocketed the Glocks then carried the rest of the guns to the aft deck by way of a short ladder on the starboard quarter.

I helped Louise climb onto the platform with Leo's help. Then we both pulled Leo onto the deck with Richie pushing from the tender. The little boat struggled to escape the tie lines as the waves continued to wash over the deck, making it difficult to keep a foothold. Richie was the last off. As he stretched out to us, one of the lines let loose and he tumbled into the water, Leo, Huck and I barely hanging onto him. I saw the pure terror in his eyes. "I've got him," yelled Leo over the tumult of the storm, and slowly I felt Richie move away from me and out of the water, Leo screaming and cursing Richie all the way to the deck. "People and things understand me better when I curse," Leo would explain later, finally able to laugh about it.

Richie landed like a large beached mammal onto the deck next to Leo. "Jesus, Holy Christ!" he gasped as he lay face down on the platform. The rest of us collapsed around him, like a team that had just won a tug-of-war contest.

"Gotta secure our boat," said Louise, eyeing the tie-down lines stretched tight as the dinghy struggled against the fury of the storm. She tried to get up but a wave washed over the platform and knocked her down.

"Let's do this together," I said. She nodded.

Louise was closest to the lines so she scooted to the gunnels and grabbed one line, trying to pull the dinghy back to the yacht. While she held the line, Leo and I grabbed the other line and between the three of us forced the tender through the rolling waves and back toward the platform. We held it steady while Richie—now over the shock of his near drowning—and Huck reached over the edge of the platform, both of them dangerously close to washing over the side, grabbed the rope that circled the top of the tender and pulled the boat in tight so that it was finally parallel to the platform once again. And then, with the effort that it takes to raise the main tent in a Barnum and Bailey circus, we heaved the dinghy up and onto the deck. We held it in place—hell of a job—while Louise ran the tie-down lines through the nylon rope that runs along the top of the boat used for hauling it, and then made a triple figure eight to secure the lines to cleats on either side of the deck. What the hell. The best we could do in a storm.

That done, I watched Louise pull herself up the ladder while the waves tried to knock her off and wondered when the ship was going to come alive with a whole crew of Russian mercenaries rushing us. But no one was stirring on the boat—except us. I began to wonder if we were on a ghost ship. And as Louise reached the top of the ladder and disappeared onto the aft deck, I saw the tail end of a helicopter. It extended over the end of the top deck. I had seen it earlier when I put the binoculars on the boat.

I thought at the time, it made sense. They would need a helicopter to transport body parts quickly, like a heart or a lung, fresh and vibrant, to clients after a surgical removal.

Each of us in turn fought the wind and rain that beat on us as we climbed the ladder to the aft deck. Richie almost tripped into a small swimming pool as he made his way through some deck chairs to a bar against the bulwark just to the left of sliding glass doors. I was sure he wanted to check the contents of the bar, but he passed right by and tried the doors. They were open. We followed him inside.

When I pulled the doors shut, we stood in a darkness as black as pitch. I whispered for Richie to stop and pulled my Glock. It was fitted with night sights. I checked the room, now clearly visible to me. A salon. With leather couches and chairs and another bar, this one with a polished mahogany front, tiled top and lined with half a dozen stools with seats cushioned a rich red.

Beyond the salon was another set of glass doors. But the stairway off to the right intrigued me. A ladder to the cabins below, I figured. I headed toward the ladder. The others followed. At the base of the stairway my foot sank into a carpet that I could sleep on. Before me was a long hall lined with what I assumed were individual cabins. The first few I figured as quarters for the crew with the more luxurious cabins forward. A flicker of light seeped under the cabin door closest to us. Richie was right behind me. I motioned him to one side of the door while Louise and I slid over to the other, backs against the wall. I could now make out the forms of Huck, Leo, and Santiago without the Glock's sights. I motioned for the three of them to move down the hall to cover the other cabins—just in case.

Louise slowly turned the door handle—no sound. Then, when light appeared in between the jamb and the door, she opened it quickly and held her gun at a surprised man, sitting in a lower berth, reading. Richie and I were right behind her.

"Silentio!" whispered Louise, almost in a full voice. The man dropped his book and held up his hands, his eyes as wide as a Hunter's Moon.

There were two other men in the room, one in the berth over the reader and another in a lower berth on the right side of the cabin. Both had been sleeping. They weren't any longer.

So there we were, Louise and I and Richie, our guns on the three men who now had their hands up. No one talked for a few tense moments. Then Santiago appeared.

He spoke to them rapidly and firmly in Spanish. Thank God for the horseman. They nodded their heads, vigorously. "Si entiendo," the man with the book said.

I leaned into Santiago's ear: "How many crew members are there?" He stared at me. I looked at Louise. She translated what I had just said to Santiago and loud enough for the crew to hear.

"Seis," the man with the book said.

"Where are they?" I said turning to Santiago. This time the bookman understood.

"Siguiente cabina," he said, pointing through the wall to his right.

Uh-huh. Neighbors. "Tell him we need the rest of the crew in here," I said.

The man nodded quickly, indicating he understood.

"I'll go with him," said Louise. "Make sure he doesn't sound an alarm."

She nodded to Santiago and the two of them headed out the door to the next berth.

They were back within two minutes with three other crewmen—Latinos—looking nervous and confused, rubbing their eyes.

"Ask them who's the captain of the boat?" I said. "And where is he?"

"Senor Kolya," said the man with the book. "Entiendo Ingles," he said.

"Where is he?" I said.

The man looked confused. "Where?"

I looked at Santiago. He explained.

"Aqui," the man said, looking surprised and pointing to the top deck.

"Santiago, quedate aqui con ellos," I said, pointing to the crewmen. I needed someone to stay with them.

"I will stay," he said. Serious.

"Pedirle que lo que esta delante," I said to him, pointing up the companionway. I wanted to know what we were walking into.

Santiago spoke rapidly to the man with the book. He replied just as rapidly. My Spanish, I vowed to work on it. I was running out of words that I knew.

"Tres cabanas, salon y cocina," Santiago said, then he turned to Louise and continued in Spanish.

"He says that the man told him the Russians had closed off the galley to make an operating room," she said, flinching as she came to 'operating room'. I did too.

I asked him how many people were onboard besides the crew.

Louise and Santiago translated.

"Ocho," bookman said.

"Russians?" I said.

"Si."

"A doctor?"

The man nodded.

I looked at Richie. He shrugged. "Nine to six. Fair fight." And he studied his Mossberg, turning it over in his hands. The room was so quiet I could hear the rain and waves punishing the boat. This storm's never going to end, I thought.

And so we headed out, picking up Leo and Huck who were in darkness at the end of the hall. Santiago remained with the crew. Just in case.

"Anything?" I whispered to Huck.

"All's quiet, hombre," he said. "Big chief and me had it covered. Rooms are quiet. Must be topside drinking vodka or asleep."

I took the lead back up the ladder to the main deck. I didn't need to use the night sights any longer. My eyes had become used to the dark. We were back in the salon. The glass doors I had seen earlier were directly ahead. I eased the doors open. Noiseless so far. Another, larger lounge. The furniture in this salon was sleek—retro: plasticized chairs and form-fitting lounges. Large pillows were arranged around an oriental carpet that fronted a large screen TV. Home-away-from-home.

Several bottles were sitting on a bar that stretched across the far wall to the right of the TV. There were some empty glasses there. I went over to check one of them. The ice had melted. I could see it was a first class bar with a polished wood finish and a brass rail running the length. I would have to stop in some evening.

It was then that I caught the odor of alcohol. It wasn't from the bottle of scotch—it was the hospital kind—coming from the area beyond the salon. Two sets of solid double doors blocked the way at each end of the room. The floating hospital's operating room.

The wind was picking up again. Minutes earlier I could see—though only vaguely—through the transom-like windows overlooking the lounge. Now waves were pushing their way over the deck and slamming against the upper deck so a constant stream of water washed down the windows obliterating the view. Tropical storm? More like a hurricane. I looked at Huck. He shrugged and nodded. If he said 'Kemo Sabe' one more time, I was going to kill him. He didn't.

The four stood around me at the bar.

"Let's do this," I said, telling Richie, Leo, and Huck to take the doors to the right. "Louise and I will enter here," pointing to the double doors nearest us.

"This is gonna be good," said Richie, staring at the double doors. "Fuckin' Count Dracula in there."

"You got that right," said Louise, checking her gun.

We eased the doors open together—*quietly* I signaled, a finger to my lips. Light poured out into the lounge from what looked like a hospital emergency room, a sharp odor of alcohol attacking my nose, harsh bright lights filling every corner of the room—including a man in blue scrubs who was leaning over an operating table. There was someone else in scrubs standing near him.

Then I saw him—pulling a gun. Another man—he had been sitting on the far side of the room, not in scrubs—but now he was standing—aiming at Richie and Leo—and I screamed at him. He turned and I fired three or four times in rapid succession. Red patches appeared across his chest like small dye marks from a paintball gun.

Only I was using a Glock. And the man lurched suddenly as though he was hit with a baseball bat and fell back into the wall like a man thrown in a bar fight. The men in scrubs watched the whole scene like two actors told to hold their positions and shut up.

I checked the room quickly. No other Russians visible. Richie and Louise were moving along the perimeter of the large area, opening doors and slamming them shut. Leo was hurrying over to me. I knew what he was thinking. His granddaughter.

I looked past the two men in scrubs who were standing with their hands over their heads. It was a young girl on the operating table. A white sheet partially covering her body. Her stomach was exposed where there was an open incision, blood seeping from it. Bottles of liquid, with plastic tubes running to her arms, hung from two metal stands on either side of the table. She was obviously anesthetized. Leo was now standing over her, breathing hard. I thought he would have a stroke. But he looked down at the girl on the table and said, "It is not my Taisia—thanks you, God!" And he leaned on the table, breathing more slowly now.

"Oh this poor, poor, young girl," said Leo, touching her face. "This poor, poor girl."

The man with latex gloves, bloodied from the surgery, was staring at me as I approached him, my gun leveled at his mid-section.

"What have you done to her?" I said. Leo translated.

"Nichego," the man said. "YA tol'ko chto nachal."

"He just started," Leo said.

"Then close her up," I yelled. I turned my eyes away from the young girl. Furious.

He seemed to understand what I said. But Leo translated anyway, taking the doctor by the arm and shoving him toward the operating table.

"Somebody oughta operate on this asshole," said Richie, shaking his head in disgust.

I nodded. "Uh-huh. Maybe take one of his eyes out. That coldness rising in me again.

It was deathly quiet in the room as we watched this monster, this wretched and abhorrent man of medicine—if that's indeed what he was—who steals the life-organs of children, go back to work. I couldn't hear the storm above the silence.

"Someone's going to have to stay with this guy while he finishes sewing this poor girl up," I said, turning to Louise. "Would you?"

She nodded. Her gun was now holstered. But she laid her hand on it as she moved in closer to the table.

"Don't shoot him," I said.

"Self defense?"

"Absolutely."

"I'm guessing Kolya and Remi must be on the bridge," I said. "They may have heard the shots, so we have to move fast." I looked at the body on the floor. "We've accounted for three of the Russians. There are five more."

"Where is my Taisia!" Leo said to the scrub assisting the doctor. The man shrugged. Then Leo said something to him in Russian. The doctor stopped what he was doing and said, "With Mr. Kolya," and then went back to work. Leo moved toward him, red with anger. I grabbed him by the arm, still picturing Maryana, about to be hurled into the sea.

"He needs to focus on the girl. Later," I said. Leo calmed down. The Russian returned to sewing up the young girl, looking back nervously over his shoulder to check on Leo. I needed to get the big man out of there.

I told Leo to check the rest of the cabins, figuring there was a good chance Taisia was there—despite what the doctor said. He was eager to do that.

"Check on Santiago, also," I said. "See how he's doing with the crew. Then come topside. Bring the crew with you if you have to. We'll need help," thinking of the five Russians who were still loose onboard.

I motioned to Huck and Richie to follow me. As we made our way topside by way of the inside ladder, I could feel the power of the storm bearing down on the yacht like a massive pressure cooker. I struggled to maintain my balance on the stairs. There was no light in the stairwell so I used the Glock's night sights. The ladder consisted of a narrow, metal, circular stairway that led to the upper deck. I thought of the movie, *The Spiral Staircase*, in which a terrified, mute girl is pursued up a spiral staircase by a crazed serial killer.

Huck's rifle clanked against the stairway. I jumped and Richie bumped into me.

He turned back to Huck. "Why don't you tell the world!"

I waited a moment until Richie calmed down then opened the hatch at the top of the ladder. The wind blew me back into the stairwell knocking me into Richie again.

"Geez, Coop, my hand." I didn't apologize because a rain of shells hit the decking as I fell back.

"Christ! I guess they know we're here!" said Richie, hanging on to me. I reached up and pulled the door shut.

"I think the shots came from the pilot house on the upper bridge," I said. "You two go back and take the outside ladder to the upper deck. That should bring you around and below the bridge."

"There's thunder on the bridge, and lightning in my hand," said Huck, waving his alligator gun at me. Huck. Native American philosopher.

I watched them disappear below. They would gain access to the outside ladder from the salon and a walkway that extends along the starboard side of the boat—and they would get soaked in the process.

There was no sound now except for the wind as it screamed and whistled through the cracks in the door. The gods of the sea were at work.

Several minutes passed and I heard yelling and the sound of activity on the upper deck. I started to open the door again when a roar shook the boat like a hurricane ripping off the top of a house, blowing across the deck in a tidal wave of noise.

I forced the hatch open and peered out onto the deck. Flashes came from the bridge and I heard the clatter of shells against the hull. Too close for comfort. But by keeping the hatch open, I had a shield against the shooters as well as a good view of the aft deck where the helicopter was sitting, its rotors thrashing at the wind.

Several forms were huddled near the chopper, their heads low beneath the blades. I fired three shots just above the copter blades, afraid of hitting Taisia if she were there, then dropped back behind the door. Another volley of shells erupted from the sky bridge and ricocheted off the metal door.

"You will kill the girl!" yelled a man in broken English. He was holding someone in front of him, and moving toward the open door of the helicopter. Taisia! I thought. A man standing near him fired in my direction. I fixed him in my night sights and fired three quick rounds that drove him back against the rail. He stayed down.

"Stay off the copter!" I yelled.

"Hooy Tebe!" the man said and continued to move toward the open door of the copter. I think he just told me to go fuck myself.

I was getting set to rush the copter when I heard a shotgun roar behind me. I turned and watched as flashes of gunfire lit up the wheelhouse. I hoped we were winning.

Time to move. So I ran toward the copter, firing into the blades. Before I got there, a man burst from the aft deck and slammed into the Russian, wresting the girl from his grip. I grabbed her arm before she fell and pulled her away from the blades. I told her to wait while I turned back to help Leo. Too late. Leo had raised the Russian over his head and was spinning him as though it was a Vince McMahon WWE wrestling match. Only this time there was no mat to break his fall. He threw the Russian onto the hard deck, screaming, "You would take my little girl to make revenge on me? You would do that?" And he stared down at the Russian, whose body was now bent back on itself, blood starting to ooze from the back of his head. "You must pay for what you have done, myasnik!"—so this was 'The Butcher'—and I couldn't see the Russian's eyes from where I was—he must surely be dead—and I saw the tattoo on his arm—a snake wrapped around a fish knife and I remembered that Kolya used a fish knife on his victims. So here he was. This trafficker in children. This myasnik. This butcher.

And Taisia had watched it all, like a child in the front row of a horror show, mouth open against the rain, staring first at the body lying on the deck, then at her grandfather who stood over him. Then he went to her and took her in his large hands and looked into her face.

"My little girl," he said softly. "You are now safe," and he hugged her, her shoulders shaking as she put her head against his chest.

The helicopter pilot was standing speechless in the copter door looking down at the scene, and he raised his hands as Louise appeared behind Leo and yelled above the storm for him to get down. And when he did, she pushed him onto the deck, face down, and locked his hands behind his back. And then I remembered the shots on the bridge and turned to see Huck and Richie dragging a man between them. They dropped him on the deck in front of me.

"Remi," said Richie. "There's another guy in the cabin." He paused. "He's deceased." I didn't ask how. "So KGB. Not so tough anymores, huh?" said Richie to the man on the deck as though he could hear him.

"Is he dead?" I asked.

"Nah. I hit him in the head with the shotgun. Didn't want to waste good shells on this piece of shit."

Remi moaned and mumbled something in Russian.

Leo had joined us, his arm around Taisia's shoulders. I looked at him, remembering his promise to kill them all.

As though he had read my mind, he jumped in. "Not to worry. Remi will be good prize to take back to U.S. police. KGB man caught by Americans private detective and by Russian grandfather of kidnapped girl." He said it proudly. But I heard him mutter something in Russian under his breath. I caught one word: *mertvets*. And I knew what that meant. "He's a dead man."

And then like a big bear he hugged Taisia. "Moya malen'kaya vnuchka!"

His little granddaughter. But she wasn't really that little anymore—only in the eyes of a grateful grandfather, I suppose. And yes, she was young. But not her mind. She had lived through horrors no adult would ever live through.

So finally, it was over. All but the damn storm.

69

COUNTING THE DEAD

Reality hit when the storm intensified and a violent surge of water almost swept the deck clean. I thought of the tender and wondered if it was gone. It wasn't. Santiago and Louise had tightened up the lines with the help of the ship's crew. When they finished the crew came topside talking excitedly with the rifleman.

Louise called me aside. "They are worried about what's going to happen to them," she said. "They said they didn't do anything wrong."

"The girl on the operating table. How is she?"

"Resting. The re-stitching went well and the doctor has sedated her. She will sleep for a long time. Poor kid."

I nodded and waited for more.

"No worries. The doctor is too scared to pull any more shit. But just to be sure, I locked both him and Igor in one of the cabins—with help from the chief of the boat—that's the man who did all the talking in the cabin. So we're good. Let's just hope the girl comes through this without major damage." And then, shaking her head, she demanded, "What kind of people do these kinds of things?" Not really a question.

I shook my head and thought of what Nietzsche said: "In the last analysis, even the best man is evil." Maybe he was right. But if that's so, then this is beyond evil. And I couldn't imagine anything as black as that.

"Let's get below," I said.

Louise and I watched a procession of men heading into the stairwell to get out of the storm. Richie was supervising Huck and Santiago as they prodded the pilot and carried Remi, still unconscious, down the stairs. Leo and Taisia were right behind them. I motioned for Louise to go ahead of me.

The wind and rain tried to follow us down the ladder as I worked with the hatch to pull it shut—it had been partially unhinged by the wind as it banged against the metal frame of the upper deck. I finally slammed it in place. Silence for a moment—at least more than I had in hours. The storm was still hurling waves against the yacht, but the sound was deadened now—only the wind whistling as it tried to break the upper deck door free once again. It was enjoying its work.

70

THE RESCUE

"They paid for me to go to Ohio—for the study," she said. "Me and my friend, Geza. They promised $2,000 dollars for the payment. Each. It was too good to pass up, Mr. Cooper," said Taisia, wiping her eyes as she said it, *and did I understand?* I said I did understand and not to worry. She was the victim, not the bad guy. She seemed relieved.

Leo was with her, his arm around her protectively. "Moy malen'kiy Taisia," he murmured, and it calmed her. *My little Taisia.*

A Coast Guard cutter was waiting off the port side of the ship when I went topside. Huck was in the wheelhouse and had alerted me about their arrival. It was parked near our yacht. The cutter had already launched a boarding boat that was heading toward the stern of the Bering Cross. The storm had subsided somewhat, the rain had stopped, but Triton was still stirring up trouble from the depths, the waves rolling like the gods were fighting beneath.

"I was able to raise them on the radio," yelled Huck from the bridge. "They weren't no more'n a holler away."

The first men onboard were in full combat dress, carrying assault weapons, new Hecklers it looked like. Right behind them was Captain Jaime Welder. Stiff and straight as ever. I remembered him from a rescue last year when we chased kidnappers through the Everglades. Richie, Huck, and I had lost our boat—I should say destroyed it—when I rammed a boatload of smugglers trying to carry children out of the country. So this was a second appearance for him— and me. And hopefully the last.

Welder's mustache made him look older than his thirty five years though it was blond, no gray showing anywhere. He would look good on the side of a Wheaties Box. "Build Strong Bodies, Kids, So You Too Can Join the United States Coast Guard."

"Y'all are in Cuban waters you know," he said, looking at the helicopter with its busted blades, then at Huck and Richie walking toward us.

"So are you, Captain," I said.

He nodded. "Let's get you all off this boat first. I'll have my men captain both your yacht and this vessel back to the Coast Guard Station. I understand you have some bodies onboard," he said, looking around to see where they were.

"That's right. Two Russians are on the bridge in the wheelhouse. One is below. We also have some prisoners." And I told him about Kolya, the doctor and his assistant, Remi, and the pilot. I hoped no one would ask about Maryana.

He shook his head. "You been busy, Cooper." I'm sure he didn't mean that as a compliment.

"We'll help with the transport of the prisoners," he said. "I'm figuring we'll turn them over to Miami Police when we land."

361

He stood for a moment, thinking. I was wondering if he was going to handcuff us all. We had encroached on Cuban waters, ignored the orders of Homeland Security, and put the Coast Guard in jeopardy by forcing a rescue in another country's waters. Good thing the Cuban government didn't have much of a navy.

Then Welder looked up at me.

"This is the second time I've rescued your..." and he stopped. I could see he was debating about what to say. I helped him out.

"...ass. And I thank you, Captain." But we had caught a big fish. And he knew it.

"I understand you have an MPD officer onboard," he said.

I nodded. "Detective Louise Delgado."

"That's fine. I'll turn over the prisoners to her. Might as well make that transfer right here then," he said, looking around at the sky, still an impenetrable wall of blackness. And the storm was still an angry, stinging, force out there on these seas just off the coast of Cuba. And it dared us to venture out in it, tossing waves against the deck as a sign of its power. Rain began to mix with the spray, cold and chilling when you don't have any gear.

"This is going to be tricky," Welder said, ducking against the weather, his hand raised against his eyes to check the route to the cutter. The sea seemed to grow meaner as he watched. "Let's get you the hell off this water and back to land where you belong."

The landing boat took us in groups of four to the cutter. By the third trip, the energy of the storm had ebbed enough to let the moon slide through. It rode low in the sky, laying a path of silver across the water that still chopped at the boat. I watched as the final boatloads departed—Santiago Cavallero and part of the crew of the Bering Cross; then the other crew members—I watched them climb safely on board the cutter; then Remi and the doctor and the Russian pilot—each boatload riding in silence—and I watched as Richie, Louise, and Huck crossed the moon's path. And then there were only three of us left.

I climbed aboard the final boat with Leo and Taisia. I could hear her breathing, interrupted by a catch now and then as she stifled sobs, and I heard Leo, breathing smooth and soothing, as he kept his arm around her shoulders, and I thought back over the nightmare we had lived through—no dream here though—we would not wake up in the morning and say *wow that was a fucking scary nightmare I just had*—and I could hear the breathing of the boat as it carried us steadily toward the cutter, and of the night—yes, it breathes as well—and, of all things, I swear I could hear Maxie's breathing. And I promised him, right there onboard that boat, talked to him like he was alive—I had never done that before. Never in these eight years promised him that I would find him. Why hadn't I done that before? Could I ever forgive myself for not doing that?

And I stared at the Blood Moon. And knew immediately what I had dreaded all these years. That if I found Maxie, I would find him dead—not might—would. And that's too much to expect of any parent, isn't it? I was hoping Maxie would understand that.

And when I climbed on board the cutter, Louise was reaching over the rail. And she looked into my eyes, and I was certain she knew. I took her in my arms and held her for what seemed to be an hour—it may have been longer because the moon seemed to change its position in the sky as we held on to each other…and I watched it fade toward the day.

I didn't see blood on the moon. But it was there. The blood of Geza, and of Tania and Sly, and of April, and the girl on the boat, and China, all intermingled with the blood of Maryana and her friend, and Kolya, and of the Russians we had killed on the Bering Cross, and of everyone else whose blood was spilled on the fields under the October Moon.

71

EARLY SATURDAY A.M., OCTOBER 23

"I need to talk with Remi, Leo," I said, once we were settled on the Coast Guard cutter. "There are some things I need to get straight."

He looked at me briefly, then "*You* need to get settled? *You* need to get settled!" And a silence grew around us.

"I'm sorry," I said. "Of course you need to do the same. But are you ready to talk to him without doing some major damage?"

I needed some closure on Remi—his part in the body parts business, in the killing of Geza, in the murder and dissection of April's body, in the kidnapping of Tania and Sly, in the brutal surgeries. And this would be my only chance before Louise turned him over to Homeland Security, and let's face it, I wanted to know if he might have some connection to my own son's kidnapping—small chance of that—but...if he did, I wanted to be the one who found out, not DeFelice, not Louise, not some stranger working a case who didn't know Maxie. And if Maxie

365

was dead, I wanted to know *now*. I wanted to know before we got to shore. And what the hell—if Remi was responsible, then...well...but that was unlikely. As I said, I just wanted to know.

Leo agreed to help as a translator. *A neutral translator*, I reminded him.

Louise let me have some time with him. *No problems, Cooper*, she said. *I don't need any problems. I got enough already being out here with you in Cuban waters.* She had him handcuffed to a lower berth.

Remi looked at me and growled. He didn't need to growl. I already knew he wouldn't talk. And he spat at Leo. And for the first time I didn't see anger on Leo's face—I knew that wasn't a good sign. Then Remi spat at me, and Leo lifted him out of my hands—by the hair—and then dropped him—a small clump of Remi's hair—bloody hair—in his fist. And he shoved the bloody mass into his face, speaking to him in Russian and bringing his other hand back in a fist—his large hand—a hand as big as the end of a sledge hammer—and I saw fear in Remi's eyes as he wiped blood from his forehead and stared at it—just a flicker of fear—like a match in the night in the front lines of a battlefield—and Leo talked to him—Leo, the interrogator—talk about police brutality—talked quietly to Remi—about his family (СЕМЬ́R)—perhaps something like *How are your children (ДЕТИ)? Your wife (ЖЕНА) ? Are they well? How would they be without you? Could they survive if you weren't around?* And the fear was there—the match that wouldn't go out—and Remi began to talk—to raise his hands like *I get it*—and Leo began to translate—*he says he didn't kill Geza—can't blame me for that, he says—Kolya killed him—ordered him killed—the doctor was responsible for the girl's surgery—he suggested it, I just wanted to sell the fucking children, not torture them—* and this was an important part—when I told Leo to ask about April—The Russian shook his head and said I should *talk to the Irishman's wife.* The Irishman's wife? *Jackson,* I thought. *You mean Jackson?* And he didn't answer. And *I didn't kill her,* he said, spitting out blood as he tried to talk. The Irishman's wife?

I let that go and told Leo to ask about my son—eight years ago—did he have anything to do with that? And he shook his head. Or did the others? And he continued to shake his head, *no.* Maryana? *No!* Kolya? *No.* And I grabbed him by the shoulders as I asked—and Leo was also screaming into his face, and I started shaking him, his head bobbing like a rag doll—and I choked him, my hands wrapped tightly on his throat, so tightly that I felt his Adam's apple move where it shouldn't go, back and forth across his throat—what else was I to do?—a fair exchange for the life of my son—even if he didn't do it—a fair exchange—but the violence of the struggle—the sounds of the struggle mixed with pounding on the door—then the door swung open and Louise and Welder and some Coast Guardsmen broke though and saved the Russian—this kidnapper of children—this butcher—this devil who stole their organs and sold them for profit—and I wanted to scream as they pulled the Russian out of my hands—*he deserves to die!* And they pulled me away and they pulled Leo away, and wrestled us to the floor—and that's all I remember of that incident—except that I thought if we killed him who could really blame us?

LATER SATURDAY MORNING, OCTOBER 23

It was midmorning when the cutter pulled into the Miami Coast Guard Station. The skies were now clear and the whole lot of us, the crew of the Russian boat, the illegal Cubans, Leo and Taisia, Richie, Louise, Huck and I were standing against the rail watching the ship pull into dock. A small gathering of people on shore stared at us. Several medical emergency trucks were parked behind them. I spotted Rodriquez next to DeFelice, his hand over his eyes against the sun. Neither of them looked happy. Jason Eisenberg was there also—off alone. I didn't see any others from the media. No TV reporters, no cameramen, no one that I recognized from *The Herald*. It was a small party.

I recognized Phillip Michael Thomas. He was standing with a tall, thin man in a suit. I wondered if it was Cleveland Wong. They were in conversation with several Coast Guardsmen. They looked my way as the crew tossed the lines ashore. I knew I was going to catch hell—from a lot of people. But we had accomplished what we needed to do, even though there were still unanswered questions. April for instance. But Taisia was home safe. That's all that mattered.

Louise put her arm through mine.

"My I have this dance, mister?" she said, smiling. I summoned up what strength I had and led her down the gangplank with the others to meet the welcoming committee. Paramedics met Taisia as she disembarked with Leo. Others boarded the cutter to take care of the girl who had been cut open by the Russian doctor and to treat the others that needed medical attention.

Captain Welder was talking with several guardsmen and pointing to the two boats that were coming in behind us: the Bering Cross with its cargo of dead bodies, and the yacht that we had taken across the Florida Straits to intercept the Russian trawler.

"Cooper!" said, Jason, the first one over. "I hear you found your girl. Congratulations! And how do you feel now that it's all over?" he said, pulling out his notepad.

"Put that thing away!" I snapped. "This isn't *Good Morning America*." I really didn't need this right now.

But when he actually looked like he was embarrassed, I felt kind of bad. Kind of.

So I said: "You look good—considering. How's your recovery?"

"Good," he said. "It's still hurts some—when I lift my arm." He paused. "And don't tell me that old joke about the doctor's advice—*Don't do that anymore*," he added, smiling.

I nodded and smiled back. Best friends again. After all we had been through a shooting together.

"I'm just glad it's over, Jason," I said. "It's over."

He nodded. "Okay, tell me the story. The whole thing. Between you and me, this is Pulitzer stuff," he said, sticking the end of a pencil in his mouth. Ready to write.

"Give me until tonight," I said. "Right now, I'm…" and I shook my head… "tired." The man's going to win a Pulitzer for his persistence alone.

"Come on, Coop," Louise said, and started walking toward Rodriquez and DeFelice.

"I'm not even going to say it," said DeFelice as we approached. "Same bullshit, you stupid idiot," and he put his arms around my neck and whispered, "but I'm glad you're okay, partner," and he pounded me on the back. When I pulled away his eyes were watery. "God, I was worried about yous guys," he said, looking over at Louise. Then he gave her a hug.

"Welcome back, Kotter," said Rodriquez, breaking in on the reunion. "I'm not going to get into the fact that you kidnapped one of my detectives," winking at Louise, "and forced her to accompany you into Cuban waters…" and he hesitated… "but I gotta say you did okay. But son of a bitch, don't ever do anything like that again or I'm gonna throw your ass in a cell." And he paused. "And I mean it!"

"But anyways, glad you're back." Then, "DeFelice thinks I should give you your old job back," and he looked over at DeFelice and shook his head. "But he's an idiot." A pause again. Then a smile. Then, "Interested?"

I didn't respond. He hit me on the arm a couple of times. A guy thing. We stood and watched the man with the suit and Captain Welder walking toward us.

"That's Agent Wong with Welder," said Rodriquez. "The man you ignored. He doesn't look happy, does he?" giving me that *This is going to be good* look. Wong was shorter than Welder, and stocky.

I had asked Welder what would happen to the Cubans, explaining how Santiago had helped in the rescue operation. He said it was an immigration issue, but in his experience, they were usually pretty lenient with Cuban nationals trying to escape the Castro regime.

"I see you made it, Cooper," said Cleveland Wong, not holding out his hand.

I started to say something.

"Don't tell me your story," he said, holding up his hand. "I don't want to hear it. I would probably have to lock you up—and your buddies." Clearly pissed. Welder was shrugging his shoulders like *not my problem.*

"So..." I began to say.

"So, Cooper, at least you had a good outcome"...cop talk..."and you did what we could not have done. "And..." he hesitated..."I don't know how you and your *groupies* pulled it off—and survived," he added. Ouch. Groupies?

"Partly with that man's help," I said, pointing to Santiago, who was still huddled at the pier with his four friends, waiting for permission to come ashore I figured. I waved for him to come over.

"I'll talk to ICS," he said.

"You are ICS," I said.

"Enforcement," he said.

"Keeping the homeland secure," I said.

"As long as people like you don't fuck us up," he said.

"Ouch."

"You better hope that's the worst of it," he said. "Next time..."

"I'll stay out of trouble."

He turned to the rifleman and his friends. "I hear you've been a brave man, Mr. Cavallero," and he turned to me. "Does he...?"

"Understand?" I said.

Cleveland nodded.

"He does," I said.

"I have English," said Cavallero, smiling and shaking the agent's hand.

"So, we go to Chokoloskee Island?" Santiago whispered to me, using his hand to shield what he was saying from the agent.

72

THE REUNION

DeFelice offered to give us a ride to the Keys to pick up our vehicles. We took him up on it. I wondered how we were all going to fit into his unmarked until he pulled up to the dock in an Escalade.

"Nice car," I said. "How'd you rate this?"

"Homeland Security," he said. "Thank Agent Wong," and he jumped from the driver's side and got the rear door for Louise and Taisia. What a gentleman. Then Richie, Huck and Leo piled into the rich interior of the Escalade, Richie making comments like, "Shoulda been a cop!"

We headed for US 1 and the Overseas Highway.

"So, Lou, how'd this guy rope you into an illegal activity?" said DeFelice over his shoulder to Louise. Always the wise guy. "Lucky you didn't lose your badge."

"Fuckin' cops," said Richie under his breath.

"What'd you say?" said DeFelice to the back of the SUV. "I can still beat your ass, Marino, baseball bat or no baseball bat. Remember that."

I don't think I ever saw the two actually fight when we were kids. But they trash talked a lot. Just like now.

372

"Fuck you guys care about is rules. The little lady...
Ouch!" Richie moaned. "Louise!"

I looked around.

"I ain't no fuckin' little lady," Louise said to Richie who
was looking at her as if to say, *What the hell?*

"Anyways, I'm defending you, Louise," he argued.

"I don't need your defense," she said with heat. That's
Louise.

"Anyways, Lou, good work. Thanks for helping to keep
this nutcase alive," said DeFelice. Then, "You know, Coop, I
thought you and me was close. This is the second time you
go on some crazy, Rambo type gig and don't tell me till it's
over. What kind of friend don't ask for help?"

I told him I was sorry. "Next time," I said.

"Yeah, yeah," he said. "Heard that one before, didn't I?"
He had. I didn't want to count the times. Like last year in
the Everglades—chasing kidnappers.

The house was black when we turned onto Avenue A
and into 1st Road from the Overseas Highway. It seemed
so long ago when I saw the face in the window. Yet it had
been only twenty four hours.

DeFelice dropped us off and said his good byes with
all kinds of warnings like, *Drive safe and stay in touch for
Christ's sake. Call me.* I said, *Sure*—like I always do—and
he said, *Uh-huh*—like he always does—and he drove away
to fight the late afternoon Miami traffic.

LATER THAT AFTERNOON

The sun was at half-mast in the west as we left the house on
1st Road and headed toward Oceanside and my house on the
edge of the swamp. Louise was with me in Richie's Land

Cruiser; Huck, Leo and Taisia were riding with Richie in his rental Jeep. Rodriquez had given Louise a pass because of what we had broken up: a Russian gang selling body parts in the U.S. Jason had the inside story and was playing up the Cooper/Delgado team: private investigator and Miami PD detective rescue a University of Miami girl from butchers, returning her to her Russian grandfather and mother. Rodriguez loved that. And the story would develop into a series of investigative articles dealing with the international trade in body parts, Jason said. Pulitzer stuff.

Louise was leaning against me as we hit the bridge that would carry us back to the mainland. We just missed the south Miami late afternoon traffic, hitting the Oceanside city limits just after 6:35 p.m. Fifteen minutes later we were on Midnight Drive heading west toward the Everglades and my home. In the west clouds were lined up along the horizon. They were laced with an orange hue, residue from a sinking sun. The night air was on its way, so I opened the windows to catch its coolness.

"You want a job as a private investigator?" I said. "We would make a good team."

"Who would be in charge?" she said, poking my ribs as she continued leaning.

"I would be," I said. "My business."

"Just like a man," she said. "That would be a problem. I need to be in charge. I like being on top."

"Whoa," I said. "Are we mixing metaphors?"

"I hope so," she said, and snuggled closer.

"Do you believe what just happened out there in the Florida Straits?" she said. "We attack a boat that's almost three times our size, shoot up some Russians, capture the crew, rescue not only a Russian girl, but also another victim, and save her life. Then we kill one of the most notorious traders in the body parts industry and his girl-friend, and arrest another. And finally I don't lose my job, and you don't lose your license even though we crossed over into Cuban waters. And we're being called heroes. Go figure."

"Go figure," I said smiling, and held her tightly.

73

THE LIGHT'S ON

It was 7:30 p.m. when we turned off Midnight Drive to the road that leads to my home. The porch lights were on. So was almost every other light in the house.

A man was leaning against a post on my porch. He was in darkness, backlit from the lamps that hung on either side of the screen door.

"Welcome back, Cooper," said a familiar voice, then he shifted and I saw who it was.

"What are you doing here?" I said. I could see the smile, the darkness accentuating his white teeth. Boyd.

"Congratulations, Coop," he said and moved away from the post, swung down the stairs, and walked toward me with his hand extended. I took it.

"For what?" I said.

"For doing what we paid you for. Killing Kolya." And he smiled a big smile as he shook my hand. "Mr. Santangelo sends his best."

"How did you find out?"

"Your reporter friend called Mr. Santangelo. He's a good man."

"You tried to kill him."

"You say. Boy oughta stay out of the woods unless he's huntin'."

"Uh-huh," I said.

"Whaddya doing here, Boyd?" Richie said, climbing out of his rental, car doors slamming and feet hitting the gravel. I kept my eyes on Boyd. Trying to figure out why he made the trip all the way down here.

"I'm here in peace, pal," Boyd said, holding up his hands.

"Don't fuckin' call me pal," said Richie. "I ain't your pal." What the hell was wrong with Richie?

Leo and Huck had just climbed out of the Durango and were standing behind Richie.

"Fuckin' redneck," I heard Richie say. "Probably killed April 'cause she's black." I hadn't talked with Richie about my conversation with Remi.

The other cowboy from the training camp in Wayne National Forest stepped through the screen door and took Boyd's place at the porch post.

"Everything okay, Mr. Boyd?" he said, not moving his head as he stared at Richie and me. Boyd waved him off.

"Mr. Santangelo paid you to get a job done, Cooper," he said, holding out an envelope. "You did it. Simple as that."

Louise reached over and took it. She opened it up and studied the contents. I could see it was cash.

"Why did you hire me, Boyd?" I said. "You could've taken care of those Russians yourself."

Richie moved toward the porch, walked up the stairs, and leaned against the other post, opposite Darren, Boyd's buddy. He and Darren in a staring contest.

Boyd shook his head. "Mr. Santangelo don't pay me to look for missing people, Cooper."

I noticed he didn't say he doesn't kill people. He just said he's not paid to find them.

"Those boys were tryin' to take over The Man's territory. He wanted you to take care of it. You did. Simple as that," Boyd continued, running his hand through his gray beard, then feeling for his mustache. I wondered if Remi was talking about Boyd—"the Irishman."

"Besides, those boys was engaged in selling body parts. That there's against the Bible," he added, smiling. "You found them, took care of them. Period. End of story." Then he walked over to a bush by the porch and spat in it.

"April," I said. "You didn't like her."

Boyd looked puzzled, then smiled and glanced over at Darren. "Okay, I get it. Cooper thinks I killed that negra girl. Did I do that, Darren?" he said, turning sidewise to me. That smile again.

"Now why would I do that, Cooper?" He moved a chew around in his mouth.

"Maybe because she's black and she's with a white guy," Richie suggested, still leaning against the porch post, "seein' as you are a racist hillbilly, red-fuckin-neck pig."

I had to give Richie credit. He got about as many epithets in a single sentence as he could. When he threw in 'pig', I saw Boyd tense.

"I hate Communists, fags, Jews, negras, and guys like you, Richie. But I don't kill them. I'm a God-fearin' Christian," he said as red veins appeared in his cheeks. He turned and spit black juice out of the side of his mouth in Richie's direction, not bothering to go back to the bush. I thought of the Mail Pouch sign. "For a good chew…"

"I didn't kill your girl, Cooper," Boyd added, turning back to me and wiping his mouth with his shirt sleeve.

Uh-huh, I thought. Maybe so. That leaves Jackson and maybe Sonya. *The Irishman's wife?*

"This the girl's grandfather?" said Boyd looking over at Leo. Trying to be friends now.

I heard the sound of tires against gravel. A black car came around a bend of the road, its headlights hitting my house squarely in the windows, the reflection throwing the yard into daylight. I shielded my eyes to see who it was. The driver pulled behind the Jeep and Land Cruiser, scattering dust, shut down the motor, and opened the door. It was Jackson Lawless. Damned if it wasn't! Before his feet hit the ground, I was at the car.

"What the hell!" I exclaimed as Jackson straightened up and faced me. "And how did you know I would be here?"

"Just took a chance, Coop. I was tired of waiting and doing nothing. So I jumped in my car and headed down. Looks like you're having a party!" he said, looking around at the small crowd that was staring at him.

"Welcome to Florida, Doc," Boyd said. I hadn't noticed the similarities between the two before: mustache growing into a beard, same height and build, graying hair. Maybe they were related. Stranger things have happened in the Valley.

"I called you, Cooper. You never called back," Jackson said as he slammed the door and followed me to the lawn party. I could smell liquor. "You could give a shit the cops are after me."

Jackson looked at Boyd as he passed by, "Is this one of the bad guys you're chasing?" saying it loud enough for Boyd to hear. That's Jackson. Always trying to start trouble.

Boyd moved the chew around in his mouth then spit— not too far from Jackson's feet. Jackson staggered around it and moved toward Boyd. I pulled him back.

"So, Coop, wha's going on?" he said, turning back to me. His breath. By God, I figured he would blow at least a .20. Lucky he wasn't picked up and lucky he made it this far without killing himself—or someone else.

I told him about the Russians and said that they may be the ones who killed April.

"The fuckin' Russians killed April?" he slurred over the words and lost his balance momentarily.

"Perhaps," I said. He looked at me.

"Perhaps? Who else 'perhaps,' Cooperman?"

Cooperman? He had never called me that before.

"Maybe you killed her," said Boyd, loud, so everybody could hear. "Man had a reason," he added, turning to me and nodding at Jackson. "The girl wouldn't break it off, right, Lawless?"

Jackson glared at him and tensed. I've seen that before. Fight time. Trouble is Boyd loves to fight too. Those Irishmen.

"You redneck son of a bitch," Jackson slurred. He swung at Boyd but missed by a wide mark. Boyd laughed, backing out of the way, easily. It was a miracle that Jackson had made it from Ohio. Alcohol must be part of his blood supply.

Richie helped me get him into the house and onto the couch. He was out cold before he hit the pillows. I let him sleep. The "sleep that knits up the raveled sleeve of care." But Macbeth couldn't sleep because he had murdered the king. I wondered about Jackson. Could Boyd be right?

74

BACK TO OHIO

He had slept long enough. I woke Jackson at 9:00 p.m. and told him we needed to talk. He sat up, rubbing his eyes, and looked around. I think he was about to ask where he was when he finally seemed to focus and noticed that I was there.

"What?" he said.

"You're still drunk," I said. "Can you talk?"

He nodded. "I can talk."

His breath still reeked. I turned away. At least he didn't call me Cooperman.

I told him about what Remi had said: *Talk to the Irishman's wife.* And what did he mean by that? Jackson stared at me—as though I said something in Usbecki.

He shook his head, as though he was shaking free the cobwebs that had formed over the past days. Then, "What? The Irishman's wife? What the hell is that supposed to mean?"

"I think he meant your wife," I said.

"That makes no sense," he said. "Boyd's probably Irish. Hell, half the Valley's Irish."

"Right," I said. "Good point."

Jackson looked completely confused. It was so quiet I could hear it.

"Hell, I don't know what that means," he said finally.

"Maybe we need to talk to Sonya," I said.

"Yeah," he said. "Maybe." And he sank back into his funk. The alcohol was still outnumbering the blood cells running through his veins.

"Where the fuck you guys goin'?" said Richie as he watched Jackson and me packing up the rental.

"We have some unfinished business in the Valley," I said, looking over at Jackson. I knew he wasn't comfortable with Richie so I didn't explain. "Tell Huck I'll see him later and tell Louise I'll talk to her on the road."

Richie nodded but had the sullen look he has when he isn't happy with me. "I gotta do this one alone with Jackson," I said when Jackson had settled into the car. "Personal thing."

He nodded again. "Call me," he said. I nodded back.

We had a lot of time to think as the hours of the night turned into early morning. The sun began to creep over the horizon and light up the foothills of the Appalachians as we neared Mount Airy, North Carolina. Jackson was driving now, and we hadn't said a word since we left Florida. He was sober.

"Hell is going on?" said Jackson to the rising morning—shaking his head as he stared at the distant road.

"Maybe Sonya has friends from Saint Petersburg?" I said into the silence.

He looked over at me. "And what the fuck is that supposed to mean?"

And that was the last thing we said to each other until we crossed into Ohio at South Point, skirting the southern end of Wayne National Forest.

"How are we going to do this?" I said, looking out at the forest as though an answer was waiting out there—somewhere among the trees that were dumping their leaves for the coming winter.

We pulled into Dunkin' Donuts in Riverdale at 9:30 a.m. early Sunday morning, worn out, unshaven, and stinking from too much time in the car, from no break, and from the lingering effect of Jackson's alcohol. We had spelled each other by simply pulling over and switching drivers. I felt like I had been hit by Mike Ditka when I pulled myslf out of the driver's side.

"Damn," said Jackson. "I felt better after my high school football games. At least I had a reason to hurt. This is just crazy."

We ordered coffee, a couple of bagels with cream cheese, some hot, glazed donuts, and sat down. The bagels were obviously not water bagels, but the coffee was great. *The country drives on Dunkin'*, they say.

Nobody else was in the place except the girl behind that counter who was staring at us. I guess that was a factor of our appearance. I probably would stare too.

"Tell me what's going on, Coop?" said Jackson after a few minutes of moping over the coffee.

"What do you know about Sonya's background?" I said.

"Her background? What? Who's the private dick here?"

"All right. Look, I just need to talk with Sonya. Have you called her to tell her we're coming?"

"Yeah. About three hours ago—you were sleeping. I didn't tell her you were with me." Confession.

I nodded. We finished our coffee, got some refills, and headed out.

"You going to call her again?" I said. "Let her know?"

"Nah. No sense. Let's just get this the hell over," and he revved the motor and pulled onto Highway 52.

Sonya rushed over to him as he came up the stairs to the porch, asking why he had left without telling her. He didn't say anything.

"Cooper!" she said. I was standing off to the side. "You didn't say Coop was with you when you called, Jack." There was a question in there.

"Cooper found the Russian girl he was looking for," he said. He was evaluating her as he said it.

"Oh," she said, as though *and what does that have to do with your disappearance?*

But then, "That's such great news, Coop! I'm so happy for you. Congratulations!" But there was an air of puzzlement behind that happy smile. Then, shaking off the confusion of the last few moments, she apologized for keeping us on the porch. She took Jackson's hand and told me to come in.

"I'll make some coffee," she said and headed for the kitchen.

Most crimes aren't solved by evidence or through the deductions of clever detectives—like me. No. Cases are usually solved because the perpetrator confesses to the

crime. Why would someone confess? I would have to say, I
don't know. Guilty conscience? The fear that they're going
to be caught? Perhaps they just want to be caught. I'm not
a psychologist. Just a philosopher turned detective. I used
to study the meaning of life. Now I know there isn't any.
It's an irrational world. And, in that world, there are four
kinds of people: there are those who are mentally ill—and
you try to understand them. Then there are the ignorant—
you can understand them, but they will never understand
you. Thirdly, there are the average Joes—like you and me.
Right? And finally, there are those who are just plain evil. I
never thought such people existed—until I became a cop.
And I thought about what Einstein had said: *The world is
dangerous not because of the people who are evil, but because of
the people who won't do anything about it.*

I was wondering where Sonya fit into this picture as I
watched her pour the coffee.

She noticed that I was staring. "What?" she said.

"We need to talk," I said.

Sonya poured herself a cup of coffee, sat across from
me, and waited.

"Jackson mentioned that I found Taisia." Sonya nodded.
"She had been kidnapped by several Russians—two of the
kidnappers are dead. One is still alive." Sonya was watching me intently. "Maks Remizov." She blinked and looked
down. *She knows him,* I thought. "I had a chance to talk
with him." I paused for a reaction. "You know him?" I said.

She began to shake her head... "He told me to talk
to you about the killing of April," I said. "Why would he
do that?"

She was silent for a few moments. Then she looked
away. People always seem to do that when they don't know

what to say. Maybe she was picturing Remi. Perhaps talking to the police. About her. And then she turned back, looked at Jackson first—angry—then at me.

"Is he a friend?" I said.

I could see it on her lips—she hadn't said anything yet—but it was there—the confession—*I didn't mean for anything to happen to her—I was just so angry!*

"I didn't know what I was doing!" Sonya said—almost a scream.

Damn! I thought. *She did do it!*

"What?" Jackson demanded, clearly stunned by her words. "What?"

"I hated her and I hated you for loving her," Sonya fumed, turning on Jackson, her face blood red. "After eight years… and you have to fuck one of your own students! How could you do that to me?" rising out of her seat, her fists clenched, looking like she wanted to pound on him, Jackson backing away, more from amazement than fear, and she lunged at him and caught him as he fell back, trying to strike him with her fists, missing mostly, her arms flailing about like wounded helicopter blades. Then Jackson righted himself and grabbed her by the shoulders, squeezing them and leaning into her face:

"What did you do!" he yelled, his scream setting my teeth on edge. And Jackson held her tight, bringing her face into his: "You killed her! Why?" and he shook her, his long arms almost raising her off the floor.

And she screamed, "I didn't!" And I tried to pull him away from her. But his body relaxed as Sonya cried and he pulled away.

"I didn't kill her!" Sonya yelled again, her hands out like a supplicant, spittle floating in the early sun now streaming through the window. "I didn't kill her." And Jackson just stared at her.

"But I might as well have..." she said. "I might as well have," and she shook her head. "How could you...?" She was looking at him, bearing down on him. Hurt and anger pouring from her eyes like tears.

Jackson didn't say anything. He just stared at her in disbelief.

"My father was KGB," she tried to explain, watching Jackson to see his reaction. But he just continued to stare. "He is retired now—but still he has connections," and she stole another glance. Jackson stared without emotion.

"And..." I said, urging her to get on with it. .

"And I told him about you and..." hesitating "...and he said Remi was here in the Valley and that I should tell him about you and the girl and if Remi, damn him, didn't do anything, he would..."

"Do what? Kill me? Kill her?" Jackson was losing it.

"I never said anyone should kill anyone!" she said, like a defendant in a murder case.

"But you know these people and you knew what they would do. So you told Remi and he said, what? I will scare her? I will hurt her just a little? And for what price? How did you pay him? In kidneys?" And he paused, wiping spittle from his mouth. "What the fuck did you think he would do?"

And Sonya tried to say something and Lawless waved her off, the Furies having taken over, and he buried his head in his hands... "And we had broken it off...we had broken it off!" he yelled, looking up at her. "And you decided to execute her! How could you do that?" and he stared at her as though he were staring at a stranger. And Sonya was frozen in her place. No tears.

"I hated you," she said. "And I still do."

I heard car tires hit the stones in the drive and went to the window. Passarelli climbed out with a uniform right behind him. I had called him on the way while Lawless slept. It was a good thing I had.

I told Passarelli the whole story—about Kolya and Remi, about boarding their ship and rescuing Taisia, about Tania and Sly, and finally about Sonya and her connection to Remi and the death of April. He shook his head and said it was a hell of a story and told the uniform to read her rights and cuff her.

Soon everybody in the fricking city would hear the whole damn story: Jason would tell it in *The Plain Dealer;* the readers would tell it on the evening news. And the story would probably make CNN—that is unless the Coast Guard could stifle it so nobody would know they were in Cuban waters. And a lot of people would be hurt—Jackson—April's family—maybe the children, Tania and Sly—but what the hell, that's not my problem—the story, that is. I had found Taisia. And Leo was happy—no, ecstatic. And I had found April's killer—or should I say killers. So my job was done. End of story—for me. And if that sounds heartless, then let me tell you that in this world, in this evil world, a man can only do so much. You have to leave the rest of the rotten garbage to others. At least I had taken care of some of it, even if it was only a single piece of garbage on a single day.

AFTER THE WAR

HOME: THE EVERGLADES

SUNDAY EVENING, OCTOBER 24

Halloween was coming—my favorite holiday. I thought about Sonya, all the way back to Florida. Jillie and I had known her for over eight years...and yet... Just goes to show you. You think you know someone. I pulled off the interstate at a motel in Perry, Georgia around 10:00 p.m. I had drifted off about three times, actually going off the road the last time, the rough edges of the berm waking me up. So that's why I stopped. And I dreamed of crazy stuff all night. It's no wonder...considering what had happened the past forty-eight hours.

MONDAY MORNING, OCTOBER 25

I headed out early this morning—having had enough of those dreams—no breakfast. I exited at the Welcome to Florida, Free Orange Juice sign around 9:00 a.m. The sugar gave me new energy—the donut did too. By the time I pulled into my drive in Oceanside the sun was high over the Everglades.

The Land Cruiser was still parked there. I had forgotten about Jackson's car. It was sitting behind the Cruiser. I guessed everybody else had called it a day and headed home.

"Finally decided to come home?" Richie said, banging out the screen door ahead of Sammy. Huck was right behind him.

"My old buddies," I said.

"Only friends you got, Coop," said Huck. "You got my private eye badge?"

"Not yet, Kemo Sabe," I said. "Need to pass the test first."

"And what test would that be?"

"Cooper's multiple choice test."

He stared at me. Was I serious?

"You willing to work for low wages?"

"I ain't made dime one yet, cowboy."

"Money is the root of all evil."

"Ergo I am *the* most virtuous injun you ever seen," he said. Huck, the Mark Twain of the Everglades.

Richie shook his head. Disgusted. "Real funny, Huxter." Then he handed me an envelope. "From Leo," he said. "Said to give this to the great detective Cooper." He paused as I took it. "It's cash. I already checked." He was smiling. "You won't have to work much in the future, ol' buddy."

I almost felt guilty. Was that legal? With three paying clients—Santangelo, Jackson, and Leo—I could finally go shopping at Whole Foods. I would share some of it with my new partner, Louise. And of course, with Richie and Huck. I figured a case of Sam Adams for DeFelice. Maybe two. Oh hell, maybe three.

"Oh yeah. Louise said she expected a lobster dinner—at the Ritz," said Richie. "Soon. Call her."

I handed them both an envelope. "We did well," I said. "Share the wealth."

Richie and Huck both looked at the envelopes, turning them over in their hands almost at the same time.

"You sending us W2s?" said Richie.

"You ever get a W2?" I said.

"Nope."

"Then, no," I said.

"Phew," said Richie. "That was close."

"What the hell's a W2?" said Huck. That's Huck. Probably never filed a tax return in his life.

Huck shuffled down off the porch and held out his hand.

"Pardner, I've got to hit the trail. And thanks for this," he said, holding up the envelope. "Got some gators to catch before the night's over. There's a couple big ones the law says I can harvest down by Chokoloskee. Join me later?"

I told him, *thanks*, but *no*. Had some catching up to do myself—thinking of a glass of wine and my hammock.

"I didn't see your truck. Where'd you park?"

"Around the back. Not too far from Herman. Wanted to keep him company. It gets awful lonely back there, Coop." He paused, then headed for the back of the house. "You oughta take better care of him," he said, his back to me.

"You don't plan on shooting him, do you?" I said.

"Nah. He's my friend...and yours."

Richie just shook his head. "Man's crazy." But I knew he liked him—deep down.

After Huck pulled out honking and waving, Richie and I hung out in the backyard with a couple of beers. Sammy had crawled up on Richie's lap, purring like a lawn mover as

Richie scratched behind his ears. The three of us watched Herman and the Swamp for a few more hours until the sun began to drop to late afternoon. He had said he just wanted to spend a little goddamned quiet time with me for once. I appreciated it.

"By the way, Boyd said to call him. Said he might be able to help you find Maxie," Richie added, rubbing Sammy's belly now. And after a pause, "Guy's full of shit, Coop. Don't trust that bastard." He stared at me for a few moments, then threw up his hands. Sammy jumped to the ground. Irritated. "But anyways…that's what he said," and he could have added, *the bastard*.

I nodded.

"Well, buddy. Time for Uncle Richie to hit the road. Give me a hand packin' my Cruiser." And he got up and headed for the house. I pulled myself out of my chair, went in through the back porch, and helped him pack and load the Cruiser. "Can you get the rental back for me?" he said, as he climbed in. I said, *No problem.* Then,

"It's nearly 5:00 o'clock. Sure you don't want to stay the night?"

"Nah, Gotta get back," he said, wistfulness in his voice as he pulled the door shut. "Ma's missing me."

Richie always looked sad when he left. I think he couldn't help but think of our days in the neighborhood. We were always together. Usually in trouble. But always together.

"You come visit soon," he said. An order.

"You bet," I said, knowing full well that it would be him who visited me again. He couldn't resist coming down to help his old friend.

"You need me to help find your son. Call." Another order.

"Thanks, Richie," I said, and waved as he headed out toward Midnight Drive. I saw him look in the rearview mirror. He stuck his arm out the window and waved back.

I was alone again. Almost. Sammy was rubbing himself against my leg. That doesn't mean he likes me, which he does. It means he's ready for his special meal of the day. Tonight, it was going to be chicken livers. I had picked them up at Publix several days ago. It was not really that long ago when we headed into the Keys to find Taisia. Several days.

I went to the fridge and pulled out a bottle of Chardonnay—Columbia Crest Estates. I grabbed a jelly jar— that's what I drink my wine in—held the door for Sammy, and headed for the hammock in the back yard, far enough from Herman so as not to worry.

As I lay there, I thought of what Boyd had said to Richie. I thought I would call him in the morning and ask him what the hell he was talking about.

I had spent enough time looking for other people's missing friends, sons, daughters, spouses. I knew it was the fear that I would find Maxie dead that kept me from looking as hard as I should have. Jillie was right. I needed to handle it—the fear, I mean. Or was I being a crazy idealist? Shouldn't I leave that horrendous job to a third person? Who's uninvolved emotionally. Who would just report the terrible news to me. That would be bad enough in and of itself. But to find Maxie's body myself! *Don't do it*, I thought. *Don't do it.*

But, deep down, I knew I would.

I lay back in the hammock and stared at the early evening sky. I could see the stars emerge as the sun lost its light. And I thought about all that had happened these past October days. The children. The bloodshed. The evil. The Indians were right. The autumn fields run red with the harvest kill.

I watched the Blood Moon rising.

ACKNOWLEDGEMENTS

It's time for me to acknowledge the people who made it possible for me to write and publish *Blood Moon Rising*.

First, let me thank my readers: John and Stephanie Coburn, Ryan Conrath, Scott Nelson, Jane and Glenn Trout, James and Helen Conrath, Jack and Melissa Conrath,and Christine Bohanan. Thanks also to others who have supported me in my writing efforts: Robert Freedman, Don and Lucy Hand, Raymond and Susan Imbrigiotta, Mandi Thurston, and James Powell, Esq. You have all been so marvelous!

A special thanks to Jack Driscoll, a PEN/Nelson Algren Fiction Award and Pushcart Editor's Book Award winner, and the author, among other notable works, of one of my favorite books, *Lucky Man, Lucky Woman*. Jack has not only guided me in my early writing efforts but has continued to help as I work on my skills. Thanks, Jack. It never ends, does it?

Tristram Coburn, who originally served as my agent and is now in the publishing business (Tilbury House

Publishers) and who continues to help, has been key in my development as a writer. Thanks, Tris. *Blood Moon Rising* would not be what it is today without your insights about the content and your editorial direction. Thanks for hanging in there.

There are others to whom I owe a debt of gratitude. Randy Wayne White, one of my first reads when I came to Florida, has continued to encourage me with his constant and important reminder to "Persist!" And thanks also to another famous Florida writer, Tim Dorsey, who continues to inspire with his great stories about the myriad of characters in the Sunshine State that make writing about Florida such an interesting adventure.

Thanks also to Chandi Riaz and her team at Arc Manor Book Design, the designers of both the interior and the wonderful cover of Blood Moon Rising, and to Shahid Mahmud, the Publisher of Arc Manor Publications. You have both made it a beautiful publication. A special thanks to J. Michael Orenduff, author of the *Pot Thief Mysteries*. I enjoyed my time with you on your "Talking Books" radio show. And to Julie Glenn, host of *Gulf Shore Live* on WGCU, an NPR affiliate. Thanks for making my appearance on your show a comfortable and delightful one. And how can I not mention the two hosts of our book launch at Tipsy Cow in Southwest Florida, Jim and Andy Palmisano. Kathleen Donaldson, a former law enforcement officer, continues to help me with the complexities of police procedure.

Thanks also to Dr. Phil Jason, reviewer extraordinaire for the popular, *Florida Weekly*. I appreciate his insights into my writing. He should know about writing, as Professor Emeritus of English at the United States Naval Academy and a poet. Martin Lipschultz has been a constant with his remarkable photography. He rendered the first photograph on my website that makes me look remarkably like one of my idols: Leonard Cohen.

And thanks also to a fellow author, David Harry Tannenbaum, who has penned, among other works, the remarkable *Padre Island Series*. It stars two of my favorite detectives: Jimmy Redstone and Angella Martinez.

And what can I say about Ryan Conrath, the one responsible for the website at www.richardconrath.com, and for his editorial insights and his help with rendering my books into Kindle.

And finally, last but surely not least, a deep bow and salaam to my lifelong partner, chief editor, muse, and constant inspiration, who has spent endless hours, days, and months listening to the reading of my books, editing them, commenting on whether the lines are true to the scene, and without whom *Blood Moon Rising* would not be what it is today—and I guess, by now, you must realize that I am talking about my wife, Karyn Marie. A simple 'thank you' is just not enough.

AUTHOR'S NOTE

Blood Moon Rising is a work of fiction. Some of the places exist only in the mind of the author. For instance, there is no city south of Miami named Oceanside, nor a town in Ohio named Muskingum, nor a college by the name of Concord. I switched the names of town and university to protect the innocent. Other places, streets, and restaurants are for the most part real, although the details may have been changed to suit the author's fancy. You must understand, writers love to tell stories.

Coming Soon! The third and final book in The Cooper Series. The following pages are a preview of the action that takes place in book three, *A Cold Copper Moon*.

A COLD COPPER MOON

Prologue

EIGHT YEARS AGO

The screen door slammed after him as he ran across our porch, down the wooden steps that front our house, an old colonial, and into the yard, now freshly green from the recent rains. He threw a baseball into the air and caught it—he always did that—and then ran in circles as he tossed the ball, scuffed from falling into the dirt, watching it into his mitt, laughing each time he threw it into the sky, a little higher each time, and he would do that until I would come home—Jillie would tell me— and then we would play catch. But he would have to practice in the meantime.

And I was watching him now—in my dreams?—*as the ball sailed higher and higher and floated into a cloud and then dropped out of the white. The boy lost it momentarily, then reached out for it when it appeared once again, and missed it. It hit the ground and rolled toward the road, slowly at first*—and I held my breath—*until the ball caught the edge of an incline and continued its descent more rapidly*—I must be dreaming— *Maxie chasing quickly, laughing at the ball as though it were something living, playing hide-and-seek, his hair blowing in*

403

the wind like the wheat in the nearby field, the mid-morning sun bright on his face, and he took the incline quickly and hurtled down after the ball until it came to rest in a ditch bordering the road, settling in some mud and stones at the very bottom of the incline where he reached for it, rubbing the ball against his pants to wipe it clean of the grime from the ditch.

Then a man stooped down and said, "Let me help you with that"—I tried to warn him!—*and Maxie looked up at him, this stranger with an odd voice, not at all like the voice of Anthony, who owned the antique shop on Main Street, nor like mine, nor like anyone that he had ever heard, and the man took the ball from him and said, "Let's go to my car and get a rag and clean this ball up for you, eh?" And he took the boy's hand before he could answer and led him to a black car, opened the door, and said, "Now let's see if we can find that rag shall we?"*—and I reached out for him—*And he asked Maxie to look in the back seat to see if he could find it because his eyesight wasn't that good anymore, and the boy did and he felt a shove and fell forward into the seat and heard the door slam almost at the same time as he heard his mother call out, "Maxie...Maxie, where are you?"*—and I tried to call out too—*And Maxie knew that she would be coming to the door and looking for him any minute. But the car was already moving quickly ahead and Maxie couldn't see the door of our house opening as he looked out the back window of the car, and I could see the fear now rising in his eyes and choking him, and I saw him look into the front seat where a second man had risen up and was now reaching for him, and Maxie was trying to call out for me*—and I tried to reply—*but fear must have closed his ears.*

And I watched helplessly as they passed Anthony's Antique Shop.

Blood Moon Rising, semifinalist winner of the Royal Palm Literary Award, is Richard Conrath's second novel in a trilogy featuring Cooper, a private detective, who searches for his young kidnapped son while trying to track down other missing people.

Conrath is a former Catholic priest who left to teach philosophy in a small college while freelancing for papers like the *Cleveland Plain dealer and Sunday Magazine.* He left teaching in 1984 and began a series of three-year stints in administration as a college vice-president, president, and then as headmaster of an American school in Turkey. It was there, during the darkness of the Turkish winters, that he began to write his first mystery.